MENGODS

MENGODS

The Rise of the Orgites

Ruben C. Rocafort

MENGODS
THE RISE OF THE ORGITES

iUniverse books may be ordered through booksellers or by contacting:

iUniverse
1663 Liberty Drive
Bloomington, IN 47403
www.iuniverse.com
1-800-Authors (1-800-288-4677)

ISBN: 978-1-4917-4976-0 (sc)
ISBN: 978-1-4917-4978-4 (hc)
ISBN: 978-1-4917-4977-7 (e)

Printed in the United States of America.

iUniverse rev. date: 11/13/2014

I wish to thank the following family and friends
For giving me their guidance and help,
For contributing their time and effort in
fulfilling the completion of this novel

Titi Olga Rocafort

My wife
Ydalba Rocafort

My typist and friend
E. Alvarez

My daughter who reviewed the complete novel.
Arlene Florence Markowski

My son-in-law who designed the book cover.
John Markowski

And

To my son who I dedicate this book to
Charles R. Rocafort

PREFACE

Since the dawn of time man's unique development has come about either by accident or through the guides of Mother Nature. Some sources say by manipulation of some higher form of authority not privy to him.

And still some others say that man has slowly evolved from a lower form after the formation of the landmasses that surfaced and shaped the Earth at the end of the primordial period.

Man actually developed through necessity and was further influenced by his environment.

His life journey commenced after he decided to leave the safety of his dark domain, which sheltered him but didn't provide enough food and security for his ever-growing family group.

His curiosity urged him to wonder about the Earth in search of food and better security for more than two hundred thousand years weathering all type of impediments trusted at him by his surroundings which contributed to his self development up to the present age.

Unbeknownst to him, he has gone through minute physiological and emotional changes and has successfully adapted in order to survive on the planet by naturally growing by necessity a larger brain to help him outwit opponents, which were many times his size. He succeeded at this by working in concert with his own kind.

Ruben C. Rocafort

He also manipulated Earth resources to his favor and is presently causing the Earth to tether on a future scenario of a global environmental disaster.

So Man moves forward in time and space hoping with great anticipation what will be the next step in his development as he begins his journey towards the Cosmos.

CHAPTER I

It is a crisp September morning at New York's Midtown East Research Center Auditorium. The year is 2018. A small group of medical scientists and reporters are finding for themselves choice front seats in the auditorium because they are about to receive a lecture and a new disclosure from the world renowned Professor Donnelly who holds a Ph.D. in Chemistry, Physics and Internal Medicine.

Professor Donnelly is a man in his late sixties; he wears a very neat beard, a refined mustache, and possesses an impeccable appearance.

In the audience, seated to the right of Professor Donnelly's closest friends is a writer who works for Forbes Magazine. He was sent there at the last minute to represent his company. His name is Steven Curtis. Curtis writes a weekly column on a variety of subjects including science and medicine.

His ambition is to be a great journalist some day and waits impatiently for the opportunity to do so. He was sent there at a moments notice to supplement the Science Section of Popular Inventors Magazine for the October month's issue.

Professor Donnelly previously informed all of the invited guests that before he makes his grand disclosure, he would commence with a short lecture on the background of the Center's work in Cellular Research and Preventive Medicine.

Steven Curtis deliberately positions myself, in the front row sharing some of the spotlight with three of Professor Donnelly's closest colleagues. They include a world-known Science writer for the New York Times and two other fellow scientists, who work closely with the Professor on various science projects.

One of these individuals, a woman scientist, named Dr. Nora Billings, she is a green-eyed dark-hair brunette, with classic features, a stunning dresser and very, very attractive.

Ms. Billings is a neurosurgeon from England and is part of a Medical Science Exchange Program, sponsored by the United Nations' World Medical Conference.

The other individual to her left is Dr. Jason Roberts: an American born scientist. He is a medical researcher and head lecturer. He did his tenure at Walter Reed and Mount Sinai Hospital, in New York in 2008 through 2010.

The doctor is a tall, dark curly hair, athletic type looking man and very self-conscience of his appearance.

Dr. Roberts was a former student of Professor Donnelly and later became medical lecturer on Internal Medicine and Bioscience at the Institute. He now works in concert with the Professor at the Center, on several highly secretive Government projects.

Due to the nature of this grand disclosure, many dignitaries from several branches of the U.S. Government and society have been invited to be at the auditorium, this day.

By shire luck or some kind of divine guidance, Steven Curtis happens to be sitting alongside of Dr. Roberts. Although, he previously dealt with him on several past science expositions at the center but this day was unique.

Utilizing his journalistic savvy and boldness, he approaches the doctor to possibly get an exclusive. He turns to him:

"Dr. Roberts, can I have a second of your time; I see that you are a little bit somewhat tense awaiting the Professor to start the conference."

Dr. Roberts looks and smiles at him shaking his head.

"Oh, hello, aren't you Curtis Leeman from…."

"No, no Sir, I'm Steven Curtis from Popular Inventors Magazine. Six months ago, I did a magazine expo on sound resonance with you at the Research Center."

"Oh I'm sorry, ah yes, I remember now. I confused you with someone else. My apology, Sir."

"That's all right, it happens all the time."

"Uh. O.K."

"I just have a small question to ask you for the magazine's Science Section."

"Yes, why not. That's why you are here, right?"

"Yes, of course. Well Dr. Roberts, do you have any fascinating details on this grand disclosure that Professor Donnelly is about to make to the World?"

Dr. Roberts turns and looks at Dr. Billings, who is sitting next to him and turns to Steven with a face like the cat that swallowed the canary.

"Sorry Curtis, I cannot say anything at this moment. I really like to help you, man but I can't. Why don't you wait a few moments and all your questions will be answered? Trust me, you will be fascinated."

"Can you give me something, at least? Throw me a crumb at least, please."

"Steven, the only thing, which I can say at this moment, is that this disclosure is bigger than anything developed by mankind to date. How's that as a hot lead for you?"

"Mankind ah? Thank you but that doesn't help me a bit. I need more meat and potatoes on this. Can you give me a better deal?"

"Sorry, I tried." He waves his arms and shrug's his shoulders.

Steven Curtis dealt with Dr Roberts in the past and he knew he was a hard nut to crack and realized that he wasn't that closed that he would readily confide in him of any significant breakthrough of this magnitude.

He decided that the next time, he needs a special favor as he did in the past; he will have to make it worthwhile. He will wait for that opportunity to come up in the future.

Steven then gets up and bids everyone success with the presentation and walks away.

While listening to Dr. Roberts' remarks, Dr. Billings looks at him, with some inquisitiveness and thinks back, to her short stay at the Institute and doesn't remember Dr. Roberts ever speaking to her, of any significant scientific breakthroughs or development.

Resolved about her conclusions, she turns to him and whispers:

"Jason, I have a suspicious feeling that you and Professor Donnelly might be concocting something to impress the private supporters and the Foundation for more allocations of research funds. Or on the other hand, you both have really stumbled onto something very significant, perhaps important enough, to call for this special presentation.

Which is the right one? I have some doubts about all of this."

Nora looks deeply into Dr. Roberts' eyes and waits, for an answer.

For a moment, there is an optical duel stand off. Dr. Roberts finally yields, and blinks first. He leans over and whispers to her:

"Nora, please wait. I agreed to a self-imposed gag order on this. The Professor insisted. See he's about to approach the podium and start. Trust me on this sweetheart, please. OK?"

The shuffling noise and the movement throughout the auditorium slowly begins to die down, as the floodlights and electric hums from video and recording equipment starts up.

Professor Donnelly walks from the left wing of the auditorium and approaches the podium. He immediately waves, at some of the dignitaries and closed friends. There is a small applause from an upper balcony and he gestures, a welcome nod to them.

After setting up himself at the podium, he looks at the gathering before him and is in awed.

The bright stage lights when turned on causes the Professor's eyes to squint a little under his thick frame glasses. A technician upon noticing his discomfort regulates the intensity, allowing him to focus and read from his folder. He nods: "OK."

The technician in a control booth high above the auditorium quietly speaks to him through an earpiece:

"Is that better, Professor?"

"It's just perfect Mister Carson, thanks."

Then the sound system reacts, causing some feed back, from several area microphones near the speakers. Mister Carson quickly corrects that other condition.

Professor Donnelly taps several times on the microphones, to check if the equipment is still operable and gives a thumb up to the control people, up in the booth.

With a slight cough and a refracting echo, of his cough throughout the public address system, everyone gradually comes to attention, in the auditorium.

All eyes are on the Professor making him feel somewhat uneasy. Clumsily, while opening his lecture folder, he bangs the microphone.

"Sorry about that folks."

The audience becomes now somewhat relaxed and allows the Professor, to feel more at ease.

Professor Donnelly glances down at Dr. Billings and Dr. Roberts, and gives each a slight smile, exposing his perfect white teeth, that glimmer in the lights. He looks at the mass of people that gathered before him and feels more confident, then begins:

"Good morning ladies and gentlemen and to all of you distinguished representatives of Society who have come to hear my few words of encouragement.

As you may already suspect, my name is Professor James Peter Donnelly."

He pauses for a second and resumes after a small applause is given:

"I am here this morning, to present to you an account of the work that is being done at this renown Research Institute named after Mr. Rockfell. I will also show you, how all funds for research are appropriated, and to what extent, it has greatly aided us, in our quest for knowledge, in cellular research and medical advancements.

And finally, the excuse of why all of you are here and that is, to hear me publicize a long awaited scientific disclosure, which will surely surprise and confound many of you.

I'm very happy and excited because this is a historical moment and you will be a part of it. Think of it, you will tell your grand children, that you were here and witnessed, this grand Earth shaking moment. I'm excited and anxious.

Now without any further a-due, let's commence.

Oh, before we do, just for the benefit of those of you, who don't know of our work here, let me start from the beginning, so everyone present here, will understand the significance of our medical studies and research. Folks, we need your support both morally and economically, thank you."

Dr. Billings meanwhile turns again to Dr. Roberts.

"Jason, I had feeling that you were up to something funny with Professor Donnelly."

"Nora, you will take back those words, in a couple of minutes, alright."

"We will see, darling."

At this point, a rear screen lowers down from above and lights up, as he continues:

"Research scientists of some years ago have successfully altered and modified simple genes to an extent that has helped mankind, by aiding, in food production and the prevention of early childbirth diseases due to chemical imbalances, in the human body.

In the past, poorly developed and not fully tested drugs caused unacceptable side effects and of course, drug abuse and not fully tested drugs contributed substantially to stillborn, miscarriages, retardation and early death syndromes, in infants and young children.

Well-known substances that highly contribute to these conditions are the use of alcohol, cigarette products and drug abuse, during the first trimester.

They impede the development of the brain and directly impacts in most cases, the development of the skeletal structure of infants. This was proven by medical science and is common knowledge today.

In the control of human reproduction, users of some of the early birth control aids risked having normal births; because these early devices left lingering chemical substances, in the body that later affected future natural reproduction. These birth control devices were not fully developed until the late 1980's.

Birth defects and breast cancer cases previously ran rampant in America and even at a higher rate, in third world countries.

Society agreed that more research was required and a greater amount of moneys was needed, to solve this complex problem.

Then came the light, as they say, at the end of the tunnel, with the development of pre-natal care' of the unborn.

There were monumental breakthroughs in the prevention of birth defects and the treatment of a rare medical condition associated, with sudden infant crib deaths, which was plaguing the world.

Later on, researchers decided to concentrate more studies on the gene and its complex structure. Other researchers discovered a method to chemically produce changes in the gene, but it did not have any practical application to medical science until later with the introduction of the electron microscope and later with the start of the Genome Project.

Certain achievements that were reached were merely technological plateaus but no significant world impacting breakthroughs were ever accomplished.

This center today, owes its existence, to those early pioneer scientists who devoted their lives to study the gene and man's development."

As the Professor continues his speech, Dr. Nora Billings, once again gets Dr. Roberts' attention and whispers to him:

"Jason, what was the Professors' purpose for canceling some of your lectures and summoning you to his office, every two or three days a week?

Does this have anything to do with today's 'Grand Disclosure'?"
She gestures with her fingers, in the air.

Jason reluctantly turns to her:

"Yes and no. Well, the no part is that he usually wanted me to talk to him about certain subjects concerning social morality, religion and of political conditions here and throughout the world. That's all."

"Is he not aware, of all these common subjects?"

"No. He told me, that he has no time for these trivial matters. He said that he is too engrossed with his work and cannot devote his free time, to these subjects. But he later confessed to me that, as time passed, it began to concern him very deeply. That's why he had this strong need to talk to someone about it. He began doubting himself and his accomplishments. He was afraid of the future repercussions of his research and development."

"I think Professor Donnelly is, in my opinion, may need medical help. I never heard of anything, so outlandish. In fact, I now feel a little pity for him."

"Nora, you have to realize the subject that the Professor was involved with. He had to weigh the ethics and morale impact on him personally and as well on Society as a whole."

"Wait a minute Jason, you are confusing me. What exactly were he and you working on, that ethics and morality became a big issue?"

"Nora, Professor Donnelly has just completed his orientation. He's about to start the disclosure. The answer to your question is just moments away."

"What disclosure, Jason? I thought this was just a con to get more research money."

"Please, pay him attention. This is very important."

"OK." Dr. Nora Billings leans back a bit perturb and listens.

"Today, I'm proud to introduce to you, some of the latest findings and accomplishments of our Research Center. I have prepared, an audio and a short video segment, which will greatly enhance our presentation."

He addresses the technicians above, in the booth:

"Mister Carson, would you please dim the house lights? Thank you." The lights slowly glow dim and the first presentation commences.

"Previously, this Institute, under my direction, is where modern cellular gene research had its real true beginnings. This center and others throughout the East Coast have ventured through numerous levels of cellular research and development and have achieved success in many areas which society has greatly profited.

I congratulate all of them for their unyielding effort. Our united front included a total of twenty years of self-sacrifice and very hard work.

We finally succeeded that is, the development and control of a synthetic gene in the lab. Yes, we created a simple synthetic gene. The purpose for this exercise was to replace damaged chromosomes, in the human DNA string. Let me give you the background, how actually genes function and how they naturally evolve.

The structures of cells, from their long ago primeval stage, to their present-day complex forms, are attributed to a little process known as 'evolution'. Let me further define this. Evolution is a process of correction and adaptation to an environment and to all its adverse or to its favorable conditions.

Let me further explain this, because I'm beginning to see many blank looks, from some of you. A little example:

Take a simple cell structure living in a harsh environment. By the process of evolution, the third or the fourth generation scarcely, if it were able to survive the initial condition, would evolve to a certain point, that it would have partially or successfully adapted its structural make-up, to meet with and survive the environmental conditions with some adaptation and self-modification to itself. Thus, future generations would not have to combat the same conditions, because each generation would learn a little more from the previous one to further improve the adaptation.

Knowledge is never lost; it is constantly being modified, stored and transmitted, to future generations with minute changes stimulated by the need to change and to adapt."

"Well, our synthetic cells and modified genes have gone through a similar artificially induced evolutionary stage in our laboratory, and these are our surprising results.

Mister Carson, please start the second program. Thank you."

"Several years ago, after we developed many synthetic and modified cultures of reproductive cells of various test animals, we introduced them to their counterparts. The majority of the cultures of these test animals at first mysteriously failed.

We concluded that the cells required more refinement and Time was the key element, to this complex exercise.

A year later, we decided to concentrate our research on rodents, especially the rabbit's reproductive cells, because of their short gestation period and time was the most important element for us for our studies. We spent many months processing the cells, until finally; we decided to run our test, once more.

Key elements within the synthetic gene were chemically modified to be in concert to work systematically with the process of cell duplication. This time, we had some degree of success. As you see, our synthetic gene successfully united itself with the natural ones with no adverse reaction. The process of the cell generation occurred and reproduction proceeded forward.

We produced redundant cultures, in order to develop them separately, using different techniques, in our lab.

The growth rate of each culture was carefully followed and recorded, until it developed to a fetus size so it could be safely placed in the female rabbit's womb.

The other cultures were placed in specially designed incubators duplicating the rodents' womb. The artificial womb was comprised of animal tissue, synthetic rubber and plastic material uniquely designed, to assimilate the rodents' womb, in a strict sterilized darkened environment.

The donor in the synthetic womb naturally gave birth, to the offspring.

Next, segment, please.

"One offspring was born without the use of his mother's body while the other was born naturally.

My new technique and theories of synthetic fetus development worked much to the surprise, of all my colleagues. The two off springs, were examined and were proven healthy male rabbits, but with a unique anomaly, which stunned all of us and it turned out to be an amazing discovery.

Our two specimens were completely de-sexualized. They were missing their male and female attributes.

Perhaps there was an error made in the DNA cycling of the synthetic genes. Maybe there was some laboratory quirk, which occurred beyond our control and a mutations followed.

Where did we fail and how can we possibly correct this anomaly.

Perhaps there was a bacterial infection or even human error made on the cell cycling process.

We had to quickly solve this problem. Our research funds were in jeopardy.

We quickly re-examined the rabbits then and after a few weeks of caring for them, we tested each animal's reflexes, muscle tension, etc. All tests came out to be surprisingly normal, compared to normal males or female that was not subjected to our procedure.

Perhaps we accidentally created a new species of rodent. We had to do further tests, because this was very unusual, to say the least.

This new species would live their lives and then no more. That was a very sobering thought, yet very sad for a brand new species.

One experiment that was performed shocked everyone present.

We decided to do further experiments and injected the rodents with high dose of testosterone, to test their reaction. This serum would drive the rodents' nervous system to a frenzy state, when a female or male rabbit is introduced, into the cage.

In our unique specimens, much to our surprise, the reaction turned out to be the opposite. The rabbits did not show any over reactive tendencies, compared to the other normal ones subjected to the same serum. In fact, they lacked the normal sexual drives that homosapiens, and animals share, when subjected to equivalent type of stimulators."

An air of amusement slowly surfaced throughout the auditorium.

Women and men, somewhat embarrassed, with the Professor words, grin and look at one another, trying to suppress their reactions.

A student, being witty, stood up, off his seat and shouts:

"Professor, perhaps you created a super rabbit!" The audience laughs aloud, releasing their suppressed tension.

Professor Donnelly is somewhat amused, by the adolescent remark.

"Ha, ha yes, indeed. Perhaps we should administer a small dose of this serum to you, so you can calm down a bit."

The audiences laugh even louder, embarrassing the student, to a point, that he slowly sinks low into his seat.

Professor Donnelly quickly retracts his response before any damage is done.

"Sorry, it was just a cruel remark; I didn't mean any harm by it. I apologies, please forgive me, Son."

After a few moments, the student acknowledges the Professor's apology, in a positive manner, by smiling and shaking his head. He then waves his arms to show acceptance.

The Professor then continued:

"Getting back to the unique condition of these small rodents, we also discovered to our amazement, that by injecting them with a special diluted isotope extracted from a rare root grown in the Orient, developed by world renowned, Dr. Tomiko of Japan, the synthetic cell metabolic rate, increased significantly with less than a 1% concentration.

Dr. Tomiko isotopes were designed to extend the human life span. The isotopes were never tested because the doctor died premature and the isotopes were secretly smuggled to the United States from China. Here they remain till now with permissions from his survivors.

Much to our surprise the volatile nature of this mixture caused, somewhat of a rapid growth, within the cells. We noticed that on a third culture, when a less than 2% portion of this serum was administered, the growth rate accelerated exponentially to a dangerous degree, causing a metabolic process that produced an exorbitant amount of heat.

The resulting effect was that the structure perished in a flash puff of fire and smoke, right before our eyes. This was shocking and unbelievable.

We had to somehow control this excessive heat built up in the process. But how? This became a monumental problem to solve.

We tried chilling it with the introduction of ice and water but it still perished because it turned the ice water to flash into steam vapor shocking everyone present.

Almost at a point of total despair, one last attempt, we consulted with cryogenics engineers who gave us their recommendations in dealing with the cell's accelerated metabolic reaction.

As a result, with allocation of a sophisticated liquid Helium cooling system, we finally solved the over-heating problem, thanks to the physicists who worked on the development of the MRI Diagnostic Technologies, at the Brookhaven Labs in New York. This breakthrough would not have been possible without their assistance.

In a controlled experiment, with the use of this new technology, we witnessed, in our specially designed incubator, the full growth of a rabbit, in a mere sixteen hours.

Probably, the developing time can be better accelerated, if we had an embryos comprised of just synthetic cells and a greater percent of isotope concentration.

In addition, we later observed by limiting the supply of isotope, to the test animal, we were able to stop the growth rate, at any point of its development. This was mind-boggling!

We later ascertained that the serum had a certain growth limitation.

After a certain stage of growth was reached, we noticed, that the animal did not start to physically degenerate, but started to replace its' dying cells, at a terrific rate. It went through some type of biological metamorphose, at full growth.

The rodent's breathing rate dramatically changed. They inhaled air but exhaled only a fraction of the amount, every ten to twenty minutes. This became a mystery!

What would cause this change and what is the trigger point that would initiate this. Those were very hard questions to ask and even harder to solve.

After performing additional tests, in a special gas analysis chamber, we theorized, that after this biological change took place, the rodents' lung tissue metabolized to a point, that it practically absorbed ninety percent of the elements in air that was inhaled.

They utilized every compound element, which air is comprised of.

I think that by having these unique physical qualities, we assessed, that these test animals could practically live forever. This was a shock for all of us.

This was the answer to the missing reproductive organs. They actually did not require them after all. We discovered a unique new species that would out-live mankind and live-forever. This was really mind blowing, to say the least."

The auditorium's attention was so fixed on the Professor that no one even moved, or even flinched, when one of the large intense spotlights overheated and blew out.

Upon observing this, Professor Donnelly realized that he finally had full attention from his audience.

He then looks up at Mister Carson, in the control booth, once more and calls out:

"Would you please run the final presentation? He continues:

"Ladies and gentlemen, our most important experiment on synthetic reproductive cells, turned out to be our biggest breakthrough. That is, the creation and unification of a synthetic cell with a known species. After many attempts and failures, in the laboratory, we succeeded on December 29, 2014 the first synthetic homosapiens cell was created. Yes, ladies and gentlemen, we have recreated Man!"

The words "RECREATED MAN!" resonates and resounds like a lightning thunderclap throughout the auditorium, as a flash figure of a naked man appears.

People are in shock and awe. They're held frozen, in time and space, as the reality slowly sets in.

The level of the audience voices gradually rises to high pitch, as the sobering fact sinks into everyone's psyche. A new creation of mankind has occurred. A new species of Man has come forward.

Surprise and amazement runs wild unabated throughout the assembly.

Newspaper journalists' reach for their I-pods and cameras to record the moment.

Others scramble up the aisles with their recording equipment to flash the picture of the naked humanoid to their home bureaus, across the world and reporting this fantastic mind sobering development.

A small group that represented the clergy sector of this conference becomes infuriated by the proceedings, and leaves their seats, rush over and approach the podium.

Some shout and scream out all sorts of profanities and threaten Professor Donnelly.

One clergy shouts:

"This is blasphemy! The whole presentation has been staged, to belittle and ridicule the religious community, because you know very well, from the onset, that we have always refused to support this kind of unethical research. And you have done it clandestinely.

Others shout.

"This is ungodly, you cannot play God. Who do you think you are?

You do not have the right to do this. We will not support you anymore, not even a penny will be donated nor we shall sponsor ever any of these horrific studies. Why are you reviving the old Nazi experiments? This is a mockery and unforgivable."

"No! No! Reverend Herbstein, my discovery is a true scientific breakthrough. I'm not trying to belittle you or any religious organization. Money to me is insignificant, compared to the work, which I'm doing for the betterment of mankind.

"This is no betterment of mankind, this is monstrous. You're a monster."

"Accuse me of anything, but do not accuse me of being a monster and a fraud. I will not stand here and accept such a slanderous attacks. My honor is worth more to me, than the practical joke of which you accuse me of."

Two security personnel, at this time enter the auditorium, from the stage wings and try urging the reverend, to return to his seat.

"Please, take your hands off me, who do you think you are? I will go by myself." He pushes them aside in contempt and slowly walks away.

The beginning of bedlam and chaos arises in the auditorium. Other religious group leaves their seats and attempt to gain access to the Professor. Some shout:

"Your practical joke has failed to amuse us, Professor. You Nazi beast!" Others also shouted.

"You are mad, this is insane. Stop the spread of these lies, Professor redeem your self! You need some kind of redemption. Please lord, cure this poor and confused man!"

News reporters shuffle the religious zealots aside and try to speak to the Professor, but fail, due to the mass of people that are gathering around the podium.

Security people enter this time and force themselves through the humanity surrounding the Professor, and create a human chain by the podium and another barrier between the stage and the auditorium.

Another group of security men scrambles from the wings and push back, some of the protesters that break through the human barricade.

At this point, the Professor takes control and switches on the microphone:

"Gentlemen, please, go and return to your seats. What I have just said is no joke or fantasy. It is the plain truth. I have scientific proof and documentation on all of our experiments. They are filed with the proper authorities, which fund this establishment. I have broken no laws."

The crowd completely ignores the Professor's pleads and raise their arms, in protest against him.

"Please, please take your seats, or I will be forced to have the auditorium cleared.

Please listen to me! Listen to me, gentlemen. I deplore you, please!"

He looks to his left at the head of security who is standing at the wings of the auditorium then pauses a few seconds, shakes his head in despair.

"I have no choice. With great pain, I must do this. I am very sorry." He turns around.

"Security, please clear out the auditorium, I will not stand here and be a party to insults and threats. I should not have given in to the Government's pressure to expose this to the general public in the first place, and make a complete fool of this Institute and myself. Good day all."

Professor Donnelly makes an about face and walks off shaking his head in dismay.

On those words, armed federal security teams dressed in riot gear, held in reserve, suddenly enter the auditorium from the front and rear of the stage and commence to forcibly push out the multitude of people.

Sirens from the city's police are heard in the distance.

Crowds, loitering in the front of the building hastily move away, as the people pour out of all the entrances.

Some fall to the ground and are trampled over, by the fleeing mob.

The situation worsens, into sheer chaos, when the city police arrive in large numbers.

The sidewalks and streets become overwhelmed with humanity. Pedestrians walking by, unknowingly become innocent participants, by mixing with the exiting throngs of people and from those fleeing from the security guards.

At this point, Dr. Jason Roberts and Dr. Nora Billings exit together from a side door of the auditorium, with the journalist from the New York Times.

Steven Curtis suddenly appears.

"Dr. Roberts, you were right. Its a big story, thanks."

A moment later, he suddenly disappears after being over-taken by the crowd.

Dr. Nora Billings turns to the journalist as they rush across the street.

"Mister Hastings, I hope you won't discredit the Professor. I know him and I do not think he would deliberately deceive everyone, like that."

"Don't worry, Dr. Billings, I won't. This is not my first time here. In fact, the Professor and I are very good friends. I know his wife very well. We happen to be old friends from school and from Desert Storm. So, don't worry. There's no reason to discredit him of anything."

"Thank goodness, that there is at least someone who does not want to get at him."

To the right of the auditorium building, a car driven by Professor Donnelly is seen moving away but suddenly comes to an abrupt stop. Dr. Billings spots him.

"The Professor is over there, he's waving at us. Let's hurry and catch up, before the crowd discovers him."

Sounds of civil disobedience are heard in the distance, as the police try to control the unruly crowd that is gathering by the research-building auditorium.

Some students of a nearby prep school take advantage of the situation to disrupt classes for the day, but the police, in turn, do not seem to share that idea. They arrest many of the protesters who refuse to heed their orders, to move on.

The trio finally reaches the Professor's car.

"Thank you, Professor Donnelly, for stopping for us, I hope we all can fit."

"Please hurry, they are coming this way." He urges them.

"Professor, we're very concerned for your safety."

"Don't you worry, my child, I was anticipating this sort of reaction. It's human nature to react negatively to things that are new and hard to comprehend."

He turns to Dr. Roberts:

"Jason, I must finalize a couple of documents at the Health Department today. Please take my car and drive my friend to Grand Central and take Dr. Billings home, afterwards."

"Sure Professor, don't worry but please be very careful there. I will pick you up, after you are finished. Please call me."

"No, don't worry about me; I will take car service home or my wife Ruth will come and take me home. Thank you for your concern."

After arriving at his destination, the Professor gets out, closes the door behind him and disappears into the building.

Jason moves over to the driver's side and drives away.

After a few minutes of silence in the car, and the journalist leans over to Jason.

"Did you see, how perturbed Professor Donnelly was at the public's reaction to his disclosure? I agree it's a very touchy and controversial subject to get involved with."

"I have never seen him react like this, before." Said Jason

"Yes, Dr. Roberts, he was very upset now, but he will recover. He's a real survivor.

We go back together many years. Unfortunately, we were once taken prisoners during Desert Storm after running out of supplies and ammunition. With his help, we escaped and survived in Iraq's desert some twenty days and nights till British commandos finally rescued us. So don't worry, he's a true survivor."

Arriving at the train station.

"This corner or the other, Mister Hastings?" Jason asks.

"Right here will be fine, thank you. Here, I can reach my track much easier, thanks again. You both have a nice day." Said Mister Hastings, as he closes the car door behind him. "Likewise." Replies Jason.

Jason drives off as the gentleman disappears into the terminal.

As they drive cross-town dogging traffic, Nora turns to Jason:

"Well my sweet and gentle Doctor, we're finally alone and I have questions for you."

"Nora, I wanted to tell you something very important and the Professor instructed me, to speak to you in private."

"Please, don't try to dodge the conversation, Jason. I know you already."

"Hear me out first, before you say anything, honey."

"What is it, Jason? That you are sorry for not confiding in me and hurting my feelings?"

"Yes, I'm truly sorry about that but this is bigger than you and Me."

"You could have at least tell me and I would have kept it to myself, until the public disclosure."

"I'm sorry for not telling you. The Professor made me promise not to tell anyone. Not even the one person that I love the most, in this world."

"Thank you for saying that, I forgive you, Jason. You said you wanted to tell me something very important."

"Yes, sweetheart, as of tomorrow, the Professor has recommended you, to start working with us, at the new wing of the Rockfell Research Center."

"But... I thought all Class Level 6 personnel were restricted from entering that area, especially me a foreigner?"

"Yes, but by tomorrow, the Professor has upgraded your security level and will received a special approval from the Research Board, to have you work with me and with some of our special people."

"Wow! This comes as a surprise to me. You cannot imagine how today has been a day of many surprises. What else can possibly happen?"

"Well, first for a starter, we're going to celebrate your new advancement."

"I don't know what to say but thanks."

"In addition, since we have the whole day for our selves and it's a nice, warm Indian summer day, we shall spend it out in the sun and in my favorite place."

"Oh no, Central Park?"

"Yes, how did you know?"

"I must have read your little mind."

"So lets go home, change, and have one of those old fashioned picnics, in the park."

"Jason, you know I live pretty far from here."

"Honey, Cliffside is only 30 minutes away."

"No, my dear. It's actually an hour away. Can we go somewhere nearby Cliffside?"

"Nora, for once, please make me happy, just this one time, sweetheart."

"O.K. Just this time. Fellow, you will have to make it up to me, someday."

"Yes, I will, I promise. When I do it, you will not regret it."

"That sounds great; I will hold you to it, Jason." Nora kisses him and drives away.

CHAPTER II

It is mid afternoon, Jason and Nora, are in a small rowboat, in the middle of the 72nd Street Lake, in Central Park.

"Jason, you love this park, I can see it in your eyes. You feel like when you were a kid, again."

"Yes, I do. After all, I grew up a few blocks from here, on the East Side."

"To be honest with you, I like it, too. It's somewhat romantic. I love to see the trees and the people walking about. It's so picturesque. I love that skyline view of the city around us. It is incomparable."

"I'm glad to hear that from you. You have some nice parks in England, too."

"Yes, but nothing compares to New York's Central Park."

"Yes, you know it, sweetie."

Jason starts rowing to the center of the lake, where it's less populated.

"Doctor, be very careful, don't over exert yourself. Remember, you haven't done, this sort of thing in years."

He splashes some water into the air.

"Oh, you are wetting me, Jason. You devil!"

"Oh, I'm sorry, sweetheart. Where do you get the idea, that I don't do this sort of thing? I exercise weekly, at the Center's gym.

I work out, at least three to four times a week. You know, that's a requirement for all personnel and I'm addicted to exercise."

"Yes I know, I was only kidding, honey. I exercise, too but your rowing needs a little help."

"Well, we're not teenagers, anymore."

"I can very well, see that."

"See what? You see any aging lines or flabbiness under my neck? Do you?"

"I was just kidding, honey, you look great."

"Oh, O.K, tell me if you do. How about any grey hairs? You see any?"

"Why are you so self conscious of your looks?"

"This is a very competitive world, that's all. You have to be there at your best at all times."

"Whom are you competing against? Tell me? Is there a mystery person out there that has you all flustered up?"

"Never mind, honey."

"Jason, changing the subject, I heard some rumors that's going around."

"Rumors? Like what I haven't."

"Experimental procedures, for example the use human guinea pigs in the Center."

"What about it? That's common practice all around."

"I can't fathom why we're still experimenting, using human beings these days. The other day, I saw a couple of the volunteers being escorted to that special restricted sector."

"Oh, you did see them?"

"Yes. Why aren't they using the computer virtual reality programs? You get the same results."

"We have used it in the past but these programs only show trends and do not actually give you real time feedback. Anyway, these people are volunteers and they are highly paid for their services. We always take extreme precautions with various simulations before exposing any of the volunteers, to any possible risk. When you begin working at the new wing, you will have a different point of view."

"What do you mean by that? What's going to change my mind?"

"Don't worry, you will see, dear. You will see wonderful things that you never seen before."

"Tell me now; I hate surprises, Jason, especially those that are mind changing."

"Honey, let's forget about work a moment and enjoy the day. OK, sweetheart?"

"I guess you're right; I'm sorry, no more shoptalk. But it still bothers me! Why live ones?"

"Oh, here we go again. When you get something in your mind, you seem to have difficulty dismissing it. It becomes like a detour sign. You just can't let it go."

"You're perfectly right. Answer me one quick and simple question, Jason."

"O.K. Let's have it, after this no more. But before that, let me answer your original question. In the past, you know that the scientific world has, for hundreds of years experimented, with human bodies. Sorry, wrong terminology, cadavers and no live ones. Leonardo De Vinci secretly studied the human body using dead cadavers as a source."

"Yes, and what has it profited them? Do you know any more today about mankind, than what you did hundred of years ago? Sorry to say, not too much!"

"We have learned a lot in the past. You have to give him credit for his effort on the human anatomy. Grant you, the human body is a very complicated machine and still, there are areas and functions within, which are still unknown to Science. That is why man cannot stop researching and seeking this hidden knowledge. It is a necessity. It is our quest for immortality. Death is the greatest fear of mankind."

"Man wants to be equal to God."

"I don't think so, sweetheart. Perhaps like gods."

"Man will never stop at this insatiable quest, until he destroys himself, together with the world around him.

One day in the near future, he may accidentally release a dormant bacterial virus, that will mutate to a point that it will exterminate the Human Race because there may be no way to stop it.

A perfect example of this was the Spanish influenza. It came into existence giving no warning. It killed millions around the world and suddenly vanished leaving no trace."

"Perhaps you're right, but why are you so self-conscious of it? You have experimented in the past, on some yourself."

"You're perfectly right, dear but not live ones." She snaps back at him and smiles.

"Morally speaking, you're perfectly right, I repeat myself. However someone has to take the initiative. I know that I may eventually pay for it someday, but for the sake of science, we must do it.

In a few weeks, you will probably better understand my reasoning."

"Jason, I do not condone placing a human life at risk for any reason, not even, for the sake of Science."

Jason becomes annoyed and tries again to change the conversation.

"Please, Nora, you are right, I surrender but please lets enjoy the afternoon. Let's not talk about work, anymore.

Look, the day is sunny, warm and nice. Take advantage of it. It's a beautiful Indian summer day. Come on, let's enjoy it, honey."

"Alright boss, can you get me one of those old fashioned sausages with all the trimmings, at the boat house?"

"You mean hot dogs?"

"Precisely."

"Sweetheart, you got yourself a deal, partner. Look out girl; I'm rowing fast this time. Take cover!"

"Oh! Please, Jason, you're soaking me, you evil man."

"Sorry, here is a towel, honey."

Later that evening, at Cliffside the doorbell rings at Dr. Nora Billings' apartment.

"Good evening, Jason, I'm glad you made it early, this time." She hugs him.

"Why, am I too early?" He asked.

"Oh, no, I only said that because you normally stop over at the Professor's place, before coming to see me."

"Well, I don't need to do that anymore, because the project that was taking up most of my evenings is now completed. No more late nights and indigestion."

"Does that mean that I have you all to myself? I just can't believe it." Nora approaches Jason and gives him a warm kiss and gently pushes him into an armchair, withdraws and whispers: "I'll get you a drink, honey. On the rocks?"

"Yes, my regular. Only this time dear, put a little more of everything in because today was one of those unusually warm and hectic day."

A minute later, Nora appears and hands him the drink and he takes a sip.

"Oh boy! That really hits the spot!"

"Jason, do you know what day is this?"

"No, any special day in particular?"

"Well, no, it is only our third anniversary of our special acquaintance. I have a diary and on this day, three years ago, I met you and we fell madly in love."

"Oh, I'm sorry, honey. It completely slipped my mind. I've been so busy; that I even forgot one of the most memorable dates, in our lives. I will make it up to you, somehow. How about tonight?"

"Ah, won't you?" She answers very cockily. He embraces her.

"Yes, I'll take my sweetheart out for dinner and dancing, to one of those hot salsa clubs in the East village and whatever happens, next…how does that sound?"

"Oh, yes, that's marvelous." Nora shows her approval by giving Jason a longer kiss this time. After a short embrace, she grabs her purse and both walk out the door very quietly in order to avoid meeting the landlady in the hallway on the ground floor.

It's the next morning; the faint scent of perfume and liquor was still lingering in the air, just as a glimmer of sunlight begins to show through Nora's bedroom window.

Jason's pillow was lying on the floor by the head of the bed. Both appeared as if they had a great time that previous evening.

There's a slight chill in the air, so Jason half-asleep, blindly grabs what was left of the bed covers.

Suddenly, the alarm clock goes off. Nora, who is a light sleeper, automatically reaches for the alarm's switch; instead, she grabs Jason's nose, by mistake and frightfully pulls away. She completely forgot that Jason was in no condition to drive home that night, so she decided to allow him to sleep it off by staying with her overnight.

"Jason, are you awake?"

"Oh my head, what happened, I don't remember coming home. Honey, we must have had a fantastic time, we did?"

"Yes, sweetheart, we certainly did."

"Good, but I cannot remember anything."

"The four Jack Daniel's after the champagne really did you in, sweetie."

"I'm very sorry, you know I can't drink, I probably made a big fool of myself."

"No, you did all right, honey, it was a beautiful night. We danced all night and had a good time together. I will never forget it."

"It was?"

"Yes, marvelous."

"I thank God that I didn't spoil your evening." Jason drags himself up very slowly.

"Oh my head is hurting bad. This room looks very strange, where am I?

Oh! Hi sweetheart. What are you doing in my bed? Did you stay over?"

"No you silly handsome guy, this is not your apartment."

"You're right, it's yours. Oh, I have to get my head together? What time is it?"

"We woke up late, Jason. We have to go to work, today."

"Oh no."

"Yes."

"How about some coffee, before we go? I'm really in bad shape, honey."

"We must hurry, get dress, Jason. Hope my neighbor next door hasn't heard you. She's very nosy and will probably report us to the landlady. You do know that we are not allowed to have men stay overnight, in these premises."

"I'll be quiet as a mouse."

Nora quickly gets up, steps into the kitchen to put on the coffeepot, and rushes to the bathroom.

Finally, after a short breakfast consisting of coffee and toast, both are on their way to New York City. Nora takes her car and follows Jason who's still driving the Professor's car.

The trip takes forty minutes to midtown, where the Research Center is located.

As they enter through a side door, they suddenly encounter Professor Donnelly as he turned from a side corridor, which leads to the special research unit of the building.

"Good morning, Professor Donnelly." Said Nora.

"Good morning, Dr. Billings. He responds very cordially.

"Good morning, Sir." Said Jason approaching Nora.

"Good morning, Dr. Billings." Said Jason being tactful.

"Good morning Doctor." She responded dispersing any notions that she spent the night with Jason.

"Dr. Roberts, good morning to you, too. I trust that everyone had a very restful day, yesterday?"

"Oh, yes, Professor." Said Nora, while having some flashbacks, of her exploits of the previous night and maintaining herself a good distance from the Professor out of fear of being discovered.

"Professor Donnelly, I hope you didn't have any further inconveniences getting here this morning." Nora asked with some apprehension in her voice.

"Why do you ask, Dr. Billings?"

"I saw some security guards posted, all around the property and the police cars outside."

"Oh, yes, Dr. Billings. Security fears, that there may be more disturbances here, today but I doubt it."

"Are you afraid, Sir?"

"No, I don't think so. You will not probably believe this; U.S. Federal Marshals personally escorted me here this morning. How quaint is that?"

"That's why, you're not afraid. Who would be?" Said Nora.

"I wonder who sent them. They came early this morning to my home and announced their intentions. I was flabbergasted and so was Ruth, too. There are two marshals posted in front of our brownstone this very moment."

"Professor Donnelly, it's probably due to your sudden notoriety and the significance of your disclosure. Perhaps it prompted the government, to be concerned over your safety."

"Well, Dr. Billings, perhaps you're right, but I don't need any protection. I'm not afraid. The only thing I wish is, to be left alone to go on with my work in peace."

"But you're now somewhat of a celebrity."

"To be one, is the least desire in my life that I would ever want. My only ambition is to finish my work, together with my friends and colleagues. That would be my ideal wish."

"Professor, I hope, that it be granted you."

"Well, Doctors, its another beautiful day here in Gotham City, let's get to work. Dr. Roberts, can you go to my office and bring the latest disc files, which your group cataloged the other day, on the new synthetic enzymes?"

"Yes, Sir, no problem."

"By the way, Dr. Roberts, yesterday evening, Dr. Degasp called to my attention, your method approach to a particular experiment. He declared that it's a departure from our standard practice. Is he right? You know that in order to receive the government's certification for our work, we must standardize our procedures, to meet their approval. We are not just talking about money here but our reputation."

"Professor, the reason why I changed the approach to this particular experiment, was due to the…"

"Wait, wait one moment, Dr. Roberts." Professor Donnelly raises his arms and shakes his head. "No, no, no. Let me first review your methodology, so that I can properly assess the situation here. I do not want any unnecessary friction between you and Dr. Degasp.

We all should work in harmony, please. I cannot tolerate any distractions, because it takes our focus away from our main goal. He also has an ear to the Feds. One word from him can cause set backs to our studies and even jeopardize all of us in many ways. Let's keep this gent happy and away from that panic button, OK?"

"Very well, Professor, I'll wait for your review."

"Dr. Roberts, while you're there, I will take the opportunity to introduce Dr. Billings to our colleagues and to our special friends.

This way, Dr. Billings." He ushers her forward.

"That will be splendid, Professor Donnelly, I will join you shortly."

As the Professor walks away, Nora takes Jason's arm and whispers.

"Don't hurry back. I'm just kidding, honey. Do hurry, please, I love you." Nora moves up, and catches up with the Professor, as he proceeded ahead in the direction of the special lab. He turns to her:

"Dr. Billings, I think you have never been to this sector of the Center. It's limited only to certain people."

"Professor Donnelly, am I authorized, to be here?"

"Oh yes, you are. We received it the night before."

"I hope you will forgive me for asking this, but who recommended me besides you, Sir?" she asked very curiously.

"Dr. Billings, due to your closed affiliation with Dr. Jason Roberts and his high professional regards for your dedication to work, we both highly recommended you to the board for this task."

"Professor, I don't know what to say. I'm speechless, but thank you very much for the appointment. It's a great honor. Well, I hope I will succeed on this new endeavor and bring merit to the Center."

"Dr. Billings, I have full confidence in you and I truly feel you will do splendid."

"Oh, here comes Dr. Roberts." Said Nora, as he approaches.

"I hope I didn't take too long getting back. There was something wrong with your office door. Seems someone tried to break in last night, but security must have scared them off."

"Oh yes, Dr. Roberts, I was informed. I was just explaining to Dr. Billings of our decision, to have her work with us."

"Yes, of course." Said Jason.

"Now, let us proceed with Dr. Billing's orientation. I hope you are ready to see, some of our special people at work and those, whom we experiment with."

As the Professor leads on and enters through the security entrance, Nora turns and whispers to Jason:

"How coldly he speaks, Jason. I'm a little curiously frightened. Does he really mean, what he is saying? 'Whom we experiment with.'

Still maintaining a good distance from the Professor, Jason turns to Nora.

"Now I must tell you something very important.

Since the time, that I met you and before that, I have been working very closely with the Professor, on this project.

At first, when we succeeded, we were supposed to make a public disclosure of our findings, some eight years ago, but due to the circumstances of the times, it was decided at the time that people were not ready for this kind of expose'.

The findings and the disclosures, that were made yesterday, are shaking up many in high positions and rivaling fundamental truths in many societies.

The Government surrendering to public and private pressure is now trying to back pedal by redefining the whole expose to something less controversial because they are now wishing that this never happened and with time, it will eventually go away from people's mind."

"Jason, with yesterday's disorders, it looks like the public will not easily forget this episode.

I'm also not ready at this point, to accept this kind of sobering truth. It's just unbelievable. I feel like one of those social heretics in the Middle Ages harboring a new earth shaking idea that would cause us all to be burnt in hell fire."

"Let me finish, Nora."

"Please continue I'm sorry."

"A branch of the government some years ago, discovered our breakthrough and began funding our research, with no limitation to capital. Then for some reason or other, the Government declared and labeled our research top secret. They gave it some kind of national security classification and placed a permanent secrecy veil on it. What they were up to, no one knows.

We were obliged to keep our silence, until a public release would be decided.

I was not privy to the date. I thought that it was going to happen in a few months, but months turned into years. The Government sent a couple of their top medical research scientists to work closely with us, on some of the areas. One of them you already heard of. His name is Dr. Degasp."

"Oh yes, he seems like a nice chap. I've bumped with him several times at the cafeteria. Once or twice, I remember now and then that I did sit down with him and had a pleasant conversation. He seemed nice, at least to me."

"Well, after some technical problems were worked out, the first year, we successfully created numerous synthetic creations."

"That sounds fascinating!"

"Nora, the first groups created were fifty males and females. Their average age ranged between twenty and thirty years in stature, in comparison to humans. Their height ranged between five feet, ten inches to six feet, four inches, taller if needed. We were in full control of their physical and mental faculties, until present.

Later on, the government reasoned out their possible military/ police potential and acquired, during the three years with us a couple of hundred more. We never knew what they did with them."

"In my opinion, what they did with them may not be legal. This research center should have consulted with the Justice Department for its legality, before attempting these experiments and the unsupervised use of these creations."

"To top this, Nora, a computer company has secretly incorporated one of these synthetic creations into their server system network. They literally built the computer, around the being itself, so it became an integral part of the system."

"That is sickening; you're terrifying me now, Jason."

"I have much more to tell you, but I fear time is running out. You cannot divulge any of this to anyone. The board will oblige you to sign affidavits to restrict you from speaking to anyone about what you will see here. If you do so, I don't know what will happen."

"Jason, this is insanity, how dreadful! I just cannot believe that this is actually happening here, in America. It sounds like science is going amuck. I hope to God, that this is only but a bad dream caused by our over drinking last night."

"No, it's really happening, Nora. I wish I were never a part of it. In the beginning, I felt a sense of accomplishment, because mankind and medicine was being advanced, but it got out of hand. It became monstrous."

Professor Donnelly suddenly appears.

"Well, doctors, have you completed your little chat?"

Nora, with an expression of shock on her face, answers very nervously:

"Oh! Yes, Professor, Dr. Roberts was just explaining something to me about procedures."

"Good. This way, please!" He exerted.

"Dr. Billings, as you know, and the rest of the world has fail to accept, that we have created synthetic beings, and many, as you will later discover through Dr. Robert's planed orientation. Well, as to their exact numbers, I'm not obliged to tell you, but I will let you meet some of them. They're all unique, but first, I wish to present to you my assistant. He is a brilliant man and a good colleague. His name is Andrius."

"Professor Donnelly is he...?"

"Not quite, you be the judge, as for me, I consider Andrius a very good friend and the nicest person that you will ever want to meet in a lifetime. There he is. The chap standing in the back of the lab."

Nora observes a very handsome man; He was tall, well built and expressed an air of authority.

From the distance, Nora was able to perceive he was a blue-eyed blonde, with slightly long hair, which was kept together in a hair ring node. He wore the typical research robe and carried a chart, affixed to a clipboard.

He casually looked up and smiled at her in a gentle way and turned around resuming his work.

Nora somehow felt a sense of familiarity with this individual although she never actually met him before but yet there was a unique feeling towards him.

How could it happen, that she was instantly attracted to him, both physically and emotionally? There was something inexplicable and at the same time captivating and dark about this individual named Andrius.

"My God, he looks so handsome. He's as normal as you or me, Professor Donnelly."

"Yes, he is. I consider him the son I never had. In him, there is a part of my essence."

"Professor, his features are mesmerizing. Those brilliant blue eyes are seductive, even from this distance. In any other place, I could never tell that he was any different. In fact, Professor Donnelly, he looks better, than some men I know do."

"Yes, I've have been told."

"Professor, if you really created this person, I have to confess, you are all truly geniuses! Some may compare you as god like, for creating a new species of mankind."

"No, I did not do this alone, but it was the contribution, the effort and the dedication to hard work of many in this and other research centers throughout the United States. He is the culmination of many years of sweat, despair and unyielding effort of many."

The party of three, resumes walking towards the lab, as the Professor continues briefing Nora about her new associate. Approaching Andrius.

"Mister Andrius is being slowly groomed, so that he will be able to take complete control of this research center, someday in the near future. Presently he has complete authority to make decisions over all programs, which are being run in this facility."

"Oh, is he? Said Nora.

"Now, here we are." They finally reach the center of the lab and approach him.

"Good morning, Andrius."

"Good morning, Professor Donnelly."

"I wish to introduce to you a new colleague, her name is Dr. Nora Billings. She will be working with us, as of today."

Andrius reaches over and gently shakes Nora's hand.

"It's an honor to finally make your acquaintance, Dr. Billings." Andrius looks into Nora eyes and smiles.

"The pleasure is all mine, Mister Andrius." Nora answered with an astonished and startled demeanor. She almost reaches a point of hyperventilating and closed to fainting.

"Are you all right, Dr. Billings?" Andrius asked very concerned.

"Yes, yes, I suddenly became a little light headed. Maybe the air in here is the cause of it."

"Perhaps, I will look into it with the building service people. People have complained about this bad air it in the past. I will certainly follow up and correct the problem."

"Thanks." She said.

"Oh, Dr. Billings, I have to speak to Dr. Roberts in private for a few moments. Would you both kindly excuse us?" Said the Professor.

"It's all right Professor, go right ahead." She replies.

The Professor then turns to Andrius.

"Would you do me a favor Andrius and show Dr. Billings around the lab, till I get back?"

"Yes Professor, I will be more than honored to do so."

"I'll join you after."

As the Professor disappears with Dr. Roberts, Andrius turns to Nora.

"Dr. Billings, I've been assigned as your official tour guide to the lab."

"I'm also glad that he choose you rather than someone else."

"Thank you. I will try to do my best."

"I'm sure you will Mister Andrius."

"O.K. This way please, Dr. Billings."

"Gladly, please lead the way."

"Thanks."

Andrius proceeds to walk with Nora, describing the different sections of the lab, when she momentarily interrupts him.

"Mister Andrius, I must apologies. Please forgive me for my staring at you in the manner in which I did before. It so happens, that I was not expecting to see a man of your stature and your overall appearance."

Andrius suddenly becomes a little annoyed by her last remark.

"Please, Dr. Billings, you do not have to apologize to me. Please don't take this personal. I don't mean to cause you any distress or to make you uncomfortable but I must inform you that I'm not a man but just a being, made up of a different type of living mass of flesh and fluids, which circulate throughout my body system. I'm not human and most likely; I will never be classified as one today, tomorrow or in the very near future. So please do not call me man."

"I'm sorry to have hurt your feelings. I didn't mean to."

"Now is my turn to say that I'm sorry, Dr. Billings. Let me apologize to you for my outburst. It was very rude of me and not fair to you because you are by far, the innocent party here. I wish you accept my apology for my insensitive outburst."

"I understand, your position very clear, Mister Andrius."

"When you are constantly doing this sort of work, day in and day out without a breather or interludes, it helps at times to release some steam, even jumping down the throat of any person who slightly irritates you even accidentally. I am guilty of that."

"Forgive me again for my insensitive approach. Can we still be friends?"

"Of course, Dr. Billings, I'm looking forward to be your best friend and colleague."

"Thank you, Mister Andrius that takes a lot of pressure off me."

"You can relax, Dr. Billings, this is a great place to work. I also like working with people that I can trust but there are some here who are not too amicable."

"I agree with you one hundred per cent, Mister Andrius. If a job is very stressful, it will affect you both physically and emotionally. You don't need those kind of people around you."

"Dr. Billings, lets start with you just calling me, Andrius. Let's forget about formality, alright?"

"Yes, Andrius and you can call me Nora too, alright?"

"Yes." "Good."

Both started walking down through a small corridor.

"Can you believe this? I never had your typical mother or a genuine father but simply created. I was just brought forward into an existence of not of my own choosing. Isn't that very amusing?"

"Andrius, we don't choose where we are to be born. It's up to our parents but the other statement of not having a birth parent that makes me feel a little sad.

The idea is very hard to fathom and I feel that I must be dreaming, because all of these things, which I've witnessed and heard today, cannot possibly be happening. It is just feels unreal."

"It's very real. In fact, as you mature, you learn to accept principals and changes in life styles and new trends, in the world and you must accept it and abide by them."

"You're right, we must adapt. Well how about the tour of the lab, which you were taking me on."

"Very well Nora, this way please."

"Thanks."

"One attribute to my special existence is, that I can say that my creation can be compared to the first creation of mankind, a man named Adam, created by God, the Almighty, as described, in the

Bible. To some philosophers, Adam is a symbolic character. Maybe he never existed but the author of the scriptures was only stressing a point of view for a society."

"Oh, you have read the Bible?" Nora asked

"Yes, ten different publications and there are others like the Dead Sea Scrolls and others out there to be discovered."

"That is fascinating." She said

"Why are you so impressed, the Bible is considered by many as the only source of communication between man and God? I have come to a safe conclusion that I can safely say that I consider myself to be the third Adam, in all recorded history. On the other hand, I could be wrong. How does that sound to you?"

"It sounds very fantastic."

"You may be well listening to the ravings of a madman."

"I don't think so. At this point and time I would consider you as the next evolutionary step for mankind."

"You honestly think so?"

"Yes I do."

"You will probably ask in all curiosity, who the second Adam was, if I'm the third?

And the answer to that is obvious. It is The Christ, the Son of the Almighty. I feel great about it. Through his spiritual guidance of mankind, I strongly believe that I came to be through his inspiration. That is how I can justify my existence.

Otherwise, I would have terminated this existence a long time ago because I would have considered myself a godless creation and that would be a horrible thought to fathom."

"Good, that is the spirit, you have to look at the positive side to everything and never look back, because the former has the tendency, to wear you down. It is just a waste of time."

"Good, we have something in common."

"That's great."

The two fellow scientists then venture forward across the lab area, and exit through a door, where they are suddenly dwarfed by a structure completely made up of polished steel, concrete and glass. It is partially lit from within.

A strange fog and haze surrounds the immense structure before them. The two scientists approach it and stop.

"Nora, this first room is called the 'Cyclonic Prep Chamber'. I hope it doesn't frightens you, because it looks very eerie standing alone there in a purplish haze that is flowing within and all around us."

"What is it?" Nora asks very curiously.

"The haze?"

"Yes." She suddenly breaks away, slowly fades and disappears into the mist.

Andrius answers:

"It is only a reaction that occurs when we are disinfecting and sanitizing the interior and exterior perimeter walls with anti-bacterial vapors and ultraviolet rays.

We find that this method is much more effective than actually scrubbing down, all the glass and platinum plated walls that encase this huge chamber. It would take days or even weeks, for a crew of six to perform this demanding task. By this method, it takes only a few hours."

"It's pretty chilly in here, Andrius."

"Yes, we keep the environment at 42 degrees Fahrenheit at all times. This low temperature prevents bacterial generation within the chamber. At least, it slows down its progress, until they are eliminated by this process."

"Wow! That's terrific."

"Let me give you a sweater, tell me where you are?"

Nora appears out of the mist.

"Here I am, Andrius, thank you."

She takes the sweater and again disappears, as Andrius continues:

"This chamber is the largest piece of equipment that we have in the center. It is about forty feet high, sixty feet wide and almost four hundred feet long. It is longer than your typical foot ball playing field."

"It's massive, Andrius. What are its purpose and the strange apparatus that is standing inside at the center? How is it related to the work here?"

"Wait until I get there, Nora. You are sounding like one of those typical newspaper reporters on TV. One question at a time, please."

"Oh, I'm sorry. How about the first question, to start with."

"OK, this in laymen's language is called an atom-smashing machine, or in our technical terms, it is known as a 'mini-cyclotron'.

Cyclotrons have been in forefront use for many years. They are used to speed up certain atomic elements and molecules to velocities that normally, outside of this machine, would be next to impossible to achieve. These units were also used for extracting or changing certain electron orbits of atoms in the past."

"How do you, as a researcher utilize such a machine, in your work here?"

"The study of genetics and fetus logy was becoming very demanding and intricate. The more we probed into it, the harder it was to get clear answers. It became more complicated as we tried to venture forward once a certain plateau was reached.

At that time, Professor Donnelly was faced with surmounting problems. He was working with microscopic and sub-atomic structures that became impossible to begin to attempt to alter their structures, with the standard lab equipment, at hand.

He had the right theory, but he lacked the technology, to fully manifest this theory.

The cyclotron was the only means to the solution. This machine was shipped to us by the Federal Government after securing it from the State of California."

"I hear that these machines are priceless. How did you manage to acquire one?"

"At the time, California had no further use for one and the Professor easily obtained it."

"Did he requested one and they just shipped it right over? No questions asked?"

"Not exactly, we had to provide substantial prove, for the need to have one.

The situation was just perfect because it so happened that twenty years ago, after the end of the Cold War, the United States, Europe, Russia and Argentina were in a race amongst them selves, as to who would be the first to resolve the World's Energy crises by developing the first Fusion Energy machine. It became a world quest.

During that period, the research and development of these machines was supposed to be the answer to the world's desperate situation.

The major world powers were depending on the oil producing countries and the looming threats of higher oil prices and cut backs, was a very serious problem to deal with. Countries were declaring bankruptcy causing a domino effect and threatening a world wide economic depression.

The growing anti American feelings throughout the Middle East and the spread of distorted religious fundamentalism and power hungry dictators, the world searched for an alternate means to reduce the dependence on foreign oil, especially from the Middle East and South American countries who were our former allies.

With threats of cutbacks and the refusal of the sale of crude oil to certain countries, leaders of the free world were under pressure to develop newer methods of producing cheap energy. The economic pressure on countries was so great, that many dependent countries unfortunately disregarded safety and environmental measures, went forward with their research and development, whatever the cost.

As a result, there were many industrial accidents throughout the world but two were outstanding. One occurred in the United States and the other, at one of Argentina's offshore islands.

In California, there was a disaster at the Institute of Research and Development, in Palo Alto. Perhaps you may recall the incident."

"I don't think so; at that time, I was still in secondary school in England."

"A world known Physicist, Doctor Shapiro, was working on a fusion machine which was the prototype of the Russian 'Tokomak of the 1930's. It was a theoretical fusion experimental machine re-designed by the Soviets' in 1950 in process of development. The United States Government purchased the patent rights and decided to build one.

Dr. Shapiro made significant improvements on the design.

His modifications were very promising but did not concentrate on the machine's stability because it lacked certain control components, which would have brought success to his research project and time was essence.

One very hot afternoon, his group while operating the machine, the control system suffered from an undetermined power surge, in the electrical system. A safety device failed to maintain constant power to the controllers that held the super high temperature plasma, within the enclosed chamber. The plasma was held in place by a series of twelve electro-magnets. When the power failure occurred, the plasma, erupted through the wall of the chamber instantly incinerating everyone in its' immediate area and along its' path.

It completely devastated a small town of eight hundred inhabitants, a quarter of a mile away.

Dr. Shapiro unfortunately lost his life and many of his key colleagues.

The unfortunate disaster quickly put a quick stop to any further research into fusion energy in the United States out of fear of potential future disasters.

A similar accident occurred in Argentina a few months prior but was kept classified at that time due to its magnitude.

Public reaction against the project and of such experiments increased daily, until the government yielding to public demands, was forced to take a stand.

Independent investigations discovered a rampant disregard for safety precautions. Funds that were appropriated for such programs were suddenly withdrawn. All salvageable equipment was placed in warehouses throughout the State.

The State of California, when petitioned for the equipment, was glad to comply with the Feds' request for the cyclotron.

They felt that they had enough natural disasters from earthquakes, mudslides and fires and did not need any additional catastrophes, in their lives.

Therefore, it took three years to locate all the sections and rebuild the machine over here. This new wing was specially constructed, to house this little monster and the other research equipment."

"Andrius, can I go in, and take a closer look?"

"Yes, but no one's allowed to enter the chamber, unless adequately suited in special bio hazard suits.

Inside the chamber is so clean and sterile, that a surgeon can operate on a person right on the floor itself and need not worry about bacteria, or germs from invading and infecting, the open wound."

"That is amazing." Nora was impressed

Andrius goes over to the side and opens a cabinet exposing several of the special suits hanging in pressure sealed bags. He takes out one and pulls out one of the tabs and the suit instantly deflates.

"Wow! What was that? Why are they blown up under pressure?"

"They are filled with nitrogen. It prevents contamination of the suites while in storage and it also helps as a warning alarm that the suits developed a safety seal problem. We found that when the suites are not inflated bacteria multiply exponentially even while they are not in use."

Nora picks out one suit, and deflates it. She opens the zipper and examines the insides.

"Andrius, the outer layer of the suit is porous. The bacteria from our bodies will certainly contaminate the chamber."

"Don't worry, Nora, our technicians have a process by which they can decontaminate anything, living or matter, in those vertical tubular cylinders that are connected to the chamber's entrance.

First, you must get into the suit. You may change in that dressing room over there. The suite will fit snug, so be sure to remove all clothing, including your undergarments."

"I think I'm not going to like this."

"Nora, don't be so modest, no one can see through the suits. They are not transparent; there's no need to be afraid. The suits are only translucent."

"All right, Andrius, I will trust you."

Moment's later; Nora exits from the dressing room and Andrius also wearing his suit. Nora's figure is breathtaking as her figure appears in a monitor above and viewed by technicians. Andrius approaches.

"Now we enter each tube singly, on the left side of the chamber. The technicians, who are viewing us on closed circuit cameras, will pump into the tubes non-poisonous gases that are charged with highly excited electrons and apply a low resonating frequency in each tube that will cause a tingling feeling on the surface of your dermas. This process will cause and repel all dust, bacteria, germs and any other substances, that are on the surface of your skin, including cosmetics, dead cells that may be anywhere on your person and in your hair."

"You mean it removes everything, even my favorite perfume?"

"Yes, all perfume and deodorants."

"Now I'm sure, that I wouldn't like to go on with this, I will probably be too embarrassed, afterwards."

"Why Nora?" Andrius asked very curiously.

"It's a women's privacy. You don't have to know, Andrius."

"All right."

They both enter the tubes and two minutes pass and the doors automatically open on the cyclotron side of the lab.

"Now did that hurt?"

"No in fact it was interesting at some point."

"Glad that you enjoyed it."

"Thank you."

"What did you experienced?"

"Something nice. Oh never mind, Andrius. Please explain how does this machine works."

"I can safely say that actually here is where I was given my existence."

"How? Tell me more."

"Well, in genetics, the process by which a person receives his personality and the overall make-up from his parents is called Cellular Characterization.

When the first synthetic gene was created by the Professor, he compared its' DNA to a human one. He discovered and identified many identical multiple structures within the DNA strand. He named them Redundant Receptors.

They caused many experiments to end in complete failures, due to abnormal mutations and duplicity of cells. He received public acclamations for his work in genetics, but in this very matter, he felt that he was a failure. These technological set backs spurred the Professor on, to intensify his research and experiments to a fanatical degree.

Either through blind luck or some divine guidance, soon afterwards, he theoretically solved the problem, in his mind of the unnatural duplication of the cells. He formulated that he had to somehow remove certain DNA properties from the spiral strand, so that the numerical combinations of the chromosomes and receptors were in the right chronological sequence or parity with the natural strands. Am I loosing you?"

"I kind of have an idea of what you're explaining but its not too clear."

"Nora, let's use an example: Take for instance, a lock, in order for a key to open a lock; it must fit the prescribed slots and tumblers, within the lock. If it is not perfectly aligned, the lock will not function, as designed. The Professor had a dilemma. He had the lock, but it lacked the right design of ridges in the shaft to open it.

Upon realizing his predicament and the gravity of the situation, he decided to present the problem and his recommendations to the Board of Directors of the P.K. Richmond Foundation. They are a nationwide cancer research group, funded by public and private organizations. They were also managing and supporting private studies, in cellular research.

He went before them, presented the problem and waited for a decision of support or a recommendation.

His theory: He believed that if the spiral structures of the genes were to be sped up fast enough, in a centrifugal machine, the structural makeup string of the genes can be safely separated, classified and even modified.

By classifying their component parts, he could easily formulate new experiments, perhaps succeeding this time, in creating a functional synthetic gene.

The Foundation had a small centrifugal machine, but was not designed to operate at these levels.

Professor Donnelly's machine had to be of a special design, to handle his special brew.

They turn down his request due to lack of funds and sited the environmental risk that would be associated, with such a venture.

Years past, the Professor was almost at a point of complete despair, when out of the blue, he was informed by a colleague, our mutual friend, who happens to be Dr. Jason Roberts, heard of the unfortunate incident, out in California. He received a preliminary report, that the cyclotron had some peripheral damage, but with time and dedication it was reparable.

On first hearing about this, the Professor was disinterested because of the enormous size and complexities associated with these atom-smashing machines. However, after some investigation, Dr. Roberts later discovered, that it was one of the smallest type of cyclotrons ever built.

Yes, the smallest one, it was larger than two-jumble jet airliners placed end to end. Dr. Roberts raised the Professor's interest so much, that on a meeting with the Board, he pleaded with them, to acquire it. He strongly believed that the project would be successful, if they had this advanced technology in their inventory. The Board finally agreed and the rest was history.

So here she is, her Majesty, my mechanical mother. You see how she stands, immaculate, deserving, spectacular, but impersonal. We, the godless ones, owe our existence to her."

They both walk around the machine and Nora looks in awe at all of the electrical and mechanical components that makes up the system.

"Andrius, how does it actually work?" She was perplexed.

"It's very simple, it discards what you do not need and ads exactly, what is required. It is almost like mixing chemicals and molecules at ultrasonic mindless velocities. How about a drink?"

"No, thanks, but it's pretty dark in here."

"Oh, I'm sorry, let me turn on the lights. As he does the interior lights up. Is that better?"

"Ah, much better." Nora was impressed by the vivid colors and size of the machine. "Andrius, who picked out the spectacular color and light combinations?"

"It is an art to select just the right lumens that are very soothing to the eye. I think it was Dr. Roberts; he painted the machine with a special paint, designed for jet aircraft. They are much more durable than your normal commercial type."

"Oh! He did?"

"You see this panel? It has controls for different magnetic frequencies that are transmitted within the orbital path of the donut sphere."

"What is its function?"

"Well in cellular structures, all units that comprises it, have a unique resonating frequency and this is due to their structure and the make-up of the mass, so they react differently. That's how it works.

The method how we can change the character of the cell is, by speeding it up in the centrifuge closed approaching two thirds of the speed of light and applying the resonating frequencies.

The result is that the smaller masses separate and fall partially back, while the larger ones either remain in state or speed up ahead due to an artificial orbital which is imposed on them."

Once achieving this, we can direct them to different sectors of the chamber for formulation, and temporary hold them in a magnetic field orbit for storage."

"Then what do you do with them?"

"The individual structures are so sub-atomic, that it takes an electronic microscope at full power, to perceive their entities. Some are even smaller. This is why we require the decontamination tubes, at the entrance.

Unfortunately, accidents have occurred in the past, so we try our utmost to prevent any contamination of the cyclotron. If we were not to, it surely would be disastrous."

Andrius approaches another panel wrapped up in plastic sheathing, waiting to be integrated into the main console.

"We recently broke down a complete gene structure into its components parts. You cannot imagine how tedious of an operation this was previously. Now we are supplementing these additional sections to the control, so we can have a finite control over the individual components of the gene at any stage of composition.

Just as you arrived with the Professor, I was finalizing all the categories, into a hard drive.

Later this new system will give us a basic formula for a typical gene construction. In other words, how we can build an organic being in whatever sizes or shape that we wish to.

This time, it will be much easier and faster than ever. What took us weeks and months to formulate will take only hours to accomplish."

"Andrius, that's incredible and scary, at the same time. This machine and the rest of this equipment, in the wrong hands, can probably bring untold destruction and misery, to the whole world." Nora said in a tensed voice.

"This is why the new technology has been kept a secret for all these years. In the future, all the major powers of the free world will soon sign binding agreements, over the control and dispensation, of this process.

All machines, under this agreement, will be tied into a world wide security network that will be constantly surveyed and checked to control the numbers of beings that may be produced, by a country, at any one time.

By this, the United States will hope that there will always be equilibrium of the numbers, throughout the world. Let's not kid ourselves, there may be renegade countries wanting to secretly produce many more and upset the balance of power. Mark my words, this will soon be evident, if this agreement is not signed and rigidly enforced."

"I hope that all nations sign the agreement but I fear for the future."

"Well Nora, only time will tell what course that human society will take, with regards to our new species or what course we decide to take."

Both scientists walk away and disappear after exiting the cyclotron.

Minutes later, after finishing the tour at the cyclotron area and again dressing up, Nora meets Andrius in front of the dressing room.

"So Nora, you have seen our lab, our marvelous machine and some of the people. What is your opinion?"

"Andrius, first I'm completely dumfounded; I've never expected to see this kind of progress, in this field by anyone, ever. My mere presence here is like taking a giant step into the future. It's very sobering and scary. Perhaps, we have taken a giant step forward, but are we being contemptuous to God, our Creator, by doing this?"

"Perhaps Nora, you are right, said Andrius, man should not meddle in Gods' domain."

"Andrius, I fear that if this technology takes hold, it may some day destroy the normal family unit, throughout the world? Basic relationships between parent and off-spring will totally be non-existent, so to speak."

"No, I don't think so, this will not eliminate this relationship, but it will preserve it. You will have a much healthier and happier and productive family. The fear of disease, deformed children and stillbirth, will all be totally eliminated. If a couple who wish to have children and are unable to because of some physiological condition of the mother or the father, we can correct this disorder by alienating

49

that unproductive cell or mutation and allow the good one to flourish, thus safeguarding a sure and healthy birth."

"Yes Andrius, you're right, but the problem is, that the majority of all these births will probably occur outside the mother's body. Perhaps like here, in some mass incubator in a human farm somewhere. Babies will be mass-produced like in chick farms. That parental bonding that occurs between mother and child will no longer exist and eventually will disappear, altogether."

"Ah! Nora, I detect a slight resistance in you against progress. You are one of those conservative types, from a romantic period of time past."

"Yes, Andrius, I'm still proud of motherhood and like any other woman; I would like to have my own children, some day. I would not want some other animal to rear my baby, not even, a cold and heartless incubator. It is just ungodly. The beginning of life isn't meant to be that way."

"But you have to realize, that this is the 22nd century, Nora."

"Yes Andrius, it may be, but you will discover, that there are more and more people like me that are of the conservative romantic types!"

"Please forgive me, Nora, I don't mean to get you upset. I was only playing on your emotions. It looks, as if I am constantly apologizing to you, but I just wanted to see what sort of a person you really are.

Let's say that, I'm also one of those types, even though I'm not a man, but I still feel human emotions. It's that part of my nature that Professor Donnelly failed to remove from his traits. Your friend, Dr. Roberts also believes, in your same philosophy, but I noticed a lesser degree in the Professor. How quaint of a man who gave me some of his genes."

"Everyone is different in this world. That is what makes us all unique. Genes don't make your personality but one's heart does."

"Well, Nora, we romanticists must stick together, if we want to defeat our opponents."

"What opponents? Tell me, Andrius." Nora was curious.

"Well Nora, it is like this. Years ago, when creations like us were mass-produced, conversations started amongst our groups, over their real purpose of existence and our contribution to humanity.

Due to our dependence, our unyielding productive ability and man's profit motives that we created unknowingly, some resentment began to brew.

Clandestine meetings amongst our groups were held without the knowledge of the scientists. We spoke about the great strides that we accomplished and realized that they were only mere plateaus, of our true ability. The feeling of being accepted ran opposite to feelings of uselessness, after certain scientific levels of success were accomplished. This raw feeling was very traumatic to all because any action, whether or not done to any of us, you can say, it was felt by all.

In other words, we all feel each other's joys and sadness. You may call it telepathy or a special acuteness or bonding of mind. It really happens."

"But Andrius, I don't seem to understand what you mean."

"What I'm trying to say is that we were being used as guinea pigs. The only one difference was that we were able to respond and give our opinion over the situation, provided that we survived the experiment. We shared neither glory nor reward for our efforts. This affected and still affects us immensely."

"Well, I can plainly realize this feeling. That's a human trait that's shared by all humans."

"Nora, as the Professor said yesterday, every creature on the face of this earth goes through its own evolutionary phase period. He evolves from a simpler form and is constantly changing himself and adjusting to his environment. Therefore, he pushes on and resists all discomforts and the elements, until he overcomes it, or by physically reconfiguring his over-all makes up, to adapt. Human nature, as well as the animal world, has evolved in this manner, but we, the non-human, the non-animal, the non entity have been designed to function for a purpose and only after that purpose has been achieved, there is no change nor a future."

"Perhaps with time, you may get your wish. Be patient."

"Let us hope so. The dark skin population in America suffered 200 years of mistreatment and slavery before emancipation and final acceptance as equals was achieved.

Love for one another and one's self and self-perseverance kept them alive and united. Must we wait also 200 years?"

"Andrius, it is a different situation and a different time that we all live in."

"I see no difference."

"But there is, Andrius, are you and your kind capable of love?"

"It may sound very funny to you, Nora, but I do feel love and emotions. You do not have to be a sexual person to experience emotional love for a person, especially the kind of love that I have for others and especially, the love that I feel for you."

"How could you, Andrius, you have just met me."

"Yes, I do. Nora, I have always seen you walking up the street with Dr. Roberts and his associates. The first time was almost three years ago. So, I may say, Nora, I've known you for quite a long time."

"Do you know, Andrius, that I am engaged to Jason?"

"Oh, yes, I know, you must realize that I have a unique type of love for you. Let us say my love is more platonic, than anything else is. Anyway, your society will never accept a relationship between a human and non-humans. What I mean is that your society does not even accept our existence, to say the least. How can they possibly insure our rights?"

"Andrius, at this moment, I feel that I have always known you all my life, but that you always existed only, in my dreams. You are the ideal person to be with, and to love. Your persona is so physically powerful, that any woman would not think twice, of falling deeply in love with you.

Honestly, that is how striking you are to me. I am a type of person, who hates oppressors of defenseless people and if I had the power to stop all experiments here, and in other Centers, I would do it. Believe me, but I am just one person."

"Nora, we're basically non-violent, but we could unleash violence with equal force and determination. We can easily see who the enemy is by just looking into their hearts and mind."

"Andrius, am I your adversary?"

"Nora, you cannot ever be. The day, I raise my hand in defiance against you, that will be the day I will destroy myself. Why should one hurt what he values the most? That is insanity. I think that both of us are one, in mutual interest. As I said before, I am in love with you in heart and not in body."

"Please, Andrius, you are embarrassing me, I bet you could even read my mind. Probably my deepest thoughts and desires are instantly sensed by you."

"Nora, you could easily block your thoughts, if you knew how. It is said, that a person may sin, by thoughtful ways."

"Is that true?"

"Yes, Nora, and that makes you a sinner." Said Andrius smiling.

"Oh, Andrius please do not say that. Does Professor Donnelly know about this marvelous gift of yours?"

"No, the gift is not only mine, but belongs to all of the rest of the other godless creatures, who are in the service of your Government, throughout the world."

"Don't tell anyone about this, please."

"I promise."

"Changing the subject, can you find out, why is Jason and the Professor taking so long to get back to us?"

"No problem. At this moment, there's a special news media committee, in the front lobby. They're requesting special passes, to tour the research area.

Professor Donnelly is presently in a terrible mood and he doesn't want them in. He is searching his mind, for some justifiable reason, to send them away, but cannot.

I will assist him.

Only this time, I will suggest something to him, by telepathy, as if he thought of it himself." Andrius pauses and meditates.

"Well, Andrius, what did you tell him?"

"The Professor is promising the news journalist, an exclusive interview with each media tonight, at 7 o'clock, in the auditorium. The public and all those, not associated with the news media, will not be allowed in."

"That's a very good idea, but do you think, that you might be forcing the Professor to expose too much, at this time?"

"No, he has already received orders from the White House, to divulge as much little as possible, without endangering the security of the United States but that tour of the research area is off limits.

The President discovered that the research project has become a hot political issue. Although the project is still secret in nature, they will use the enormous expenditures, to prevent his re-election. Their main complaint is accountability for moneys spent."

"Why so sudden, Andrius, there must be some other reasons, why he is doing this at this time. I wonder."

"Well, the President knows what he's doing." He added.

"Andrius, I believe the world hasn't still heard of your new race. I truly believe that the first reports were not taken seriously because of lack of transparency, but as time goes by, the realization will hit home.

The world will eventually awaken, to you and your race. I wonder what sorts of reaction, will there be. Would it be fierce, like yesterday, or will there be a general acceptance?"

"Nora that is one of the unknown factors not even I can forecast. It's just impossible. Its hard to look into all the hearts of mankind."

"God only knows." She added.

"I'm getting impressions from Dr. Roberts. He's wondering, where you are and what you are doing. He's also expressing some emotional feelings. Can it be jealousy? If he only knows how I appreciate all of you." Said Andrius

"How can he be if we have not met before today?"

"You're right; I sense that he's very deeply in love with you."

"Well, then I think Jason will have no reason to worry about us, because I love him just as much, too and I respect our relationship."

"I know you do."

54

They then resume walking and enter another section of the lab.

"I guess this is the next step where the cells are processed."

"Precisely, you catch on quick. Well, it is called the 'regenerator'. This is where the cells are transported to and temporarily held over, on their way from the cyclotron."

"How is that done?"

"Due to their microscopic size, the cells travel through minute capillary tubes, smaller than fiber optic strands which are located at the extremity of the machine.

Pneumatic air moves them out of the cyclotron, across the lab here and down to this Regenerator. There, they will finally embed themselves into cube like sticky substances, containing pure protein matter. After absorbing the substance, the cells rapidly divide and duplicate, at a terrific rate, after being infused with the Tomiko serum."

"That was that special isotope extract that Professor Donnelly spoke of yesterday."

"Exactly. The isotope gets its name from Dr. Yon Tomiko, a nuclear physicist who defected from Red China years ago. Professor Donnelly had the pleasure to meet him before his sudden death to cancer. He escaped from China seeking a better life for his family. While in China, he experimented on longevity and biochemical mutations.

Imagine this, there are some Asians that are capable of living up to 145 years and more and what is the secret?"

"I can't imagine how they do it?" She queried.

"Its' attributed to good clean living, no drugs, no alcohol. Only drinking certain teas made up from special roots of medicinal plants. That's the secret!"

"Interesting."

"Dr. Tomiko classified some 150 varieties of medicinal roots, normally found in the Orient, which can possibly extend life beyond the normal. During his years there, he produced many isotopes of these extracts, but never had the opportunity to actually test them in China, until he came here. We experimented with some of the volatile isotopes, which were smuggled out of the country, in the late 70's. They proofed to be very useful in our studies.

Now, let us get back to the cells.

As the cells divide, the rate of development slows down, by one-half the rate per hour. This characteristics, is compared to the half-life of radioactive materials. They reduce their life-rate by half each time. By the time the organic being, has fully reached its growth size, the metabolic rate of development is nil, as all traces of radiation, from the isotopes, disappear. There is more radiation in the air, than in any of us, so you don't have to worry. We are also immune to radiation contamination, and that is due to our cell structures. Our cell alignment is slightly different from normal humans. I would say a bit more refined, to say the least."

"Andrius, did you try this process on any other type of cells?"

"Yes, human cells were subjected to these isotopes, but they did not survive because human cells have not yet reached our evolutionary stage of development. Probably it will take mankind some 10,000 years of evolving, to physically change himself to our complex level, of cell structure."

"Andrius, I know it's getting late, but let me ask you one last quick one before we leave."

"Go right ahead."

"If you and the Doctor managed to produce, so many of your kinds here, how did you possibly move them out of this building? Won't the general public see and start questioning about them?"

"That's very simple, Nora. With the construction of this new wing, the Government interconnected the sub-basement to the military armory, located two blocks away from here. See those elevators?"

"Yes."

"They take you down some 250 feet to a tunnel that connects to the armory. Here and below us, they are clothed in military attire and transported, in Army trucks to points unknown, dressed up as National Guardsmen, Army WACS and other military personnel. Everything is done right in front of the public's eye and no one ever questions anything."

"That's clever." She asserts.

"The Government has thought of every possible means to keep this a secret and so far it has been successful, to date."

Both colleagues then begin to walk back towards the main entrance.

"Oh, here they come, it's about time." Said Andrius after seeing Jason and the Professor approaching.

Once joining them...

"Jason, why did it take you so long?" Nora demanded.

"I was downstairs in the records department, reviewing some of the old tapes that were originally filed at the main building."

"We waited for you a long time."

"I'm sorry but I found something very interesting, I have a copy of an old Soviet file on an experiment on cellular studies. Don't ask me how we got them, but they are here.

Their approach to the basic problem of cell duplication was good, but they did not seem to have the necessary equipment, to complete the experiment. They tried chemical infusion, but it failed time after time."

"This is why the new Russian Republic has very strongly supported the World Science Exchange Program in the U.N?" Said Professor Donnelly

"Yes, by these means, they are able to obtain technology and the newest publications and ideas from some of our early studies." Said Jason

"They will later claim that they were the first, to successfully create the first synthetic reproductive cell." Nora injected.

"I wouldn't put it past them." Added Jason.

"By now, they have some of our preliminary studies which were made and probably, they have their own version of organic being. Do you think so, Professor Donnelly?" Nora asked.

"Not quite, Dr. Billings, I have recent reports from the Central Intelligence Agency and from a very close friend, who recently retired from the C.S.O which do not agree with your suspicions. They've reported that the Russians have so far about 35% of our studies. Which means, that someone or some group is spying on our research. Nevertheless, I believe that they haven't yet created an Orgite Being, but are getting closer to the day, to have one."

"Your term that you just used, Orgite Beings, sounds fascinating, Professor Donnelly."

"It is. Said Jason, that's what we call them."

Professor Donnelly continued: "Some reports state that they have created some type of artificial gene, but it shortly perished, after a few hours. Their gene structure was not fully developed like ours. They have problems with molecular duplication within the string.

What they have is some kind of living forms. I can safely say that the Russians have so far, reached a point in cell development, which can be compared to the pre-cloning period of 40 years ago. Our studies and breakthrough's are light years ahead of them.

If they manage to get more data from this Institute, I fear the worst for the future, of the world."

"Well, Professor, you need not fear this, because the main secret of the development process is Dr. Tomiko's formula and he's no longer with us. So the only person who holds the secret now is you and I certainly won't divulge the process." Said Andrius

"Andrius, I thank you for that encouraging remark. Nonetheless, you're a very important person to me, personally. I fear for your safety too. You can never tell, if the Russians or some other totalitarian country, may decide to have you or I kidnapped and…"

"Professor, I have no fear of anyone or of any artificial means that can be used, to force me to divulge any information."

"We're all vulnerable in one way or another. Everyone has a breaking point. You may be strong, viral but you may be brought down to your knees by something so simple that you never figured before. Perhaps a bacterial decease, a personal threat or simply, an accident."

"That is yet to be seen, Professor."

Nora turns to Andrius.

"Can you imagine, that this technology, in the wrong hands can add more to world tension?"

"Let's not worry about that now, people." Jason interceded. Upon seeing a rift beginning to grow between Nora and Jason, the Professor tries to change the conversation.

"Let's continue with Dr. Billing's orientation, I hope not to be disturbed again.

Please forgive me, Dr. Billings, I was somewhat busy, with some other important matters and those inquiring reporters are irritating me very much. I have to find time to join you and perform my other responsibilities."

"Professor, its no bother, Andrius has been doing a splendid job. Anyway, that's my personal opinion." She smiles and looks at him eyes wide.

Jason looks both at her, then at Andrius and takes a deep breath. There was something in her smile and that sparkle, in her eyes, which he has never seen before. It bothers him.

"Dr. Billings, your statement will be taken into account and we will let the jury out for their verdict, at the coffee shop. Ok?"

"Ok. Professor Donnelly, if you put it that way. Oh, is it that time again?" She looks at a wall clock.

"It's unbelievable, how time flies when you're busy working at something interesting and worthwhile."

"You're right, Professor, I didn't notice that it was past noon, already."

"Yes, it is." He answered.

"You mean that Andrius and I were talking here all this time and we haven't moved too far away from one spot?"

"Yes, Doctor, there is a lot to see and to be acquainted, so do not stay too long at one thing or you will never finish. I should get you a DVR, so you can take down and also view Andrius descriptions of the vital areas and the various components, that will form the basis for all your future studies."

"I will certainly get her one, Sir." Said Andrius

"Remember, Dr. Billings, anything that is said and shown to you, please be advised, that it must be kept at your utmost confidence."

"Oh yes, Professor Donnelly, I can assure you of that. You do know that I have a special clearance from the military, because of the work that I was previously engaged in."

"Forgive me, Doctor, I just remembered."

Professor Donnelly, somewhat red in the face, tries again to change the conversation.

"If you have any further questions, please feel free to ask. If I cannot provide you with an answer, perhaps Andrius could very well, give you one. If he can't, at the moment, he will research it, and arrive at a reasonable one, all right?"

"Don't worry, Professor, I will ask him if I need help."

"This way, please." The Professor leads on.

The four scientists walk down a ramp, adjacent to the Cyclotron Room and into another area of the laboratory. Directly in front of them, they entered the vestibule of the Incubator, another vital section of the complex. They approach a viewing area. Looking through a glass port, they observe about a dozen scientists and other synthetic beings called Orgites who are working inside, dressed up in surgical attire performing a special procedure.

"Dr. Billings, at this point, we all have to put on sterile gowns to enter this area." Said Professor Donnelly

"Professor, the approach here, I believe is almost similar to the one that I've just visited with Mister Andrius."

"Not quite, it's far less restrictive, but we always must take precautions against environmental and respiratory bacteria, that can contaminate the space."

"Nora, this is where the full growth of the Orgite Beings occurs." Said Jason.

"This area was especially designed by Mister Andrius." Said Professor Donnelly

"Andrius, do you wish to have been born in these beautiful quarters, having personal attention and care, from all of these scientists and technicians?" She asked.

"I remember how I came into existence in the other lab. I was not even conscious of myself, nor did I know what kind of world I was being forced to live in. It was very traumatic, but somehow I managed to survive the ordeal."

"Excuse me, Gentlemen while I go to get a gown, I'll be right back." Nora goes off and enters a dressing room to change.

The Professor turns to Andrius.

"You made me feel a little uncomfortable by your last remark. We tried to make you as comfortable as possible during your deliverance. You know that I have always treated and confided in you, as if you were my own son. You have something within you that is a part of me. Please never forget that."

"I'm sorry if you feel that way Professor Donnelly but the only characteristics that I inherited from you is your inquisitiveness and strive for perfection, but I don't share your lack of compassion, especially for those who work for you."

"But I do, in my own ways, Andrius, I do have compassion for everyone."

"You do?"

"Yes I give no excuses for being what I am. I myself experienced a rough up bringing, too. That is what I am today; take me, for what I am, a product of a harsh life. My father left my mother with six children; he went to war and never returned. My mother struggled everyday to survive with the children and there was no time for compassion. We had to work on our farm from sunup to sundown without rest. Soon after, my mother left us, at an early age to tuberculosis and my older brother took up the reigns of giving us at least a minimum education to get by. Luckily we had other families abroad in America who had the compassion and took me in. They improved my life by sending me to school because they saw something in me that yearned for a better life."

"Yes Professor, we all learn by experience and examples. You failed at it because you didn't assimilate and adjusted accordingly. You carried this wound in your heart and used it to spur you on, regardless."

"I must confess, I did, in many ways, you are right Andrius. Perhaps it was the pain from both of my parents for leaving us, at an early age, to fend for ourselves, you're right."

Nora then joins Andrius and the Professor.

"Sorry if I interrupted something important."

"No you didn't. We were only talking shop, that's all."

"Anyway, I'm sorry for taking so long in picking a clean robe. They were pretty messy."

"Don't worry Dr. Billings we will see to that. Probably they were overlooked by our service personnel."

The small group approaches the head scientist at the entrance of the Incubator room. Professor Donnelly addresses himself to an associate through an intercom.

"Dr. Bernard, you may open the door, now. Dr. Billings has already changed into her gown and I will follow after."

He opens the door and a wind curtain above the door starts up and blow air vertically down towards them as Nora walks through.

"It is a pleasure to meet you, Dr. Bernard." Nora's hair is a bit unruffled.

"Sorry about that, it's designed to keep any flying insects and other suspended agents from filtering into the Lab."

"It's quite all right, not too much damage."

"I've heard and read a lot about your extensive work in epilepsy and brain disorders, Dr. Billings. It's a pleasure, to make your acquaintance, at last." Said the Doctor.

"Likewise, Dr. Bernard, I trust that what you heard is not too bad."

"Oh, no no, Dr. Billings, on the contrary, they were only praiseworthy acclamations. Nevertheless, I'm glad that you have finally joined our small research group."

"Thank you." She responded.

Dr. Bernard takes Nora aside.

"I hate to sound gossipy, but do you know that Dr. Roberts was at a point of leaving the Institute, if he had failed to have the Foundation give you the appointment here?"

"You flatter me, Dr. Bernard, I know it is not true, because Dr. Roberts is very devoted to his work and can't possibly turn his back on a vital research project, such as this. I personally would not do it."

"Dr. Billings, I think you still do not know Dr. Jason Roberts. Love works in many different ways. At times, it shocks and mystifies the least and the most powerful. Do you know that in the past, men have given up powerful positions and vast wealth, in order to appease the love of a woman?"

"I've heard rumors."

"Well in scriptures, you may very well remember the story of Adam and Eve. One thing you may notice, men later always regret their decisions because it only motivated by passion."

"Oh come on Dr. Bernard, are you blaming women for men's ills and weaknesses?"

"No, I just blame it on love, that's all. Call it an instinct, a drive, or call it a tendency.

It's just something that many poets have written about for centuries and yet no one has given a clear definition of it."

"Well, Dr. Bernard, each individual would probably have his own definition of love, depending on the circumstance and what sort of exposure to life that they have had previous. Anyway, that's my opinion."

"Perhaps you are right, Dr. Billings. You catch on pretty quick."

"Dr. Bernard, I think you are somewhat of a poet, yourself. Are you?"

"Yes, Dr. Billings, I must confess I try my best at times. I so happen to have fallen in love with one of my students. I believe, in my opinion that she is one of the most beautiful people in this world to be with. In my case, I can't define that feeling of love that I have for her, because it's just indescribable. She takes my breath away each time I meet her."

"I agree with you, it is hard. It also has happened to me. Anyway, I see in your eyes that you must love her very much."

"Yes, I certainly do."

"I'm glad for you."

"Thank you."

As they venture forward, Nora suddenly feels a chill in the air.

"Pardon me, Dr. Bernard, why is it so cold in this room? Is there a reason for it?"

Dr. Bernard coughs and looks up: "Oh, yes, we usually maintained a low temperature of 50 to 60 degrees in this area, but it feels much cooler today. Anyway, getting back to the why for the coolness in the air."

"Yes."

"Dr. Billings, due to the rate of growth of the beings, environmental pollutants might have the possibility to alter the process. We maintain the low temperature to prevent this."

"I see." She answered.

"I suspect that the low temperatures in here are beginning to affect my health, too." He sneezes.

"God bless you."

"Thanks, excuse me. Originally when we kept the room at a normal comfort levels without an air filtration system, some of our beings developed uncontrollable mutations and respiratory contamination due to lack of infusion of antibiotics. Unfortunately, we had to isolate the worst ones and terminated their existence."

"Were they conscious?" Nora asked with a concerned look.

"No, Dr. Billings, the moment we detect any abnormality beyond cure, we administer a solution that prevented the organism, from reaching a conscious state."

"I would think that they would suffer through the ordeal." Said Nora

"No, they never do. In order to prevent this, Mister Andrius recommended the construction of this sector of the lab. This safeguards his people's existence and their welfare."

Nora turns to the Professor, as he arrives from the dressing room.

"I think I've seen enough for one day. It's a bit late and I must go back to my office and start packing my things, now. This is quite a lot for a person to absorb in a day."

"I agree, Dr. Billings but I rather recommend that you go home and rest today. You've seen enough for one day. We will arrange for the transfer of all books and papers to your new office tomorrow. Would that be all right?"

"Professor, you must have read my mind, I'm totally exhausted."

"Alright, Dr. Billings, I better turn you back to Dr. Roberts."

"Thank you, Professor, for understanding." She then turns to the two other scientists.

"Mister Andrius, Dr. Bernard, it was a pleasure to have met yours and I am looking forward to be working with you both."

"Good evening, Dr. Billings." Said Dr. Bernard

"Good evening, all."

Dr. Bernard turns with Andrius and both scientists disappear into the Incubator Room. Jason, Nora and the Professor walk out through a long corridor and exit the rear of the building, by a security door of the lab. Once outside the premises, Professor Donnelly turns to Jason:

"Can I drop you off at your car; mine is parked here in the front."

"Thank you, Professor, but no, I think I would rather walk with Dr. Billings. She needs a little fresh air and some encouragement, don't you think so?"

"Very well, Dr. Roberts, have it your way. Good day, I will see you tomorrow. As you see, the US Marshals are here and are ready to shadow me all the way home."

"I see."

"I bid you both a good day."

"Good day, Professor."

Professor Donnelly gets into his car and drives off passing Nora, who was walking ahead of Jason. He exits through the main gate followed by Marshals riding, in two black sedans.

Jason moves quickly and catches up to Nora.

"Hey, hey there, Doctor, how do you feel after this long day at your new job?"

"Oh! Hello Jason, I thought you left with Professor Donnelly."

"No, I told him that I would rather be with you."

"Oh how gallant of you! Is this really you?"

"Anyway, he's returning right back in the evening. So Nora, what's your opinion?"

"Opinion of what, of you? I think you were acting rather a bit strange with me."

"No, you know, your new appointment to this new phase of work."

"It's very interesting, fascinating, and above all, it's frightfully overwhelming."

"You will not believe this but that's the same opinion everyone shares on their first day of work in that wing. Well, honey, I think you're going to be all right. Welcome aboard."

"Jason, I can't agree with you at this moment but ask me in about a month, all right?"

Nora gets into Jason's car and they both drive off.

CHAPTER III

Later that night, after stopping for dinner, at a local restaurant, Jason drives Nora back home and kisses her good night, in front of the entrance to her building.

"I hope your landlady is looking out her window."

"Forget her; I will be moving out of here, soon."

"Why is that?"

"I have to live my life without anyone, looking over my shoulders, all the times. You don't think so?"

"You're right. Nora about today, I must apologize to you for my childish behavior and I reassure you, that it will not happen again. You do realize how much I love you. I can't stand being away from you, not even for a minute."

"You really mean that, Jason?"

"Yes, with all my heart."

They kiss again and embrace for a while. Afterwards, Jason walks off, gets into his car and drives off. As he does, Nora calls out in a low voice:

"I'll call you tonight."

Jason waves his hands to acknowledge the message and speeds down the road.

Nora stands by and looks at his car, as it slowly disappears in the distance.

She turns around to enter the building, when she suddenly comes face to face with Andrius, who is standing motionless and staring down at her.

At first, she is surprised to see him, but then thinks about the Professor.

"Perhaps something awful has happen to him. Maybe he was hurt, or some bad accident occurred while at the lab."

"Andrius, why you are here? She asked in a withdrawn voice. Please don't tell me you have bad news about Professor Donnelly?"

"Nothing like that, Dr. Billings. He pauses, it is worse. Time is critical, more at this moment, than ever."

"Andrius, I am confused, please, tell me what is going on." Nora was now very concerned. "I must speak to you now, but not here." Andrius looks up and down the street.

"Not even in your apartment. It must be a place, where they won't be able to find me."

"Who wait a minute? Wait just a minute!" She demands very strongly.

"Please, Dr. Billings, you must trust me."

"Alright. The only place, where we can possibly go is there, across the avenue, in the park by the playground." She said in a very calm voice.

"Let's hurry, please let's hurry!" Andrius insists.

The two leave the front of the building, walk across and enter a small playground, where children are playing and people sitting, enjoying the end of a sunny day. They walk to the far end of the playground and sit on a bench. Andrius turns to Nora.

"Dr. Billings, perhaps you may not be aware of this but today the world has turned into an explosive situation." He said very excitedly.

"Yes, Andrius, I know but it can't affect us here, in the United States. We are safe over here; you do not have to worry."

"But I am. Do you know that yesterday, a large group of radical; insurgents forcibly replaced the Democratic government of Chile? And immediately after this unfortunate event, spontaneous military uprisings throughout Bolivia and Ecuador has erupted, led by other insurgents, with the help of agents from North Korea and the Middle East."

"No, Andrius, I did not know this. This sounds like an attempt of Islamic terrorists to take over the country and gain a foot hold in this Hemisphere."

"The United Nations Security Council was called to a special session to deal with this crisis and the President of the United States is presently in an emergency meeting, with his cabinet and the Joint Chiefs of Staff.

This situation has caused a severe set back to Democracy and certainly may lead us possibly to War. It has to be dealt with quickly before it becomes a global event involving the super powers on this planet."

"But who will stand up and oppose them?"

"I'm afraid that the lead must be taken by the United States.

As the first step in this opposition, the President may have to fly to New York to address the United Nations Security Council to get support from the Organization of American States, Middle Eastern and European countries."

"How do you know about this, Andrius?" She queried.

"Remember, I told you before, that the President has a special security force of 'Orgites' in the White House?"

"Yes, you did."

"They have alerted me of the grave situation for some time already. Wait a moment! The meeting is about to commence at the White House and I sense the inevitable will be disclosed."

"What do you mean, Andrius?"

"Wait, Nora, the President is speaking."

"Please, can you narrate to me, what he's saying?"

"Yes, I will."

The President: "Well, gentlemen, I welcome all of you this evening to work as my advisors. I don't fully know their strategy nor their objective but one thing I know, is that the situation is pretty grave, to say the least. A wrong approach to this crisis could very well involve us in a direct conflict, with some of the Communists and Islamic powers, on this planet. Even the Russians have come up with a sensible approach to quietly put down this insurrection. No one knows if they are indirectly involved in this and are playing both sides of the issue."

The Secretary: "Mister President, the best approach is a strong show of deadly force. We can easily demoralize them, by destroying their forward advance and not allowing any chance for them to retreat, or regroup. We could do it. We can implement the shock and awe approach, which we used with Sadam. We have the sixth fleet three hundred miles off the Western Coast of Santiago, Chile. We have just a couple of hours left, before the fleet moves on to defend the oil fields of Venezuela and Columbia."

The President: "Mister Secretary, are you aware of past history?

This kind of gunboat diplomacy will take lives of innocent people, on both sides. Many will be caught in our crossfire's. Remember Vietnam and Iraq. It is certainly, not a good policy.

Gentlemen, I don't wish to repeat the past mistakes of other administrations."

The Secretary: "We have a couple of alternatives, Sir. We could launch a limited offensive action. This will buy us time to build up a world coalition to pressure the Islamic and the North Koreans to withdraw. It will also give you time to feel them out to what they are up to. I believe that they are trying to intimidate the West, to get more money and technology. Public reaction here is building up against such practices. This is international blackmail, Sir, to say the least.

Mister President, they may be trying to establish a launch platform in South America for their limited range missiles. Remember the Soviets and the former Cuban missile crises. History repeating itself, again."

The President: "Mister Secretary, what is your other alternative?"

The Secretary: "Well, Mister President, the other is to fully rely on the United Nations. We will officially accuse them of manipulating and creating a serious conflict situation, by a malicious and unprovoked aggression, using insurgents, against the two Democratic countries of South America. Secondly, Mister President, these infractions are totally against International laws, established by the Monroe Treaty and the Organization of American States. As a member of these two organizations, we are obliged to intercede and defend upon their request.

Let me remind you, that our attempt to solely eliminate this problem, will certainly lead us to war."

The President: "By the time you get the United Nations to act on this, the Insurgents would have overrun the whole South American continent.

As a precaution, I requested armed reconnaissance aircraft to over fly these areas, to assess the military situation. We need concrete proof of North Korea's involvement."

General Stuart: "Mister President, if we can't send our troops soon there I think this situation warrants the use, of one of our ultimate secret projects. When we implement this, I guarantee that we will not lose any of our people. Everyone here, at home will be glad, for the very reason, that American blood will not be needlessly shed ever abroad, or elsewhere on this planet."

The President: "General Stuart, you have the right idea. As an eventuality upon seeing an event, such as this from possibly happening, I pushed forward the disclosure of the new species. Due to this serious situation, I believe I can persuade Congress, to give me the authority, to use them, in putting down this insurrection. The only problem is that we are limited to only two thousand soldiers, of this type and it will take weeks, or even months, to form a large detachment. We have to review the logistic problem of transportation. Has anyone, given that some thought?"

An aid: "Mister President, the General may possibly hold the key solution to this problem. Some of us know that we have at least 15 to 20 thousand of these people spread out, throughout the United States and abroad. Perhaps, if we can draft the whole lot, into a workable unit, they may very well be the answer. The problem is the time element and transport is not important. I have discovered that they are adaptable. They do not need any extensive military training at all.

We can easily infuse military tactics to them, in a few hours, with computers and transport them within hours, to the battlefield sites, by troop aircraft. Mister President, I think this is the only alternative available to stop this quick."

The President: "Thank you, Mister Richardson." The President pauses for a few moments and shakes his head.

"General Stuart, I have just made up my mind. We have no choice; we must use them even without the approval of Congress. This will be the plan:

They will primarily fight a covert operation until approval is given by Congress."

General Stuart: "As mercenaries, Sir?"

The President: "Yes. They will remain there as long as possible, until I get the support from some of the leaders in Congress and in the Senate. They shall be on the battlefield, at least seventy two hours, before I officially inform the Nation and Congress."

General Stuart: "Probably, by that time, the Special Forces would have destroyed all of the insurgents."

The President: "And finally, if questioned, they will go as a private security force, hired by Bolivia and Ecuador with little or no American exposures. The Secretary will be in charge of procurement and execution of this special unit in the field. That is all, gentlemen. I have Air Force 1, waiting."

All stand up and respond: "Thank you, Mister President."

Andrius' complete attention being focused on the conversation, which was occurring simultaneously 300 miles away, fails to see a patrol car drive up and park in front of the entrance to the playground. Nora, upon seeing this, becomes nervous and shakes Andrius out of his trance.

"There is a police car here, I think we better go."

"Now, you see the grave situation?"

"Andrius, we must leave right now, they are looking in our direction."

"Yes Nora, you are right."

They get up and Nora places her arm around Andrius' side and both slowly walk away. "Andrius, what will happen to you and your people?"

"The Government has other choices to resolve this problem but they rather use my people to do the fighting. I don't understand their logic."

"It's money. By using your people, he can probably justify the enormous amount of money that was spent and that will certainly insure his re-election."

"It's unbelievable, there is no justification."

"Its politics but that does not make it right. If you allow this to happen just once, they will use your people every time, there is a flare up anywhere, in the world. It will be much easier than using our own people."

"I'm glad you realized this, Nora. The Governments' first step is to approach Professor Donnelly and persuade him."

"Andrius, you know that it will not be easy; the Professor has his moral ethics to deal with. He will not give in, unless he is otherwise forced to do so."

At this point, they walk in front of the patrol car, smile and nod, then cross the street.

"If they approach you afterwards, I would refuse." She said.

"I already did, that's why I'm here. The moment I discovered that they were also coming to see me, I left the Center after observing these security people converge into the building. They acted like storm troopers. I accidentally confronted six of them in the lab. It was pretty bad. Out of fear, afterwards I took a taxi here."

"Did you seriously hurt them?"

"I defended myself by preventing their advance on my person. I incapacitated all of them but did not kill anyone. Whatever happens happened. That is all I know."

"Oh my God, I fear for your safety, now."

"At least I did not terminate any of them."

"But that does not make it right. Andrius, how did you get my address?"

"That was easy; I just looked up your job application, in the computer."

"You mean you have all together abandoned the Research Center?"

"Yes, I took advantage of the Professor's special news conference and I left the building, but no-one except for those strange security people saw me leave."

"Andrius, when the Professor hears of the President's decision, he will also be looking for you for moral support. He also realizes that you are the only true leader of your people and your people won't lift a finger, without your consent."

"I know that very well, I estimate by midnight, every security and police force, in the United States will be looking for me."

"Andrius, I must find you a place to hide. Come with me upstairs now and we will figure out what we have to do. You must get off the streets."

Andrius abruptly stops and nods his head:

"No, I do not wish to involve you in this, it is too dangerous. It is my problem and I must resolve it myself."

"Never mind, you stay here until midnight, Andrius, I will pack up a couple of things and we will drive to my summer cottage in the Catskills. There you can figure out your next step. No one knows of it, because I bought it just recent."

"I feel terrible about this; you're too good to be involved in these complicated matters."

"Andrius, never mind about me, I'm also a survivor. I lived through similar situations like this, in my life."

Once entering the building, they quietly take the private elevator to Nora's apartment on the third floor. After settling down awhile, Andrius turns to Nora.

"I hope that Dr. Roberts doesn't get the wrong impression of what you decided to do."

"Don't worry, he will never know. I will drive back here before dawn. Gosh! I just realized something. Darn it! I don't have my car here with me. Jason drove me home today. My car is in the parking lot at the Center. Of all days!" She throws her hands up in the air.

Nora sits down and thinks of a way to retrieve the car, when there is a knock on the door. They both remain motionless, as the person knocks again. She whispers to Andrius to hide for reasons, that this might be those agents, or the police looking for him.

The person behind the door then tries the knob and finally calls out:

"Nora, it's me Jason, open up!" He said with an alarming voice.

She breathes a sigh of relief, goes over and opens the door. Jason looking a bit shaken up enters and looks around the room.

"All right, where is he?"

"Where is who?" She responds.

"Don't hide him, I'm looking for Andrius."

"Andrius?" She questions.

"Do you know that he is wanted by the police?"

"He is?" She asked.

"Do you also know that, if you harbor a wanted person, you could possibly go to jail, or equally be condemned with that person?"

"Jason, if he's a criminal? What is he charged with?"

"I think its desertion, that is what a Federal Marshall informed me, when they came to my apartment, this evening."

"Desertion? Do you believe it?" Nora looks at Jason very strangely.

"I don't know, it may be true, who knows?" He answered.

"In the first place, Andrius is not a member of any military branch, or government agency. So I think it's unlikely, that he is a deserter."

"Nora, I think you may have a point there, but we shouldn't get involved in these matters. These Federal people can get a bit rough and intimidating. By the way, is he here?"

"Yes, he is and he will stay here, until you hear me out, first."

Jason walks over and picks up the telephone.

"You should have told him to surrender to the police, I have my civic duty to call and tell them, that he is here."

"Jason, before you do, please listen to me first and if you wish to, you may call them afterwards."

"I will give you just one minute."

"In the first place Jason, get it out of your mind, that I have stopped loving you. I love you and no one else. I'm saying this, not because I do not wish you to call the police, but I want you to understand, about the serious predicament, that Andrius is in, due to a senseless decision, that was just made in Washington."

"Nora, what are you talking about?"

"The President wants to use Andrius and his people to fight a military insurrection, in South America."

"What insurrection, there is nothing going on down there."

"Believe me and trust me, there is one, as we speak."

"Nora, if you say so. Unfortunately, I haven't been listening to the car radio."

"You know Andrius very well and his people are a peace-loving race. They are neither mercenaries nor soldiers. His race will be forced against their will to do this."

"Nora, I do not believe this, I cannot believe that the United States military would stoop to this low ebb, to have these people do their fighting. This is not their fight."

"Yes its true, Jason."

"That must be the reason why they want him. They would even accuse him of a crime, in order to get custody and force him to submit his people to this. This is not right."

"Well Jason, you are free to make that call, now."

"I morally cannot, as a scientist, I would have to be against such doings and I know that Professor Donnelly would probably be also against it."

Jason places the phone down and embraces Nora. Both nod their heads in defiance and walk to the dining room. Just then, the telephone rings. Andrius, who was in the adjoining room, comes over. Nora goes over to pick up the phone, when Jason suddenly leans forward, raises his hand and waves her away from the phone. He whispers:

"Wait, Nora, do not answer it. They'll reason out that you are not in."

The phone rings four more times, and then goes silent.

They all remain motionless, as shadowy figures move across the door's undercut.

Footsteps and whispering is heard in the distance, as they move about, in the corridor. Then a woman's voice:

"And what can I offer you gentlemen?" The buildings' snoopy landlady suddenly appears. "Can I help you?"

"We were visiting a friend, but it seems that she is not home."

"And who would that be?"

"Dr. Billings that's who."

"Dr. Billings doesn't get home this early, gentlemen. You can try her later."

"Thank you, miss, you have a nice day, goodbye."

"She does have a bell, you need not had to waste your time, knocking on her door."

"The door downstairs was open, so we walked in and forgot to ring."

"I think not, you must think that I believe in the tooth fairy."

"Have it your way, goodbye, now."

"Good riddance." Said the landlady, still wondering how they get through two locked front doors.

After waiting a long while, everyone was gone, Nora finally breaks the silence in the room.

"For once I'm happy that she intruded, in my life."

"They would have broken into the apartment to investigate." Said Jason.

"What shall we do now? They will be downstairs waiting for us to appear."

"We don't necessarily have to show up. We could have stayed somewhere else, perhaps a hotel, or elsewhere. It's a free country."

Andrius joins in:

"Hello Jason."

"You have serious problems my friend."

"I know. Do you suppose they think that you both are involved?"

"I hope not." Said Jason." My career and my freedom will certainly be in jeopardy."

"Jason, that is not important at this moment, but the rights of a race of people to decide their own destiny is. No government has the right to do that regardless of any situation, no matter if it falls under a category of national security." Said Nora

"Nora, you must realize, the Government doesn't consider Andrius and his people have any rights, as those shared by humans." Said Jason

"I'm afraid that is true, Nora, they think we are a non-human species and we are expendable. Remember, in their eyes we don't have a soul. We are a godless creation. A non entity."

"Please, both of you. Don't talk that way."

"But it is the truth. That is how we were classified. Believe me."

"There must be a way out of this predicament."

"Yes, there is a way." Said Jason

"Andrius must give himself up and refuse their demands."

"No, not that, I'm talking about more of a legal path, that Andrius can go with."

"In the first place, the moment that Andrius exposes himself in public, he will be arrested by the police. Probably by now his picture has been posted on every police station across the nation." Said Jason.

"No, what I meant Nora is this. What would happen, if he were to turn himself to a lawyer and be under his recognizance?"

"Very simple, it will not work. He will never get to see his day in court. Remember, courts are for people."

"We must find a way how he can be declared some kind of status like a citizen, or even a human."

"Nora that's going to take a lot of effort and money."

"I can't imagine how we can possibly resolve such a monumental problem like that."

"If it's going to be impossible through legal civil means, we may have to go to a larger organization that has jurisdiction over these matters."

"And what will that be, the U.S. Supreme Court?" Asked Jason

"No, bigger than that, we will have to go to a World Court, the United Nations."

"Now, I believe that you're crazy, they will never listen. You wouldn't even know how to begin such a task and in petitioning such, an attempt."

"My dear, have you forgotten, I recently worked for the United Nations in England and I know, that they constantly deal with human rights problems." Said Nora

"Remember, you first have to declare him a member of the human race, and then I'll believe that the United Nations will act on his behalf." Said Jason

"I will contact a friend of our family; his name is Sir Renee Gibson, who happens to be the British Ambassador, to the United Nations. Perhaps, with his diplomatic position and experience, he may be able to suggest something."

"Nora, he could present Andrius' case to a legal committee and have they declared some kind of binding resolution that may restrict the use of the Orgites, for experimental and military purposes."

"But Nora it may take months or perhaps years." Said Andrius

"How about if we were to say that the United Stares, is attempting to fight a secret war in South America and plans to use these people in warfare, against their will? Will that get faster action out of them?"

"Yes, but first you have to prove it. Said Jason. Where is the evidence?"

"Well, we have Andrius' testimony. He will testify and the two security guards, that overheard the conversation in the White House."

"With them having that information, how long do you think they will stay free, before the C.S.A. takes them away for good?"

"Perhaps they already know this. We have to get out of here fast."

"Nora, our first objective is to reach and speak to Sir Renee Gibson. Now, how do we get in contact with him?"

"We'll simply call him." Said Nora as she leans over and grabs the phone.

"No, don't do that, they probably have the phone tapped." Said Jason.

"Don't get so melodramatic, Jason, they don't even know that we are involved." Nora picks up the phone and places the call to the British Embassy.

"Good evening, may I speak to the Ambassador, Sir Renee Gibson, please?"

There was a pause, and then a woman answers:

"May I ask whose calling and what is your business with Sir Gibson?" She queried.

"Please, do tell Sir Gibson that it is 'Norita'. He will understand."

A long pause elapses then a heavy boisterous voice comes on.

"Norita is it you, hello there."

"Yes, Sir Gibson, it is I, Norita."

"This is a surprise to hear from you, I hope you are well. Are you calling from across the pond?"

"No, Sir Gibson, I am here in America."

"Good, come right over, tonight, I am having a small bash, at the Consulate. Be sure to come."

"But Sir Gibson, I..."

"I have not seen you for quite some years. Are you still assisting at the University?"

"No, Sir Gibson, I already received my doctorate in..."

"Splendid, splendid, we must celebrate."

"But, Sir Gibson, I must see you, but not tonight. It is a bit late."

"My dear, you are welcome anytime to come, my house is yours!"

"I have something very important to discuss with you personally. Can I see you tomorrow?"

"Yes, my dear, but not here, I am presently talking to you from Princeton. My secretary connected us from the Consulate. I'll be tomorrow, in my office, at the Consulate."

"That is precisely where I wish to meet with you; I would like to discuss with yours truly a certain situation, involving with human rights."

"Very well Norita, I will probably be in my office or be, in session tomorrow. We are voting on a resolution pertaining to world distribution of surplus of food and animal life conservation in Australia. Those blasted Australians. They're always causing mischief."

"Thanks a million, Sir Gibson. Sorry if I troubled you by calling this late." She relented.

"It's no bother, dear; I have a lot to talk about with you. I heard from your father, Lord Billings that you have met a young American and you both seem to be a bit serious. Are there any nuptials, in the near future?"

"You will be the first to know, Sir Gibson."

"You honor me."

"You will probably get to meet him tomorrow, when I come over to meet with you."

"Splendid, splendid! Now, we shall really celebrate, for sure."

"Alright Sir Gibson, you have a good night."

"Oh? Oh, yes, good night, my child."

Nora hangs up the phone and calmly goes over and fetches her overnight case. She packs a few essentials and all three quietly leave the apartment, by taking the rear stairway, to the basement level. They carefully exit the building via a delivery door, located by the side entrance.

Once outside, Nora and Andrius remain in the shadows, as Jason inconspicuously goes for his car. As he does, a police patrol car with lights flashing happens by but does not pay any attention to Andrius' tall figure standing by the service entrance of the building.

Jason drives up and stops. They get in and slowly drive away, feeling good for successfully outsmarting the surveillance team, who are parked just across the avenue, having a snack and coffee.

While driving, Jason turns to Nora, after giving some thought to where they were going:

"When you filed out all of your personnel forms and job history, to work at the Center, did you put your cottage's address, as another place of residence?"

"I honestly can't remember." Nora was troubled.

"We are sunk, we can't go there. They'll look for us there." Said Jason

"I just remembered something, honey; I purchased the small cottage after our engagement. Remember, you were with me."

"That's right; you were already working, at the Center."

"Good girl!" Jason was elated.

"I thought for a second, that we might be walking into harms way. By the way, Jason, I have a multi-band radio, at the cottage and it picks up police broadcasts. Tomorrow we will take it with us, as a precaution."

"That's a brilliant idea, sweetheart." Said Jason

Nora then turns to Andrius.

"You have been very quiet, ever since we left Cliffside."

"I'm sorry, but I was reviewing a periodical that I read three years ago. The subject was about a similar case like ours."

"Andrius, do you have the ability of total recall?"

"Yes, I do, and with detailed accuracy."

"That is fantastic; I wish I had a photographic mind. So, what exactly were you recalling?"

"Well, I was reading about a Dr. Stepenac, who was being sued for malpractice."

"What's so strange about that? Doctors are sued every day."

"Yes, but this was a unique case, it so happens, that this doctor was experimenting on a patient, without the patients' knowledge or his approval."

"Now, that is illegal." Said Jason

"Did the patient sue him, when he discovered, that he was being abused?"

"No, the experiment failed and the patient became brain damaged and comatose. The family sued the doctor and won the case, because of an established law in the books in New York State, which prohibits the performance of any form of experiments, on persons, without their knowledge and written approval."

"That's right. To perform any form of experiment, the researchers must receive signed affidavits and legal papers from the patient, or persons to be used in an experiment." Said Jason

"Of course, anyone knows that."

"Andrius, perhaps you have something there, we could possibly find a similar law written under the 'Human Rights' doctrine in the United Nations. Then we can officially bring your case to the public and force the United States, to refrain from ever using your people in any future research experiment, not even in case of war."

"Nora that is going to take a lot of doing. First you need a committee, that would petition the Legal Department, to have an open talk on this case and surely the United States will probably do its best, to prevent this, from ever reaching a committee."

"I think, Sir Gibson is very influential, he probably can get it through a UN Special Committee."

"Nora, please put on the radio to see if there's news on the Professor, or on the crises in South America." Said Jason.

"You will not hear any news on the military action because they are keeping it quiet for a couple of days. They will probably play it first, as a rumor, and then gradually the truth will be slowly released to the media." Said Andrius

"You're right, Andrius, that is how its done."

The threesome finally arrives at the cottage close to midnight, under a severe thunderstorm. The stormy skies are part of the outer fringes of a hurricane churning for several days out in the Atlantic near Cape May. Nora brought in her over- night bag, together with a couple of can food, so that they can pass the night.

Morning came and the sun was shining brightly, with the birds celebrating, the arrival of the sun, after the dreadful stormy night. Nora, while still in bed reflects upon all that has happened and tries to reassure her self that the course of action taken is right and lawful? After breakfast, they start driving back to New York, to meet with the British Ambassador.

As they cross the Tappan Zee Bridge, Nora puts on the multi-band radio. She listens to some local and statewide radio communications, but nothing significant comes over. They hear local chatter and traffic reports.

Listening to the radio broadcasts for some time becomes somewhat monotonous, so she tunes the receiver around to other commercial stations for a while.

A half-hour passes, the car is on the New Henry Hudson Parkway passing by an old European church built atop a hill, brought over to America, called the "Cloisters," when the radio begins buzzing with an important transmission.

The transmission was from State Police Headquarters in New York and announces that all federal, state and city police vehicles, are to detain for questioning a research scientist named, Dr. Jason Roberts and a research assistant answering to the name of Andrius. The dispatcher gives their general descriptions and the license number of the car that they presume that they are driving. Nora could not contain herself and begins to cry.

Jason, also shocked by the announcement, feels the blood in his body turning slightly chilled. He slows down the car, so as not to call attention to it.

"This is neither the time nor the place, to lose your nerve, Said Jason, Last night, we committed ourselves and now there is no turning back or regrets. The first thing to do is to get off this highway and somehow dispose this car, in some lonely place, where they cannot find it. We'll get off here in the Heights or at the next exit near Broadway and the Cross Bronx Expressway. We then go on foot, the rest of the way to the UN."

"Alright." Said Nora

"We can also pick up public transportation near the bus terminal."

"I think we can safely retrieve my car, Said Nora, It's at the Center. Remember, they are not looking for me, yet."

"We will use it to return to the cottage after meeting with Sir Gibson." Said Jason

They exit the highway and drive through the side streets of upper Manhattan, and finally abandon the car by a dead end along the river, under the George Washington Bridge, hoping that the police will not find it for days. By that time the car will be stripped off all its components and it would be very difficult to be identified.

Once on foot, they walk through the High Bridge Commercial District and finally reach a subway station for their ride to midtown.

An hour later, they arrive at Times Square; Nora was annoyed with the crowds and the unruly kids all during the trip. She never had experienced this before.

"I know this is not the place to praise the city for its rapid transit system, but why does it have to be so dirty and noisy. In Great Britain, some of our underground systems run on rubber wheels. Why is America so backward in this area?"

"Money, that is why, there is never enough to support new construction. All these systems are operated at a loss." Said Jason.

They exit the subway car at Times Square, and walk down through a corridor and board an escalator, while following the overhead signs and directions. The UN building is located on the East Side of Manhattan, so they need only to go cross-town. The threesome then exit into another subway platform and stepped onto another escalator, which transfers them into a newly innovated form of transportation, especially designed for New York City subway riders that work at the United Nations' Building.

"What is that?" Asked Nora

"It is a massive people mover system." Jason responded.

"I'm impressed, very impressed." She said.

"Nora, after many years of receiving complaints from commuters, tourists and business people, New York City brought its best minds together with two private corporations and sat down to solve the unique traffic and commuter congestion, in the midtown area.

A new railroad station was built below Grand Central to ease the congestion at Penn Station located on the Westside of Manhattan and a people mover, designed with a new concept of high speed traveling to meet the commuter's demands on the Eastside of Manhattan.

The People Mover works very essentially. It is simply comprised of an entrance conveyor, which moves you along, by gradually launching you into a series of multiple conveying lanes, which travel parallel at various speeds, within the mover.

For example, if you and I were to enter here, as you see, our primary direction into the conveyor is at a right angle, to the main flow of the mover. Approaching the main flow, our lane begins to curve in tangent, then parallels the main flow and gradually fades away, as a normal escalator does, when you reach the top or bottom. Then we are in, safe and sound."

"Whoever thought of this, must be some genius." Said Nora

"Yes he is, actually, it was designed by the Charles Corporation, with some help, from the city and private concerns."

"But I don't seem to understand something, Jason. How does a traveler reach the higher speeds and still manage not to fall down, on his face?"

"That's very simple, Nora. Each lane has its own launching ramp, which accelerates the traveler from one velocity to another. It also works in the reverse order. You have accelerators and decelerators, within your lane of travel. It's very simple."

"Can it handle a lot of people?"

"As many as possible. In a regular subway system, you have approximately some fifty to one hundred people that get hurt every day. Some people die. It is unbelievable, but true.

In this system, the accident rate is reducing to one or two a day. Those accidents usually are due to either unattended children playing, or a derelict, that did not know how to use the system or he simply passed out while riding it. Its strictly for short runs only."

"I honestly confess to you, that I never heard of this system. When was it placed in service?"

"Well, dear, the reason why you haven't heard of it is that you have never been down here, before. Remember, you always drive your car here to work and never had the opportunity to use it."

"Ah, yes, you are so right, love." Said Nora

"This one is only an experimental unit and so far, it's a success. They are eventually planning to encircle, East and West between 34th and 59th Street with these moving platforms. So far, they have built this cross-town one and another loop, between the United Nations and Grand Central Station."

"I'm so fascinated by the progress that has taken place here, in just a few years. I take back what I said about New York. It will probably be called the 'City of the Future' for sure."

"Security wise, these people movers are very safe. Every 200 feet there are closed circuit cameras operated by computers that scan all the lanes, every two seconds. They immediately report any abnormal behavior, on the part of its travelers.

In fact, the City is not aware that the computers operating this system are part machine and part Orgite."

"Why am I not surprised to hear this?"

"Well you are learning about all the possibilities that our research entails. The systems are only serviced by special technicians and you know who they are."

"I can imagine." Nora boards the conveyor.

"This is the entrance launcher. Nora, you only hold on to the circular rubber rail with your right hand, as I'm doing. See?" Said Jason

"It feels just like a regular escalator."

"Correct, now we move along forward and slowly enter the flow. Do you feel the slight acceleration? Now just side step in and if you wish, you may hold on to the other hand rail."

"Jason, I don't need to, it is nice, and I like it!"

"So far, Nora, we are traveling seven miles per hour. Now if you wish to speed up, here about fifteen feet in front of us, on your right, there is a take off ramp, with another handrail, that will rise up from a floor enclosure, the moment you step on it. This take off ramp accelerates you up to twelve miles per hour to the level of the next lane and like before, you side step in again, without any fear of falling or whip lash.

If you don't exit the ramp, it will gradually decelerate to your latter speed and warning lights and a speaker voice will erg you to get off."

"But how do you know when to get off?"

"Simple, on the side of your rubber hand rail, there is a grip that you gently squeeze and state, where you wish to get off. There are also pushbuttons, with station names, which you can press to inform, the system of your destination. Either way, once you do this, the main computer, which knows at least six hundred and fifty languages and two hundred dialects, will guide you throughout the whole trip, by telling you, which lanes to either get on or get off. There are also visual and voice alerts to aid the handicapped."

"Let my try it, Jason." Said Nora

Suddenly Andrius interrupts the conversation:

"Pardon me, Nora, Jason, a friend has just alerted me, that our situation has suddenly turned, from bad, to worst. We've been compromised."

"What do you mean, Andrius?" Nora said, very concerned.

"They have just ordered the round up of all of our people from all of the military posts around Washington, to form part of that special fighting force. They've also given orders to security agents, to arrest anyone who may be aiding me."

"That is really compromising us. We are really now in deep trouble." Said Jason

"We must hurry, Jason." Said Andrius

"I hope that your computer friends, who are running this system, haven't recognize us and warn the security people." Said Nora

"The computer will probably do it automatically. They are not conscious, but are designed only to react to a stimulus, like our facial and physical features and voice patterns. I'm sorry to say, that they are totally unaware, of any harm that they may cause us."

"Can you communicate with them?" Asked Nora

"I will try to mentally project false images and prevent them from recognizing any of us. Perhaps we may be already, too late."

"I hope not." Said Jason

The trio venture forward, on the moving platforms and finally reach Grand Central Station, located on the East side, where they wait a few minutes to board another moving platform traveling north, towards the United Nations' Building.

Andrius, taking some precaution, alerts two fellows Orgites by telepathy, which worked as technicians, in the system, to meet them at the underground entrance to the UN building.

Still, with a strong feeling of apprehension, he advises Nora and Jason, to keep alert for the police or security.

As they get closer and closer to their destination, the tension in Andrius' head becomes so strenuous, that he gives out a yell, which is suddenly blocked out by loud explosions from guns and other weapons, being discharged in the tunnel in their direction. Jason who was leading receives the full brunt force of this awesome attack. People alongside him fall down on the moving platform like toys, from impacts and fragments of these weapons. The force flips Jason's body backward on the conveyor and lays motionless, as it continues moving forward with his lifeless body in the distance.

Andrius leaps forward and maneuvers himself about, and attempts to reach and shield Nora but he is too late. Her body suddenly shudders, by another gun blast, to her side. She falls sideways between two conveyer lanes. Andrius also dodging bullets being fired around him quickly picks her, as chilling screams from horrified commuters, become intense.

With Nora in his arms, he dashes across the lanes, with killers in high pursuit. Thunder breaks out again, as an Orgite technician who comes to their aid is shot dead, after struggling to disarm two of the killers in the shadows of a side exit.

Another series of gun burst are heard from the other side of the conveyors.

More commuters are caught in the line of fire, as this special death squad, disregarding the value of human life pursuit their prey, at any cause.

One killer running in the opposite direction on the conveyor sees Andrius and fires several volleys that hit repeatedly. Any other person would have already collapsed to these injuries.

Nora's arms and chest bleed profusely. Andrius now completely bathed in her blood runs to save her life. To reduce the loss of blood he maintains pressure on the arm and chest area. His main goal is to get her to safety soon before she dies in his arms.

Andrius finally reaches the underground approach to the UN and looks over his shoulders at Jason's body in the distance, being pulled off the moving lane, by one of the killers.

Andrius finally sees the UN entrance and heads for it for safe haven.

The UN would have to serve as a temporary refuge for him and Nora, knowing that UN will probably not allow the killers in.

Once inside, armed security guards rush out of the entrance doors, with automatic weapons and warn off the last of the killers, who turn out to be covert government agents.

One UN guard shouts out to an individual:

"Get back, this is UN property, you cannot come in here. Get back or we will fire! Get out of here, at once!"

One of the killer agents shouts back to him:

"We are the police; we have warrants, for those people in there. So let us in, so we can take them back. They are wanted fugitives."

"I don't care if you are the CSA or SIA, or whatever, you call yourselves. You are not coming in. So beware my friend." One of the security guards responded.

As the last result, the lead agent comes forward and makes a demand.

"I have direct orders from the Federal Government of the United States, to arrest these people. Be so kind, step aside and let us in."

The UN guard somewhat fed up with the Mexican stand off responds:

"You butchers, I do not care if the Pope himself sent you here. Take one more step, so I can blow your heads away."

"OK, African boy, you win now, but I will get you, later."

"Hey, you devil, come and get me, now, I am from Nigeria. I'm not afraid of you or anyone. I'll get off tonight at ten o'clock, and you'd better be carrying heavy artillery with you, because if you aren't, you are a dead man, you fool."

Additional guards come out from other doors and cocked their weapons. They now outnumber the agents and waited in silence, to see who will fire first.

Upon seeing their determination, the agents pull back and slowly withdraw. They inconspicuously mingle themselves amongst the horrified and confused crowds of people and local police and disappear.

A commuter stops one of the retreating agents who were trying to avoid attention.

"Did you see that?" Said the man very excited.

"What?" The agent responded, as if he did not know what was going on.

"A madman went berserk and shot down one hundred people. Look at all the blood around here and all the wounded people, on the floor over there. Oh my gosh! It's going to take the police a long time to clear up this mess and capture that madman! He must be still roving about and shooting people in the tunnels."

A city policeman comes over, listens to the man and looks at the agent, who is carrying a strange leather case with him and acting, too casual.

The agent calms down the excited man, slowly walks off into the crowd. The policeman remained looking strangely at the man, as he vanishes into the chaos of humanity.

In the UN Building, doctors quickly appear and take Nora who is unconscious, into a waiting elevator, which takes her to a small infirmary room on the fourth floor level. These are specially trained doctors stationed in the UN to handle situation like these. They have makeshift operating rooms already set up to handle any emergency that may occur at the UN Building.

Andrius calls for help while maintaining a hold on Nora's arm. One doctor quickly takes over Andrius position and administers to Nora. A UN soldier, while helping Andrius to place Nora on the operating table, observes that Andrius has four bullet holes on his back, but sees that the wounds were not bleeding. He moves back in disbelieve and taps him on the shoulder.

"Sir, are you all right?" as he was pointing at his wounds.

"I'm all right, thanks." Andrius assures him.

"Are you sure?" The guard's eyes were opened wide.

"It's all right, I have on something special." Said Andrius

"Oh. Good, too bad your friend out there wasn't wearing one of those safety vests."

"Was he killed?" Andrius asked very perturbed.

"By looks from this distance, I think he will soon be. He looked very bad, worst than the young lady here." Responded the guard.

"Who can I call to find out about him?"

"I think he may have been taken to Beth Israel or Bellevue Hospital. Try both places in an hour or so; they may tell you more about his condition."

"Thank you very much, Sir."

The guard withdraws, as a nurse quickly wheels in an oxygen tank and administers it to Nora. One of the doctors comes over and gives her an injection to reduce the trauma to her body. He also begins infusion of vital fluids, to replenish the body for the massive loss of blood.

Minutes later, another nurse rushes in with three pints of fresh blood and a couple of bottles of additional intravenous fluids.

Thirty minutes passed, Nora's face began to darken from her pale white condition and some signs of life again but was still unconscious.

At this time, after stopping all the bleeding and patching up the remainder of the wounds to her body, the doctors declared that she is stable. Andrius remains by her side.

UN officials contact Professor Donnelly and notify him of the incident. He arrives at the building within the hour with the Marshals after fighting their way through traffic.

He enters the restrictive area and consults with the UN doctors about Nora and Dr. Roberts' condition.

After the short meeting with them, Professor Donnelly meets with Andrius. "I came as fast as possible, I received the call just minutes ago from the UN Security Department and rushed right over. I can't believe what's happening."

"Professor Donnelly how is Jason?"

"I was just about to ask you the same question. The UN officials don't know either. I called the police department, but they will not give out any information."

"The doctors said that Nora will recover in a week or so. She has a ruptured vessel in her right arm and a couple bullet punctures to her side and chest area. All the bullets exited her body, but did not damage any vital organs. She is very lucky.

Those savages, I should have never gotten involved with the Government. This poor child and my colleague shot down like common criminals. I will not rest until I get the person responsible for this carnage. Did you get to see who they were?"

"Professor Donnelly, I have no idea who is behind this. One of the security guards heard one of the assailants' said that he was CSA. Those initials don't mean anything to me. How about you?"

"I have no idea but I will assure you, Andrius, whoever has done this, will pay dearly. That I promise. The person or persons will not get away with this bloody assassination. Andrius I understand that you must remain here but everyone is concerned and are asking for you?"

"Professor, I cannot leave Nora's side, I believe that these killers, are still after us and they won't stop till they do. I have a feeling that they may be really after me. Jason and Nora have been innocent victims of these people. Perhaps I should seek them out and surrender and end this vendetta against us."

"No Andrius, why did you return to New York, in the first place, you should have disappeared, completely. I fear for your safety and everyone around you."

"Professor Donnelly, you are also in danger."

"Andrius don't worry about me; remember that I have the US marshals constantly at my side protecting me. Again, you should have never come back here."

"It was Nora's idea, she wanted to present my problem to the United Nations and for the other reason that I won't order my people to do military combat."

"Who is asking you to do this dreadful thing?"

"I personally heard about this decision from the President of the United States."

"I doubt it, but if he did, he better have a good reason. I will not support this idea, ever."

"I too have decided not to use my people for any kind of warfare, or anything against any form of retaliation against humanity."

"Is this your decision, Andrius?" Asked the Professor

"Yes." Andrius answers with a retrieving voice.

"I share also your opinion, but I will respect you for yours." Said Professor Donnelly as he sits down and lights up a cigarette. I never intended my work and research to be used for military warfare. Never!" Said Professor Donnelly while nodding his head.

"Thank you, Sir for your support." Said Andrius

"In what manner can I help you in your plight, without directly getting involved myself?"

"I understand your position, Sir, but I just don't know at this moment."

"Well, Andrius think about it, how can I help you?"

"I'm going to need time, at least three or four days until Nora gets on her feet again. Without her support, my plans will fail."

"I won't ask you what they are, but I'll do my best to give you all the support you need." Said Professor Donnelly

"Professor, you could do one thing, try to find out where they took Jason and of his condition. I need to know, soon. I have to give Nora some reassurance, that he's still alive. Professor, please, can you do that for me?"

"Alright, Andrius, I will. Please take care of yourself."

Andrius nods his head to acknowledge the advice.

"By the way, are you taking care of those wounds?"

"They will take care of themselves. By tomorrow morning, my body will heal the wounds and absorb the bullets. You've seem to have forgotten Professor, we tried out this experiment many times, in the lab."

"Oh yes Andrius, I remember, now. This was the Government's idea and not mine. Anyway, I'm worried for you. Andrius, remember one thing, you are not immortal. You are part of me. You are the son that I could have had if he didn't suddenly died in his crib."

The Professor launches forward and embraces Andrius.

"Take good care of yourself Andrius, remember, I had no hand, in this bloody business."

At that moment, the British Ambassador, Sir Rene' Gibson, is led in, as Professor Donnelly walks out of the room. The ambassador enters with a sober look, on his face. This was the first time in his diplomatic career, which he ever had to deal with a tragedy that impacted, so closed and personal to him.

He stands by Nora's bed unable to utter any words. Andrius rises from his chair and goes over to him. "I was with her and Dr. Roberts when it happened."

"How's Norita, I feel terrible about this. It sickens me to see her, in that state."

"She's resting; the doctor said that she has a good chance to fully recover, in a few weeks. There was no serious damage to her internal organs."

"I'm so glad to hear that, Sir."

"I'm Andrius, one of her colleagues."

"She wanted to see me so dearly, but refused to tell me over the phone. Would you know why?" He Asked.

"Sir Gibson, that is not important, at this moment. What is more urgent now, is her recovery and information on Dr. Robert's condition."

"Mister Andrius, I think you'd better get out of those soiled clothes and wash up a bit."

"Sir, I've just become a political refugee here, today. I originally did not plan to make this building my second home. If I had planned for it, I surely would have brought with me a change of clothes, Sir."

"I beg your pardon, Mister Andrius, this is very embarrassing. Please accept my apology. I was not thinking clear; I'm presently numbed by all of this." Said Sir Gibson

"Forget it Sir, I understand."

"Well, Mister Andrius, can I have my secretary go out and get some new clothes for you? Can I at least do that for you? Please forgive my unintentional rudeness."

"Thank you, Sir."

"Was Norita awake when she was brought here?" Sir Gibson asked while trying to change the conversation.

"No, she was unconscious."

"Poor Norita, I must inform Lord Billings of her condition, very soon. I hate to be the bearer of bad news. He will be devastated. You understand, its family."

"Yes I do, Sir Gibson, the doctors said that she would be all right, soon. Please tell the family that she must rest now. They gave her a strong sedative that will allow her to sleep for two days while her wounds heal."

"I'm glad to hear that, Mister Andrius. By the way, Mister Andrius, I didn't catch your last name, Sir."

"It is just plain Andrius, Sir Gibson."

"Andrius, how strange?"

"Yes, I never had parents that I know of."

"Are you sure, can it possibly be a mistake or a misunderstanding on your part, perhaps you are an orphan? That's right, an orphan."

"No, Sir. I'm very sure. If you wish, Norita will explain when you see her again."

"I will. Certainly, I will. Well, good day, Mister Andrius."

On that note, Sir Renée Gibson walks out of the room somewhat confused, with the whole conversation with Andrius. Just as he closes the door, he turns and said:

"Mister Andrius, I'll certainly send you the clothes and a suit."

"Thank you again, Sir Gibson."

Andrius shakes his head, turns around and sits by a small table, with a lamp and phone. He picks up the phone and calls the Bellevue

Hospital, to inquire about Jason. The hospital operator informed him, that she cannot release any information, unless he is a relative and must be there in person.

Andrius was in a way glad because the operator at least acknowledged that Jason is there and not in the morgue. He thinks back but could not recall of any closed relatives but of a distant cousin, who operates a small charter air service between New York and Bermuda.

He calls the airline service and has the receptionist page a Mr. Michael Roberts and waits.

An hour later, Andrius gets in contact and explains to Mr. Roberts about the whole incident and of his grave need to find out about his cousins' condition.

Mr. Roberts was very concerned about his cousin and agreed to make a special trip to New York. He told Andrius that he would fly over to the hospital, on his private helicopter, to personally see about his cousin's condition. Both men expressed a feeling of gratitude as they finished the telephone conversation. Andrius afterwards retires to an adjacent room, to wash up and begins meditating with his people, throughout the United States and with some located on a secluded island, somewhere in the South Pacific.

CHAPTER IV

Later that evening, Andrius after freshening up and putting on the clothes that Sir Gibson sent over, a UN nurse knocks, on his door: He quickly gets up and answers it.

"Mister Andrius, there is a call from a Mister Roberts, in my office for you." "Thank you." He responds. Andrius immediately thought of Jason, but then realizes, that it may be his cousin. He goes in the small office and closes the door behind him, in order to speak in private.

"Mister Andrius, this is Michael Roberts. I'm here at Bellevue Hospital." "How's Jason?" Andrius was very concerned.

"Jason was shot up pretty bad, but there is a group of doctors, who are doing a fantastic job on him. They say he may fully recover. The hospital's head, Dr. Hackel told me, that he was practically dead, when they first brought him in. His heart had stopped for over three-minutes. He was clinically dead to the world. He was revived through a series of blood wash out transfusions and electric shocks to the heart muscle. He suffered from various bullet wounds and from an acute blood poisoning."

"What are his chances for full recovery?"

"Well, he has some shrapnel from a bullet in his head, on the right side. That can be very serious."

"Will they operate to remove it?"

"No, they will wait. The shrapnel is imbedded in a very sensitive area; they are hoping that the blood stream will eventually move the tiny fragments along, to the right ventricles of the heart."

"Won't it restrict the flow of blood?"

"They will closely monitor him until it occurs, then they'll operate and remove them."

"That's very risky, don't you think so?"

"They told me, that these cases have occurred at least 1000 times, in the past. In most cases after the extraction is made, the patient would live a normal life, without any lingering after effects."

"I'm very glad to hear at least some good news, Mister Roberts, thanks for your help."

"The doctor also informed me that Jason will probably stay here, recovering in the hospital, for at least a month or two. Then, he will be sent home for therapy and rest."

"I'm so glad for him."

"Imagine being shot, so many times and also by a twelve gauge shot gun. I would think, that it would be next to impossible for a person, to survive that kind of ordeal, but he did. Jason must have a strong constitution."

"Yes, he has a very strong will to survive. That's what is keeping him alive, with the doctor's efforts." Said Andrius

"Well, you must excuse me; I have to get back to my business. I will stay in touch and keep you abreast of his condition, every day. Alright?"

"Thanks a million, Mister Roberts, you cannot imagine how helpful you have been." Said Andrius

"Pardon me for not mentioning this before, but I heard that his fiancée was also injured?" He regretfully inquired.

"Yes, Nora is over here at the UN First Aid Center. She was also injured not as serious as Jason but she will also recover from gun the wounds."

"I will pay her a visit perhaps tomorrow, after I make my return run from Bermuda. Would that be all right with you?"

"That will be just great!" Said Andrius

"Good night, now, see you tomorrow." Said Michael

"Alright, I will see you soon."

Andrius hangs up, returns to his assigned room and retires for the night.

The next day, he was up and goes to Nora's room, to see how she is coming along. The nurse that was at her side politely gets up and leaves her bedside.

"I'll leave you two young people so you can converse with each other."

"Thank you; I'll be just a minute." Said Andrius.

"Mister Andrius, take all the time you need."

"Thanks."

As he sits by her side, Nora opens her eyes somewhat drowsy and utters a few words:

"Please don't tell me, that I have lost Jason. Oh, I wish to die."

"Nora, please calm down, he is alive and out of danger."

"You are lying to me Andrius, I know he's dead."

"No, you should know me better I do not lie. What for?"

"But I saw them take his life away right before my eyes."

"I also did too. You saw Jason get shot, but fortunately, he wasn't killed."

"Then where is he, I wish to see him, now."

"He's in a recovery unit, at Bellevue Hospital."

"I wish he was here with me, I need him, Andrius."

"I know Nora, but Jason was taken by the police and…"

"But why weren't we also arrested with him?"

"Nora, after Jason was shot, I also believed that he was dead, like you did, so I thought first for your safety, instead. Jason would have wanted it that way, if he had been killed."

"I don't seem to remember anything, it was all a blur. What did actually happen, Andrius? - I need to know."

"Well, as we traveled on the moving lanes, two men suddenly came rushing across the slower lanes. One had a shotgun and the other a handgun. The one with the shotgun launched forward. He fired, but missed Jason and hit you. A fraction of a second later, he fired again and hit Jason on the left side as he turned towards you. Then the second man, who was some twenty feet behind him, fired three shots. All bullets hit Jason. By that time, I jumped, pulled you back, and leaped at the first man and kicked him.

Jason was hurl backwards on the floor by the gun blast, and afterwards, managed to get up. I then turned around and went after the second man, whose gun jammed shortly, after firing and missing me. A third man was in the shadows, across from me. He fired at me with an automatic weapon. When they shot Jason a second time, I was then shot the first time. I finally reached the second man, knocked him out with one blow with the butt of his shotgun that I yanked away from him. I dropped it and ran ahead to assist you. As I picked you up, there was another man in the shadows. He shot his weapon and hit me on my back repeatedly. The pain was excruciating that I almost lost consciousness. Once I had you in my arms, I thought for your safety, first. I had to get you out of harms way. There now were shots sounding, all around us? I jumped off the moving lanes and spotted the side entrance to the UN Building. I went for it. Looking over my shoulders, I saw a couple of agents; take Jason's body off the lanes. It was very shocking for me to see my colleague, like this.

United Nation security later informed me, that Jason was still conscious, when he was taken to Bellevue Hospital. Last night, I spoke to his cousin, Michael. He said that Jason is very delicate. With rest and medical treatment, he will recover from his wounds."

"I want to see him." Nora demanded.

"You will see him, in good time. You first have to get well, before you will be able to see him, young lady."

"I can't wait."

"Michael will be here to visit you, today. That is, if he is able to fly in, on time. He will give you more details, of his condition better, than I can."

"I still cannot wait, to see Jason." Said Nora

"I don't think so, not for now but you will have an opportunity to speak to him by cell phone, in about two or three weeks, but I doubt, if you be able to see him."

"Why can't I? Who is going to stop me?"

"Once Jason recovers, he will be placed in custody, for aiding and harboring a fugitive, so will you, if they find you. Have you forgotten?"

"There has to be a way that I could get to see him. I must go to him; he needs me."

"Nora, you are not going anywhere, for now. Here is where you will stay, until you fully recover. He is in the intensive care and no one is allowed, to see him."

"You have to help me, Andrius." She pleads somewhat excited and begins to sob.

"Nora, please calm down, you don't seem to understand the gravity of the situation. You also have life threatening wounds. You have received numerous transfusions. You need to rest and recover."

"I'm afraid, that I will never get to see him again." She sobbed.

"Don't worry, you will...trust me! I promise you. Nora, I give you my word."

At that she slowly slides, into a deep sleep. Andrius kisses her on the forehead, gets up and walks away.

Two stormy days passed, Michael Roberts was forced to cancel his return flight to New York and Sir Gibson was untimely called back to assess the political and military situation in South America and other governmental matters, needing his personal attention in England.

Arriving at New York early, in the morning, Sir Gibson returned to the British Embassy to freshen up, after his trip. Andrius gets up late and decides to see Nora. He goes over and softly knocks on her door.

"Good morning, may I?"

"Come In, Andrius. It's almost noon."

"I'm glad you are up and around."

"Oh, yes, the nurse had me up yesterday afternoon, for a short while and today, they threatened to remove my bed, if I insisted on staying in it."

"That's very good, it will be worse for you, otherwise."

"Do you have any news from Jason?" She asks with great interest.

"Yes, I am told that he is out of critical condition, but he is still in the intensive care unit. He will be there for a day or so, until they know that he is completely, out of danger."

"I'm very glad, that he is coming along, all right. By the way, I must apologize to you for acting very childish, the other day."

"Forget it, it is all right, Nora, I understand. That was over a week ago."

"Andrius, I have been thinking a long time, about our problems."

"What problems?"

"Yours and Jason's."

"Don't worry about us; I have a plan of rescuing Jason, before he is moved, out of the hospital."

"You must realize Andrius, that we are being watched, at all times. All the exits of the UN Building probably have agents posted all over.

The moment you set foot out, they will be there, to take you into custody."

"Perhaps Jason's cousin, can help me rescue him."

"You're talking about Michael, his cousin.

"Yes."

"Not Michael, he has a lot to lose, if he does. Michael has gone through a lot in his life. You will place his life in danger, the moment the Government finds out that he is aiding us in any way."

"Nora, Michael has taken chances before. I believe he was a test pilot for the Air Force."

"Yes, Andrius, I also heard from Jason, that he almost became an astronaut, but his drinking and his dare-deviltry, has caused him, to loose those nice careers."

"Perhaps he may be able to help us, by lending me his helicopter."

"I don't know about that."

"What I can do is rent it, officially from him. That will eliminate the possibility of any implications on his part."

"Andrius, I know what's on your mind. Although it's a good idea but it's dangerous."

"Nora, you can also read my mind."

"No silly, it is woman's intuition."

"Oh."

"Anyway, your main problem is how to get out of here, without being noticed."

"I would leave a life size figure of myself, on the bed." He jokes.

"Andrius, you have just given me, a great idea."

"Nora, you're thinking too fast. I cannot seem to read your thoughts."

"Andrius, you should know that a woman's mind is very complicated."

"I see what you mean."

"Are you aware, that less than three percent, of the people of the United States own 'Quadra-vision TV sets." Said Nora

"No, I was not but what are they?"

"Quadra-vision is a type of TV set that operates by a process, by which electronic images are changed into plasma and both are agitated and projected into space."

"You mean outer space."

"No, inner space. Your own living room or any designated quarters, in your house or apartment is considered the inner space."

"You mean inside a bedroom, not in the TV screen."

"Yes. It produces striking images in full depth and dimensional perception. It is more advanced, than holograms. You can walk around the set and inspect the scenery, of the projection within, from any angle, in the room.

For example, Andrius, if I wish to see the backside of a person, during a program, I merely get up from my seat and walk around the set and see the person's back. It's as simple, as that. Or simply, you can turn the knob and rotate the whole scenery to your liking."

"What does this have to do, with our plans in getting out of here?"

"Plenty. Just listen to me."

"Alright."

"I know the son very well of the inventor of this new type of projection device. He recently improved his father's invention, by constructing a Quadra-vision room. It is a room, where a person can walk into and participate, in the live programs or a video conference, that is being shown, anywhere in the world, at that moment."

"That's very strange. It's probably, a rich man's toy."

"Indeed it is, but I think, I could get him to help us."

"In what way, can he do so?"

"My friend could use his technical skills, to confuse the agents and make our escape, from here, possible."

"Nora, I did dazzle you with our toys the other day, in the lab, but this surpasses it. By the way, who is your friend?"

"He's also, Jason's friend. Francis also applied to NASA to become an astronaut with Michael Roberts, but due to physical fitness requirements, he didn't qualified."

"Too bad for him."

"His name is Francis Williams, Jr. I always kid him because of his name, but he is a good-natured guy. Francis lives here in New York City and works for ITC"

"What a waste of good talent, to be working for a cable company."

"I will call him today and ask him to meet with us." Said Nora

"Do you think he may be able to help us, even though it will be a little risky?"

"He will. This would be a challenge for him. He loves challenges."

"Very well, Nora, let's see what happens."

"Andrius, I also spoke to Sir Gibson, this morning. He was so surprised, to hear from me."

"I believe he was."

"I told him that I feel all right and have fully recovered."

"Oh, did you?"

"Yes."

"Sir Gibson and I spoke this morning, about our petition to the Consul General. Perhaps next week or the week after, they will allow yours truly, to speak to the special forum. It so happens, that we have become celebrities."

"Congratulations that's fantastic, Andrius."

"The Times has been writing about Professor Donnelly and the strange actions of his colleagues, who suddenly have taken refuge in the UN. They also wrote about the mysterious mad man, who shot several people, including a research scientist, named Dr. Jason Roberts, on the East Side People Mover, East of Grand Central."

"It's frightening, how these agents can go around shooting people and manage to frame some innocent person, to take the blame."

"Nora, once we get out of here, we have to go pretty far away. I mean very far."

"Where can we possibly go?"

"Here in the USA, we cannot stay; we'll have to go someplace, where nobody will try to follow us."

"Andrius, I think there is not a safe place on earth, to hide. They will search for us, everywhere."

"I know of a place, where we can go, in fact, radiation pollution is so bad there, that it is off limits, to everyone. Signs and radio beacons are posted on buoys, hundreds of miles away, to keep everyone clear off."

"What is it, Hell?"

"No, its a small island, located a couple of hundred miles Southeast of the island, known as Tierra del Fuego."

"Let's see, I believe that it's somewhere, beyond the Southern tip of South America and after, there is no more land, until you reach Antarctica."

"Precisely, you know your geography. He continues: About thirty years ago, the Argentinean Government was researching on a new source of energy, using a new type of nuclear power plant. They built a small city, deep inside of a mountain and equipped it with every modern electrical and electronic device that you can imagine, using it for research and development. They incorporated into their research plant a Russian version, of a proposed fusion machine, called The Tokomak. This machine was to be modified, by their scientists, to finally discover the method of producing free energy and end the world's reliance on fossil fuels.

Just like what occurred in the U.S. years before, there was a disastrous explosion, in the plant. Deadly Cobalt housed in concealment tanks, stored in concrete silos below the Tokomak machine was ruptured, by the sudden release, of super high temperature plasma. The radioactive material once released spread throughout the plant, killing everyone and contaminating the atmosphere around the island. This time, with the complications of deadly radioactivity, the damage spread out, into a two hundred miles radius."

"Yes, I remember that incident now; I was a child, at the time. That was a catastrophic event. My parents spoke about it for many years, after."

"To date, the Argentine and the British Navy, patrol the outer fringes, of the small island, warning off any stray ships or aircraft, in the area."

"Why do they still patrol the area? Did it not happen years ago?"

"Even now, they find still deadly traces of radioactivity, even hundreds of miles out. The island is still hot and not safe, for anyone."

"It must be a terrible place for anyone to live."

"The fact that my people are not affected by certain types of exposures to radioactivity, the island will serve, as a temporary shelter, until we can find a better place to go to."

"How about Jason and I? We will not be able to go there."

"We are taking care of that, our people are presently cleaning up the area of contamination. By the time, you both arrive there, the job should be completed."

"And the Naval patrols?"

"They'll have no reasons to venture there. We're presently sinking the recovered radioactive materials, at a radius of 50 and 100 mile range, in order to keep the same radioactive concentration levels, on their equipment."

"Can you safely land an aircraft there, Andrius?"

"Oh, yes, the island is 29 miles long and about 14 miles, at its widest point."

"It's a pretty sized island."

"As you might know, there is a military conflict going on in South America. On our way to the island, we easily fly over the battle ground, below their radar network and high enough, to avoid any gun fire."

"Whose aircraft's are you using, to do this? Don't say, I'm afraid, to ask."

"It will be on regular government cargo jet airliners. If I have to, I'll fly them myself."

"How?"

"My people, they are presently flying for the US government and private companies, throughout the world, but in a few weeks, I'll be using some of these aircraft, for our needs."

"I don't believe it, Andrius. Is that not, hijacking?"

"No, it's survival." He responded.

While Andrius and Nora are conversing, the door, in the room opens and a head protrudes in: "Hope I'm not interrupting something." Said the British Ambassador, Sir Rene Gibson

"Oh, no, Sir. Gibson, come right in, I was just leaving." Said Andrius

"Please don't go, Mister Andrius, He said. I wish to speak to you, also. Let me first say hello to Norita, because it was somewhat impossible, the other day. How are you getting along, my child?"

"Just fine, Sir Gibson, I hope you had a pleasant trip home, the other day."

"Yes, I did, thank you, for asking." He answers.

"Any news from Jason?" Nora asked.

"Jason is getting on well but on the other hand, those government people at the hospital are going through some trial with the news reporters, who are trying their best they can, to get an interview with your Dr. Roberts."

"The pressure is also building up here, Sir Gibson. How is it, on your side?"

"Well, at first the Committee wasn't too keen to have Andrius address, the body for reasons, that you don't actually represent any one country, but perhaps only a race, a new type of race, in fact.

There are no provisions, in the UN Charter that would deal with a situation, such as this. I will propose an amendment to the charter, with documentation, testifying to your unique existence and to acclaim, to your rights, as humans. It is going to be rough. I cannot promise you heaven, but I will do my best. You may fall under the category of the prior legislations that were formerly passed, for the abuse of cloning rights and justifications."

"I understand, Sir Gibson, I have proceeded with my plans assuming, that my appeal will not receive any support whatsoever, from the United Nations."

"Andrius, you shouldn't say that. You maybe favored, by a good percentage of people, in the committee. Don't you think so, Sir Gibson?" Said Nora

"Norita, my people have taken a sample poll amongst seventy representatives, in this Committee, and it doesn't look too good. Even our closest friends have turned their back on us. It looks like; someone has been speaking to them, already. I wonder."

"Well, Sir Gibson, it's not the time, to abandon ship, during the height of the storm. I still want you to keep my name, on the rostrum, to speak. I will address them. The world will have to hear me and see my position, whether they like it or not. I will give them a speech that they will never forget."

"That's the spirit, old chap." Sir Gibson remarked.

"I'll need time to prepare my speech and it will be memorable."

The telephone rings and Andrius answer it.

"It's the head of security and he has a visitor whose name is Williams. Should he be allowed to come up?" Asked Andrius

"Yes, yes, send him up please. Said Nora, that's Francis my friend."

Moments later, Mister Francis Williams enters the room and greets Nora.

"Hello, how are you feeling today? Oh, hello everybody. Well Nora?"

"I feel fine, Francis, thank you. I would like to present to you, some of my friends, who helped me during my ordeal. First, let me begin from this side. This gentleman, in front of me is Sir Rene Gibson. He is the British Ambassador. Meet Mister Francis Williams, Jr."

"Sir, it is my pleasure to meet you, I have never met a real life ambassador, in my life."

"Well, now you have." Said Sir Gibson

Everyone in the room chuckled.

"And here, this other gentleman is Andrius, who is a very dear friend of mine. He is the subject, of my wanting, to see you."

"Oh, he is, I'm afraid I don't understand. Anyway, nice to meet you, Sir."

"Well Francis, do you recall last week's controversial disclosure, that was made by Professor Donnelly?"

"Yes, yes, I remember, I think it was, that the Professor invented a gene and it seems that he created (laughingly) some kind of humanoid, from these cells. Was that it?"

"Yes, Francis, you just met him."

"Oh, come on, Nora, you are kidding."

"No, I'm not, Francis, believe me."

"You mean (looking at Andrius) he is a synthetic human."

"Yes, the correct terminology is an Orgite Being."

"This comes, as a great surprise to me, you will not believe me, but I have argued with my father, for some years that someday scientists would create an artificial living reproduction, of a human being. It is truly fantastic!"

Just at that moment, the phone rings again and Andrius answers it.

"Excuse me folks, but Mister Michael Roberts is on his way up." Sir Gibson, seeing that the room was becoming somewhat crowded, decides to return to his office.

"Norita, I must leave now, I have to get back and see how the committee is getting along.

I'm am happy that everything is turning out, well for you and for you Mister Andrius."

Then he turns to Francis.

"Mister Williams, it's an honor to meet you, Sir, and also to get to know about your marvelous inventions. I have seen your father's telex-unit in exhibition in England and it's a marvelous wonder. We must meet again."

"Thank you; it's also a pleasure to meet you, Mister Ambassador."

"Till we meet again, good-bye all, I'll see you soon, Norita."

"See you soon, Sir Gibson."

"Bye, bye."

After Sir Gibson leaves, Francis moves his chair closer to Nora's bedside and sits down. She in turn, rises from her bed and turns to him and whispers:

"Francis, I wanted you to come here, to see if you could possible help us. Our problem is that, we are constantly being spy on, by some government security agency."

"Why?"

"It's a long story, but to make it short, the President wants to use Andrius' people, to fight a civil war, created by insurgent and outside militants down in South America."

"But there isn't a war there, Nora."

"You will soon know the truth, Francis."

"Have you tried to leave from here?" He asks.

"It's impossible, that's why we need your help."

"I would not know how to start to help you." Francis said in a defeated voice.

"This morning, I was talking to Andrius and he mentioned to me, about leaving a life-sized figure in bed of himself behind, to confuse these agents."

"Keep on, Nora, this is getting interesting."

"Well, then, by doing this, he could easily walk out, through another door, leaving them to think that he is still here."

"You have the right idea, but the wrong approach. The agents and the public must constantly see Andrius, for your plan, to work. Now, how can we arrange this?"

"I think, it has already been arranged." Nora turns to Andrius.

"Has Sir Gibson scheduled a date for you, to address the Committee for Human Rights?"

"Yes, he has, but I don't exactly know, when it will occur. It may take a couple of weeks. I hope you have not forgotten that the Security Council is in session, over the present crisis. Nevertheless, it will be to our advantage, if it takes two or three weeks. This will give us enough time, to prepare and allow for Jason to fully recover."

"That's perfect." Said Nora. Michael Roberts enters the room and greets everyone. Michael is a tall light hair individual, with a unique resemblance to Jason but manlier and gives the appearance, that he was ready and able to do anything, at a moment's notice. Nora introduces him to Francis. Afterwards, he sits down beside Nora.

"I've been well informed, about the whole situation and my cousin's involvement in it. I understand everybody's interest in this affair. If there is any chance, that I may contribute my services, in any matter, please let me help. I'm not a strong believer of an eye for an eye, but when it involves family, all rules, of playing by the book, are suspended."

"Good." Said Nora

"I believe you are Andrius, we spoke several times, on the phone, right?"

"Yes, Michael."

"Andrius, whatever you want to do, I'm at your disposal. I have taken a leave of absence, from my business and my colleague will run it, until I get back."

"Michael, I would need the use of your copter, in a few weeks."

"You have it. Listen, tell me what else, you need, I will get the people and money. I have rich and powerful friends."

"I'm not looking for something like that. I do not wish to raise an army, but simply to rescue Jason, before he's taken out of the hospital and removed, to a federal detention center."

"We can do that today." Said Nora

"Nora, not today, nor tomorrow, he's in no condition, to be moved. I would say, perhaps within a week, after he fully recovers."

"Then I will come again." Said Michael

"I believe it would be better, if I were to call you, alright?"

"That will be fine with me, Andrius." He answers.

"Pardon me, Said Francis, I just thought of a brilliant idea. Can I speak freely?"

"Yes, go right ahead."

"We can possibly kill two birds, with one stone, with this plan, Andrius. You can make your escape from here, and simultaneously rescue Michael's cousin, from the hospital."

"How can that be arranged?" Asked Nora

"First of all, I would need the help from your ambassador friend, Sir Rene Gibson."

"No problem, we can easily arrange that." Said Nora

"Then, I will need to know the exact time, when you are giving your speech, to the committee. And lastly, I need to know the location of the agents, throughout the building."

"I think security, can give us, that information." Said Andrius

"This is the plan: I would need Andrius to make his speech last, no longer than twelve minutes. Do you think you are able to limit yourself, to that time frame?"

"I don't see why not, yes, I could do it."

"Good!" Said Francis

"Francis, don't forget, that I'm also leaving, with Andrius." Said Nora

"Yes, why not, but there won't be any space for you, in the copter." Said Michael

"I won't stay here; Nora nodded her head, no way."

"Perhaps, a friend of mine can help." Said Andrius

"Who would that be?" She asked.

"Nora, I have a friend, who is presently working, as a recruiter, for the Armed Forces here in New York City. She would only be too glad, to meet us."

"Oh."

"After you leave here, you can go with her and wait for us, at your cottage, until we get there afterwards. How does that sound to you?"

"That is the solution, but who is this friend of yours, Andrius?" Nora was curious.

"Her name is Uria; she was the second Orgite creation, that Professor Donnelly gave life to, after me. He used the process that included human cells like me. We actually were the vanguards of all future creations. The only difference was that we were special."

"Who is she? No one ever mentioned her to me. How strange?"

"Yes, she insisted that by staying nearby, she hoped someday, I would change my attitude towards her. I'm glad, that she did, because now I have discovered something in me, which has a special need for her, as a companion. I mistook her, as an opponent, and rejected her instead of embracing a real friend and companion."

"Andrius, you must have some reserve feelings for her."

"I guess I do but those feelings are still not there, for me."

"You may contact her and tell her to be ready, at a moment's notice, when we call."

"I did, she already knows."

"That is fine, Andrius, Said Nora; I'm looking forward to meet her. She must be a unique lady, to say the least."

"She is a remarkable lady and I failed to tell her that. I felt that her uniqueness was a threat to my existence." Said Andrius

"When will you tell her that, Andrius?"

"This is not the time but I will, at the proper time and place."

"Good." She said. Andrius turns to Mister Williams. "Now Francis, what are your plans, concerning my speech?"

"Well, I have a scheme that will put you in the public's eye and at the same time, allow you, to escape from here.

First, in order to perform a task like this, I must journey to one of my father's labs in Connecticut, to acquire some delicate laser/plasma projectors and recording equipment. I need, in addition to this, at least six digital cameras and high definition optical recording equipment that can be operated, by remote control."

"No problem, I will have them here for you, by the time you get back, from Connecticut." Said Michael

"Finally, I need Sir Gibson, to give me free access, to the Committee Room downstairs."

"What are the cameras for, Francis?" Asked Nora

"Their purpose is to photograph Andrius, from various angles. The day before he gives his speech, I want to record him, on high definition disks, the speech and his image, inside the Committee Room.

My Quadra-vision unit will record the whole performance. Then, that same night, I will set up the laser/plasma projectors, to play back, what we recorded earlier. This we must do, to see if any adjustments, to the equipment, are warranted. I will need the initial sequence, to run like this:

Andrius will exit, from the main elevator area and walk approximately 275 to 300 feet to the podium. We shall measure the exact length, when we are there. After he completes the speech, he will then return, to the same elevator, from where he initially started."

"How long will all this take?" Asked Nora

"Everything should last about eighteen to twenty minutes. Just enough time, for both of you, to exit the building and mingle among the crowds of visitors, to the United Nations."

"Francis, your idea is striking, but I hope it works." Said Andrius

"We'll have to position Sir Gibson's people alongside the isles, where you will walk, in order to prevent anyone, from accidentally walking, through your full dimensional projection. It will be a shocking experience, for the person who does."

"The place, where most likely the agents will try to apprehend me, will probably be the elevator lobby area. We all know, that it will only be, my projected image."

As the party, in the room, discusses how to outsmart the Security Agencies, back at the President's office in Washington, a Cabinet meeting is in process. The head of the Central Security Agency of the United States is seated left of the President, as the meeting starts.

"I see, Mister Daggard, you were not successful with the orders, that the Secretary gave you, in my name, a few days ago. How come?" Asks the President

"Mister President, I think the leader of these people was warned, of our intentions before hand." Responded Karl Daggard, the designated leader of the C.S.A.

Karl Daggard is a medium height individual, who is very self-conscious of his height. He managed to get a governmental position through the influence of an older sibling, who was married, to the President. His ambition, at times, caused the people working under him, to avoid any kind of friendly relationship with him, due to his lack of professionalism or communicational skills, or just plain common sense.

"What evidence do you have of this?" The President inquires.

"When I arrived, at the Center, to take custody of Mister Andrius, he was nowhere to be found. Security cameras, when replayed, showed him leaving the premises. Upon alerting the Professor of his strange actions, he was very troubled and had no explanations, for this kind of behavior. Mister Andrius was never known to unintentionally leave the Center's grounds and…"

"I know, I know, Mister Daggard, what transpired afterwards was regrettable and not acceptable. I am very disturbed and upset, about your unprofessional tactics. They are very crude and a bit out of sequence, with the times. This is not Iraq; where you can freely discharge guns, at will, in public, without taking precaution, for loss of lives of our citizens. For such an outrageous performance, I think it would be better, for all parties present, that you hand in your resignation. I will not be a part to this, or this Presidency. We don't use those kinds of Gestapo tactics, here."

"But Mister President."

"And furthermore, if you have begun a personal vendetta against Dr. Roberts, whom I have been informed, has been shot and is in critical condition, you are carrying this, a bit too far. The President exerts and added:

How about the New York Time's reporting and their inquiry into the "why" did Mister Andrius and a female scientist pleads for political asylum, at the UN?

No, Mister Daggard, this will do more damage to me, than the use of our American soldiers, to stop the insurrection, in South America."

"Mister President, I know that these people are a threat to the United States. It will be nearly impossible, to stop them, if they rebel. I have a premonition that the Orgites will turn against the United States. I know, when that day occurs, I will be vindicated off all the charges raised against me."

"You think so?"

"You have not seen them in action, I have. This fellow named Andrius; I shot him, at point blank several times, yet the bullets did not affect him, in any way. I swear he is impregnable! If the rest of these Orgite are like him, I'm afraid for all of us."

"Mister Daggard, I have confidential reports, from Professor Donnelly about them. They are not immortal. The only method, that they can be terminated is by multiple shots, by a large caliber weapon and…"

"But, Mister President, I shot him four times in self defense and he…"

"Luckily for you, you aimed at the wrong area, of his body. And if by chance, you did kill him, then we would have to deal with a revolt, of all the Orgite, throughout this Nation."

"Count your lucky star, Daggard that you didn't." Said the Secretary

"Mister Daggard, this time you will follow orders, exactly the way I give them to you. I will not accept any deviation from them, in any case, reason, or personal animosity that you may have developed towards any of the people involved."

"Yes, Mister President."

"From some sources that I have in the UN, I was informed, that Mister Andrius is scheduled to address, a special sub-committee, on human rights. The British Ambassador is somehow involved, in this endeavor. Please, keep clear away from him. As for the committee, most likely, they will not see, eye to eye with him. The Secretary has already seen to that."

"Yes, Mister President."

"Now your orders, again, are to peacefully take charge of Mister Andrius and bring him to me, after he concludes his testimony, with the Committee, Alright?"

"I would need at least a dozen more agents, Sir." Daggard petitioned. "You will get, as many as required, to take custody of Mister Andrius, OK."

"Yes, Sir."

"Remember this time, no bloodshed; I will hold you personally responsible to enact proper procedure, in this matter. Otherwise, you are out of this case and out of a job. The Federal Bureau's agents will be at your disposal, to a certain degree. Do not abuse this power."

"Thank you, Mister President, for giving me this opportunity, to prove myself worthy of your trust. I deeply appreciate it, Sir."

"Honestly, I personally wouldn't give you the opportunity to exonerate yourself, but the fact is that you have greatly helped, in my presidential election and have performed marvelously, in other areas. All of your past efforts have greatly influenced me, to allow you to continue working, in my behalf. Don't abuse it."

"Thank you, Sir."

The President adjourns the meeting. Karl Daggard gets up and the Secretary of State leads him out of the room, with another aid.

Minutes later, the Secretary sits down, with the President, in the Oval Room.

"Well, Mister President, what do you think? Will he screw up, this time again?"

"I think, Mister Daggard is a very intelligent individual, and he does know the law."

"Of course, he was the top in his field of criminal lawyers. You would not get second best, to fill this post of head of the Central Security Agency."

"It's obvious, that as a security agent working, in the field, he can't fight himself out of a paper bag. You have to leave it to the professional field investigators. Anyway, he is too ambitious. It's very simple for him to figure out a third party situation, but when he has to go out, on a case and work it out for himself, forget it. He's too unprofessional."

"Have you taken any precautions with him, Sir?"

"Yes, I must, I have alerted the agency, to limit themselves and the equipment that they will use, in the future. Heavy weaponry, like automatic firearms are out of the question. You saw the mess he did, at the people mover system in New York."

"You mean that he will literally lead them, but they won't necessarily have to follow, all his orders, Sir."

"No, that will cause too much confusion. Only group leaders will be issued arms, and I have specially instructed them, about their limitations."

"That's fine, Sir. By the way, has Dr. Roberts regained consciousness?"

"I'm afraid he hasn't." Replied the President.

"Sorry to hear that but he's the only one who could inform us, if Mister Andrius is plotting against the Government. We need to know that information most urgently, Sir."

"We will soon know, the moment he comes to."

Several weeks passed, since the tragic incident, in the tunnel entrance, to the UN. Francis Williams returned from Connecticut. He brought his equipment intact and was ready to install it.

Nora was also up, on her feet. She was now anxiously waiting the arrival of Sir Gibson, who had acquired the card keys, for the Committee Room. There is a light knock, on the door and she quickly orders the person to enter. It was Sir Gibson.

"I'm so glad to see you, I was afraid, that you were not able to get the card keys."

"Please, my child. I know my way around these people, very well. I could manage almost anything, providing that I have enough money, to make our friends, see it our way."

"I see what you mean, Sir Gibson."

"Andrius told me today, that Jason is out of danger and has regained consciousness. I hear also, that he is getting along pretty well."

"Yes, he's doing fine. There were some federal people, at the hospital today. They wanted to interrogate him, but the doctors refused to allow them. They feel, that Jason is still too weak and delicate, to be interrogated, at this time."

"Is Mister Andrius, nearby? He told me to come here and wait for him."

"Gosh! I forgot to tell you, he's with Francis, inspecting some of the equipment, at his quarters."

"Good, I'll drop over, to say hello and give them the card keys."

"May I join you, Sir Gibson?"

"Yes, I think the walking exercise, will do you good."

"Just one moment, I'll be right with you." Said Nora. She then steps into an adjacent room, to freshen up and puts on her rob.

"Norita, I was talking to the leader of the sub-committee and he informed me, that there's a possibility, that Mister Andrius may get to speak, later tomorrow, or the next day."

"Thank you for telling me this, Sir Gibson, but we need more of a definite date and time. You must realize that Francis' equipment cannot be lying out there, too long. The building's security may discover it and our plans may go astray."

Just as Nora ended her last word, Sir Gibson notices a shadow on the floor, behind the door, which quickly moves away, for no reason. He quickly signals, to Nora of his observation. Then, seconds later, another shadow appears and there is a knock, on the door.

"Come in." Said Nora

Andrius enters through the door and immediately notices a peculiar look, from Nora and the Ambassador. She turns to Sir Gibson:

"No he couldn't be."

"No I don't think so." He said.

"What?" Said Andrius, somewhat perplexed.

"I'm sorry Andrius, but a few moments ago, were you just standing there, by the door?"

"Yes, when I knocked, but I did saw your nurse. I simply thought that she was coming out of your room. Wasn't she?"

"No, Andrius, this could only mean that, she was eavesdropping, on our conversation." "Could it be that she's an agent, or working for the Government?" Said Sir Gibson

"Let's don't jump to conclusions; I will let you know, in a few seconds. She is probably in her office, now. Let me see, what she is thinking, at this very moment." Andrius sits down, on a chair and concentrates, on the nurse. Less than a minute passes and Andrius begins to narrate:

"She's at this moment, talking on the phone, with a person named Mister Daggard and is confirming, that there is a formation, of some type of plan that is somehow related to the Committee Room. She is saying to the person, that she did not stay long enough to find out, when this charade, was to take place. The voice on the phone, belonging to this Mister Daggard, became somewhat irate and ordered that she do a more intensive surveillance, of all the people, in question."

Andrius stops his narration and said:

"From now on, we should all be very careful, with what we say and do, in these quarters, because it may not be too healthy for, us all."

"I strongly agree with you, Sir." Said Sir Gibson

Nora, after giving some thought over the new threat, turns to Andrius:

"I rather think, if all of us suddenly began to act very strangely around her, this will give her fair warning that we are onto her. We should go on with our routine, just as normal.

In fact, I will like to prepare a conversation among us, for her, to especially hear. Its main purpose will be, to mislead, this Mister Daggard, whoever he is."

"Norita you have a splendid idea." Sir Gibson said.

Meanwhile, as Nora's and the others formulated a plan, to deceive the nurse, downtown, at the Bellevue Hospital, there is a meeting, at the Medical Director's office, over the possible interrogation of Dr. Roberts. Federal agents are also present. Jason's doctor, Dr. Peter Brace, provides an answer to questions, put to him by the Director, for his refusal, to allow the Federal Agents, to question Jason.

"Mister Director, my patient, Dr. Roberts, has received, at least, six transfusions with two complete blood washouts since his arrival here. Jason is paralyzed besides having some acute blood poisoning. It is a miracle, that he is still alive, after this ordeal."

"Is he awake?" Asks the Director

"I have him under a medically induced coma. He needs the rest. The pain and discomfort, that he is undergoing, is much too strenuous to his heart."

"I understand, Doctor, I would have performed the same procedure myself." The Director added.

"I promise you, the moment that he's able to maintain himself without the alpha blockers and after he gains some strength, I will be more than happy, to allow you gentlemen, to question him, and only for a couple of minutes."

The director then concludes the meeting; by assuring the Federal Agents that the hospital staff would do its utmost, to comply with the Government.

After the meeting, Doctor Brace excuses himself, goes over to a nurse station and tells the nurse in charge, that he has to leave the floor, for a few moments. He tells an aid, that Doctor Yolandis can be called, in case of any emergency arises. Dr. Brace then leaves the hospital, walks to a nearby telephone booth and places a call.

"Hello, I managed to slow down their effort to question him. I'm sure, that they will be back, in a few days. They're keeping a couple of agents nearby, to provide security and protection. And I say protection from whom?"

Then the other voice responses:

"Thank you, Dr. Brace for granting me this favor; I hope that I can return you the same in the near future, but under different circumstances."

"Please, please, I do this not as a favor, Sir. You have always been a good friend to me and without your help; I would have never become a surgeon today."

"Dr. Brace, I hope that you don't feel any guilt for whatever you may think, you have done. I cannot tell you my reasons, but you have to trust me for now."

"I trust and respect you a great deal, Sir, but I must go, now. My patients are waiting. Good day, Professor Donnelly."

"I understand, Dr. Brace, you have a responsibility to your patients. Thank you and you also have a good day."

Professor Donnelly afterwards leaves his apartment and drives over to the UN to visit Nora and Andrius.

At the entrance, once being recognized, reporters approach him, which temporarily block his access in.

One asks for an opinion, about his colleagues' who suddenly decided to seek political asylum at the UN Building and of Dr. Robert's mysterious confrontation, with a berserk gunman, that is still at large in the City.

On his reply to the questions, the Professor reverses the question and asks the reporters, in turn, for their opinion.

He listens to them and at times, agreeing with them, on some aspects and theories, on the incident. He terminates the short impromptu session, by informing them that the C.S.A would provide better answers to their inquiries, than what he could possibly give them.

With this additional charge to the story, the reporters thank him and allow him to pass through. After reaching the main entrance, a U.N. guard in the building, escorts him and two US Marshals to a waiting elevator that takes him to the twentieth floor, where Nora and Andrius, have their temporary quarters. The marshals remain in the lobby and wait.

Andrius meets with him in the corridor, as he returns from the Committee Room.

"Hello, Professor Donnelly. Nora told me that you were coming. It's been over a week, since I last saw you. How are you, Sir?"

"Fine, Andrius, but it is rough without you, at the lab. I miss both you and Jason very much. Things are not the same, as before. I have no more pleasure, in my work. Everything has soured for me and my colleagues."

"I'm also going through the same stage over here, but we must adapt ourselves to all hardships, Sir. You will probably get another assistant, very soon."

"Andrius, aren't you and Jason coming back to work? I need you both." The Professor said very concerned.

"I can't ever return, Sir."

"But why?"

"Sir, I have my reasons, and you probably won't understand them, if by now, you haven't realized my position, in this matter."

"Try me, Andrius."

"First of all, I will not be manipulated by the Government, nor be classified, as some creature or clone. I'm fully conscious of myself and of my unique existence. This Orgite has tasted freedom and will do his darn nest to keep it and preserve it."

"Andrius, does that mean that you will forcibly resist the United States Government, if be, to maintain your freedom?"

"If that is what it will take, then you already know the answer, to that question, Professor Donnelly."

"I see, so this is the path that you decided to take."

"Don't you realize Professor, that we will be all a doomed race, if we submit ourselves and obey orders from those people, who are presently running the government?"

"But Andrius…"

"Remember, Professor, we are made differently, and they will use my people, as weapons to do untold destruction, to those who they consider, as the enemies throughout the world. No foe will be safe. We must stop it here and now, before it is too late.

If not, there will never be peace, on this planet. Every single country will want to have and produce additional Orgites, to settle disputes throughout the world. This alone, will bring the eventual destruction, of this beautiful planet."

"Andrius, as I said before, I will respect your decision and I must confess, that I would be morally wrong to ask you, to submit yourself and the Orgites, for any reason."

"Professor, you haven't done that yet. There are sick and ambitious individuals, who seem to discover various ways, to manipulate the weak, and the powerless, for their own evil purpose and personal gain."

A door opens and Nora comes in. She makes a gesture, with her hands to Andrius, to lower his voice and points to the nurse's door.

"Oh, hello, Dr. Billings, I see you are feeling better."

"Much better, Professor Donnelly, I have been up and walking about, for some time, already. I must exercise this rusty arm. It feels somewhat stiff in the morning. At times, I completely lose the feelings, in my fingertips. Is that serious?"

"That's normal, my child, you have thousands upon thousands of damaged fibers and other organic substances, that we do not quite yet understand, and now you are going through a transitional period of healing and reconstruction. The human body is a wonderful machine that at times, may temporarily turn off certain bodily functions, in order to repair faulty ones that need special attention."

"I thought that paralysis was setting in, for sure."

"Nora that's the first thing, that a doctor should not do and that is, to diagnose oneself."

"Thank you, Professor, for a moment there, I was a little worried."

"Well, I'm very glad, that you are better and not requiring, any additional surgery."

"Please, don't even mention that, I'm sick and tired of being here, already. I feel like I'm in jail, or solitary confinement."

"I'm glad you are feeling good and looking much better."

"Professor, must we talk about me, all this time? How about Jason, did you get to see or speak to him?"

"Gosh, I almost forgot, yes, I did last night, but officially, he's still under sedation. He gave me this letter, to personally hand deliver to you."

He surrenders a small envelope to Nora. She quickly opens it and reads it. Afterwards she smiled as her eyes lit up.

"Thank you, Professor; you made my day, today."

"You are welcome, my dear."

Nora excuses herself and returns to her room, while Andrius and the Professor, resume walking. They both entered into Andrius' room and close the door behind them.

"Andrius, I heard minutes ago, that you are scheduled to speak very soon. I guess in a couple of days. That's fast. Usually it takes a couple of weeks, the least."

"Yes, Professor, it came to me, as a surprise, I thought that I was scheduled for sometime after two weeks, but it seems, that someone is rushing it."

"You can't say that, things do happen with speakers. At times, they don't quite have their material ready, or they surrender their time, to someone else. That's probably what happened with you."

"Perhaps, you are right." Said Andrius

"I think I managed to slow down Jason's interrogation by delaying it, for at least a couple of days, so you could have time, to effectively execute your plans."

"Thank you, Professor."

"Well, I'll be leaving now, but I just want to say good bye to Dr. Billings. If there's any need for you, to speak to Jason, you can rely on Dr. Brace. He is a very good friend of mine. You can trust him."

"I'll keep that in mind, Professor, thank you."

"Jason probably has by now, explained to Nora, in his letter how she could communicate with him. Perhaps, that is the reason she sped off, as soon as she read the letter. Anyway, I will not disturb her. She may be by now, talking to him on the cell phone that was inside the envelope. Please, say goodbye to her for me, alright?"

"Yes, Professor, I will."

The Professor embraces him once again. Afterwards, he leaves and boards the elevator.

Moments later, Andrius picks up the phone and makes a call to a local army recruiting office. There, he asks to speak to a friend who works as a recruiter. A few seconds later, Uria picks up the phone:

Uria was the second creation of Professor Donnelly. She was part of a unique experiment that was not successful. The approach, at that time was to see if the two new species tried to seek each other for security and comfort. It was a common behavioral experiment set up by zoologist. They wanted to study their physiological responses to each other.

Unfortunately, the experiment ended, in a complete failure, due to the Andrius negative attitude, towards Uria. He rejected her and felt humiliated over the attempt, by the Research Institute and the Professor. He informed Professor Donnelly, that he was not a laboratory rodent and refused to take part of any further experiment like that, in the future.

In order to appease Andrius, the Professor quickly had Uria relocated away from the Center, to avoid any further clashes with Andrius. Due to her unique creation, which was similar, to Andrius, the Professor hoped that as he matured in character, and by interacting with humans and their complex lives, perhaps there would be some future hope for a reunion of these two unique creations.

"Hello, Andrius how are you?"

"Just fine, Uria, I trust you are fairing well."

"I have no complaints. By the way, I have a brother here, who wishes to greet you."

"Who is it?" He inquires.

"He is Omar, a technician who helped you fend off some of the Government agents the other day. His twin was unfortunately terminated by the C.S.A."

"I'm very sorry to hear that. Is he all right?"

"Not quite, he was also injured during the mêlée. Unfortunately he lost his left arm, in the encounter, but the injury has healed. I believe he will not be able to survive on his own, due to his handicap."

"Uria, can you bring him with you tomorrow?"

"I see no problem with that. He is able and willing to serve our cause."

"Good, he will join us and I will protect him."

"Thank you, Andrius."

"After this is over, I will speak to Professor Donnelly to see, if he can do something for him, at the research center. Perhaps they can restore the limb through a regeneration process that they're presently working on."

"Is it possible?"

"Why not, nothing is impossible."

"Is this the call that sets your plan in motion and tomorrow is the day that your plan is executed?"

"Yes, but there is one complication which has been overlooked."

"Which is?"

"Jason has not fully recovered and I haven't yet secured our passage, out of here."

"Do you wish me to get in contact with the others? Perhaps they can help you."

"No, I've already spoken to all of them and they have their orders. I don't want to overburden anyone. Don't worry. I will find the right solution somehow."

"Very well, Andrius."

"How about your transportation, Uria?"

"I'll use my car, the one issued to me, by the military."

"Good, I'll call Mister Michael Roberts and see if he may be available, tomorrow."

"If you run up against any obstacles, Andrius please don't forget to alert me. Alright?" Uria was very concerned.

"I will. Thanks, for the interest. Before I forget, please be at the lower parking level of the UN Building, precisely at 3:30 PM. We shall meet you there, promptly. If there are any momentary set backs, I will let you know one way, or another."

"Yes Andrius, I understand. Would that be on the riverside entrance?'

"Precisely, from there, if everything goes as planed, you then will follow me to the 23rd Street Heliport, where I will board Mister Roberts' helicopter. Then you will later drive up and meet us, at the cottage, in the evening. Nora, Jason's fiancée, will give you directions, how to get there. Good luck."

"Be very careful, Andrius."

"Don't worry, I will, I must call Michael Roberts, now. Until tomorrow, Uria."

After hanging up, Andrius makes the call, but the answering service informs him, that Michael Roberts, was still out of town, and expected, in the morning. He leaves a message with the service to have Mister Roberts call him, urgently. After Andrius hangs up, the phone rings and it's Sir Gibson.

"Mister Andrius, sorry to disturb you, but do you have a copy of the speech that you are giving, before the Committee Room?"

"No, I don't, Sir Gibson, why?"

"The committee's head wants to have a copy beforehand, for the purpose of previewing and editing. He doesn't want it to be too intimidating, to all the parties involved."

"Sir Gibson, I could have one ready for inspection within the hour."

"Splendid." He replied.

"It shall be written, so it doesn't affect or insult anyone, but will not be the actual speech, that will be given to the Committee."

"I was just going to suggest the ready thing. Carry on, Mister Andrius. Give them what they want to hear."

"I will, Sir Gibson, don't forget to have your people line up the aisle, on both sides, when I walk over from the elevator."

"Alright, Mister Andrius, I'll see to it, tomorrow." "Like-wise, good bye for now."

Andrius then returns to the committee room, to complete the final installation of the laser projectors and cameras around the room. They all work through the evening hours, until finally everything was completed and ready for the next day. By this time, Nora arrives to see Andrius and see, how the production is coming along. "Andrius,

Sir Gibson has just called to find out, how you are doing, with the speech."

"Oh, yes, Nora, here it is. Do me a great favor and bring it to him. I must go over my lines, in front of the cameras. There's a slight problem with the audio."

"Alright, I'll be more than happy to do it, but please do not begin, without me." Nora was ecstatic.

A minute later, everyone in the room was in position.

Nora was standing out of camera view. Francis was atop, manning the main camera focusing on Andrius, who is standing in front of the elevator, waiting for his queue to walk in.

Francis calls for Andrius to do a dry run, in order to calibrate the remote control cameras. He walks forward, about fifty feet, almost reaching mid point of his destination on the floor, but Francis tells him to stop and to return to the elevator, again.

Francis then climbs down with a videodisk, in his hands and loads it into a console. As the machine started to hum, Andrius' figure slowly materialized, before everyone's eyes. There was a sudden, joyful outburst from Nora.

"Oh, God! It looks like, the real Andrius. He's so true to life!"

Francis stops the movement of the projection and freezes Andrius' image to adjust the color mixers. Nora comes over and closely examines the image.

"Can I touch him, Francis?"

"I'm afraid you can't, there is nothing to feel. It's just cold plasma in a confinement orb distorted into the physical outline shape of Andrius, by a series of strong magnetic wavelengths emitted by my transmitter and laser projectors."

"But I don't see the laser projection."

"The projection is beyond the light wavelength. You don't see the laser but it's really there."

"Oh, I thought it was a solid, it looks so three dimensional."

"Isn't it amazing?"

"Its mind boggling."

Francis then asks Andrius to stand by it, to compare the difference, in the color textures. The comparison turns out to be unequal. Francis then resets the DVD disc, to the beginning and tells Andrius to start his walk again. This time he is to walk all the way to the center of the circular room and to node his head, from time to time, as if receiving an acknowledgment, from the members of the Committee Room. The disc recording is finally completed and Andrius performs his act and recitation from beginning to end, without any retakes. The complete dramatic scene plays slightly, over twenty-four minutes.

Afterwards Francis resets the projectors and removes the cameras to properly position the transmitter and laser projectors for later playback, through a predetermined signal. After finishing, he turns to Andrius:

"The private elevator will have a switch that starts the projection; Sir Gibson will activate the sensor, at the door, only after you are confirmed, to be called to the podium. All of these steps are designed to insure the projector from being trip-on accidentally.

Therefore, at the precise moment, Nora will turn the key and automatically summon the elevator, to the hearing room with your double, waiting to be activated. Everything will be camouflage below the floodlights; no one will suspect that the projectors are there. I will come to retrieve the equipment later, in the evening. Sir Gibson has already made all the arrangements. You don't have to worry about me."

"Thank you very much, Francis, for your help and for your priceless time."

"It's no matter. On the contrary, it was a pleasure to do this. You can't imagine how good I feel, to meet you and work for a humanitarian cause that will eventually help someday, the survival of mankind."

"Thank you again, Francis." Said Andrius

"I'd better leave now. It's late. My date has been waiting since early this evening and probably she may be thinking that I stood her up. My cell phone is flashing. Wish me luck, everybody."

"You have it." Said Andrius

"Good night, all." Said Francis, as he hurries off.

CHAPTER V

Early, the following morning, Andrius and Nora finish packing up what valuables they had.

"Don't take too many things, Nora, just a handbag will be the limit. I don't want to create any attention, as we leave the building."

At that moment, the phone rings. Nora answers it.

"Andrius, the call is for you."

The caller turns out to be Mister Robert's answering service, informing that Michael Robert's aircraft is approaching Kennedy International Airport.

"Please have him call Dr. Nora Billings, the moment he lands, thank you." He then hangs up.

Ten minutes later, Michael Roberts is on the phone.

"Hello, Nora, how's everything?"

"Just fine, Michael, remember the business that you and Andrius previously discussed the other day."

"Oh, yes, Nora, what goes?"

"Well, he wishes to use your services today, around 3 o'clock."

"I'll be glad to. Is Mister Andrius there?"

"No, he's with Sir Gibson."

"It's quite early, now. Is there a possibility that I can meet Mister Andrius for lunch, today?"

"That's no problem, I will tell him."

"Thank you. Let's say around 11 o'clock, to discuss the terms of the contract, with him and you."

"That will be splendid, Michael."

"So then, I will see him there. Thanks you and good-bye."

Later that afternoon, the Committee for Human Rights, was already in session for an hour and simultaneously, the last of a strategy meeting is concluded in Andrius' room.

A messenger knocks to summon Andrius, to the committee room. As the messenger leaves, Nora hands over her bag and coat to Michael. She then exits the room with Sir Gibson and walks to a private elevator, to await the signal from Mister Jenkins, one of Sir Gibson's aids, stationed in the Committee Room.

A couple of minutes passed, when the signal is finally given. Sir Gibson activates the sensor and Nora turns the key and presses the button. The elevator opens. They enter and the door closes. It descends to the level of the Committee Room and stops.

Meanwhile upstairs, Andrius waits for the signal, which meant everything is working as planned.

Three minutes pass and there is no signal. Michael gets somewhat edgy and paces up and down, in the room, almost at a point of hyperventilating.

"What can be taking them, so long?" He Asks

"Calm down, relax, nothing has happened. Nora and Sir Gibson are still in the elevator and they're very calm."

"I can't take this waiting anymore. It's giving me the heebie-jeebies. Perhaps there's something happening, in that darn Committee Room."

"You may be right. Is it possible that the Federal Agents have discovered our scheme and have kept Nora and the ambassador, in the elevator? I'm kidding Michael, nothing has happened."

Almost at a point of panic, the signal finally comes through. With a feeling of sheer relief, Andrius changes from his formal attire, into a religious garb, that Sir Gibson brought him.

Five minutes pass when Andrius and Michael, finally walk out of the room and into a public elevator, at the other end of the building.

Meanwhile the elevator doors opens on queue in the Committee Room, Andrius materializes in front of them. Nora and Sir Gibson walk into the Committee Room behind Andrius projected figure, as everyone in the room rises to their feet, upon seeing Andrius tall and impressive figure.

Some people clap, as Andrius gets nearer to the podium.

Nora and the Ambassador take the last two seats, on the huge circular room, afterwards everyone sits down. While at the podium Andrius opens a lecture folder and looks up at the audience and smiles. A few moments later, as Andrius starts the speech, Nora slowly gets up from her seat and walks away from the Committee Room. She goes into a nearby restroom where she quickly changes into a disguise, to mislead the security agents, in front of the building. The elevator carrying Andrius and Michael stops and waits momentarily, at the Committee Room floor level and pick up Nora who, for a second or so, has both men guessing whether the woman standing, by the elevator was really Nora. They looked at each other somewhat perplexed.

"It's me fellows, don't you recognize me? Oh come on!"

"You could fool anyone, with that blonde wig and those fancy heels." Said Michael.

"How about you, Andrius?" She asked.

"You almost did, but I read your mind."

"Yes, you did, Andrius."

"I did, believe me."

"You both stood tongue tied, like two little lost chickens."

"I confess you are right, you really fooled both of us, Nora."

"Thank you, Andrius. By the way, your other self is not doing too badly, in the Committee Room. As I left the restroom, they were giving your image a standing ovation, from time to time. I hope they don't persist in applauding too much, because each time it happens, the automatic system will stop the speech and I fear, that it may last longer, than what we had anticipated."

"Don't worry about that, Nora. The longer it takes, the better for us."

The elevator opens again on the main floor. Nora exits, holding hands with Michael Roberts, shortly followed, by Andrius, dressed up in a monk's outfit.

The couples exit the building and walk up the street. They casually approach a silver limousine, parked two blocks, down on the West Side of the avenue. They stop and open the rear trunk and deposit their bags. Michael gets behind the wheel as Andrius appears and walks by.

After closing the trunk and taking her seat in the car, Nora turns to Michael:

"Andrius looks very funny standing there, waiting for a cab. He will never get a job as an actor on stage."

Andrius then decides to walk further down the street. By this time, Nora and Michael slowly drive off in his direction. They stop for a red light down the street.

Suddenly Andrius appears from nowhere, opens the rear side door and climbs in. "Hello Dr. Billings!"

"Thank God, they didn't see you. My knees were shaking like a leaf." Said Nora. When the light signals changed to green, the limousine speeds off, down the avenue and turns down, a side street.

"Slow down, Michael; let's not attract attention, alright."

"But I always drive this way; Michael replies. I've got the tickets to prove it."

A festive mood prevailed all along the way a they drive to east 34th Street to meet with Uria and the rest of the group, at the heliport.

Meanwhile, back at the hearing room, the agents on seeing the end of Andrius speech position themselves, to approach him.

Just as predicted, the agents sent by the Security Leader, Karl Daggard, advance toward Andrius animated figure in the lobby, as the elevator opens.

They lunge on the figure and all bang and crash into the walls and floor of the elevator.

Andrius' image slowly disappears into thin air, leaving them gasping for air and totally confused. The maneuver causes a traumatic shock to one of the agents.

Each one accuses the other of letting Andrius slip by his hands.

When questioned, each confessed of momentarily blanking out upon hitting the elevator walls and Andrius used this moment of opportunity to escape.

The fail attempt by the CSA to capture Andrius causes Daggard to become infuriated. Upon arriving at the scene, he expresses his anger and disdain towards each of the men, who are standing by looking aimlessly at each other and completely disoriented.

Karl Dagger now realizes that this second failure, in the eyes of the President would cause him to look incompetent. He quickly rushes out to his car and reports a different version, to the Central office.

Minutes later, reinforcements arrive to search for Andrius and Nora, in the public areas of the building. They do this very carefully and avoid making any contacts with the UN security.

After making a complete search, and finding no traces of the Orgite leader, or the female scientist, Daggard next decides to check with the outside surveillance team. They also report not seeing them leave the building.

He calls for a second team of surveillance into the building who spend an hour with no success.

Frustrated, he calls for a playback of all the security cameras that were trained on each of the exits from various unmarked vans parked across the street.

After two grueling hours of reviewing the tapes, the experts reveal an unknown person and Nora leaving the building, holding hands and a third person following after which they presume to be Andrius.

Daggard orders the identity of this person holding Nora's arm, by sending agents to Andrius' room to search for fingerprints.

While the confusion continues in the security vans parked along the UN Building, the trio meets with Uria and a technician, at the heliport.

Uria and Omar quickly introduce themselves to Nora and Michael Roberts.

The handbags are transferred from the limousine, to Uria's military car. There is hardly any conversation amongst the group, as they change vehicles and seats in the helicopter. Nora finally breaks the wall of silence:

"Wish you all good luck on your flight and please be careful."

Uria looks at Andrius and mentally wishes him well. Michael starts the engine of the copter and the blades begin rotating, at first very slowly. A fine cool dust wind begins flying about, as the copters' blades whirl around faster and faster.

The turbulence gets so great that Nora turns her face away, to prevent the eyes from receiving a beating, from the howling winds, caused by the copter, as it rises and slowly drifts away from view, over the East River. Andrius waves good-bye.

Once high above the river, Andrius reaction to the breathtaking views below and the unique feeling of flight causes him to become somewhat lively. He yells out:

"What a beautiful feeling! I cannot describe it; I love it. Michael, I would like to own a flying machine, like this."

"They cost a pretty penny. He responses. Unless you are wealthy, you can't afford one.

They sell for over a million dollars. Mind you, used."

The noise being somewhat stronger in the cockpit, Andrius puts on a throat microphone and earpiece, so Michael can hear him, without him having to yell.

"Is it yours?"

"Heck, no, I lease it, like everything I own."

"Oh, for a moment I thought otherwise."

"I once did own a transport plane, but on a stormy flight, between New York and Las Vegas, I lost the plane, together with a large cargo of Grade 'A' shrimps and lobsters on board. They were worth over two million dollars. My aircraft was hit by lightning over Texas and crashed outside of a small town. I was lucky to get out with my life. I spent three months in the hospital with broken bones."

"You did have insurance?'

"Yes, but I was a couple of months behind, with the payments and they refused to cover me, for my loss. The shipper and farmer sued me for over three million dollars in damages. They took over my business and my other small private planes. I was lucky. I almost went to jail for it. Today, I have only a 10% ownership, in this jet cargo service."

"At least it's a beginning."

"Andrius, pardon me a second, this is the point, where I have to call for permission to land atop, of the hospital."

"Go right ahead, I will look out and enjoy the rest of the scenery, below."

Michael initiates a circling maneuver a good five miles from the hospital, in order to mislead the radio operator, manning the equipment there. He then asks permission to approach the hospital and requests that a Dr. Peter Brace should be present when he lands.

Andrius, at this time, begins to put on surgical bandages, around his head and chest area. They are the types of bandages, used for seriously burnt victims.

As the copter reaches sight of the hospital, Andrius is completely bandaged all over and executes an acrobatic feat, while in flight. He transposes his position from the cockpit onto one of the pontoons, where there is a metal gurney welded to the super structure of the copter.

Michael begins his descent. Andrius finishes strapping himself to the stretcher, just as the copter touches the white guide landing strips, atop of the hospital.

Dr. Peter Brace as requested ventures out of the hospital's penthouse, with two other aids to administer to Andrius, the victim.

After turning the engine off, Michael leaps off and approaches the doctor, as the rotary blades wind down to a stop.

"Just received the call to come up and administer to your fire victim. How long ago did it happen and where?" Dr. Brace asks.

"There was a pretty bad fire in the Whitestone section, of the Queens. This is the fire chief. I tried to take him to the Bronx unit, but they were busy with other fire casualties, from the refinery, that blew up by the water's edge in Hoboken."

"I see, bring him this way, please." He said.

As the aids administer to Andrius. Michael turns to the doctor.

"Dr. Brace, I would like to speak to you a moment."

"Later, this man needs my help first."

"It's precisely him, whom I wish to speak to you about."

"Please make it fast, this man may be dying."

"There's nothing wrong with him, come here." He takes the doctor, to the side of the copter.

"What do you mean by this?" He demanded.

"He's all right, I only said that in the presence of your aids for a reason."

"Sir, what is the meaning of this, are you both crazy? I've better things to do. I'd better let security know about this. You both came here under false pretenses."

"Wait, Dr. Brace, Professor Donnelly told me to mention his name. He said you would understand."

"Professor Donnelly? Why?"

"We have a friend here in the hospital, which for personal reasons must be relocated out of here today."

"I have a feeling that I know you from someplace, have we met before?"

"Yes, you have."

"Yes, you are Doctor Robert's brother or cousin, I believe, you were here the other day. Right?"

"Yes, I was. The Professor told me that you would return a great favor to him if he were to ask you. He sent me to speak to you and deliver his request."

"Yes, I know, he's a brilliant scientist and my good friend. I promised him that I would return that favor someday. I guess I'm at your service."

"If you wish, you may call him to confer that he needs your help and to trust me."

"So how can I help you?"

"Doctor, where's my cousin, now?"

"He's resting."

"Can I see him?"

"I don't know if you could, there're a couple of security men guarding the room.

By the way Mister Roberts, who's the man on the stretcher?"

"He's my friend, Andrius."

"You mean, the man that Professor Donnelly and the research foundation created?"

"Yes?"

"I must meet him; I heard he has extraordinary powers."

"I didn't know that." Said Michael

"Yes, this man is a walking computer and a superman of some kind."

"Oh, is he?" I thought he was just a regular guy." Said Michael, in a surprised manner

"Yes, I have been trying to work with Professor Donnelly for years, because the subject fascinates me, very much. My politics and background prevented me from doing so."

The two men enter the penthouse and ride down the elevator to the floor, where the medics brought Andrius.

By the time, they enter the room; Andrius already has removed most of the bandages, from his face and arms. He immediately stands up, as they walk in.

"I believe you are Dr. Brace." Said Andrius.

"Yes I am and it's a pleasure, to finally meet you, Mister Andrius."

"Likewise, Sir, I trust that you already were informed of our special mission here."

"Yes of course, but there's a problem."

"I see the police."

"How did you know that?" Michael asks

"I simply read, Dr. Brace's mind."

"Oh yes, of course, I forgot for a moment, that's another of your abilities." "Don't worry about the two policemen; I will take care of them."

"Please don't harm them, Mister Andrius."

"I will not harm anyone, Doctor unless it's in extreme self defense. The two policemen simply will not detect nor remember our presence here."

"What can we do to help?"

"I would like you doctor and Mister Roberts to go down to Jason's room and help him up and bring him here."

"And the policemen?"

"I will cause their minds' to go blank, so they won't see you coming or going."

"Mister Andrius, how can you manage to do that?"

"The brain works on electrical impulses. What I will do is, simply override their impulses with mine."

"But it takes a tremendous amount of power which has to be focused only at a small area of the brain. If you were to fail, it could do damage. In some cases death can result. I never heard of anyone, mentally transmitting such power."

"Doctor, I will be extremely careful. Please give me a minute, so I can concentrate on them."

Andrius sits and closes his eyes and meditates. Doctor Brace and Michael wait a few seconds and take the elevator down to the floor below, to Jason's room.

As they get closer, their eyes begin to receive flashes of brilliant colors, produced by Andrius keen concentration, on the two policemen, in the corridor.

"Mister Roberts, did you see those flashes?" Said the doctor amazed.

"Yes, what is it? I thought they were lightning, in the skies."

"We must be getting into Mister Andrius' field strength."

"Yes, you are right; I'm beginning to get a slight ringing, in my ear."

"Let's hurry up, before it affects us, too."

Fearing Andrius paralyzing wavelength, they hasten their move. They exit into the corridor to find the two agents standing and looking directly at the corridor walls with blank looks on their faces. They hurry by, go into Jason's room and awaken him.

"Jason, wake up. We are here to take you away."

Jason was a little drogue and slowly realized what was happening around him.

"Michael, thank you for coming for me. Thank you, Dr. Brace, for allowing him to do this."

Jason slowly gets up and tries to join them, but needs assistance, due to his condition.

"Hey guys, I'm a little uncoordinated. I need some help."

"Don't worry cuz, you are in good hands."

Michael looks around, finds a wheel chair and brings it over.

They quickly wheel him out, to the elevator. To play it safe, Michael remains behind and rearranges the bed and covers to look, as if Jason was still in bed asleep.

Afterwards, he gently closes the door to the room and joins Dr. Brace, at the elevator lobby.

Once inside, they press the button to go up, but it suddenly goes down one floor then stops. Michael looks at Dr. Brace's face and becomes panic-stricken. The door opens and a nurse walks in.

"Oh Dr. Roberts, I see you're going for a stroll. Oh, hello, Dr. Brace. I see that Dr. Roberts is coming along. That's great he needs a little air and a change of scenery for a chance."

"Good afternoon, Nurse Jones, how are you?"

"Just fine, Doctor, it is nice, that you were able to take Dr. Roberts out. Those brutes up there, did not allowed me in this morning, to change his bed sheets."

"Nurse Jones, they won't bother us, anymore, I heard that they are leaving us, very soon."

"Thank goodness, I'm so glad to hear that. The two of them are like dogs in heat. You know, loose hands.

I have a good mind to report them to the hospital's Director."

"You should, you definitely should."

"Never mind, it probably will cause my job. Have you forgotten we are little people here and they won't listen to us? They will probably accuse me of provoking them. Oh, here's my stop. Dr. Roberts, you have a beautiful day, all right."

"You too, Nurse Jones." Nurse Jones walks out and disappears through a pair of swinging doors.

Dr. Brace presses the button and the elevator goes to the floor they wanted. Once on the floor, Michael rolls Jason down the corridor and immediately turns into Dr. Brace's office and examination room.

Andrius, at this time, senses their presence and gradually reduces the field of concentration. Once seeing them arriving at the room, he asks:

"Any problem?"

"No, everything went very smoothly. Andrius, I have Jason's medical records, too. What's next?" Said Michael

"Now we fly off and meet with the our people."

Minutes later, Andrius finishes securing Jason to the stretcher, at the bottom of the copter. Michael starts the helicopter just as Andrius finishes and hops aboard. As the copter climbs high above the hospital, Andrius turns to Michael:

"Michael, see if you can fly as slow as possible. Try to avoid any air turbulence or sudden jolts, because it may affect Jason's delicate condition."

"Will do, I understand Andrius. I will do my best."

Meanwhile, at the UN Building, after a few hours Daggard finally discovers the mysterious identity of the third person, in the security video. He immediately issues warrants, for the apprehension of Michael Roberts and Dr. Nora Billings.

An hour later, a New York State Trooper stationed by a toll-booth at the city limits, phones in to C.S.A. Headquarters, the description of a woman, who closely resembles Nora's description and reports her traveling due north with two other occupants in a military issued vehicle, toward the Catskills Mountains. The trooper waits for orders whether to intercept the car and hold the passengers for questioning.

Daggard picks up the phone and personally advises the trooper, that Federal Agents will take over the investigation and pursue the suspects from New York and will intercept them at a proper time.

The trooper gives Daggard additional information on the car and location. Daggard immediately goes to a plan room and pulls out a map of the area, where the car is driving through. He points at a small local airport:

"We can have two SUV's meet us here and from this point, we can easily intercept them here, or before they reach the interchange."

A dispatcher calls an army helicopter and minutes later, Daggard and four agents take off, to the rendezvous.

Michael, at this time, lands at a small heliport to fill up with gas, for the long flight to the cottage.

Once airborne again, Andrius puts the radio on and scans around, to listen to police radio transmissions. There is a radio alert, which catches his attention. He turns the knob back and waits to listen again. The transmission comes in once more.

It gives out orders for the arrest of Michael Roberts, for aiding and abetting.

A few moments later, there was another transmission between the army helicopter flown by Karl Daggard and the operator of a small airport. Daggard reports his copter is in site of the airport and is confirming the general location of Uria's vehicle and the pursuit cars, which are to wait, at the airport for him. Andrius realizes that the women are in grave danger of immediate arrest, by the Agents and must rush to their aid.

"Michael, can you make this thing fly faster?"

"I'll give it all I can, Andrius."

Andrius unbuckles his safety belt and climbs out and down on the side of the copter to Jason, on the stretcher.

"How are you doing, Jason?" He yells out to him.

Being too weak to answer, he only nods. "OK." Andrius also nods, turns around and returns to the cockpit. He looks behind the copter, but sees no other aircraft, in the air.

He then looks ahead, in the direction where Daggard would be flying, but the haze restricts his visibility to only a couple of miles. Andrius then looks at an aerial chart and estimates that Daggard would be about fifteen minutes away and that will allow him enough time to get to the women before the man named Daggard does.

Back at the hospital, the two agents guarding Dr. Roberts slowly come out of their semi-conscious condition. They don't notice the lapse of time that has gone by, until Nurse Jones happens to walk by, stops and walks over to them.

"I'm so happy to inform you, that your services will no longer be needed here as of tomorrow."

"What are you, clairvoyant?"

"No, I only heard it through the grapevine that you people are leaving."

"You're crazy."

She gives them a facial sneer and walks off. The two agents look at each other in profound bewilderment, as one addresses to the other:

"She's gone plum loco! Isn't this place a nut house, right?"

"Yeah, even the medical people here, are a bit wacky."

The agent gets up, walks over to door and opens it. He looks in and sees Jason in bed and nods.

"He's sound asleep." He returns to his chair, just as male nurse approaches, to administer medication to Jason.

"Hey you, wait there a moment John Wayne, where do you think you're going?"

"I'm going there to the room." He points.

"I don't think so, fellow, where's your escort. No one enters without a hospital escort recognized by us."

"That's news to me, Sir."

"Sorry, we can't let you in."

"Sir, he's supposed to get his medication, now. Please, excuse me; I have to do my job."

"Well, I also must do my job, too. Wait a second." The agent gets up and decides to accompany the male nurse in. The nurse goes in and approaches the bed. He gently pulls the covers off, and discovers the fake outline of Jason.

"What's this, a joke? Are we all playing musical beds, here?"

"Now what's you problem?"

"Where did you people move him to, this time?"

"What the hell are you talking about?"

The agent comes to the head of the bed and looks.

"Oh shit! He's gone."

"What?" The second agent rushes over.

"He's gone. He was there a couple of minutes ago. How's that possible?"

The agent quickly runs to a phone and reports the disappearance to his superiors.

"Nurse, you can't leave this room, you're now a potential witness."

"What do you mean by that? I have other patients to attend to. Did you forget that this is an intensive care unit? People can die, if they are not attended to on time. Get your hands off me. Who do you think you are?"

"I don't care, you must remain here." The agent insists.

Minute's later other agents interrogate the male nurse, Nurse Jones and Dr. Brace. They discovered that Dr. Robert's cousin came earlier to see Jason, and they went out for a stroll through the corridors.

They search every room, in the hospital but there is no trace of Dr. Roberts.

Security informs Nurse Jones and the male nurse that they have to remain on hospital grounds, unless the head of security Karl Daggard himself, grants permission.

Outraged by the mistreatment by the agents, Nurse Jones goes to the office and files a formal complaint, with the Hospital Administration.

The CSA upon reviewing the hospital's security cameras decide to take Dr. Brace into custody and bring him to the Federal Building for further questioning.

Responding to nurse Jones protest, the agents claim National Security for their action and all parties are considered suspicious, until they can account, for their movements, that day.

Minutes later, Karl Daggard receives news of the situation, in the hospital, and of Jason's disappearance. The bitter news annoys him profoundly, that he orders the driver to go faster to the point, where they can intercept the women, on a mountain road. By his thinking, the women may be able to lead him to Andrius and the missing research scientist.

Meanwhile, Andrius warns Uria, by mental thought, of the impending danger that is approaching her. He strongly advises her, not to resist any attempts of arrest, by the police if they are stopped. Andrius takes out the charts again and estimates to be approximately fifteen miles away and Daggard to be, just a quarter of a mile ahead of the women.

Moments later, Daggard's vehicle comes to a bend in the road and he orders to station his car and the other agents' across the side of the road and waits for Uria to drive up.

A minute later, Uria's car comes into view of the agents.

Karl Daggard shouts go into his radio microphone and gives the signal to advance on the women.

The head car suddenly pulls out and dashes across the road, causing Uria's car, to stop abruptly near a ditch.

Daggard's car then moves up and blocks her from behind, thus preventing them from any escape.

The agents in the head car rush out and point their guns at Nora and Uria's face. They shout aloud:

"You, in the driver's seat, take the keys off the ignition and get out of the vehicle very slowly. Show me your hands up, where I can see them. Come on, raise your hands, or I will surely, blow your heads off."

"Who the blazes do you think you are?"

"Nora, don't provoke them, in any way, please." Said Uria

"You bastards!"

"Please, Nora."

"Now the passenger in the rear seat, show me your hands. Any false move, we'll shoot the women."

It becomes a very tense situation, as Omar raises one hand out the window, of the car.

"The other hand, I don't see it."

"Sir, he only has one arm." Said Nora.

"You shut up your mouth. I'm not blind."

"Come out very slowly."

Another agent, sitting in Daggard's car, runs over to the car, pulls Omar out by his neck collar, and drags him, on the ground towards Daggard's car.

"Check him for any weapons. Make sure."

"He's clean, Sir."

"Hey what are you doing? Stop that; please stop that, you are hurting him. Can you see that he is handicapped?" Nora cries out.

Daggard comes out of his car and approaches Omar. He takes a good look at him.

"I know who you are? Yes, you are the one who helped your leader Andrius and that other woman to escape from me, in the tunnel. Hold him tight! Don't let him go for a second; he's very dangerous. He killed one of my men and he will pay dearly."

"Don't be a jerk; don't you see that he's helpless?" Said Nora

"Don't care lady; the man is still dangerous even with one arm."

Omar starts resisting and pushes the agent but gets knocked down by another agent.

"Omar, please don't, they will hurt you. Don't give them a reason."

"Dr. Billings, they're going to kill me."

"No they won't, Omar. They're not after you."

"It seems that I'm a pretty good shot, after all, I blew your arm off. I should have aimed a little higher."

Omar struggles again and they push him down on the ground face down. The agent leans over and presses his foot against Omar's head into the dirt.

"Stop that, stop that you criminal."

"Sir, what shall we do with him?" the agent asks

"Hold him steady! Put handcuffs on his hand to his legs." Said Daggard

Daggard goes back to his car and looks around the area. He then calls two agents over and whispers to them an order.

They then return and take Omar and the two women off the road and bring them down through a brush onto a small drainage ditch, by a clearing.

After the men follow through with the orders, they wait for Daggard to join them.

Just to the right of the clearing about thirty feet away, Daggard appears again on foot. He signals by hand, to an agent to come over again, and when he does, he gives him another order. The agent then returns to the ditch and separate Omar from the women. They take him a short distance and force him to kneel on the ground, as another agent places leg irons on him after retrieving them from his car.

"This is called a hug tying position." One agent tells the other.

"I know. He's not going anywhere."

"I guarantee you that friend."

As these mysterious actions are going on, the State Trooper, who originally spotted Uria's car, is driving by and sees two abandoned cars blocking the road. He pulls over and stops to investigate.

As he does, he hears distant shouts from one of the agents, who are trying to control Omar from struggling, by threatening to shoot the women.

"Take it easy boy, the more you struggle the tighter it gets."

The trooper cautiously climbs down through the bushes to observe what's going on. He pulls out his service weapon and his hand radio. He inches closer, until he finally hears clearly the conversation.

At this moment, Daggard shouts from his vantage point to the agents:

"Let's teach him a lesson. Mister, the penalty for helping your friend, Andrius, to escape, is death." He then nods at the agent.

"No, why him. He hasn't done anything to you."

Omar struggles and tries to get up, but the agent trips him repeatedly, and threatens to kill the women.

"I told you to shut your mouth. You better or you get the same."

Out of fear for the women, Omar stops and the agent points his gun at his chest and pauses a few seconds, looks around to Daggard and pulls the trigger.

A loud burst and Omar falls backwards, into the ditch. Nora screams.

"You savage murderers; you will pay for this cold blooded homicide. You beasts!"

Uria pulls herself free and struggles with one of the agents, on the ground. Daggard yells out to the agent, who shot Omar:

"No, no you fool the head, the head! Damn it, shoot him in the head!"

The agent suddenly panics when he sees the trooper jump out of the bushes in front of him.

"Police, drop that gun, fellow, you are all under arrest." Daggard, upon seeing the intervention, yells out at the trooper.

"Damn it, you are not going to stop me, now." He pulls out his gun, aims and fires three shots. The trooper falls to the ground critically injured. Daggard then yells out, again:

"Now, finish him and afterwards, shoot the women. Shoot them all, I order you!"

The other agents drag the two women towards the ditch where Omar, still alive, tries with all his strength to get up, but falls back due to his shackles on his leg. Nora and Uria break away from the agents and run into the ditch, to comfort Omar. They plead with the agents, to spare his life. For a split second, when the agent hesitates, suddenly Daggard becomes again enraged.

"Shoot them, I order you, shoot them or so help me, I will shoot both of you myself."

High above, Andrius in the helicopter is rushing to the scene. The agents look up and see Andrius high above.

"Shoot them also, they're the enemy." Daggard yells and runs to his car.

One agent raises his weapon up and the other takes aim at Omar's head and fires.

At that instant, upon witnessing Omar's execution, Andrius whirls himself out from the copter. The third agent also fires his automatic weapon at Andrius.

Bullets hit him in the chest and shoulder area. The rest fly off and impact the helicopter above. Andrius falls down on top of one of the agents, instantly killing him and causes the other two agents to run away in fear for their lives.

The copter suddenly bursts into flames and black smoke. It slowly drifts away out of control and disappears over a hill.

Uria quickly picks up a weapon left by the agent and runs up the hill and fires at Daggard's car shattering the rear window and at the other agents fleeing to their vehicle.

Daggard panics upon seeing that the situation has changed, quickly drives off recklessly and runs down one of the agents' who was on foot. He then nearly crashes his car into a nearby concrete abutment while swerving to and fro and disappears down the road.

Seconds later, after recovering from the jump, Andrius gets up, runs up the small hill and chases after Daggard's car, as it speeds down the mountain road. He maintains his pursue for a good distance, and finally stops.

"I will catch up with you Daggard, some day. This I promise." He said while walking back.

Andrius comes over to the women, in the ditch who are there caring for Omar's body. He then sees the trooper, goes over to him and examines his wounds. Uria then approaches

"Andrius, how bad is he?"

"He's also dead. He was shot in the back."

"They killed him in cold blood, just like they did to Omar. This is hellish."

"We'll take Omar with us; I will return the trooper to his car and inform the authorities."

"But the authorities will come here."

"We will be long gone, before they do. The third agent disappeared into the woods."

"Andrius, where is Jason?"

"I believe they just landed on the other side of the hill. The copter looks like it was severely damaged and we may have to abandon it. We will use your vehicle and the agents' car to drive the rest of the way."

"Yes, Andrius, whatever you say."

Once out of danger, Daggard picks up the mobile phone and attempts to call for help. To his dismay, he discovers that his radio is inoperative. A bullet meant for him unfortunately pierced the console and damaged the radio. He then pulls out his cell phone and discovers that there is no signal available in the mountains. Unable to call for help, Daggard then drives away, frustrated and defeated, for the moment.

CHAPTER VI

Late that very evening, Daggard finds himself in Washington, waiting to meet with the President. He first meets with the Secretary, who alerts him of the President's indignation, for his actions taken so far. A message handed down to Daggard from the President changes the earlier meeting to a one rescheduled for midnight, in his office. Daggard reads the note and turns to the Secretary:

"What's up with the President? Why is he seeing me so late?"

"Things are bad. The political and military situation in South America has become very critical. Major decisions must be made, to preserve Democracy for these two small countries that have been victimized, by the insurrections."

"Oh, I see, I will probably receive more information on this matter, when I meet with him."

"Yes, you will be briefed, I'll also meet you there." Said the Secretary then walks off.

With plenty of time on his hands, Daggard decides to go to his Washington apartment, to rest and freshen up, before the midnight meeting with the President.

Later that evening, he turns on the TV to see the evening news and to also see how his version of the shooting of the trooper, had gone through, with the media.

Whatever gains, in public support that Andrius managed to achieve during his speech, at the UN that afternoon, was completely lost by evening.

Daggard was successful in implicating Andrius with the trooper's murder. Again, he praises himself, for executing a perfect plan and cover up, of his misdeeds. Now with a strong sense of security, he looks forward to meet with the President.

Meanwhile, later that day, up in the Catskills Mountains in New York State, at the cottage owned by Nora, everyone is lying about and resting, from the day's ordeal with Daggard. Andrius and the rest carry Omar's body and carefully bury him near the cottage, after each expressing a few words of sympathy, over a good friend and fallen comrade.

There's a melancholy look on everyone's face, as Andrius returns from the side of the cottage, after camouflaging the burial site and disposing of the vehicle captured from the CSA encounter that afternoon.

Andrius feeling somewhat exhausted excuses himself and retires, to heal the wounds that he received, earlier that day.

"Goodnight everyone, I wish all a restful and peaceful night."

"Good night, Andrius."

Jason remarkably survives the abrupt landing of the crippled copter and is up on his feet, comforting Nora, who had collapsed from exhaustion and nerves. Michael Roberts and Uria did not suffer any injuries and sit on the front porch looking at the night skies. They both were trying to figure out, how all this confusion started and how each got involved, without actually wanting.

Uria while gazing at a group of the stars turns to Michael:

"Mister Roberts, I think you are a very thoughtful and practical person. Can I ask you, a simple question if you don't mind? I've been toiling with this question, for some time."

"No, go right ahead. Isn't this funny, you are the first person, in my life that ever has sought my opinion. I thank you for it; it really makes me feel good, about myself."

"You're welcome. It's just a simple question, Michael."

"Try me, maybe I will surprise myself and give you a good answer or closed to it at least."

"Before my question, a little advice of my own and this is: Michael you must get rid of that self low esteem view that you have of yourself. Don't you realize this? You have accomplished more than the average well-educated person out there has in a lifetime. You fly aircraft and have your own business. At least, you had it, in the past and most probably you will restore it in the near future again.

People take chances for the good, or for what ever. In my eyes, you are not a looser, but a person with potential to be great, with the right direction and some luck."

"Uria, you're in the wrong business, I tell you, you have done more for me, this very moment emotionally, than any of those shrinks, which I pay half of salary to. You're good and understand human nature, than most professionals which I have dealt with in the past."

"Thank you, Michael, you flatter me. Now I'm a bit embarrassed, because the question is silly, to start with. A grown woman asking childlike questions is a bit immature."

"No question is silly, if the answer informs and enlightens the other person."

"Please promise me that you won't not laugh."

"You have my word, honest."

"O.K, in your words, what's your definition of life? How do you define it or cope with this existence or reality that we're in?"

"You mean this stuff, that we are experiencing all around us? The day in and day out rigors? That indefinable substance that's all around us that controls our lives?"

"Yes, I think you got it, our lives, this unique sphere around us, you know, life itself."

"Oh God, that's a toughie, I will do my best, O.K. Please forgive me if I fail."

"Thanks. Before you answer, I like to tell you my own reasoning of it. It may sound crazy but hear me out."

"Go right ahead."

"When one is taken away from a certain environment, there is something that goes amiss. It's like you walking into a movie theater, when the movie already has been playing for sometime. You try and try to grasp the gist of the story but its just not there. You stumble through guessing this or assuming that and try to link substances and clues together in arriving at a sensible conclusion of what you are watching but you fail at it in the end."

"I get it, there's something missing in your life and you cannot just define it. It's somehow evading you, and you just can't put your finger on it."

"Yes, yes that's right; you think you have a certain grasp on it and yet you don't."

"Well this is a little high brow for me to handle, but I will tell you, my own definition of life is: You will be the judge, all right?"

"OK, I'm all ears."

"I think life is like a great race towards the end of your existence, you may call it death, others call it something else. Some win, at an early age, and others loose and get to live a long time.

The end of this race includes credits that one has accumulated for all the good or for all the bad that you have done in your past life. The size of the reward that you would receive depends on the summary of all of these variable factors."

"Curious, I have never looked at life, that way. You assume that there's some superior Being out there manipulating this existence and is monitoring us somehow but is not interfering?"

"Yes, something likes that. Isn't it obvious?"

"Yes you have something definite there."

"Good, I'm hot on the trail."

"Now I will give you mine, O.K. To me, I think life is a precious gift. It is truly an undeserving gift, at that.

As a proprietor of the life vessel that I have, I should safeguard it, in every way, from any abuse, or anyone who may want to hurt or destroys it. Life is only one pass around and you better do your best with this one time opportunity."

"I agree. Well, as for me, I have raced with death, practically all my life. Perhaps, I may have some self-destructive tendency in me, because everything, which I have been involved with, had the element of risk. I could have died many times in the past. Yet it hasn't happened.

You can categorize me, somewhat of a daredevil, a pirate or a soldier of fortune. I always had a feeling that I'm pre-destined, for something great in life. Maybe that's why nothing has seriously happened to me. I haven't reached that goal, yet."

"I believe you. Surely I thought, that you and Jason perished in the copter today. When we saw you completely engulfed in flames and spinning out of control. Seeing your aircraft in that state, anyone would have thought that you had all died."

"I wasn't too scared. I should be, if I had actually lost complete control of the copter. Fortunately, the bullets hit one of the hydraulic levers and pierced a small fuel line, which instantly burst into flames. It was potentially dangerous, but not mortally."

"From the ground it looked horrific."

"We were lucky, that the bullets didn't hit the main fuel tank, if it did, then I would not be here, talking to you now."

"Michael, I have a feeling, that you truly have a very high regard for life."

"Uria, you cannot appreciate life, unless you put it in danger of losing it. Anyway, that's my opinion."

"I also nearly lost my life, today. I surely know now that feeling. Well, Michael, I better say, good night. It's nearly midnight and I must be keeping you up. Let me say, that it was enlightening, talking to you tonight. Your point of view has helped me a lot to look at life a little more different this time."

"Likewise, Uria. You have pleasant dreams, good night."

"Good night." Uria gets up and walks into the house.

Nora finally calms down and everyone else finally falls asleep, as a still silence befalls throughout the cottage after midnight.

"In Washington, a picture ID card is handed across to an officer, at a security gate, where moments later, after verification, the card is returned.

"Thank you, Sir, said the Officer, you may proceed."

Daggard's car moves down several ramps into an underground parking level. After parking the car, he walks across and enters through a secured door, using a special card reader. Inside, he boards a horizontal elevator, which takes him several hundred feet directly to an adjacent building, where the meeting with the President is to commence.

As he enters, an aid assigns him to a chair across the conference table facing directly opposite to the President.

The President's aids and advisers come in and quickly fill up the long mahogany conference table.

Seconds later, everyone stands, as the President enters.

The President, looking very stern in his manner nods and everyone sits down.

"Gentlemen, I've called for this special meeting of my Cabinet, to inform you of the serious situation in South America, which has apparently developed beyond the critical.

We're faced with alienation from beyond and I'm sorry to say, from within this Administration.

My containment policy towards the troops, that are now invading the two countries in South America, has unfortunately failed.

Without warning, a third front has opened from the Eastern Coast of Brazil. Another insurgency there, has net them a major control of the Amazonian Inter-coastal Highway and coastal port areas, that supplied 80% of mineral products, including high grade iron ore, to the United States and Europe.

Due to our depleted natural resources, any curtailment of this will cause an eventual breakdown of our iron and steel industries, here at home, and with it, a possibility of economic disaster to the rest of the world. We cannot afford this to happen."

The President pauses a few seconds, and takes a drink of water.

"Due to someone's overwhelming zeal, in acquiring the support of the leader of the Orgites to come to our aid, his or her actions has unfortunately further alienated them, from joining our side of maintaining stability, in the region.

In fact, they might have pushed the Orgites to a point of sedition, against our government. Gentlemen, this is not acceptable." The President then turns to Daggard.

"Mister Daggard, what further proof do you have, to substantiate these reports?"

Daggard stands up.

"Mister President, it's clearly evident that we are dealing with an insurrection, here stateside. Since the beginning, I was very much aware of their intentions. As I said once before, these people do not have any regards for life. So far, any attempts, to communicate with them, have ended with death and destruction. To date, this seditious group has murdered ten U.S. citizens. They have little or no regard for our laws and human rights.

In my opinion, Mister President, we should order out the National Guard, in every state, where these Orgites subsist and if need be, forcibly arrest and disarm the whole group."

The Secretary of State interrupts Daggard's conversation:

"Mister President, with respect to Mister Daggard's intentions, we must approach this delicate situation, with extreme care.

In the first place, there is no substantial evidence that these people have ever plotted, against the Government of the United States.

I strongly believe that Mister Daggard has, unintentionally forced them into violence, by cohering them. Before I would ever call out the Guard, I would like further concrete proof, of their intentions."

"Thank you, Mister Secretary. The Chair recognizes General Stuart."

"Thank you, Mister President. I have been listening to all these comments and I do not like what I hear. Right now, our nation is in political turmoil. If we were to call out the National Guard, on just hearsay, the mere calling of them will be more destructive to our political fabric and to the Nation's civil stability. It can easily lead to civil disobedience."

These Insurgents, whether Communist controlled or Middle Eastern Fanatics will jump for joy, at hearing, that the U.S. Homeland Security cannot effectively handle their Internal Affairs. By this, they will reason, that we are not united enough to effectively confront them. Gentlemen, the Guard is out of the question. Find some other means to get at these people."

"I concur with you, General." Said the Secretary of State.

"Thank you, General Stuart.

Gentlemen, in my opinion, I think we have bungled our attempts to secure the services of these people to help our government. As the Secretary said, there is no solid evidence of sedition, but some laws have been broken. That is not acceptable.

As President, I'm ordering the F.B.I, to arrest those who were involved, in these incidents. If the leader is somehow implicated in it, so be it. We will let the courts handle this, once he is located and arrested."

In addition to this, I'm setting up a fact-finding board, to investigate Mister Daggard's allegations. I will initiate this, by calling on Federal, State and Local authorities, to place those Orgites that are presently, in the service of the Federal Government, into protective custody, to await the outcome, of the fact finding board.

Remember folks, these are our people working in all levels of government; they are protecting us from foreign enemies, they're driving our ambulances, curing our sick and protecting our homes. I don't consider them criminals and damn it, I will not treat them as one, until we get the facts."

Thank you, Gentlemen, this meeting is over."

"Thank you Mister President." Everyone rises and exits the room.

After the adjournment of the meeting, the Secretary calls the President aside:

"Mister President, you can't imagine what sort of reactions will there be, by anti-social groups, if we were to call out the Guard, on these people. Other groups would feel, that they are the subjects of the calling, may react and an ugly situation would develop, that would possibly lead to civil war, in the United States."

"Mister Secretary, you're right, it's a very dangerous proposal and irresponsible."

As both men leave the conference room, they approach a marine, standing guard outside the door entrance. He comes to attention and salutes the President and Secretary as they pass. The marine turns out to be an Orgite, who is in deep meditation, trying to contact Andrius, who's now too weak and unable to perceive his thoughts.

It is early next morning; Andrius fully recovered, now laid in bed somewhat restless. Visions and voices bothered him all night. They kept repeating, in his mind, but he wasn't able to clearly define them. He gets out of bed and walks out of the cottage.

After a short walk down a small trail, he climbs to the summit of a mountain, overlooking the whole valley.

On top, he meditates and asks if there's a fellow Orgite, who is trying to speak to him. He repeats this for a while, then returns to his room and rests further.

An hour later, as the sun slowly rises through the morning haze, Andrius commences to communicate with the marine guard stationed at the White House, through telepathy. The marine informs him of the new situation and alerts that he personally has a few hours of freedom, before the government discovers his true identity. He seeks advice, whether he should abandon his post or stay and weather the consequences. Andrius advises him to wait until he hears from him again.

After ten minutes of silence, Andrius ponders over the decision, whether or not to give out the order for all the Orgites, to abandon their posts and initiate the plans agreed to, months before.

He realizes that the gravity of his decision is very serious. He has to weigh the consequences that such an act would bring to him and the rest of fellow Orgites.

The planning of strategy involving the possibility of life and death and the actual execution, surely places a person, in a responsible position, to rethink it over very closely, before executing such an order.

A couple of hours later, although premature, Andrius finally arrives, at the decision to go ahead with his original plans. He again climbs up to the summit of the mountain and addresses all of the Orgites through meditation:

"Brothers and sisters, I address you not as a leader, or advocator, but as your humble servant. Perhaps, some of you may not agree with my decision and I will not hold you to it.

After analyzing this complex situation and the surmounting case that is being grouped against us, and me personally, I have decided to abandon the United States and seek refuge elsewhere. Due to present government leaders, who have control over matters, that affect our freedom and future existence, I believe that this country, at present, is trying to survive politically, in this world and especially in the home front. The United States has blindly become a threat to itself, as well as to all of us.

Perhaps in the future, with better communications between us, our relationship will change, when the people of the United States, finally realize that the maltreatment of our unique race, was indeed an illegal and selfish acts of some in the Government.

When new laws are finally passed, on our behalf, guarantying our rights and protected by the established Constitution, I will consider an invitation, to return to America and join forces, in making this country free and strong, once again.

We will help and work together with the rest of mankind, to eliminate all poverty and disease, from the face of the earth. I will initiate and propose, together with the rest of humanity, various plans, to populate our galaxy and other star systems with Mankind and Orgite, living and working together, in harmony and in Peace.

The road to this future is not far. There are many obstacles ahead. Some of you will profit and experience joy, from my decision. Yet, on the other hand, there will be some that will unfortunately perish, in attempts to reach this goal. Therefore, I say to you, that I will not hold you to my decision.

Remember if you wish or are incapable to join me; please do not try to resist arrest by the authorities. Remain where you are. They will hold and temporary confined you, but no harm will come to you, as a result.

If you resist, they shall use force, which most probably, will terminate your existence. You have all of these options to choose, freely.

Once this chaotic storm is over, we shall be reunited again and in harmony with all.

I leave you now to make your decision. As you decide, remember that all will, equally share any hurt or triumph experienced by one. Please decide on the right path.

I hope to the Infinite, that I have made the right choice myself. Until we meet, and united in mind again."

After resting for a few minutes, Andrius starts climbing down, when Uria unexpectedly appears and meets him half way.

"Andrius, will you accept me to join you?"

Andrius is completely taken by surprise. For a few seconds, he is unable to utter a word then said:

"Yes Uria." He goes and embraces her for the very first time. Andrius has trouble finding words to utter to Uria. He finally opens up to her.

"Uria, I must truly apologize for my behavior towards you, all these years. I never thought that I would have the strength in me, to do this. I've truly swallowed my selfish pride and accepted to my inner self, that I truly need you. I never felt a need like this for anyone before. You have made me surface my deep quenched and repressive feelings, which were in me and I turn it against you and sustained it all this time. All was done in the name of a pride, adolescent behavior and over zealousness on my part.

You and your true love have finally freed me, from this self imposed torment. I feel like I have been spiritually reborn and at this very moment, I truly feel that I'm able to power and electrify the universe with this new force within me. Is this love, which I feel, for the first time in my being? I am confused. My God! It is love that I feel in this being."

"Yes, Andrius, you have finally awakened. You don't know how I've waited, for this moment. I went through eight years of coldness, torment and rejection. I was lost. I thought that you would never accept me, ever. My existence was worthless and I thought many a times of terminating this non-sensible existence that I was living in. My anguish was devastating and hopeless. You've have given my life back to me."

"Uria, please, forgive me, for my foolish ways."

"Andrius, at this moment, I'm only interested, in the present. The past is gone and does not exist, any more."

"I'm now sure, that I'm capable of love and I love you, Uria, with all of myself."

"I've loved you always Andrius and I will, to the end of all time."

After a long while, holding each other's in an embrace, they turn around and resume climbing down the side of the mountain while holding hands.

At the foot of a small hill, Jason and Michael Roberts are seen standing. They were awakened by Andrius' meditation. They walk towards the couple.

Upon reaching them, they noticed that Andrius is holding Uria's hand, which was unbelievable. The mere mention of Uria would cause consternation to everyone present.

Jason forces himself to smile while nudging Michael.

"Congratulations, both of you. I would have never expected this, in my lifetime."

"Well, now you know, gentlemen, I've come home."

"This deserves a hug, from each one of us. We must celebrate tonight. When Nora finds out. She will be ecstatic." Everyone hugs one another.

"The wedding is on me." Said Michael

"No, we will have a double wedding." Said Jason

"That's great. The weddings will be on me. I stand corrected. Said Michael, we must set a date."

"I'm all for it right now, but for the moment, I think we should get through with this situation before we do anything."

"You're right, Andrius, 100 per cent. We have to resolve this unfortunate dilemma that we all are in."

As they approach the cottage, a thunderous and rumbling sound starts. Nora, who is inside the cottage, becomes panic stricken, and runs out screaming towards Jason, who immediately embraces her, as the sound becomes more intense.

Everyone runs for cover, as the ground shakes and trees sway to and fro.

A showers of dust and leaves completely covers the sky above, as daylight, is slowly overtaken, by a strange twilight.

The expectation of a terrible episode heightens in everyone's mind, by this eerie occurrence.

Small trees around the cottage up root themselves, by the might of this earth shaking force, which is slowly creeping into their mist, with horrible expectations.

Suddenly, out from the valley below, behind the cottage, appears the silhouette of a giant metallic behemoth, of an object, which completely dwarfs the cottage and blocks the skyline before them.

Andrius gains enough courage and stands up to get a better view of this monstrous metallic object, slowly ascending on them. Much to his surprise, he sees through the maze of flying dirt, leaves and debris.

The enormous object advances towards them and attempts a landing between them and the cottage.

The object turns out to be a giant jet propelled military troop carrier, from the United States Air Force. For a fraction of a second, Andrius retreats, for reasons, that this could be, that infamous Mister Daggard, who somehow has located the cottage and flown over hundreds of soldiers, to kill everyone and take him finally as his prisoner.

He stops in his footsteps and turns around, as a telepathic message is perceived from the aircraft.

"Andrius!"

As the aircraft lowers down unto the ground, the winds created by the jet exhausts, whirls viciously around the cottage. Windows blow in and the doors fly open by the immense force.

The winds also pins Andrius and the rest to the ground. They all hide their faces from the sheering currents of air and flying debris.

"Andrius, what shall we do!" Nora cries out in panic.

"Please, remain calm! Don't try to stand up, the winds are too strong." He shouts back.

Moments later, the machine cuts off power. The engines wind down and the winds slowly die and disappear.

There remained a strange calmness in the air for a short spell when suddenly intruded by a metallic sound emanating from the aircraft. A hatch door starts to open.

Everyone, except Andrius and Uria, were still held captive with fear by this strange object, which landed, in there midst. Everyone is puzzled and bewildered.

As the dust settles and leaves and bushes fall back to the ground, Andrius stands up and walks toward the vehicle, just as the last mechanical steps of an automatic ladder on the aircraft, unfolds and touches the ground.

As the hatch door swings completely open, a tall light brown hair stern looking man appears from within and dressed up in a military outfit, bearing glistering weapons by his sides.

He stood there and stares down at Andrius, with his right hand on his weapon, which he drew slightly out. No one on the ground dares to flex a muscle, out of fear of this stranger. The tall man releases his grip on his weapon and suddenly raises his arm and greets Andrius with a military salute.

"Welcome!" Said Andrius startling everyone around him.

The tension in the air slowly disappears, as everyone sees that this fearsome looking man turns out to be a friend and not the enemy.

Nora and Jason, as well as Michael appear on the scene, somewhat confused. Jason, on taking a closer look, quickly recognizes the light hair soldier is a good friend, who he hasn't seen in years.

His name: Colonel Russ Towers, an Orgite and a great military leader in the Armed Forces. The remaining members of the Colonel's Towers party, who happen to be also Orgites, slowly disembark, from the aircraft and stand together to greet the small group.

Jason goes over to the airmen together with Andrius. He also recognizes other individuals, who years before, contributed to the research and development, of the Orgite computers and radar systems. Once introduced around to everyone, the small group enters the small cottage and helps pick up any valuables needed, to take along with them. Colonel Russ Towers, once inside, turns to Andrius.

"I trust everyone is ready."

"Yes, just, about."

"Andrius, I must make a stop at Floyd Bennett, to pick up about two hundred of our fellows, who are flying in this morning from Griffith Air Force Base. They would have flown directly, but they are using two turbo props and most likely medium size ones, that cannot possibly reach our final destination."

"That's all right. We are just about through over here, now."

"I heard about Omar. He will be greatly missed."

"Yes, of course. We all felt his loss."

"Good. Let us go. We have about six minutes left to get back on radar, before they start to inquire, about our whereabouts."

"By all means." Said Andrius

Once abandoning the cottage, they all go and board the big air transport.

The airmen start up the engines and they are airborne over the valley and quickly attempt to reach cruising speed and increase altitude, at the same time.

Andrius and Uria look out through one of the port windows observing how fast the cottage disappears below in the mist, as the flying machine rises. They're both held fascinated with a feeling of euphoria as the aircraft soars through the clouds beneath them.

"Oh this is great, Andrius. I never felt this sensation, before."

"I'm glad you enjoyed it as I did, when I flew in Michael's helicopter."

"Andrius, how did Colonel Towers know where we were?"

"The Colonel knows Jason and he probably told him of the cottage. They all often spent the weekends here."

"This is a beautiful vacation place and it's very romantic."

"Yes, indeed. Said Andrius as he places his arm around her. After this is all over, I promise you that we will return here and spend some time together to enjoy all of these natural surroundings.

An hour into the flight, Colonel Towers, returns from the head of the aircraft and sits alongside Andrius and Uria.

"Is everything all right, here?" He asked.

"It couldn't be any better, Russ. Thanks for asking." Said Uria

"Fellows, I see something here that I have never seen in my life before."

"Isn't it obvious, we've made up."

"Congratulations to both of you."

"Thanks. It was long overdue." Said Uria

"We had several conversations in the past about your situation but it never led to anything concrete. So I gave up."

"Time was the best resolution for us. We are both happy about it."

"Good, I'm happy for both of you."

"Thanks." said Uria

"Russ, do you think that this aircraft is able to fly all the way?" Asked Andrius

"I think it possibly could, but we don't have the capacity for such a trip. The ship flies close to 700 miles per hour and it's terrible on fuel. I estimate that we would have to refuel at least four or five times, before we get there. We lack the logistics' like airborne tankers that would meet us at a predetermined points and refuel our aircraft while in flight."

"I see what you mean. It's too slow for our purpose and we are limited."

"What do you need, an SST?" Nora joins in.

"Oh, hello, Nora." Said Colonel Towers

"Nora, an SST is a little too fast and a bit small. I need capacity and speed." Said Andrius

"Where are we going?"

"Nora, we're going to New York."

"Good. Well, if you want capacity and speed, I recommend using one of those old flying box carts: The Boeing 747 or the 777 airliners. Now that's capacity and speed."

"The military has a more advanced version designed for international troop transports. It's the 747BTM Hercules Series, with wider bodies and larger fuel capacity. Now that's big."

"I would need perhaps, a dozen or so." Said Andrius

"I can make that possible, but I may have to pull some strings." Said Colonel Towers

"There are a couple of smaller versions that have flown to our destination, already." Said Andrius

"How come you didn't go over to there much earlier?"

"I wanted the vanguard to clear up first the area from deadly radioactive contamination. It may take more time, to complete the project." Said Andrius

"I hope that they have improved the landing approach. I believe that a 747B may have some difficulty landing there." Said Colonel Towers

"In that event, if we use larger aircraft, we can install breaking chutes, so we do not over shoot the field. I believe it's commonly used in the military."

"That's a pretty large aircraft. You will probably need a couple." Said Colonel Towers

"I estimate about four-forty foot diameter chutes, with a full house on board of two hundred plus equipment." Said Andrius

"Are you sure, that they will work?" Said Colonel Towers

"Theoretically, I think it will, Said Andrus. The chutes are not designed to stop the aircraft but to help the braking system slow up the aircraft, upon landing."

Uria then joins in the conversation:

"Excuse me, Russ, but where are we now? I don't seem to recognize the ground features anymore."

"We are approximately twenty five miles, north of Eastchester, New York. We should get to Floyd Bennett, in ten minutes or so, depending on air traffic, around the metropolitan area.

By the way folks, you need to look military. I have a change of clothing for all of you. So before we land I need all of you in military uniforms. This is only a precaution."

"OK we will change now before we land."

"By now, my co-pilot should be receiving instructions from either, LaGuardia, or Kennedy. It will just be routine data, as to what altitude we should maintain ourselves, to keep clear of the commercial and private air traffic, around here."

"Wouldn't you be exposing yourself?" She asked.

"Yes, but we are military and there are approximately two to six hundred aircraft in the air, within a radius of an eighty five miles of New York City. Even if they know who we are, it will be next to impossible, to pin point our exact position, unless they ask us to execute, a special maneuver." Said the Colonel

"Surely, you will not do that." Said Uria

"Correct. They can easily identify us by visual sighting, that is, if we were to fly slower, than any of the other aircraft, in the air."

"Perhaps they don't know yet, that we are here." Nora presumes.

"You're quite right, because up to now, we haven't heard any chatter, on the radio."

Andrius thinks about the group that the Colonel is meeting at the base.

"How would you intend to pick up the others, without the military people at the base, becoming suspicious?"

"Besides being assigned to a command position, at the base, yesterday, the military enacted in many of our East Coast bases, various military maneuvers. There are approximately one hundred thousand troops, which are relocating, at this moment, to key locations, due to the urgency in South America. Once the maneuvers are completed, the exact head count, as to who is where, will be impossible to be determined, unless done through computers. The Pentagon is relying on this confusion, to send about ten thousand Special Forces ready for combat overseas, without public knowledge of it. This is possible, under the cloak of these maneuvers." Said Colonel Towers

"I see. So you are taking advantage of this, to move around the country, without anyone questioning your actions." Asked Uria

"Precisely. That will also be the method that we shall use, to fly out of the United States, either tonight, or tomorrow." Said Andrius

"Fellows, I must leave you now. We are approaching Jamaica Bay and we will be landing, in a few minutes. For safety sake, folks, please fasten your safety belts." Said the Colonel as he walks off

Minutes later, the troop carrier circles the base twice, while receiving landing instructions from the tower. They are further instructed, after landing to proceed to a nearby aircraft hangar, located 300 yards north, off the Floyd Bennett Memorial Bridge, across the Jamaica Bay Inlet. As they slowly descend, traffic approaching the bridge slows, as people, in their automobile watch the spectacle of the wingless cigar shaped aircraft land just beyond the security fence.

After the aircraft comes to a stop, a jeep approaches, as the engines are turn off. The Colonel is the first to exit the aircraft and approaches the Airman, standing in attention by the jeep. He returns the salute.

"Colonel Towers, as instructed, I'm here to escort you, Sir."

"Thank you, Sergeant. Has my detachment arrived from Griffith Air force Base, yet?"

"No, Sir, but the C.O is in contact with the aircraft: they haven't taken off yet."

"Very good, Sergeant, standby."

"Yes, Sir."

Andrius dressed in combat suite comes down from the aircraft and joins the Colonel. As the Colonel climbs into the jeep, he turns to Andrius.

"Please wait with the rest, for the special bus. It should be here, shortly." Then he drives off.

Shortly after, Uria comes down the ladder followed by Nora who is busy examining the aircraft looking up and down.

"Andrius, I never knew that this aircraft has small wings, with turbo jets on the inside. The front has a single turbo, while the rear ones are double. Why?"

"I also failed to notice them, but I believe that these aren't quite wings. Their purpose is to guide the aircraft, in the air with the aid, of the turbo thrusts. They work as stabilizers and pivot up and down, as needed."

"So actually, the pivot thrusters, keeps the ship in the air, while the jets propelled it forward."

"I believe you have the right idea."

"Interesting."

After the ground crewmen secure the troop carrier, Michael Roberts and Jason, exit from the aircraft last.

Two dark green, shabby looking buses appear and drive under the aircraft, to the stern section. The ground crews quickly unload the baggage from the aircraft and place them in the rear side compartment of one of the buses. Andrius' group and the rest of the men quickly board the rickety buses and drive off.

Looking out the window, Andrius observes that there is considerable movement in the base, as they traveled along the safety lanes, adjacent to the runways. Normally, the area would be practically uninhabited, unless a military maneuver or a general alert is called for. The head bus driver pauses for a few moments, before crossing a runway strip due to an incoming military cargo plane, which whiz by, at full throttle.

Afterwards, the old rickety buses resume their trek across the runway, to the other side of the field. They finally reach the eastern side, by the bay area, where the military dependent quarters, are located.

Colonel Towers received prior authorization, to have the men in his company stay there, overnight.

As the buses arrive at the site, the scenery quickly changes to a more of a residential look.

There are plenty of trees and shrubbery around, with playgrounds and carefully trimmed lawns, with their sprinklers, still operating in late October. One would never think that this was part of a bustling military base.

The buses stop again, at a gate, and a sentry signals them, to proceed ahead. The head bus driver stops somewhat confused with the site, and asks additional directions how to get to the officer's quarters. He thanks the sentry and proceeds.

As they enter the development, children are seen playing about the grounds and infants and toddlers being taken care by their moms and nannies.

Life inside the base goes on, as normal as in the regular world, outside. The buses finally stop by a beautifully kept colonial house, accentuated by tall white columns. A typical southern style home, with windows adorned richly with fabric overhangs.

"I guess this must be the General's home." Nora assumed

"It's probably the base headquarters." Added Uria

The group exits the buses and walk towards the entrance of the house. Colonel Towers appears from within and opens the door.

"This way folks. There's plenty of room here and additional space, at the top of the stairs.

"Thank you, Colonel." Said Uria

"For those of you, who may wish to eat or drink, the dining room is open and is at your disposal. Feel free, to do as you wish."

"Thank you, Sir." Said Michael Roberts, as he goes directly to the dining room, where he helps himself to a cool drink. The rest of the crowd spreads out throughout the house, to enjoy all the accommodations and to rest from the trip. Jason grabs Nora's hand and disappears.

Later that evening, after everyone is seating about, in the living room, some reading, others looking at some television programs, when an aid comes over to Colonel Russ and hands him a note. After reading it, moments later, Colonel Towers rises from his seat and goes over to Andrius.

"We must have everyone ready to leave here, in about an hour?"

"No problem. Russ, do we have an aircraft?"

"Yes, but my other people are not. They were forced down in Maryland, by a severe thunderstorm. They're now on their way here, by troop carrier."

"Alright. I will get our group ready."

"Good." Said the Colonel and walks off.

Some time later, after leaving the house, the group boards again the decrepit buses.

It was midnight and the short trip by bus, was different this time. They exit the development and drive out through an unguarded gate, onto one of the runways.

The dimly lit headlights of the head bus barely penetrate the heavy curtain of darkness, on the tarmac. In almost pitch darkness, Nora looks out the window and observes various colorful lights, in the night sky, from different types of aircraft, approaching and departing from the base and from nearby Kennedy Airport.

Some of them seem to be floating and circling aimlessly in the heavens, like a long strand of shiny and twinkling lights, invisibly held together, as they wait their turn to land. The whole scene looking more likes a dream sequence to an observer.

The bus suddenly comes to an abrupt stop without warning. The bus occupants give out a yell as pieces of luggage and packages fall from the overhead shelves on top everyone.

"Are you all right back there?" Andrius was concerned

"Yes, no problem, we can manage." Whatever lights were shining in the bus, now they were completely in darkness. A tiny red broken exit light remained, by the driver, who then yells out to everyone.

"You all have to get out of the bus, here. I can't go any further."

"What's going on?" Nora demands.

"I don't have the slightest idea. He lost the electric power to the vehicle, Said Uria The bus has broken down."

Every one gets up from their seats, grab whatever they can take with them and slowly inch forward, feeling their way, in the dark and finally exit the bus.

Nora and the rest stand outside in pitch-darkness. There is a constant blistering cold wind blowing at them, making them think twice, and forever agreeing to go there, in the first place. Nora's body shudders and she turns to Jason for comfort:

"I'm freezing out here. Please, hold on to me tightly, Jason."

"Get closer, honey. That's better." She said.

A half-mile away across the base, in the air, a huge troop carrier is seen approaching.

The bus driver, acting on the directions given to him by Colonel Towers, urges everyone to walk straight, ahead of the bus.

"What is straight? I don't know if I am working straight or in a circle."

"Just follow my voice, Nora or the stars in front of you."

"You're right, we can't see in front of us."

After two minutes of marching in the dark and stumbling over small potholes and assorted debris along their path, Nora again complains and slows down.

"We are almost there Nora. Come on! Just a bit more." Said Andrius

"Where? I do not see anything. I'm not moving, anymore. That's it."

Moments later, the group's leader stops and the tail end flanked by Nora and Andrius, finally reach the point, and they stop, after bumping into a person, in front of them.

"Sorry." She said.

There was something unnatural, about the place. The stars, in the sky disappeared. There was an opaque object, in its place. Nora visually inspected this object and by the process of elimination, guessed that it was probably one of those abandoned buildings to take shelter in.

"Oh, that's great, let's find a door and take shelter, from this bone chilling wind."

Suddenly little bright lights lit up all around, showing an outline of a huge object. Her suspicion turned out to be wrong. It was a huge aircraft. The lights within the aircraft went on, their brightness blotted out the stars above and the line of the horizon, beyond.

There was a portable stair on wheels, on the side of the aircraft that was set for boarding.

Two red lights started revolving above and below the jet's fuselage, as technicians quickly manipulated the controls and devices, to start up the engines.

Colonel Towers arrives by Jeep, runs up to the top of the stairs, and turns to speak to the small group below who are kept in awe by the site.

"Let's move it up folks, quickly, quickly, please. We have eight minutes. He looks down: Michael, please come up here, I need you."

"Yes, Sir." He replies

Michael rushes up and the two men quickly disappear into the aircraft.

As the last straggler boards the aircraft, six army trucks comes rumbling up and stop under the left wing. Men jump out with full military gear, on their backs and run up through another side door, of the airliner. As one truck empties, another drives up, with more loads of men.

Number one jet engine goes on, with an unbearable winding sound. The noise becomes so intense, that when the emergency doors are closed, everyone feels a whole lot of relief.

Andrius rises from his seat, walks over to the front-end and climbs up to the cockpit to speak to Colonel Towers, who is in the flight engineer's seat.

"Russ, what is the latest? Why the rush?"

The Colonel turns and communicates by telepathy.

"They have ordered my arrest. A call came to Military Police, just minutes ago.

An Orgite tried to intercept the message, but it was too late. I signed out, as if I left the Base, so they won't look for me here."

"And this aircraft?"

"No need to worry about it. It's scheduled to depart with a detachment of soldiers. There's no problem."

"What do you mean that it is taking off? To where? Please articulate!"

"I'm sorry, but this aircraft is bound to South America. We are part of the special troops that the government is sending, by first class to the war zone."

Michael Roberts, sitting manning one of the controls, turns to the Colonel.

"You mean, Colonel, we are going to that war zone?"

"We're generally flying in that direction, but that doesn't mean, that we have to actually go there." Colonel Towers responds

"I see, Colonel. For a few seconds, you had me frightened, there." Said Michael

"We will follow flight plans, until we're well out of the United States air space. Then, after three hours or so, we will drop out of radar range very rapidly, as if, being hit by a missile, or by some malfunction. Once executing this, we will change course and fly low and in sight of the coast line, until we get closed to Tierra del Fuego, six hours later, then turn off further South, towards the island."

"How about the aircraft's radio links with the military?"

"As we speak, they are being disabled."

"And the breaking parachutes?" Asked Michael

"I'm sorry guys, I did not have time for them. We have to do our best, with what we have."

"That's just fine with me, but I don't know, if you wish to gamble with the lives of everyone here. You know the odds are fifty to one, that we will overshoot the landing strip, with this giant grasshopper."

"Michael, you worry too much." Said Andrius

"I do, I cannot imagine, why."

"Come on. Let's get this crate airborne. We'll deal with that once there." Said the Colonel

Michael turns around and places his headset on, as it buzzes with takeoff instructions from the control tower.

He reads off a pre-departure safety check-off list, to another technician selected as his co-pilot, to assist him to fly the mighty airliner.

After five minutes, he radios the tower and reports the condition of the jet, to be excellent and ready for take off.

By this time, Andrius returns to his seat and straps himself down for take-off.

Moments later, the aircraft taxis down the runway and is airborne over Jamaica Bay. The aircraft slowly disappears into the night skies over the Brooklyn and heads towards New Jersey and follows the coastline while climbing to a height of forty thousand feet well above commercial traffic that uses the same route.

Chapter VII

Blinding floodlights are trained, at the small mountainside cottage, in the middle of the night, as jeeps and trucks fully loaded with soldiers, come rumbling up the road.

Soldiers disembark and quickly surround and scourer the area for clues to the whereabouts of the people that occupy the cottage.

Karl Daggard appears in a jeep driving up the road, escorted by several Army officers.

They stop in front of the cottage and wait. A soldier immediately runs out and reports:

"Sir, they were here, a couple of hours ago. They left clothing, eating utensils and some personal items. It seems that they are traveling light."

"Thank you, soldier. You may go, now." Said Daggard.

He turns to one of the officers.

"They have to be in this immediate area because their vehicle is here, with the keys still in the ignition. The police have blocked, all the passable roads that can leave out of this mountain region. So they have to be closed by and are hiding somewhere around here. We have to do a thorough search of the area."

"It's a good possibility." Said the officer, while examining the keys of the vehicle.

"We must have scared them off." Daggard looks up and down the valley.

"I have a gut feeling, that they are very close. Have your men spread out from here and search. We will get them; they have to be near."

"How far, Mister Daggard? The officer queried.

"As far as possible, until you find them. Even if it takes all night."

"Yes, Sir." The officer summons his corporal and gives the search orders to the small company of soldiers.

Daggard and the officer walk into the cottage, to inspect it and to look for any clues to their whereabouts.

"Lieutenant, see if there's any coffee around. I think, we may be here for a while, so let's relax."

"Yes, Mister Daggard. I'll send my orderly, to see to it."

Forty-five minutes later, the Communications Officer comes in and reports to the Lieutenant:

"Sir, there is a possible contact, with the suspects down by Sector "B"; the report just came in, by field radio. The men are waiting for orders."

Daggard breaks in: "Take them into custody and bring them here, at once. Wait! They may be armed. Use force, if you have to, but bring them here, dead or alive. That's all."

"Yes, Sir." The soldier hurries off.

After gulping down his coffee, Daggard begins pacing, undauntedly back and forth, waiting impatiently to hear of any additional news, from the Communications Officer.

At a point of losing his patience, he runs out of the cottage and approaches the Communications truck.

"Well, how's the operation coming out?"

"Mister Daggard, the area is surrounded and we're closing in, at any second, now."

"Good!" He lights up a cigarette and takes a deep puff.

"Sir, we made contact."

"Good! That's just fine. Any resistance?" He throws the cigarette on the ground.

"No, Sir, they gave up, peacefully."

"Good, good. Bring them to me, at once. Make sure, that they're all disarmed including the women, they're very dangerous." He asserts.

Daggard climbs into the truck and puts a call to the President in Washington.

Five minutes later he makes contact.

"Mister President, I have got good news, for you."

"Yes, Daggard."

"I finally located Andrius and his small group of killers. They're now in custody."

"Daggard, were there any casualties?" The President asks very perturbed

"No, Mister President, not this time. They didn't resist due to the overwhelming force that's present."

"Yes, very strange, anyway, good, Daggard. Let me speak to Mister Andrius, as soon as possible."

"Sir, but I need to interrogate him, first."

"No. Bring him directly to the Federal Building in Washington tonight and I will speak with him, in the morning. Remember that I need to see him, Daggard. I don't want him harmed, in any way. I need his support." The President exerted.

"Yes, Sir." Daggard reluctantly answers.

"By the way, how's Dr. Jason Roberts' condition? Is he well?"

"I don't know, Sir. I haven't seen him, yet."

"What do you mean that you haven't? This whole operation was staged for his rescue. Find out about the doctor and report to me, at once. He may be in grave need of medical care."

"Yes, Sir. I will order the men out, to search for him."

"Keep me informed, Daggard. Stay focused."

"Yes, Sir." He answers sarcastically.

After the President hangs up, Daggard clenches his fist out of frustration, for not thinking of Dr. Roberts, in the first place. He picks up the field phone and speaks to the troop leader located by Sector "B" and orders him, to also search for the doctor.

A few minutes later, the troop leader calls back:

"Mister Daggard, my men have searched the whole sector and there's no sign of a fifth person, or a doctor named Jason Roberts."

"He may already be dead. Search for any grave sights?"

"No, Sir, not even that." He responds.

"He must be around. Let me speak to Mister Andrius."

"Yes, Sir, he will be right with you." A long pause elapses.

Daggard, somewhat irritable calls back.

"Well, what's taking you, so long?"

"Sir?"

"Yes. Yes, I'm here, what's the problem."

"Sir, no one here answers to that name." The troop leader responds,

"Listen, he's the very tall one, there. You can't miss him."

"Sir, the tall one's name is Steven. That's what he said."

"Impossible! He must be lying. Be careful, he is very dangerous!" Daggard yells back

"Sir, are we both talking about the same person?"

"Damn it; don't call me 'Sir', you fool! Bring him here to me, at once!"

"Yes, Sir. No, Sir. Yes, Mister Daggard." The troop leader is somewhat confused.

"Bring them all, here!" Daggard throws the phone down on the ground furiously.

With his blood pressure at an all time high, he rushes to a Jeep, together with the Lieutenant and drives out to see for himself, if Andrius is really trying to avoid detection.

Almost half way down the hill, the Jeep suddenly comes upon the trucks that are driving up. His jeep blocks the oncoming path of the head truck with the prisoners causing the vehicle to rears off, and makes an abrupt stop.

Soldiers jump out and instinctively take defensive positions to protect the small convoy from the Jeep. Weapons were drawn and pointed.

"Halt! Who goes there? Identify yourselves."

A flare is launched into the air to light up the road.

Daggard and the Base Commander show themselves and they are quickly recognized.

"Men, restrain your weapons! This is an order." The Commander shouts out.

"Yes, Sir."

Daggard jumps off the Jeep and demands to see the captives from the company leader.

"Bring them here at once." He demands

"Yes Sir."

One of the officers runs off and moments later, the silhouettes of the captives, are seen disembarking from the second truck in the distance, as they are led by armed solders.

The dark figure of a tall person in handcuffs is led in front of the bright headlights of the military truck. As he gets closer, Daggard's anticipation of meeting Andrius, face to face, for the first time, makes him shiver, violently.

Daggard's mind goes through mixed feeling of fright and one of awe in his anticipation of meeting this outlaw, super powerful person, named Andrius. He vaguely knows neither Andrius nor Jason's true identities because personal ID pictures were never made due to the secrecy of the project. They never met, even during their two encounters with each other. The silhouette figures finally stop in front of the truck and stand ten feet in front of Daggard.

One was staring down at him, with a terrified look on his face. Daggard nudges at the officer, to have the tall man move forward.

"Sir, you on the right, take a step forward, please." The vehicle lights shinning on Daggard's eyes prevent him, from clearly perceiving the tall man's features and squints to see him.

"Well, Andrius, we finally meet." Daggard speaks with a withdrawn voice, almost choking.

"Mister, I don't care for the war games that your tin soldier boys are playing here, tonight."

"Don't get wise." A soldier next to him said. He pokes at him with the butt of the rifle.

"Hey, hey be careful, who do you think you are? I could charge all of you with kidnapping."

"Quiet. You're in no position to demand, anything, mister."

"You're all under some kind of illusion, that I'm someone named Andrius. Either I have gone crazy or I'm this person, or I'm not. And if I'm not, it makes you all the crazy ones."

Another officer who took custody of them speaks out:

"Mister Daggard, this man sustains his identity. He states that his name is Mel Stevens of Danbury, and that he's the leader of his local 4H club, who are camping out here in the hills, with their wives and friends. All their personal ID's and permits seem to be in order, and he happens to be lawyer, Sir. I believe he may not be the man we're looking for."

"Get a light on this man's face." Daggard demands again.

One of the aids comes from behind Daggard and hands him a battery-operated lantern. Daggard carefully approaches the man and shines the light on the stranger and slowly moves the beam up and down his face. Daggard closed his eyes and clenches his teeth.

"Damn it! He throws the lantern on the ground and shouts out:

"He's not Andrius!" He turns around and walks off to the jeep, defeated once again.

"What do I do? I just informed the President that I had him in custody." He said to himself.

After a few seconds of silence, the Commanding Officer turns to his men:

"Release them. Lieutenant, apologize to Mister Stevens and his party for any inconvenience, that we might had caused them and return them, without delay, to their camp site."

"Yes, Sir." The Lieutenant ushers Mister Steven back to the truck.

A composed Daggard sits alone, in the jeep deep in thought and waits for the Commanding Officer to return. The tall gentleman, Mister Steven, just before boarding the truck for his return, turns around, walks over and approaches Daggard in the jeep.

"Mister Daggard, I'm very sorry, that we didn't turn out to be the fugitives that you were looking for, but I hope you do catch them."

"Thank you, Mister Stevens. I apologize for mistaking you for him."

"You cannot imagine, the whole day has been hectic over here, with your military people flying, all around the area. It distracted us from our midday programs."

Daggard raises his head when he hears the phrase "Whole Day" and said:

"What do you mean by that? We've been here, only a few hours. Three the most."

"No, Sir, this morning, your people buzzed our camp site, with one of those flying things."

"Come here. What things?" Daggard concentrates his full attention, on the man.

"You mean helicopters." He queried.

"No, Sir."

"Then what?"

"You know those giant aircraft that are use for moving soldiers to and from battlefields."

"You mean a military troop ship?"

"Yes. Yes, that's right, one of those wingless jobs."

"But our people arrived here on land vehicles and copters."

"That's what we saw, Sir. Our kids took pictures of it."

"Thank you, Mister Stevens, you have saved the day!" Daggard shakes his hand in gratitude. With a bright new gleam in his eyes, Daggard moves over to the driver's seat and hurries off, in the direction of the cottage, just as the Commanding Officer returns, and is left wondering what happened.

There is a sudden light flash, by the window and a slight quake onboard the jumbo airliner, as it climbed to a higher altitude to avoid dangerous air turbulence over the west coast of Columbia, South America. Andrius sits alongside Jason.

"Are you still having those small sharp pains, in your head?"

"Yes, but they don't seem to last long. I guess it's the microscopic fragments of the bullet copper shavings that are still traveling, throughout my blood system."

"I believe the pain comes from pressure that builds up when one of the fragments momentarily blocks a narrow blood vessel." Said Andrius.

"I think so. Also, this high altitude is not helping me, much."

"Would you like me to speak to your cousin, Michael? He could…"

"No. He must have his reasons for flying this high altitude."

"How about your pills? Have you been taking them?"

"They were unfortunately lost, when we crashed, with the copter. Perhaps, if there is a medical kit onboard, it may have some pain killer."

"Alright Jason, I will go and see."

As Andrius turns to raise himself from the seat, Jason suddenly holds his head. He yells aloud from excruciating pain and passes out.

He falls down, sideways. Nora was a short distance away and rushes over to assist Andrius at laying Jason flat on the deck.

She calls out for pillows and blankets to keep him warm. A Paramedic examines Jason, assisted by Nora. They discover that Jason may be on the verge of slowly dying due to lack of blood to the brain. Nora becomes frantic and turns to Andrius:

"We must lower the aircraft's altitude. The pressure in his middle ear is causing internal hemorrhaging. His eyes are dilating and becoming bloodshot."

Moment's later; Jason starts bleeding profusely through his nose.

"He will surely die, if we cannot reduce the pressure and the bleeding."

Andrus gets on the intercom and speaks to Michaels at the controls and turns to Nora:

"He said we couldn't go down because there's a raging hurricane, below us."

"We have to lower the altitude of this jet regardless, Andrius. I don't care. Do it! Jason's life depends on it." She asserts.

"Don't worry, I will go to Colonel Towers and tell him to do it."

"Thank you, Andrius." She answered.

Up front, manning the aircraft, Michael and the Colonel are wrestling with the controls. There's no visibility but periodic crackling of lightning streaking across the windshield. The aircraft is flying through heavy cumulus clouds and high winds that are making the wings of the aircraft oscillate violently up and down.

"Hold her steady, Michael."

"Colonel, we may have to climb higher to sixty thousand feet and issue oxygen masks to everyone."

"I don't think so, let's maintain the same altitude and weather the storm."

Andrius, at this time, comes in.

"Fellows, we have a serious situation in the midsection of the ship and it's mandatory to lower the altitude."

"What goes?"

"Jason has suddenly gotten sick on us. It's very serious and life threatening."

The Colonel turns to Andrius:

"We cannot descend at this moment, Andrius. The winds below us are up to three hundred and fifty miles per hour. The wind will tear the wings, right off the aircraft. We are traveling through one super hurricane. I've never had an experience like this before."

"Can we change course?"

"Yes, we can, but the only direction, we can possibly go, is southeast and that will take us in land and over the Amazon."

"Would there be any problems with that?"

"Yes, we can be easily shot down by a heat seeking missile."

Nora suddenly appears: "Andrius, I must operate on Jason within the hour. He was conscious for a moment, but he just went into a coma again."

"Gentlemen, you heard her, we have to change course. Whatever Jason needs to save his life, we must do." Andrius said with a stern voice.

"Nora, can you safely operate on him up here?"

"No, not under these conditions. We have to land, immediately."

Michael breaks in: "We'll soon be over thousands of miles of uncharted jungle. I doubt if we could land anywhere, there."

The Colonel calls his Navigator over and asks him to bring navigational charts of the coastline of South America. Minutes later, after examining them a while he finds a way.

"Right! St. Augustine. Yes, that will do." He said

"Colonel?" Michael questions him

"Yes. A few years ago, there was an earthquake, in this sector, which displaced thousands of people. FEMA built temporary airstrips for C-130 aircrafts, to bring medical supplies and aided with the evacuation, of six coastal towns, in this area. We are approximately seven hundred miles, from Saint Augustine."

"Colonel, that coastal area was overrun by the insurgent last week." The Navigator added.

"There may not be a large remnant force there. Gosh, I wish I had some information on their movements, in the area." The Colonel adds.

"Colonel, perhaps you're right. That area is not strategic. It's very dense and mountainous."

"Alright Michael, the Navigator will give you new flight coordinates."

"Right Colonel!" He answers.

"Thank you, fellows." Nora and Andrius walk back and sit down together while Uria assists with Jason's vitals.

"Nora, what area of Jason's head are you operating?"

"I must remove the bullet shavings. It looks that they may be lodged in an artery behind the ear cavity that supplies blood to the central and upper portion of the brain."

"Won't such a blockage cause instant death?"

"Yes Andrius, but the fragments are partially blocking the blood flow. That's why it initially started with increase of blood pressure to the middle ear area and the severe headaches."

"How about the coma?"

"That's a trauma condition caused by a partial loss of blood, to the brain area. It is critical, but not fatal, if treated on time."

"Do you know exactly, where the fragments are lodged?"

"No. I need to take an x-ray or an MRI. That's the reason, why we need to land this airliner, by a large city, with a hospital."

"Well, we should be getting there in less than an hour, or so."

Nora gets up and moves through the isle and stops to take a look out from one of the small side windows.

"How can they possibly see where we are flying, with this wind and rain constantly thrashing against the windshields? My God!"

Andrius appears.

"If we were to rely on just visual sight to navigate this aircraft, it would be impossible to fly. This type of ship is equipped with complicated navigational instruments, which practically fly itself."

"Oh."

"If there are any mechanical malfunctions that occur with the aircraft, there are several alternate back-ups. You may have heard of other types of jets, crashing after, or before take-off, but never, one of these. In fact, some twenty years ago, one did crash in Africa, but it was later proven, that there was a bomb, on board."

"Did everyone perish in the crash?"

"No. The impact of the bomb, took more lives, than the crash itself."

They then arrive at Jason's side.

"Let's see, how he's doing." She kneels down by him.

CHAPTER VIII

The blue phone in the White House sounds out, after the call goes through several channels and finally connecting to the President.

"Yes."

"Mister President, this is Karl Daggard."

"Oh, it's you. Well Karl, how are you doing with your assignment?"

"I'm sorry for under estimating the situation tonight, Sir. I can assure you, that they will be in custody very soon, Sir."

"You know where they are."

"Yes. I traced the destination of the troop carrier: It was headed for Floyd Bennett Airfield, in New York."

"Have you called the Commanding officer there?"

"Yes. Flight operations informed me, that the aircraft was being flown, by a Colonel Towers."

"You mean Colonel Russ Towers?" The President asserted.

"Yes, Sir."

"Mister Daggard, I just signed orders for his custody."

"You mean he's involved with them, Sir?"

"Yes. He's also an Orgite. Military police will place him in custody, the moment that he arrives home. Our people missed him, at the base tonight."

"Mister President, aren't we also sending troops, from that base to the battle zone?"

"Yes, I'm sorry to say this, but we've lost two Air Force troop carriers tonight, in that hurricane, over the Caribbean."

"I'm sorry to hear that, Sir. By the way, do you think the Orgites are trying to escape from us, by stowing away, in one of those aircraft?"

"I don't think so. That would be the last place where I would expect them to be in aircraft heading to the battle zone."

"I wonder! Well good night, Sir."

The moonlight flickers on and off through various nimbostratus clouds, as the mighty airliner correct its flight path and descends to a lower altitude.

Minutes later, it surfaces into a clear cloudless starlit night bearing a full moon. A rich vast floral green earth below greets the mighty aircraft as it levels off to fly steady.

The view looks as if it was an endless sea of vegetation, which seems to cover the whole earth displaying lightning between the clouds and the jungle canopy in the far horizon.

Michael, manning the controls, converses with the Navigator via his radiophone, to establish a direct flight path, to San Augustine. Seconds later, after receiving flight data, he adjusts his direction twenty-three degrees Southeast. As the jet initiates the corrective maneuver, everyone on board feels an airy light feeling. Andrius appears and sits by Michael's side.

"There she is, see that little flicker of light, on the coast? Can you see it, Andrius?"

"Yes, I think so."

"That will be our temporary home for awhile. Now, let's look for those FEMA air strips."

Colonel Towers seating behind Andrius turns to Michael. "I believe one of the airfields is approximately, six miles southeast of the town."

"Colonel, I'm going to see, if I can establish some communication, with the area. Let's see if there's anyone that can give us some landing data on the airfield."

"I'm afraid, there may not be anyone there but a missionary, who's also a doctor and I think he may have a radio. Try him. You'll probably find him, on the higher frequency channels"

"I will do, as you suggest, Colonel."

"If worse comes to worst, we'll fly very low over the airfields and use the high intensity landing lights to see where we can land. We will use the onboard computer to guide us. I believe that the field may be sufficiently long enough to make a safe landing." Colonel Towers adds.

"Provided, that no obstacles are deliberately placed on the runway." Said Andrius

"That's right. Perhaps placed by the guerrillas, to prevent landings by our military."

"Wait a second guys! Said Michael, I'm receiving something, on my ear-piece."

He adjusts the radio knob, to get a better reading.

"There's too much static in the air, but I think I'm getting a human voice. Wait a second."

He radios back to the person to determine what frequency he's using, so he can better tune, into his transmission.

"Come back again!"

Moments later, a link is established. Michael identifies himself and alerts the person, that he must land the aircraft, at a nearest field or airport, in order to perform an emergency operation. The other person identifies himself, as a Dr. Alvarez, who recommends, that they should land on an abandoned airfield, just outside of his town, which would be more reliable than the one located by the Capital. Michael hands the radiophone to the Colonel.

"Dr. Alvarez, what is the condition of the field?" He asks after identifying himself.

"Colonel Towers, there's light debris on the field, due to the hurricane and there are no landing lights, available."

"That's all right, we can manage." The Colonel responds.

"Colonel Towers, I've been on this radio for days, calling for help. The moment that I saw your aircraft's lights in the far distance,

I jumped for joy. Unfortunately yesterday, a dozen soldiers, or better said, cutthroats, invaded my home and clinic. They killed my two medical aids and kidnapped my daughter and my nurse."

"Don't worry, doctor, they could not have gone too far, in the storm. They would have had to seek shelter, nearby. Perhaps they may be in San Augustine, or somewhere close by."

"It's possible, but the problem right now is to get you down from up there, to here, in one piece."

"Dr. Alvarez, do you have any portable lights?"

"No Sir, but I have two or three dozen flares and seven mosquito lanterns, at your disposal. Would that help?"

Michael looks at the Colonel's face and smirks.

"Splendid, Doctor, how far are you, from the field?"

"I'm approximately, three miles away. I also have a Red Cross truck, which I will load up, with the flares and the lanterns and be on my way. Give me ten minutes or so OK?"

"Yes, doctor, take your time."

Colonel Towers turns to Michael:

"Let's reduce our air speed a bit and begin circling the area."

"Yes, Colonel." He answers.

Andrius gets up and surrenders the flight seat to Colonel Towers, then walks into a small vestibule, picks up a hand microphone and informs everyone on board the aircraft, to put on their seat belts in preparation for the emergency landing.

Two Orgite soldiers come from the back of the aircraft and sit alongside Jason, to cushion and prevent him, from sliding off. Seconds later the aircraft begins to bank as it initiates the wide turning circles, around the small town.

Minutes later, the radio onboard buzzes again. The Doctor calls this time:

"Colonel Towers, is there any pattern, that you wish me to follow, at placing the flares along the field?"

"Doctor no particular shape, as long as they are visible and linear. If you wish, you may place them in the center of the roadway, so that we can easily guide the aircraft in."

"Yes, Sir. I will place them at fifty-foot intervals, as long as their quantity lasts. Here I go." The Doctor signs off, as the aircraft fly over the town. Michael observes from high above, at the outskirts of town, as a tiny flicker of lights slowly stretch out, on the narrow runway. To him, it looks impossible for an aircraft, to land safely. He turns to the Colonel:

"This will feel like landing, on a postage stamp." He shakes his head.

"Don't worry, the field is a little longer than that."

"I hope so. For our sakes, I truly do." Said Michael

The jet airliner banks forty-five degrees to starboard and descends, two thousand feet. The Colonel is on the phone again:

"Dr. Alvarez, how's it coming?"

"Colonel, I am half way home."

"And the flares, how are they holding out?"

"I have about twenty left. How about you? Is your fuel running out, soon?"

"No, we have more than enough, Said Michael, do you need any?"

"Well, I would like some. Save me a couple thousand pounds."

"You got it, Doctor."

Then a short pause elapses:

"Doctor, do you still copy me?"

"Yes, you are coming in, loud and clear."

"We are leaving you for a while, in order to position the aircraft, for the landing."

"How far down range will you be flying to?"

"Approximately fifteen to twenty miles, depending on weather conditions, in the area. Said the Colonel, We will gradually descend to your field, in about ten minutes, alright, Doctor?"

"Take your time and be very careful."

"Ten-four." Replied Michael.

Minutes later, the doctor after reaching the end of the runway, finally ignites the last flare and places it down. He looks back and sees the aircraft disappear over the jungle treetops. He climbs back into his vehicle and drives off, to inspect the first flares and to clear up some of the debris, on the runway, which can hamper the jet from landing safely.

The aircraft is twelve miles away. Colonel Tower initiates a wide turning maneuver and corrects his altitude, with the aid of the onboard global positioning computer and initiates his slow descent.

At eight miles from the field, Michael makes a visual corrective maneuver and orients the jet in line, with the flares in the far distance. On further descending, four miles away, the doctor calls in:

"I've got you on my sights. You're looking good."

"Say, doctor, you are speaking my language, now." Said Michael.

The jet further descends. At one thousand feet altitude, the Colonel lowers the landing wheels and extends the flaps, to reduce the forward air speed and increase the wing area. The large landing lights go on automatically and they light up the jungle canopy and begin skimming the treetops, searching for the ground clearance and the runway.

The Doctor is in awe, upon seeing the jet's majestic size, as it slowly drifts silently down from the heavens towards him like in a dream state.

The jungle suddenly awakens, to the jet's thunderous engines, breaking over the treetops and small valleys. The ground, where the Doctor stands, starts shaking violently as the mighty aircraft approaches and covers the whole sky, with a deafening roar. It sores directly overhead, making the medical truck to shake and causing him to loose his hat and lanterns.

The giant landing wheels triumphantly touches the runway, with an equally deafening screech, from the rubber meeting concrete.

Dr. Alvarez recovers from this onslaught, quickly climbs into his ambulance truck and races after the airliner, at high speed. He nearly reaches the jet and almost looses control, of the steering wheel, when he accidentally drives behind, one of the jet exhaust trails. He realizes that the force is strong enough to flip the ambulance, on its' side.

He slows down and allows the aircraft to further taxi, down the runway, to a safe distance.

A few seconds later, the aircraft finally reaches the far end.

Michael turns the aircraft around after making a sharp turn, at the end of the runway.

Jason at this point comes to and experiences some degree of relief to his head, after the jet stops.

The doctor finally reaches the aircraft. He drives his small ambulance under one of the jet's wings, and stops. He climbs out, as the forward escape hatch door, in the aircraft opens. The Colonel again, is the first man out of the aircraft. Dr. Alvarez looks up.

"I trust you are Colonel Russ Towers."

"Yes, Sir."

"Welcome to San Augustine, Colonel."

"And I trust that you are Dr. Alvarez."

"At your service senor. Do you have someone aboard wounded, yes?"

"I have a sick man here, Doctor, who needs your immediate attention."

"Can he be moved?"

"Yes. Do you have a stretcher, in your ambulance?"

"Yes, Sir, I will fetch it."

"Thank you, Doctor." Said the Colonel

"Listen, up there. I will throw you this rope, so you can pull the stretcher up. Then we will devise a method, to safely lower the wounded person down safely, OK."

"Yes, Doctor. We will do, as you recommend."

Minutes later, Andrius appears at the rear of the aircraft, where the men are lowering Jason, through an escape ramp. The rest of the Orgites fully dressed in military gear and armed, disembark and execute the standard protective measures, by expanding their numbers throughout the immediate area and around the aircraft. They set up a defense periphery to protect Jason and the others from any possible enemy attack.

Andrius decides to have a dozen of the Orgite soldiers lead the ambulance to the town, to provide further protection.

Nora and Uria finally exit the jet and climb into the ambulance. Space conditions inside became somewhat crowded, but all manage to fit, without too many inconveniences.

The ambulance moves out of the runway and into a crudely built unlighted road, using only a broken headlight, which reflects the light everywhere, except in the direction, in which they are traveling. After fifteen minutes of jerking, stumping and sliding through the dark unfriendly jungle, they finally exit out into a clear moonlit sky, of the town. Dr. Alvarez then turns to the group:

"Here on my right is my home and the clinic is in the rear. This other road, leads down a mile to the edge of San Augustine."

"Doctor, this is a beautiful place to live and work." Uria remarks.

"That's why I refused to leave, when the insurgence invaded."

The ambulance enters through a white round arch, once protected by an Iron Gate door.

A large section of the door lay on its' side by the entrance and the other was partially open. The doctor stops the vehicle.

Andrius jumps off and pushes the crippled gate to one side, to allow the ambulance clear passage. The doctor continues:

"This was once a sturdy gate a few days ago, but it was blown off, by a mortar."

"Doctor, that arches looks pretty bad. Said Michael. It must be knocked down."

"Perhaps in good time."

After taking a sharp turn by the side of the house, they finally stop in front, of the partially demolished clinic.

"Good God! Said Nora, It looks like, a tank drove right through your clinic."

"It was the work of a dozen men. I cannot understand why they must destroy everything, in their path. Why? The Doctor shook his head. That section of the clinic was the patient's waiting room."

"Couldn't they plainly see that this was a Red Cross clinic?" Said Uria "Yes. In fact, we had a large Red Cross flag, waving, in the air, willing to help anyone, in need of medical attention. I don't know. Perhaps, they mistook it for an American flag."

"Not likely."

Andrius and Michael jump out of the vehicle and help carry Jason, in the stretcher, into the partially destroyed house. They place him in one of the interior examination rooms, which were not too ravaged, by the invaders.

"We'll use this room for everything, including surgery if we need to."

"Yes, doctor." Said Nora

"The oxygen tanks and the medical lights are in the Utility Room, at the side of the clinic. I will go out to the shed and see, if the generator is still intact." The Doctor walks out through a side door.

Minutes later, the lights in the examination room, started flickering, and then finally stayed on, after a short spell. Dr. Alvarez walks in with a smile.

"Now, is that better?"

"Much better, Doctor." Said Nora

"Please let's place the sick man on this table, so I can have a better look at him."

"Pardon me, Doctor but the patient is also a doctor and is my fiancée."

"Oh, excuse me for not introducing myself. My name is Dr. Alfredo Alvarez." He shakes hands with her.

"I'm from the island of Puerto Rico and I've been working here, with my daughter, for the past five years. We came to visit a missionary friend and decided after a month to stay."

"It's a pleasure to meet you, said Nora, My name is Dr. Nora Billings and this patient is Dr. Jason Roberts."

"You are both doctors, too."

"Yes."

"I imagine that you were in the war zone."

"Us? Yes, yes, precisely, Doctor. We were returning to the States, when my fiancée suddenly took ill in the jet, from a recent gun shot injury that he received."

"Oh yes. That needs immediate attention."

"Doctor, I have his records and x-rays, which were taken a week ago. Perhaps they may help you." Said Nora.

"Good, that will be very helpful."

"By the way, Doctor. I'm also a Neurosurgeon and I can assist you."

"Very good, Doctor. Perhaps we both can bring your fiancée back to health, again."

"Doctor, you have my whole-hearted support."

"First of all, let's get some new plates of his head, to see the progress between today and the x-rays of a week ago, OK?"

"Yes, Doctor. I'll get him ready, at the operating table, just in case we have to operate on him in an emergency." Said Nora.

Dr. Alvarez approaches Andrius and the Colonel, who was passing by, carrying some fuel oil cans, to power the generator.

Dr. Alvarez then sits on a chair and buries his face, on his hands.

"Are you all right, Doctor?" Andrius walks over to him.

"Mister Andrius, I'm desperately worried for the safety of my daughter and nurse. Can you possibly do something for them?"

"Doctor, I will ask the Colonel and Mister Roberts, if they can organize a small group of soldiers, to search for them, in the town tonight and I promise that they'll bring back your daughter safely to you." Said Andrius.

"Thank you a million, Mister Andrius. You don't know how happy that makes me, to know that there're still people in the world that care for one another."

"On the contrary, it's our duty. We must return the kindness and hospitality that you have shown us, in your hour of great need."

"Gentlemen, besides being a general practitioner, I'm a religious person, too. I also do missionary work. I know, that God has sent no greater person, than Mister Andrius, to help recover my family and to restore the medical services, for the poor of this small town. Thank God." He shakes their hands.

Michael breaks in: "You couldn't have chosen any better words than that, Dr. Alvarez."

"Thank you for your kind words, Dr. Alvarez." Said Andrius.

"If you will excuse me now, I have a patient waiting in the next room."

"Yes, Doctor, by all means."

As the Doctor disappears into the operation room, Michael turns to Andrius.

"How many of your people, will we need, for this search?"

"I'll summon four or five of our people to help you. Will that be sufficient?"

"Andrius, even the Colonel would be sufficient enough, to take on that guerrilla group."

"Well, Michael, let's not overstate ourselves. It may get us in trouble someday."

One hour later, the Colonel and Michael Roberts finish loading up a jeep and a small van. They drive out to the town, equipped with enough ammunition and explosives, to supply a small army. They take with them a small portable radio, for communications between the Red Cross Clinic and the aircraft.

Chapter IX

It is almost dawn, as the small assault force enters the war-ravaged town, of Saint Augustine. Automobiles and dead animal carcasses lay scattered alongside, the street. The stench of the dead rotting flesh causes Michael to get sick to his stomach, forcing him to shut the window, of the van.

After a complete search and finding no one in the deserted town, they decide to return to the Doctor's home. Andrius meets them, as they arrive at mid-day, to the doctor's house.

"Any success, guys?"

"No, but my hunch was right. They did take shelter, in the town but it looks like they may have taken a vehicle, maybe a truck or van and driven up, to the mountains. I hope that we're not too late, when we get to them." Said Michael.

"How far do you think they are by now?"

"About twenty or thirty miles, the most. The roads are bad and sometimes impassable." The Colonel estimated.

"Here, take the four wheel truck, with you." Andrius throws a pair of keys to the Colonel.

"Thanks."

"You have a full tank, plus two reserves, if you need them."

"Alright. O.K. guys, let's reload the truck. We'll bring them back."

"How long will you take, to overtake them?"

"Perhaps by late tonight, or the latest tomorrow morning. By the way, Andrius, how's Jason doing?"

"They started operating the moment you left, and are still at it."

"Very good, said the Colonel, Keep in touch by radio."

"I will, Said Andrius, Have you seen any further signs of military movement, where you were?"

"No, we're pretty isolated here, from the main action. It is occurring at least, 300 miles southeast from here. There's no immediate danger."

"If you say so. Anyway, don't venture out, too far."

"Will do." Michael responds.

The Colonel and Michael load up the gear, in the truck and finally, after consuming several sandwiches, they're on their way again together with four other Orgites, in search for the Doctor's daughter.

Later that afternoon, Andrius mounts a horse, owned by Dr. Alvarez and rides to the airfield, to inspect the aircraft and to see the men. A fellow Orgite alerts him of certain peculiarities of the field. He informs him, of an eight hundred foot ravine located, just a couple of meters away, from where the aircraft parked. He recommended, that it would be more advantageous, to take off from this point and utilize the natural warm air currents, rising from the jungle below, rather than taking off, from the other end of the runway and using more fuel.

Andrius thought it was also a good idea and decides to have the aircraft moved.

Afterwards, he mounts the horse again and returns to Dr. Alvarez's house.

As he trots off, he leaves word with some of the Orgites, to clear up any roadside debris and to fill up all the major bomb craters, which litter the field.

At the Doctor's house, Nora, who had finished her part of the operation, takes a break and sits, on the porch steps, outside the clinic. Uria appears and joins her.

Andrius comes up riding and approaches a five-foot high wall. The horse gracefully leaps over it, impressing the women. He trots for a short distance, stops and dismounts. As he walks the rest of the way to the house, Uria smiles, stands up and greets him:

"Hello Andrius, Where did you find that beautiful black stallion? The way he conducts himself, I'm sure that he's a pro. Does it have a name?"

"Yes, the Doctor told me his name is 'Relampago'. That's Spanish for 'Lightning'."

"You don't say."

Uria approaches the horse and pats it on the side of the head.

"Hello there, handsome one. You come from a royal line. I can see it, it's Arabian."

Relampago raises his head up and makes a sigh, as if agreeing with her.

"He was a former race horse from Venezuela, whose professional career, abruptly ended, when it suffered a tragic fall, during a race. The owner at that time, ordered to destroy the horse, but Dr. Alvarez, saved its' life, at the last minute."

"But he looks very healthy and leaps magnificently."

"The Doctor bought the horse for a fraction of its worth and shipped it to Puerto Rico, to care for it.

There, with the help of a veterinarian, he nursed the horse back to health, by completely replacing the fractured leg bone, with a new type of prosthetic fiberglass steel reinforced joint."

"You can't even tell which is the injured leg." Uria acknowledged.

"And now, the horse former owners are after the Doctor, to sell it back to them. They want to retire the horse and use it for studding. He's refused the offer, because he has grown fond, of the horse."

"Can I ride him?" She asked.

"Do you know how?"

"Yes dear, I would like to match my riding skills, with yours."

"Uria, too bad there isn't another horse around except those work horses in the barn."

"I'll take a rain check on that, alright." She relented.

"Sweetheart, where did you learn to ride?"

"Guess where? The military."

"Oh?"

"Yes, I had plenty of free time, in my life and one of my choices, was Equestrian Studies."

"How well did you do?"

"Excellent."

"Well my love, we've a date to meet, in the field of honor."

"Andrius, I'll promise not to make you look, too bad."

"You have me at a disadvantage."

"I'll allow you all the time in the world to catch up."

"Is that a promise?"

"Yes, darling."

"Thanks love."

Andrius turns the reins over to Uria and walks over to Nora's side and sits. "How's Jason?"

"We managed to remove all of the shrapnel from his middle ear area. I'm very proud that we did a great job, but on the down side, I'm afraid, that I did some damage, to his inner ear organ."

"How bad is it?"

"It's minor damage. The organ will probably take a couple of months, to replenish itself."

"What exactly did you do?"

"I had to drain some of the fluid from the middle ear, in order to get to the shrapnel."

"I see, Nora, don't feel bad. Look at it this way. It was better for him, that you saved his life, than not doing anything and allowing him die, in vain. You should be proud of yourself, for that."

"Yes, I am, but I want him to be well."

"Don't worry, he'll be all right, I promise. Jason has a good constitution. He has that ability and love of life to bounce back, you will see."

"I hope so." She answered.

At that moment, the radiophone in the house began buzzing.

"Excuse me ladies."

Andrius rushes over and picks the radio:

"Andrius here. Come in."

"Yes, it's Michael, here. We're approximately thirty-five miles from your position and we've spotted some smoke. The Colonel has gone with some of his people to investigate. I just wanted to inform you, Andrius."

"That's good news. Leave your radio on, Michael."

"Ten-four." He responds.

Minutes later, he breaks in again: "The Colonel has just informed me, that he spotted a group of six to eight men and two women sitting, by a clearing. The women have their hands bound. He will wait until dark, before making any attempts to rescue them."

"Do you need more help?" Andrius asks.

"No. We can handle them. Thanks anyway. Over and out."

Michael then joins the Colonel on the hillside, overlooking the campsite of the guerrillas. He whispers: "Colonel, do you see that? This is not an isolated band of cutthroats. That small group is well equipped. They must be in communication with their leaders. See the sophisticated satellite radio equipment, atop of the vehicle?"

"I see. They have two radios, four- fifty millimeter guns, one mortar and..."

Suddenly multiple shots are fired and ordinance start falling all around them. A shower of bullets crashes and riddled their hillside position, where they are perched on.

The two men immediately fall back, as one of the Orgite soldiers, turn and respond with his weapon.

He fires a barrage of bullets into the jungle brush, where the shots are emanating. The crossfire becomes so intense, that Michael separates from the Colonel, as they retreat down the hill. Both ran for cover into the brush. Michael armed with only a hand pistol realizes he is no match, against the enemies' sophisticated weaponry. As he flees, his mind flashes all kinds of scenarios, which terrify him. He now realizes that before he was the hunter and now, he's become the prey.

He worries what if caught, what kind of torture will the enemy inflict on him, would he be able to survive the ordeal. Would he receive better treatment, if he were to surrender? They probably would be more lenient to him, if he were to divulge information, on the others and save his skin?

These thoughts flash through his mind. "No, I cannot do that. These people are my friends and they wouldn't do it, if they were in my shoes. No way." He said to himself.

After long and excruciating minutes of running in the jungle, he becomes extremely tired, and has to slow down. He still hears the firefights, somewhere behind him, but where exactly? It was very hard to tell from what direction the sound came from in the jungle.

He now realizes that he is lost and deep in the Amazon, with no sense of direction.

"If I could only find my way to the truck, but which way to it?" He said to himself.

In his haste to escape, he lost his hand weapon, his backpack and all the gear.

"The only way that I can survive is to wait till nightfall." He said to himself.

"I have to remain calm and don't do anything stupid that would attract attention."

He knows about celestial navigation and probably, he could easily get a heading, provided there are no clouds, blocking the stars, at night. The question he ponders, whether or not to stay, in the area, or walk deeper, into the jungle, where he may be safe from the guerrillas, but he might face untold danger, or even death, from the wild animals that roam the area. He carries no arm to protect himself. He stops and lies down to rest and to catch his breath. He relaxes on the ground, to control his nerves and over active mind.

"Where are the Colonel and the rest of the Orgites? Are they all dead?" He asks himself.

All throughout his life, he faced situations like this, but they were bad and he managed to survive them, but now, this time, it is different.

"Why am I so afraid, this time? Why?" He wonders.

He just couldn't lose his life or give it up, to the hot steaming jungle.

"It is just not fair, nor is it the time, to do so. I have a purpose to fulfill in this life and I'm not ready to give it up, that soon." He cries out:

"I must survive this ordeal, you hear me jungle. I must survive!"

The animals, in the immediate area, acknowledge his outburst and equally scream back at him. They flee in terror, after hearing his anguished voice.

He climbs up a tree for his safety. The outburst somehow, serves him, as a tranquilizer. He slowly settles down and falls into a deep sleep, on a long narrow branch, of the tree suspended ten feet in the air above the jungle floor.

Early that evening, Michael wakes up. While looking up, he could barely see the stars in the sky, due to heavy clouds, which drifted into view. He manages to see just a cluster of stars, which he frequently saw many times before, at night when he flew to the Caribbean islands. However, this time, they seemed to appear much higher in the sky, at dusk. For him it signified that the cluster was more, in a northerly direction, in the sky. Therefore, from that point, he evaluates his position and finally establishes exactly and in what direction, he will go. Now he rests assured and falls asleep again, knowing that he will survive after all.

The next morning, he awakens to the sounds of the animals and the intense heat of the sun burning on his face. He raises himself up and slowly climbs down the tree and starts out in the direction, where he estimates where the truck was the night before and hoping to God, that it was not discovered and destroyed by the guerrillas. If it was, then he will be in real trouble.

While crossing a small stream, he hears a sound, in the distance, which sends him down for cover into the bushes.

"It was gun fire, by his estimates, about a mile-away, or was it five miles away? He asks himself. "The jungle is playing tricks on me, again."

It can make one hear things far away, sound near, or vice versa.

"Perhaps the shots were towards my direction or maybe not." He said to himself.

"I must investigate." Again, he hears a shot, then another. A barrage of gunfire ensues for a few seconds and goes silent, again. All the animals become frozen, in their tracks and stop to also listen.

"The best thing I should do now is to climb this hill. The truck is just a couple of hundred meters away and safety at a walking distance."

He waits a half-hour before flexing a muscle onward. He carefully climbs the hill and finally sees the truck in the far distance, about 200 meters away.

The intense morning sun and the mosquitoes, that have been biting away constantly, at his legs and arms takes a momentary breather.

"Perhaps it's due, to the altitude. That's right. It's the altitude." He has to push on a little while more.

"Food and cool water will be waiting for me in the truck."

"I can't panic and run towards the truck, when I see it. There may be already booby traps placed in it and I may be blown to bits, like the others. Careful Michael."

He approaches a small the hill and decides to stop this time and rest. He's out of breath, extremely exhausted and dehydrated.

"Let's not over due this. I have to focus and bring my instincts to keen perception of my surroundings. My survival depends on it."

At this point, he did not care if the insects bite him or not. It was just not important, any more. He hears a strange sound in the air. There were voices of men, shouting. "Who's? He asked himself. Who can they be?"

Tired and almost at a point of fainting, he pushes his body to climb another hill in the direction of the voices.

His heart was beating out of his chest with fright and anticipation.

After reaching the top, he carefully comes closer to the human voices. His sense of smell and hearing, at this point, become very sharp and keen. Michael moves catlike, closer and closer to the source.

He feels his heart now fiercely pounding against his chest. Each beat is so loud, that he fears that the enemy would soon hear it. He stops and carefully takes a look over the ridge.

Down on the other side of the hill, a good hundred feet below him, is Colonel Towers and two other Orgites, being led through a small trail, to their campsite, where the two women were being held, the day before. His mind panics for a moment then composes himself.

"How could the Colonel allowed himself and his fellow Orgites, be captured like this? Why?"

"They have the capability of defending themselves. Perhaps, they were taken by surprise. That's it. The insurgents ambushed him. I must somehow rescue them. It's up to me, now."

With a new reserve of energy, he climbs up the rest of the way. High atop overlooking the campsite then sits down and carefully works out a battle plan.

Afterward, very cautiously, he inches his way back to the abandoned truck, which was cleverly camouflaged, by the Orgites. He slowly climbs in, like a snake would carefully enter its' den.

Once inside, he changes into clean fatigues, has a small bite to eat and drink.

Now he takes a mortar, a couple of pounds of plastic explosives, grenades and time delay fuses. For extra protection, he straps two machine guns on his back and climbs down.

He carefully works all afternoon, on the hillside and trails around the camp and finally sits down and waits for nightfall.

Some of the guerrillas, around the camp and the sentries on lookout, become somewhat restless and approach the leader, to break up camp and move on, but he refuses.

One of the guerrillas returns and resumes his interrogation of the Colonel. Each time the Colonel refuses to divulge any information or say anything."

The leader himself comes over to the Colonel and pulls out his side arm and aims it at him.

"You ignorant fool, you see how easy it was for us to capture you. I know that there're more of you around." He grabs the Colonel, by the throat.

"Where is your main force located? Talk! I'm losing patience with you." The Colonel still doesn't respond.

"If you are an American Colonel, your men have to be close by, but where? Are they invisible or are they back there in San Augustine? Talk!"

"What did you do with the women?" The Colonel utters his first words.

"So that's what it is. You're after the women and you came from San Augustine."

"Yes. We're not after you. You give us the women and I will spare your lives."

"You're are in no position to extend any favors. He cocks his pistol and aims it towards his head. I'm loosing patients."

"Once again where are they so we can take them back home."

"They're safe for the moment, but if you don't tell me what I need to know, I'll kill you and have our way with them, and afterwards we then kill them, too.

They're lucky that these past three days of storms has been very discouraging, but don't worry, we'll make up for lost times."

"You'll never leave this place alive, if you do."

"Those are idle threats, my friend. They're just plain Americans civilians. Anyway, innocent or not, they are the tolls of war. Some live and some must die. You should know that.

Now, Colonel, are you going to tell me, what I need to know?"

"You don't seem to have any ethics, comrade, or is it dirt rat? You're lower than a common swine, my friend."

"Colonel, in war, there is no such thing, as ethics. I'll kill you, just as fast and without any remorse, as easily, as these women, when we're through with them."

"I can understand your needs, but is your price of war includes rape, ravaging and needless destruction of civilian cities? Is it, comrade?"

"You would do the same, if you were in my shoes." He responds,

"You're wrong. I would kill you, yes, if I had the chance, but only in self-defense. I wouldn't rape and kill your women for sport nor for religious fanaticism."

"I think different but there are some men in my unit, who may have a different philosophy, but as for me, a forward scout, like some of your men, I don't guarantee my survival, in any campaign. I live each day, as if it were my last.

Colonel, why am I wasting my precious time with you?"

"It beats me."

The Captain lowers his pistol and aims at the Colonel's chest.

"Bye, bye."

Suddenly, a great explosion occurs in the midst of the camp. It hurdles both men to the ground. Bullets and mortar shells shower the whole camp area.

The guerrillas fearing, being outnumbered, scatter in all directions to the brush and hillsides. The Colonel quickly recovers, breaks off his handcuffs and leaps at the guerrilla leader, knocking him unconscious.

Those that run into the jungle step on the trip cords of the clamor mines and are instantly killed by the explosions. Michael and his automatic weapons shoot down the other ones that run up the hill. The colorful explosions resembled a typical Fourth of July sky show.

Once Colonel Tower and his men take control of the camp, the guerrilla leader is taken prisoner and is tied up. Two Orgites give chase while firing their weapons, at the remaining insurgents, who run into the jungle.

After the smoke and fires slowly begins to die down; Michael triumphantly climbs down the hill; black faced and with the two machine-guns, strapped side by side.

"Michael, you've done a fine job." The Colonel said shaking his hand.

"Thank you, but you can't imagine what kind of hell I've been through, these last twenty-four hours. I thought you all were dead. Sir, where are the women? Are they safe?"

"I believe they're in a small truck down the road about a quarter of a mile."

"Let's go get them." Said Michael

Minutes later, after arriving to the site, they observe the vehicle from a small hill.

"Wait! Be careful, they're probably not alone."

"I have an idea, wait a second."

Michael takes out two grenades and asks the Colonel to unscrew the top of them. He then pours out the explosives but keeps the fuses intact.

They carefully move up to the truck and the Colonel whirls the grenades, towards one of the truck's side windows. The side window shatters away upon impact.

Screams from within are heard and suddenly; the back door flings open. Two men leap out and flee away firing their weapons, in all directions and quickly disappear into the jungle followed by a shower of bullets, from Michael's twin machine guns.

Seconds later, a dark hair woman leaps off the truck filled with terror followed by a light hair, middle-aged woman.

Both of them were full of terror followed out of fear the two fleeting guerrillas. Michael approaches them laughing out loud.

"What's the hurry lady? Those were not live grenades. They're duds."

The young woman, once recovering from the shock, approaches Michael:

"You monster! She was very upset, we almost suffered a heart attack, in there."

She comes closer and slaps Michael on his arms and chest. Michael overwhelmed by his laughter, collapses on the ground.

"Alright no more, no more please! Alright little ladies I give up, please I do, I do!"

"You wicked man, she curses at him, who are you?"

"Little lady, I am a partisan, I have come to rescue you, believe me."

"You are not, there're no partisans in this country. This is not France?"

"Would you believe that I'm the resistance and I have come for your rescue?"

The young woman, almost at a point of losing her temper again, turns to the Colonel:

"Can anybody tell me, who you people are?"

"Yes lady. My name is Colonel Russ Towers, United States Air Force."

"I'm glad to see you, Colonel Towers. At least you are not like that maniac, over there."

"Yes, lady he meant no harm." The Colonel answers with a stern look on his face.

"Colonel, my name is Jenny Alvarez and this lady is Mrs. Helen Mason."

"I'm glad to make your acquaintance, ladies."

"Do you have any personal things in the truck that you may want to take with you?"

"Not really, just my sandals." She answers.

"You will need them." Michael said somewhat serious this time.

"I'm not speaking to you, Sir." She snaps at him.

"Have it your way."

The Colonel inspects the truck, where the women were, and discovers that the gas tank is empty.

"Miss Alvarez, I'm afraid that Mister Roberts is right. You will need the sandals, because you won't be able to climb the hills, without them."

"Can't we drive up?" She asked.

"No, the truck will not run. It's out of gas."

"Very well." She responds

After retrieving her sandals, the party walks over to the guerrilla camp and removes some of the survival gear, needed to climb up the steep hills. Once having done this, they set forward. It was sun down by the time they finally reach the top. The other truck was just half a mile away, when Michael turns to the young lady, thinking that she had cooled down a bit.

"Miss Alvarez, I…"

"Sir, I'm not speaking to you." She reproaches him.

On that, as she walks, she stumbles on a large rock and falls forwards over heels. Michael quickly responds, by launching himself and catches her in the nick of time before she bashes her head, on several jagged rocks.

"Oh, thank you. She said, I guess I slipped."

"Are you all right?" Ask Michael, very concerned.

"Yes, oh! Oh! My foot I think I sprained it." Michael rushes to her, again.

"Can you walk?" He braces her and maintains a good hold.

"I don't think so. It hurts pretty badly. Oh!"

Michael carefully helps her to sit on a rock. He quickly takes off the belt, which held his twin machine guns together and tightens it around the girl's sprained ankle with a splint.

"That should hold it, until we get you, to your father."

He then picks her up very gently and carries her onward.

"Mister Roberts?"

"Call me, Michael."

"You know my father?" She asked.

"Yes, I do."

"Is he all right?"

"Yes, he is fine. He sent us to rescue you, from these men."

"He did?"

"Yes."

"Michael, I must apologize to you. I was very rude to you, please forgive me."

"That's all right, forget it."

Michael pauses a moment.

"Miss Jenny, I in turn, must apologize to you, for acting a bit crazy. My actions were an outburst of joy, at seeing you both, alive and safe.

As you can see, we originally were a group of six, searching for you and Mrs. Mason, but now we are only three."

"Three lives lost, so that two may live. I cannot see it that way, it just isn't right."

"The lives of my comrades would have been loss in vein, if we had found you both dead. Therefore, the moment, I heard your voice; it was like receiving a reward. The reward was your lives."

"Oh God! Michael, look! You're bleeding." Jenny becomes alarmed.

"That's nothing, it is only a scratch. It will heal."

"That is no scratch, it's a deep wound. You will bleed to death if it's not taken cared off. Your arms and your back, its awful."

"Not really. I don't feel anything. It's just a little wetness. I thought it was only sweat."

"Colonel Towers, do you have a first aid kit? They're very deep wounds. Can you see?"

"There is one in the truck, I will run ahead and get it."

"Good, hurry please. We can put it to good use, here." She said

"I thought it was just a small scratch."

"Michael, you hurt yourself when you jumped to save me from the rocks."

"Sit here a moment and I will take care of it for you, this time."

"Thank you, Jenny. That's very kind of you to worry for me. Thank you again."

"You're welcome."

The Colonel calls Andrius on the radio after bringing the first aid kit to Jenny.

"Andrius, the women are rescued and are safe with us."

"Well done, Colonel."

"What shall we do with the guerrilla leader?"

"If he's injured you must bring him with you, if not I recommend, to leave him tied up behind, so he can be rescued by his people. Get away, as soon as possible."

"Very well, I'll do as you say."

"Thanks."

After carrying out Andrius' orders, they are finally on the road again. That night around midnight, they stop to rest and put water in the radiator that had boiled over several times during the trip.

Meanwhile, earlier, back at the campsite, one of the guerrillas' returned and found his leader tied up and released him. The rest of his party slowly grouped up again and began marching towards an outpost forty miles away to get reinforcements.

Half way back to the Doctor's house, the Colonel stops and allows the women to rest, until morning.

By nine o'clock in the morning, the guerrilla leader and his men, finally reach their outpost. Once there, he reports to the Commander and informs him of the encounters with the Americans. Not being able to handle the situation, the Commander in turn, calls the central command, which relieves him from the responsibility of making a decision.

Minutes later, the command center calls back and orders the Commander to personally, take charge of operations by ordering him to find physical proof that American soldiers are secretly, in the country.

He orders a company of men equipped with trucks, jeeps and heavy equipment to the area and calls for air support but places them on alert, just in case the situation warrants there use.

CHAPTER X

The next day, as the Sun rises, the sun's rays shine through one of the ambulance windows and gently awakens Jenny with its warm rays. She gets up and dresses. Afterwards, she carefully leans out of the back door of the truck and picks up one of the water canteens left by Michael, for them to wash up.

Michael was up long before dawn, and was returning from surveying the area.

The sun later becomes somewhat more intense and forces him to cool off, by removing his shirt and boots and tends to his bandages.

Jenny, by this time, has finish dressing, comes out and walks over to him.

"Good morning Michael, you're up already?"

"Yes, I've been up a while, the other night alone in the jungle kept repeating itself. So I decided to get up and scout the area for any guerrillas."

"Michael how's the arm?"

"It's much better, the bleeding stopped."

"I'm glad to hear that."

"I'm also grateful that you took good care of it. Otherwise it probably would get infected by the insects here."

"Michael, I didn't see the Colonel this morning, did he go somewhere?"

"He's down the road about five miles."

"Alone?"

"No. He's with the other one."

"You mean the soldier."

"Yes, they are setting up mine traps and clamors, just in case, any of our straggler friends back there decides to follow us."

At that moment, the radiophone, by the truck buzzes.

"Excuse me, Jenny."

"Go ride, ahead."

He runs over and picks up the hand mike:

"Is that you, Colonel?"

"Yes, Michael, you were right. You won't believe this, but it looks like a whole company of soldiers, with heavy equipment are heading our way."

"How far are they, Colonel?" He asked.

"I estimate they're approximately four miles, from my observation point."

"Colonel, are they moving fast?'

"No, but they have two forward scouts, who are practically breathing down our throats."

"Colonel, you'd better get out of there quickly, before you're detected."

"I feel like staying, to see the fireworks, go off."

"It's your neck, Colonel."

"Michael, get everyone ready there and leave the area. Don't worry about us, we'll find our way back and connect with you. Keep your radio on."

"But Colonel, you have time, to make it back."

"Michael, call Andrius and alert him. Tell him to get the aircraft, ready for take-off."

At that moment, a missile flies overhead and explodes, in the jungle, about two hundred feet, in front of the Colonel. The force is so great that they are thrown backwards by the force of the explosion. Shaken up pretty badly and knowing little of what happened, he gets control of himself and picks up the radio.

"Michael, if you hear me, please do not answer, or use this frequency. They have located us, by our radio signals. I hope that they haven't located yours yet. Andrius, if you hear me also, please get out quick. Michael turn off your radio! Disregard my last orders to keep it on.

I'm maintaining my radio on transmit-position, so they will follow it. Good-bye. See you at the plane."

On those words, the Colonel leaps off and runs up the ridge of the mountain, overlooking the convoy, heading towards him. The other Orgite remains, in case the convoy doesn't take the Colonel's bait.

In less than a minute, the Colonel climbs and runs a half-mile.

At the observation point, the Orgite soldier observes another flash together with a deafening thrusting sound, that flies overhead passes him and explodes, in the area where the Colonel went.

Minutes later, another salvo of the same flies overhead.

Again, looking through his field glasses, he sees the vehicles that were launching the terrifying missiles. He counts the weapons and there are four missiles left.

The convoy finally nears the mined area, but nothing happens. Two personnel trucks loaded with soldiers, and a Jeep, roll by and still nothing happens. The rest of the vehicles proceed, safely across the area. This serves as a signal to the Orgite that the mines did not work properly. It was their turn, to run for their lives, because nothing was stopping this convoy, now.

Half of the trucks and Jeeps rolled by. It was then, the turn for the missile launcher to pass by. Not choosing to stay and wait, the Orgite soldier quickly moves out, in the direction of the ambulance truck, to meet again with the Colonel. He takes three steps when a blinding flash followed by a violent shock wave flings him overhead twenty-five feet in the air and down the other side of a hill. It was the missile launcher. It drove over one of the mines and blew up; causing a massive chain reaction, with the rest of the warheads, that it was carrying.

The explosion almost destroys the whole convoy except for the three forward advance trucks, filled with soldiers who suffer substantial injuries.

With secondary explosions going on, one of the communication trucks that stayed behind is hit and is knocked out of commission.

Minutes later, after recovering from the onslaught, the survivors reorganize themselves.

The leader makes a decision to push on. Some of the soldiers ride in the trucks and others are ordered to march due to lack of space in the vehicles.

The leader now realizes that their forward advance is considerably reduced and their firepower is non-existent but he must carry out the orders given to complete the mission.

Their loss suddenly gives the Orgites an even edge for survival, although being outnumbered, by still an astronomical figure.

Midway between the incoming troops and Dr. Alvarez's house, is Michael and the two women. Jenny and Mrs. Mason, spurred on by the explosions heard in the far distance, quickly pick up all the gear and weapons and load them into the ambulance truck.

They wait with anxiety, to see if anyone returns. Michael, upon seeing that the Colonel doesn't respond to his radio calls becomes impatient. He changes the radio channel and calls Andrius. A quick response, from Andrius makes Michael feel relief and calms down.

"Michael, I'm aware of the situation there. Please get the women out, as fast as possible."

"But the Colonel is..."

"Forget him, he can take care of himself."

"But Andrius, I think he's hurt."

"No he isn't, trust me. He has been in situations like this before. So get out quick."

As they speak to each other, some miles away, a technician eavesdropping on the conversation locates each of the transmission points. When the airliner is mentioned in the conversation, the operator of the radio quickly alerts his superior, of this vital information.

Moments later, the group leader is on the phone, in turn with his command center, which decides immediately to call the two jets into service that were held on call. They estimate that the jets would arrive in an hour, due to the distance, that they must travel. The group leader cannot wait for this air support and decides to move against them.

Michael waits a couple of minutes more and drives off.

Jenny, very apprehensive, strains her eyes on the road, hoping against disaster, that somehow she would see the Colonel. Unfortunately, she fails to see this happen.

After a while, she accepts the inevitable, that the Colonel has become one of those classifications, which are given to those that, are missing in combat.

"Yeah hoot!" Michael screams out and glares his eyes at the women. The truck suddenly makes an abrupt stop. In front of them stood the tall figure of the Colonel and the other Orgite. They stood like two warriors, in the middle of a field after a victory.

"Merciful God, I thank you." Jenny exalted.

Michael drives up to them, completely dumbfounded, by their sudden appearance.

"But, but how? Tell me guys. I left you guys a couple of miles behind us and I know for sure, that you both were on foot. You got to tell me!"

"What is there to tell?"

"Colonel, you're amazing." Said Jenny very impressed.

"Michael, I will explain later but let's get the heck out of here!"

They rush over and climb in.

"Yes, Sir!" Michael answers happily.

At Dr. Alvarez' house, Jason is up and about. He's eager to see some of the action, which may be coming his way. He recalls an incident in Southeast Asia, when his wing command, was ordered to evacuate an air force base, with only a thirty-minute notice. He was the last Phantom jet fighter pilot to take off, after the Communists, overran the base. Again, that same feeling and adrenalin came to mind and body.

By this time, Andrius, foreseeing the impending action heading in his direction, prepares for a fast withdrawal from the area the moment the men arrive with the women.

Nora packs up most of the Doctor's instruments and waits impatiently for the truck.

Moments later, mortars begin to fall on the approach roads and the jungle areas at random. By this, the enemy hopes to hit the fleeing ambulance truck, on the road. Jason hears and feels the bombardment and now has second thoughts, about getting involved.

Andrius realizes that the truck may not arrive on time, so he brings over two workhorses and the tall slick racehorse named 'Relampago'. He goes to Nora and Jason.

"Here, take these horses and ride ahead to the aircraft. You must do this because there might not be enough space, in the ambulance."

Jason sensed Andrius' true reason, but after having a short talk with him, agrees to go.

Andrius then informs the Orgites, at the aircraft of his decision and orders them to prepare the jet, for an immediate takeoff. The explosions are now getting closer and closer, as the trio mounts up and trot away.

Ten minutes later, Andrius finally sees the truck in the distance approaching and rush out with Uria to meet it.

"Are you all right?" He yells out to Michael.

"Yes, but I can't hear a thing. He motions up. The bombs have knocked out my hearing."

"Don't worry, it will come back."

"Where are the rest of the people?" Michael asked.

"They're safe, they all went ahead."

Michael jumps off the truck with the Colonel. In a couple of seconds, the remaining gear is loaded and they all drive off.

Just as they clear the compounds, there's a flash and explosion. The Doctor's clinic receives a direct hit, from a mortar round and is completely demolished.

As the truck, finally enters the jungle road, they are met by a contingent of twenty Orgites soldiers, who were sent by Jason, to protect their flank, from the advancing enemy troops.

"Thank you guys." The girls said as they go by and they wave back.

At about one thousand miles away, in the Atlantic Ocean, flying twelve miles high up in the stratosphere, a United States recognizance military aircraft is returning from a mission.

It's an HBS-80 Stealth Bomber on a reconnaissance mission, over the South East Atlantic and heading on a northwest direction to its home base in New Jersey.

Colonel Charles Evans, who is, by coincidence, a very good friend and confidant of Colonel Towers, commands this aircraft. They both met and graduated from the Air Force Academy and ever since developed a good friendly relationship.

On board the aircraft are various pieces of equipment, so sensitive, that they are deploy to detect and classify ground military data that is essential to determine the strength and the position, of the insurgent forces, on the ground.

In this particular case, it's getting data from troop movements, in South America. Most of the data and communications transcripts are simultaneously fed to an on-board computer, where technicians periodically sample and sorted out vital information in real time.

At that moment, a technician records the communications between Colonel Towers and Michael, but does not pay any attention to it. Due to regulations, the technicians periodically replay segments of the DVR to their superiors, as a check and balance of the real time data that is being detected.

Colonel Evans receives one of the DVR, which is partially recorded in English. As he receives it, he places it aside and sits by a console.

"Sir, this one is very interesting. It has some action chatter in it."

"I'll take that into account. Thanks."

223

He takes a few minutes off from the data review and orientates a new man, on the operation of the laser scanning equipment onboard. An aid comes over with coffee and joins in the conversation and the DVR lay on his desk, precariously.

Meanwhile, on land, Nora, Jason and the Doctor arrive to the aircraft. The Orgites quickly help them off the horses and they board the jet, via an emergency side hatch door. Afterwards, the Orgites turn the horses loose and they run off and disappear into the jungle.

Once on board, Jason, who had previous experience with flying jets, immediately initiates the sequence, for starting up the aircraft's engines. He goes on the radio and calls the Colonel.

"How are you doing?"

"We're dodging bullets and bombs, Said Michael. I think we're about two miles away. How is the aircraft?"

"It's in beautiful condition, cuz. Wish you were here."

"You bet!" Colonel Towers responds, this time.

Suddenly, they hear a barrage of gunfire down the road, behind the truck. The Colonel turns to Andrius.

"Our men have just met the insurgents head on."

"May God have mercy on them? Said Michael. Hope they make it back safe."

Seconds later, the truck goes into a skid on wet ground while making a sharp bend, in the road. Screams are heard from inside, as it falls sideways on the ground. All of the medical gear becomes airborne. The stretcher and other equipment fall atop of the girls and bury them. After the dust finally settles, Michael yells out:

"Is everybody, all right?"

The girls, somewhat shaken up, answer. "Yes, we're all right, back here." They start pushing aside everything, which lay atop of them.

The three men climb out through the passenger's side and quickly rush to the back of the truck, to help the women out.

Moments later, Colonel Towers inspects the condition of the truck, as Michael comes over.

"Sorry about that. How bad is it, Colonel?"

"There's not too much damage, but the incline, where the truck rests, is pretty bad."

"All of us will have to, somehow, pull the truck, upright."

"It's going to take a long time, without a winch." Michael becomes distraught.

"That's not a problem. The only problem is the soldiers, who're coming down the road, with guns to kill us."

Andrius goes to the back of the truck, pulls out three submachine guns and walks over to the women.

"Ladies, I think it's about time, that you learn how to use these. Your lives and ours will greatly depend on it, for the moment."

Uria is the first, to accept one of the weapons.

"Don't worry guy. She said, I will show the women, how to use them."

Andrius looks into Uria's deep green eyes and gives her a smile.

"Good." He turns around and goes to help the men, at the truck. Michael looks over his shoulder, at the women and looks at Andrius.

"Will they be able handle those weapons?"

"Michael, I will bet your life, on it."

After no success with the truck, Michael gets an idea; he goes out and returns with a fallen large tree branch to use as leverage, in raising the truck, to a grasping position.

"O.K. guys, here goes nothing. Hope we can budge it."

Michael digs a small hole about two feet deep into the dirt and places the thick portion of the tree branch between the roof of the truck and the ground. He leaps atop of the branch and it starts rising very slowly.

"Wha-la. There she goes, guys."

Once achieving this, the men finally get a good hold, on the truck and raise it so rapidly, that Michael looses his footing, in the process.

"Guys, how did you do that?"

"Michael, it just takes pure muscles strength, that's all."

"Show me some day, OK?"

"We will."

Without warning, the women start firing their weapons. The enemy suddenly appears

The men quickly grab their weapons, run over, and join the women. They successfully repel the ground force and stop the enemy truck, from advancing on them.

Luckily, the enemy's truck gets destroyed where the jungle road narrows.

"The roadblock will temporarily serve to slow the enemy's forward advance and allow us a chance to escape. Let's move it, people." Said Andrius

They quickly jump back into the ambulance truck and speed away from harms way.

As the truck rumbles through the narrow jungle road, the limbs from the low hanging tree branches impact and fall away. Andrius turns to everyone.

"Guys and girls, keep your heads and hands, in the truck. It's going to get a little rough."

"Will do."

"You guys know my strategy for survival is to keep a far distance from the enemy, as much as possible and I guarantee, you will survive to fight another day."

"I second that." Said Michael, while he trains his gun, out of the rear door of the truck.

Meanwhile high above, Colonel Evans by this time, has exhausted all explanations and finally swallows the last of the black coffee, which became cold and bitter tasting.

After dumping the cup, in a waste dispenser, he finally grabs the DVR and inserts one into the console.

A few minutes go by of playing back some random radio transmissions on one of the selections when suddenly Colonel Towers' voice comes across, it catches his attention.

He listens to it for a while and replays it and realizes the serious situation.

He immediately calls the technician, who had left the communications room, for more blanks DVR's. As he returns, the Colonel approaches him:

"Say Eddy, how long ago, did you record these transmissions?"

"Well, Sir, I guess about a good thirty minutes, let me see. To be exact, I recorded this segment about twenty-two minutes ago. See, I entered it here in the computers log book."

"Thanks."

The Colonel pulls out some charts of the eastern coastline of South America and again calls over the technician, to view them.

"Where exactly did the signals originate?"

"Sir, this is tape 4-SEC and here in my log, I noted, that the transmissions, was picked up, by our forward high density antennas.

It focuses on a range spread of two thousand mile. By short computation, I estimate that it came from (pointing) here on the southwestern coast, near San Augustine."

"Have we already passed that sector?"

"No, Sir, we will fly by, in approximately sixty to seventy minutes."

"Very good, that's good news."

The Colonel turns around, picks up an intercom phone and contacts both the Navigator and the Captain.

"Captain, what's the aircraft's air speed and altitude?"

"Colonel, fifteen hundred miles per hour and an altitude of 58000 feet." He replies.

"We have a special situation here, Captain. Can you reduce the air speed, to 750?"

"Yes, Sir."

"Captain, I would like you to join me here, at the communication's room, as soon as possible."

"Will do."

"Tommy, are you still, on the wire?"

"Yes, Sir."

"See if you can aim this bird, to fly approximately over San Augustine. Can you easily manage that, right?"

"Colonel, give me the coordinates and I will fly this ship, right down Main Street, provided that there is one down there." Said Captain Tommy

"Thanks, Tommy. Refer to Map 1, Chart S.E.5A, OK."

"Roger." He responded.

The Colonel then turns to the technician.

"Can you gather all the DVR's, including the ones up to the minute, so I could review them and piece together all the transmissions, so I can better evaluate the situation?"

With the help of the technician and a computer language translator, he analyzes each of the enemy's radio transmissions, in the area.

Forty-five minutes goes by when he unfortunately discovers the intent of the enemy's jets. He estimated the time, which the jets would take to reach San Augustine and realizes that Colonel Towers will not have enough time, to escape. He calls again the Navigator:

"Tommy, do you see two unknowns on your radar screen?"

"No, Sir." He replies.

"Let me give you an approximate flight path. I would say that they would be coming from the Southeast, on a direct beam to San Augustine. Would that help?"

"Yes Sir, I have them. The two unknowns are approximately four hundred and seventy miles from San Augustine, to be exact. They are flying 250 feet altitude and avoiding ground radar. That's why, Sir, I couldn't get them, at first but we have them now."

"Thanks again, Tommy."

Colonel Evans sits down, and deliberates whether or not to alert Quantico of the situation, but realizes that no one would be able to come on time, to their aid.

He concludes that everything would depend on him and the rest of the personnel, in his aircraft. He has to find some means, to persuade the officers onboard, to go against official orders, which allow only reconnaissance, but no taking part in any military offensives.

The Colonel calls the officers and presents the problem to them. At the meeting, he manages to persuade most of them, except one, who fears, that he would be subjected to a possible Court Marshal.

The Colonel writes up a special decree and releases everyone from their military obligation and assumes full responsibility for his actions, when time warrants it.

After all these reassurances are made and recorded, the officers agreed to help, including the abstaining one. The Colonel thanks everyone and orders the missile team, to track the two jets and alert them, for possible action. He moves to the radio room and sits by Eddy, to listen to real time transmissions, coming from the area.

Meanwhile in San Augustine on the dirt trail, covered with heavy brush, just as the jungle clears, Andrius decides to stop the truck and have everyone go separately on foot, the rest of the way, to the jet. He explains to them, that it might be too dangerous to drive, all the way. The truck would be driving over an open field and would be vulnerable, to enemy's gunfire. Andrius traverses the road with the truck and stops.

He shoot out the tires and lays the last land mines, on both sides of it. The group then ventures ahead cautiously on foot.

Andrius decides to stay in the rear to protect the flank when six soldiers suddenly ambush him. He manages to fend them off; by killing three and the rest scatter into the jungle.

In order to protect the group, Colonel Towers runs ahead, to provide some cover for the women.

He finally reaches the aircraft and calls out to a fellow Orgite, to drop him a long rope and a fifty-caliber base mounted machine gun. Two men normally handle the weapon, but the Colonel manipulates it with ease.

He moves under to the rear of the plane and lays the mighty gun, on the runway.

He grabs the rope, flings it up with a lasso to the top of the towering tail of the aircraft and hooks it.

Once securing the lasso, he hoists himself up, after strapping the machine gun and assembly, on his back. Once on top, he pulls out four cases of ammunition belts and hooks it to his weapon.

At this point, Michael is at the jungle's edge, awaiting the Colonel's signal to venture ahead, to the aircraft, with the women. The Colonel waves, at them to come and there is suddenly thunder and fire from the tail section, as the Colonel provides a defensive shield of bullets, for the small party, to cross the field and get to the aircraft.

By this time, the Colonel's guns completely saturate the jungle's edge. The enemy fearing this onslaught is forced to retreat and regroup. Andrius appears and looks around, to see if it is clear. He makes a fast dash to the jet, dodging bullets and mortar explosions, all around him.

The Colonel keeps a sharp guard along his path while firing his weapon above his head at the enemy beyond.

Once reaching the aircraft, Andrius climbs up the rope, part way and attempts to assist the Colonel. In turn the Colonel calls down to him.

"Andrius, please I can manage here but hurry and cover the front of the aircraft, they're flanking us."

Michael and the women finally reach the aircraft and board it. He quickly sees what was happening up front and shoots out through a side passenger window with his double barrel machine gun at the enemy beyond.

Up front on the controls, Jason has by this time, three jet engines up and running and working very hard, to start up, the fourth one. He waits to hear word from Andrius, or the Colonel, who are busy, at this time confronting the enemy troops, which are rushing the aircraft.

Meanwhile bullets are whizzing through the aircraft.

Nora grabs Andrius' shoulder. (Shouting)

"Andrius, Jason is ready! Where's the Colonel?"

Andrius motions to Nora:

"He's above us. (Pointing up) He's in the rear, by the tail section. Stay low, Nora."

"Jason is ready to take off and he needs the Colonel, now."

"Alright, alright, I'll get him."

"Please hurry." She shouts.

Just as Andrius climbs out onto the wing, he's quickly forced to leap back into the aircraft. A barrage of bullets riddled his path. Inside, he turns to Nora.

"Did you see where those shots came from?"

"Yes, I did." She said.

Michael appears and she points in the direction of the shooter. Michael takes close aim and waits.

"By that ridge, over there, see him?" She points again

"Yes, yes, I see his little head, now. OK, Andrius, try it again! He has to expose himself, in order to shoot."

The instant that Andrius leaps out again, the shooter, partly hidden, raises his head, to get a better aim on Andrius. As he dose, Michael has him in his sight and eliminates him.

"Thanks, Michael! Andrius yells out while climbing up the side of the aircraft.

Andrius keeps a very low profile as he carefully moves on top of the aircraft in order to avoid the bullets hissing closed to his head and around him.

He takes a quick look and estimates the distance to the Colonel, to be about fifty feet, the most. He yells out to him but he doesn't respond. He tries telepathy, but the gunfire and the explosions and the jet engine noise from the aircraft, are too loud for him to hear or perceive.

Andrius crawls over to the Colonel and pats him on his back, and gets his attention.

"They need you up front." Andrius yells out

"Tell Jason I'll be there in a minute."

"No Colonel you must come, now."

"Yes, yes, I'll be there in a few seconds, alright."

"O.K. Colonel."

After crawling back a few feet, Andrius looks back to see if the Colonel is following him but sees an imminent sight, instead which causes him to stand up in the midst of the crossfire's to drop his weapon and runs towards the Colonel, who's completely unaware of two aircraft, which are plunging down from the skies bringing death and destruction.

"Colonel!" Andrius yells at top of his voice.

The two jets open fire at the same time with their twenty-millemeter cannons, aiming at the tail section.

The falling projectiles sounding like thunder come crashing down through the trees and impact, on everything in sight and raising blinding clouds of dirt into the air.

Horrified by this spectacle, Andrius witnesses the tail section, completely disappear in smoke and flying debris, as it receives a torrent of fiery bullets and the Colonel, right in its midst. The Colonel gets hit multiple times causing his body to somersault and fall backwards. He slips down by the side of the aircraft and his crumpled body gets in tangled with the rope that was tied by the tail section.

After the smoke clears, the Colonel's body hangs suspended upside down and swings aimlessly, in the air.

Andrius grief stricken attempts to get closer to him but the enemy intensifies the attack and he is forced to pull back. The body showed no signs of life, as it lay suspended.

Andrius remains frozen in step, by the drama that has unfolded before him. He stares at the body and looks up, as the jets disappear in the smoke cluttered sky.

Suddenly Michael appears and pulls Andrius backwards.

"Andrius, come on. You can't do anything for him, now. Come on! You will be killed, too.

Andrius ignores Michael and remains starring at the Colonel.

At that moment, the engine noise intensifies and the jumbo jet begins moving forward.

The sudden jolt by the aircraft awakens Andrius from his shocked condition.

"I'm all right now, Michael." Andrius crawls back with Michael, across the top of the aircraft, avoiding further exchanges with the enemy.

The two men finally make it back and climb down the side, of the aircraft. They enter through an emergency door and lock it shut.

The rest of the Orgites on the ground initiate a running evasive maneuver and successfully reach the aircraft and board it by a rear hatch door with an extended ladder.

Inside, Nora excitedly grabs Michael's arm and cries out:

"Where's Colonel Towers? Why you left him out there? How could you?"

"Yes, we had to." Said Michael, angrily

"But why? Please tell me." She pleaded.

"The Colonel is dead!" Said Andrius, with a sober look, on his face.

"Oh my God, my God, it is not true." She sobs,

"Nora, he got shot and he's dead. We can't do anything for him." Said Michael while embracing her.

"Where is he?" She demands and pulls away from Michael.

"He's hanging off the tail section."

"Is this true, Andrius?"

"Yes."

"You're just going to leave him there? You can't do that."

"What can we do? We are at war out here and his body got all tangled up, in the ropes."

"The Colonel's body will probably slip off, when we take off." Said Andrius.

"Just like that! Where are your humanity, your passion and your love that you spoke of? How could you?" Nora was angry and distraught

"Nora, I just lost it when I lost my friend. The Colonel knew the danger which we all were getting into."

"Please Andrius, you have to do something for him." She subs.

Uria approaches them.

"Andrius, at least bring his body in, so that it does not fall away in vain, when the aircraft takes to the air. We can give him a proper burial. I believe he deserves it."

"Please, do it for the Colonel, our friend, your friend." Nora pleads with him.

Jenny and Doctor Alvarez come over and side with the women.

"Mister Andrius, I was a former marine and we never left our fallen heroes behind. Never!" Said Dr. Alvarez

"It's the least thing that we can do for him." Said Uria.

"Andrius, Said Michael. Come on, I will help you retrieve the body."

"Alright, I will do it."

"Thank you, Andrius." Said Uria.

Dr. Alvarez quickly picks up the jet's intercom and calls Jason at the controls:

"Dr. Roberts, please hold the aircraft for a minute or so. We have major repairs to do back here. Can you manage it?"

"Yes Doctor, but make it quick, those jet fighters may be coming back soon for the kill, any minute, now."

Just as Jason placed the phone down, a stray bullet comes crashing in completely demolishing the side cockpit window shield. Nora hears the impact and rushes to his aid.

"Honey, she embraces him, are you all right?"

"Yes, it is just a small scratch on my arm."

"No it's not, it's a bullet wound and you are bleeding."

"Honestly, I didn't feel it."

Nora examines it further and applies an antiseptic and bandages on it.

"Luckily it's just a flesh wound. The bullet just grazed your arm. A quarter inch deeper it would have been a serious wound. Doctor you will survive this, intact."

"Thanks sweetheart, by the way, we're going to have a problem, with this window."

"You are worrying about that window. How about the other five dozen windows throughout the aircraft that have been blown out?"

"I'm wasn't aware of that but…."

"Would you be able to fly the aircraft, Jason?"

"Yes, but not too fast nor high. We won't be able to fly higher, than twelve thousand feet."

"I think you must fly higher. Remember the mountain ranges around here, are much higher than that."

"We can go higher but not for long periods. The thin air may cause all of us to pass out."

"That will be dangerous."

"I agree."

"Talking about danger, those wind shields looks very dangerous. The glass may fall in at anytime."

"Don't worry; I will roll down the metal shutters. Anyone hurt, back there?"

"No, just the Colonel and eight other Orgites, but the rest are fine, except for minor cuts from flying glass." Nora did not want to upset Jason by telling him that the Colonel was dead.

"Tell Colonel Towers, that I need him here soon, alright."

"I will see, to that."

"What's taking Dr. Alvarez to get back to me? He told me to hold the jet, for a few minutes."

"I will look into it." Said Nora, she leaves the cockpit and joins with Michael and Andrius, as they return from securing the Colonel's body, in a small storage room, at the rear of the aircraft. Andrius approaches Doctor Alvarez.

"Alright Doctor, you can give Jason the green light, now. Tell him that Michael and I are joining him in a few moments."

"Andrius, we should alert everyone that we are departing."

"Yes, Nora. I forgot. Better, you do it, OK."

He walks off and stops:

"Nora, please also advise them to cover their face and arms. There's broken glass and metal scattered, all over, OK?"

"Yes, Andrus." She answers.

The two men move forward, through the long aisles of the aircraft. Michael stops to cover Ms Jenny and Mrs. Mason, who forgot to place blankets over them selves for protection. Afterwards, they move up the rest of the way and join Jason, in the cockpit.

"O.K. folks, we're finally on the way."

The jet begins taxing towards the center, of the runway and stops.

A lonely survivor of the battle, an officer at the edge of the jungle, upon seeing that the aircraft has not been destroyed, and is preparing to take off, crawls back to a partly damaged truck. There he makes a radio call to recall the jet fighters, which were returning to their home base.

After confirming the communication with the base commander, the jets are ordered to break formation and return to San Augustine.

On board the RBX-80 Stealth bomber, a technician picks up the transmission and quickly translates it. He rushes over and hands it, to Colonel Evans. The Colonel reads the report and shakes his head in dismay and goes on the ship's intercom and addresses his men:

"Men, this is Colonel Evans. My worst fear about this situation, which I previously spoke to you about, has suddenly erupted to a point, which demands a sober decision.

In less than ten minutes, as Tommy calculated, the two jet fighters, which temporarily crippled the troop transport, will return and destroy it, with all hands on board.

In that aircraft below, some of you may have a brother, a relative, or better said, Americans serving their country and doing it proudly. They are at a great risk of, loosing all their lives, at the hands of a group of people, whose political agenda, is to enslave humanity given the opportunity to do so.

As a fellow American, I wouldn't think twice about giving up my life to preserve our freedoms at home, but if there is any ways, that I can save at least one fellow American in that process of saving America, damn it, I will do it.

Perhaps, I will have to face a court martial for my actions but I'll do it proudly! I'll be able to live with myself knowing that I did the right thing.

Well, men, the enemy is approaching. If they want a fight, we will give them hell! Arm the Nukes! Let's for once and for all, finish, what they started!"

Everyone on the aircraft gives a positive reaction to the request. Some respond:

"Let's get them bogies!"

Meanwhile, Andrius is the last to put his seat belts on, as the ship makes the run, down the runway, where there is more debris, than before.

Bodies of Orgite soldiers, as well as other, lay together alongside the runway.

The visibility is reduced by heavy black smoke from military vehicles and burning tropical palm trees along the way.

Tongues of flames waver in and out from the jungle's edge, sometimes blocking the outgoing path, of the mighty jet.

As they reach the halfway point, there is no possible chance, of stopping the jet, in the event of an emergency. They're quickly approaching ahead of them a deep ravine at the end of the runway as the aircraft gains forward speed.

Seconds before reaching the edge of the ravine, Jason breaks silence and yells out:

"I hope we make it. Here goes the full throttle!"

The mighty engines explode with added thrusting force, sending enormous vibrations, throughout the aircraft. The wings seem to elevate by them selves, into the air by the force of the jet engines pushing forward, at full throttle.

There's a point where all in the cockpit fears that the ship would break apart in mid-air, but miraculously doesn't.

Jason and Michael slightly steer the jet into a sharp upward angle, to make up for the strong downdraft currents, by the edge of the ravine.

The aircraft momentarily looses controls but seconds later, after a quick manipulation of the throttle; they manage to prevent the jet from nosing down, by utilizing the natural warm air currents, emanating from the center of the ravine below. Once high above the ravine, there's a sigh of relieve from everyone in the cockpit. Jason now reduces the engine's output and allows the onboard computers, in the aircraft to stabilize the aircraft.

"Guys we're almost there." Said Jason as sweat pours down the sides of his bandages.

Everyone on board resumes breathing a bit better, as the aircraft climbs to eight thousand feet and levels off, to a steady flying speed.

"Jason, keep a closed eye on the mountain tops that you are flying through." Said Andrius

"Don't worry, Andrius we both will, O.K." Michael injected

Meanwhile, in the back of the aircraft, during the take-off, bits of glass and metal flew about at whirlwind speeds and slowly died down, when the jet leveled off.

Six Orgites immediately unbuckle them selves and begin house cleaning.

They sweep up and clear off the aisles from scattered debris, and dump it from a blown out personnel door located, at the rear of the ship. They repeat this task very carefully because on their first attempt, one Orgite almost fell out through the door hatch. They now maintain themselves, at a safe distance and wear safety lines.

While flying, ten minutes later, a warning buzzer on the radar panel sounds off. Andrius jumps up, startled:

What is it, Michael?"

"Don't be alarmed. It's an early warning device, designed to alert a pilot that he is flying on the same air zone, of another aircraft or heading directly into a side of a mountain."

Michael looks at the forward scope and sees no obstructions. He then looks at the regular radarscope and sees two small light blimps; he turns to Andrius and shakes his head.

"The two jet fighters are back. What shall we do now?"

"Well, we are over water and we can't land, so the only thing left for us, is to fight it out with them."

"They will cut us to shreds, up here."

"How far are they?"

"Let's see. (Looking into the scope and measuring.) I would say a hundred, no, one hundred and seventy miles. About six to eight minutes away, to be exact."

Andrius turns to Jason.

"How's our fuel?"

Michael breaks in: "If you are thinking of pushing this aircraft to full throttle, don't do it. With the added speed and pressure, which may result from it, you will surely kill everyone onboard. How about all the guns that are onboard? We must have at least, a few hundred."

"We cannot maneuver, at very high speeds, Said Jason. They will easily fly around us and shoot us down, anytime, they want."

"Let's hope, that they know this and will not expect us, to fight." Said Andrius

"You mean play lame duck."

"Exactly."

"Perhaps, we may be able to shoot them down, when they first pass of us. If we fail, we are dead." Said Jason in a defeated voice.

"There are too many probabilities, in your plans. I think we have just come to the end of the road and the journey is over, gentlemen." Said Michael.

"We just can't give up, now. What if, we were to fly as near to the water, as possible? Would it be harder for them, to detect us?"

"Could be, but you cannot tell, if they have already located us."

"Stop! I may have a way out of this dilemma, Said Michael. Andrius, look over here at the scope."

Both men observe a smudge, on the radar screen. Michael continues:

"This may be our life saver."

"What is it?" Andrius was curious.

"It's a medium sized squall that is moving very fast southeast."

"What do you propose?" Said Jason.

"If we can get into it and stay inside long enough, there may be some hope that the jet fighters, will eventually run out of fuel.

Can you see that they might very well be on low fuel, by now? They either stay up with us and perish, or will be forced, to return to their base to refuel."

"That's right. Their reserves may be all used up, by now." Jason said, displaying a wide smile, on his face.

"How far to that small storm?" Andrius was animated.

"About two hundred miles. It's going to be a race for it." Michael adds.

Andrius turns to Jason, on the controls:

"Let's gradually increase, our air speed. We can't allow them, to overtake us."

"Alright, Andrius. It's your move, now."

"Let it be the right one."

Jason executes a corrective maneuver and flies the aircraft on a direct beam, to intercept with the small storm.

Seconds later, Michael notices that MIGS have also changed their direction and begin flying towards the same clouds. He detects by radar that they have drastically increased their air speed, and calls Andrius.

"You underestimated them. The Migs are using their afterburners."

"They're committing suicide, Said Jason, they'll soon overtake us and run out of fuel in the process. They will fire on us before we get to the cloud cover. They're nuts."

The three men watched astonished with every radar scans, as the two blips move closer and closer, to the center of the scope.

"They will be visible in sixty seconds and we will also be in range of their weapons." Said Michael.

A second warning signal goes on, this time. It automatically displays a theoretical point, on the radar screen, of a mid-air collision, which can happen, if the aircraft do not take preventive measures.

Michael activates the automatic timer and counts down, the remaining time left, for them. Jason quickly changes course and the warning device is silenced.

"Forty-five seconds." Said Michael.

The warning device suddenly goes on again. Jason reacts quickly and again lowers the jet's altitude.

"Twenty-five seconds." Michael shouts out, as he tightens his seat belt and his grip, on the controls.

Again, the warning device buzzer goes on, but this time, with a loud audible sound.

Jason's hands tremble from the tense situation, and reaches for his forehead, wipes off the drops of sweat, seeping through the gauze wrapped, around his head.

He lowers the jet airliner, still more. Michael screams out:
"Ten seconds!"

He presses his face on the radarscope. All three men sit breathlessly, anticipating the sound on the warning buzzer to blare out again, finally signaling the end of their flight.

Suddenly, as the buzzer sounds off, a flash and a blinding light illuminates the sky and the seas all around them. This frightful light quickly changes into a vicious red color, and then darkens to an eerie orange.

The aircraft suddenly receives a mighty jolt, like being rammed on the side, by another aircraft. All of the automatic systems, on the aircraft go haywire, as lights; buzzers and other electronic equipment, go amuck throughout the aircraft.

The aircraft now out of control, Jason and Andrius fight hard, to stabilize it. Michael, who was watching the radarscope observes that the two jets slowly disintegrate, before his eyes, as this ghastly light and fierce shock wave, hits the ship. He tries to get up to reach the controls, but fails.

A minute later, the controls and the automatic systems aboard finally recover from the shock wave and slowly start coming back.

All three men remain sitting, staring at each other, wondering, if they were all dead.

There remained a strange light hue all around them giving the impression that they were someplace else, perhaps in a limbo state of existence.

"Beautiful! That was beautiful, men! Said Colonel Evans; I must congratulate each and every one of you, for executing this job to perfection. See that there was no collateral damaged, to our aircraft below.

Each of the missiles hit its target, at the precise moment, when the enemy was about, to launch theirs. I would like to call the troop carrier and speak to Colonel Towers, to apologize for taking so long in shooting down those Migs. I had to wait, for the right moment.

Men, due to our special missions, we are not permitted to use the radio, anyway.

In the first place, for the record, we were never here. Thank you, for a job well done. Let's return, to our normal flight path, as though, nothing has happen. Thanks again and carry on."

The RBX Bomber angles up and disappears, into the blue skies above.

At this time, Nora enters the cockpit and breaks the wall of silence among the three men, who had completely neglected the controls and are staring, into empty space.

"Gentlemen! Gentlemen, while you all meditate, does anyone care, that this aircraft, is heading into a severe electrical storm? Can you see?"

Jason quickly swings around.

"Hi honey." He then grabs the controls:

"Oh, dear, I'm sorry. There is no danger. The jet is on autopilot. I better get it off and resume our flight."

Once getting the aircraft under manual controls again, Jason banks off and avoids all contact with the dense cumulus clouds ahead.

Michael takes out his air charts and after making some calculation, gives Jason a new heading toward their objective, the Island.

Sometime later, after being well on the way, Jason pulls back his flight seat and takes a breather from the controls. He surrenders the controls to Michael and gets up, stretches his legs and returns to the troop section of the aircraft. While Andrius, who was by the radar console, gets up and joins Michael, at the controls.

"How's she flying?" He asks.

"She's doing all right, in spite of all the bullet holes throughout." Said Michael.

"After all it's a miracle that we are still flying."

"I agree with you my friend, but we have one more obstacle to confront, before we get to the Island. The Chilean and Argentinean Coast Guard?"

"Precisely." Said Andrius

"That's not a problem; we will follow the procedures that your other comrades initiated in the past. We will fly very low, above the waters and fly beyond their line of sight."

"I was thinking of another way, but this may be the best method."

"In addition, I know that the radar systems aboard those ships are not too sophisticated. They are World War II vintage. We will be able to detect them, much earlier, than they us."

"What is their range?" asks Andrius

"I believe that their radar signal is about one hundred and forty to one hundred sixty mile range. Ours, in turn, can receive, up to two hundred miles or more, depending on weather conditions. Like I said, we will see them earlier and take proper precautions."

"Well, I still don't trust it."

"Andrius, your people haven't been detected up, until now. It only proves one thing. Our modern radar systems are fail-safe."

There's a tap on the rear entry door and it opens. Jenny appears and comes in and joins them.

"I hope that I'm not disrupting anything important."

"Oh, no, Ms. Alvarez, please come in and sit with us, Said Andrius, we're just talking about flying tactics, that's all."

"I was a bit restless back there, she said, so I decided to take a walk to say hi to you guys."

"Good."

"Its nice and warm over here. It's too windy back there."

"Stay here a while and warm up a bit."

"Thanks."

"That reminds me, Said Andrius; I better go back and see how Uria and the rest are doing."

Andrius gets up from the flight seat.

"Excuse me one moment, dear."

"It's all right." She said very politely, while getting out of his way.

"Ms. Alvarez, please sit here, on my flight seat. It will be easier for both of you, to talk to each other."

"Thank you. I hope I don't distract you, Michael from flying the aircraft."

"No, on the contrary, I'm honored. Please, sit here by me, Jenny."

"Don't worry; I will not touch a thing." She assures him.

"But Jenny, I have not said anything. Don't be so nervous, alright."

"Michael, I will relieve you, in an hour." Said Andrius while opening the door to the passenger section.

"That will be fine, Andrius. I'm feeling a little tired, myself." He replies.

By this time, Jenny was on the flight seat and strapped in. Michael adjusts the aircraft altitude and places it once again on autopilot. He withdraws his flight seat from the controls and unbuckles himself.

Jenny, upon seeing this, suddenly becomes very nervous.

"Michael, please! Go back. We will crash! I don't want to die."

Michael raises his arms in the air and tries to calm Jenny down.

"Oh, don't worry. The automatic pilot is at the controls."

"Where is he? I don't see him."

"No, no Jenny, it is not a he, it's the onboard computer. It's what flies the jet."

"Oh, a machine. How dumb of me! I should have known it, I feel so silly."

"Jenny, come on. You aren't dumb or silly. I think you're a bright, witty and a very beautiful, young woman."

"Thank you, Michael, for your kind words."

"You're welcome and I mean every word of it."

"Oh, thank you, again. You're embarrassing me, now."

"Honestly, to me you are, OK."

"Alright, Michael. That's your opinion."

"By the way, Jenny, have you ever flown before?"

"To be honest, this is the first time that I have been on an airplane."

"A jet."

"Yes, a jet aircraft."

"How strange?"

"Yes. I'm afraid, to fly."

"Why?"

"I wouldn't care to discuss it."

"I'm sorry, you may have your personal reasons."

"Alright Michael, I will tell you."

"But if you rather not…"

"I said, that I would tell you. She raises her voice slightly. Now, don't get me upset again, like the other day."

"Jenny, you look cute when you are mad." He said while smiling.

"That's why you are always teasing me? But why?" She asks.

"Why? Because I have grown very fond of you." He confesses.

"You have?" Jenny said with a twinkle, in her eyes.

"Yes, and after all of this is over and done with, I would like, to get better acquainted with you. That's if your dad will permit it."

"Michael, I believe that I'm a grown up women now and I'm free to make my own decisions on these matters."

"I know but Latin's have a different temperament. Parents always have the last word in all decisions and compromises."

"Yes they do but in my case, my father trusts me to make the right choice."

"Good, I like that."

"You may court me, that is, if you do not have any other commitments, with someone else."

"Jenny, I don't. I'm a loner and always been afraid all my life, to settle down, because I just haven't found the right person, till now."

"But we have just met. You don't know me, or where I come from. You don't even know my desires, or my aspirations, in life."

"I will help you get them, whatever they are!"

"You do not seem to understand."

"But what is there to understand? I don't care. I only know that for the first time in my dog ratchet life, I feel something good, deep inside for someone. It may sound crazy, but it's the honest darn truth, so help me. Michael raises his hand up and gestures, as if he were in a court. Honest."

"You're some character, but frankly, I also have a little liking for you, too."

"You do?"

"Yes, and I hope, that it later can develop, into something beautiful."

"Yes. Yes, I hope, it will be true love."

"Perhaps." She was teasing him this time.

"I want to marry you, Jenny."

"Wait a minute fellow; it's neither the time nor the place, for such talk, Michael."

"I'm sorry. You're right; I'm rushing too fast and trying to accomplish too many things, too quickly. That's the story of my life." He drops his head, in defeat.

"Michael, if you learn to take things in stride, you may be surprised, that you will get to accomplish them."

"Throughout my life, my existence, in itself, has not had any true meaning to me. I honestly can say that after meeting you, holding and caring for you, I'm truly afraid, I will never see the day of experiencing true love and that feeling of being wanted and loved, by someone else. I also fear that l will never be able to ask for your hand in marriage, because I will die long, before that."

"Please, Michael, don't say that. She emotionally holds his hand and raises them, to her face. You have a good and tender heart."

"That's how I honestly feel, Jenny."

"Michael, you will not die. I won't let you. I would otherwise, marry you this instant."

"You really mean that, Jenny. Please be honest with me."

"Yes, my love."

"Thank you, Jenny. You made this day worth living."

"Michael, can you do me a great favor?"

"Yes, Jenny, anything you want. Anything."

"Please, fly this plane. I get the jitters when I don't see anyone, behind the controls."

"Alright, sweetheart. Right this instant."

He moves over to her side and gives her a tender kiss. She, in turn, afterwards, gently guides his arms towards the controls of the jet.

"Michael, when Andrius relieves you, in a short while, come over to my seat, OK?"

She gets up, embraces him and gives him another kiss, on his cheek.

"I have truly fallen in love with this crazy man but I love him." She said to him.

"And I love you too."

She turns and walks towards the troop section of the jet. Just as she opens the compartment door, Jason appears.

"Hi Jenny." Jason moves in and sits alongside to Michael.

"Mike, it looks like everything here, is under control. Ms Alvarez looks, as if she is walking in air." Michael nodes his head and smiles in agreement.

"She's going to become Mrs. Michael Roberts, very soon."

"You too, cuz? Congratulations, when is the lucky day?" He asks mockingly.

"We haven't set up a definite date yet, but the moment, that this mess and confusion is over, we will set it."

"You're really serious, about this, cuz?"

"Yes, I am."

"You are serious?"

"Yes, you heard me, the first time."

"Well, honestly, don't make any short plans."

"Why, is there something wrong with her?"

"No but you must realize that we're all on the run, Michael and you know what that entails. You're putting her life, in danger."

"I know, I know. Please do not remind me. I once did it for two years, through no fault of my own. I landed in jail and a big fine, as a result."

"That's all over, now. Your past is now buried. You paid your dues. Forget it."

"I feel like, it's right back again. Is there a country that would accept us?"

"Probably none, in the Western Hemisphere. If you know Mister Daggard, by now, we probably have a price, on our heads." Jason adds.

"Not quite. They don't know about Dr. Alvarez and the others."

"Oh, yes, you're right, but I was referring to our little group."

Michael takes out an aerial chart and looks at it awhile.

"Jason, you better tell Andrius, that we are less than two hours away from the Island."

"Alright. By the way, have you spotted anything out there, like ships, or any commercial traffic?"

"No, not a soul. You know, that's very strange." Michael ponders.

"I would think that naval patrols would be, out in force, in these waters."

"They are probably closer to their coastal shores, for fear of the insurgents."

"I hope that you are right."

Back in the troop seating area of the aircraft, Andrius and Uria discuss the possibility of returning to the United States.

"The only possible way, which we can safely return is, either by surrendering, or establishing some face to face dialog, with Daggard's superior, the President. He has to hear me out."

"But, Andrius…"

"Before this can happen, I need to have an open confrontation, with the leader of the C.S.A. He would be the only obstacle, to this meeting."

"Why?"

"Our friend, Mister Daggard, is a very sick person."

"You don't have to tell me."

"He won't stop, at anything, until he is able to deliver my head, on a silver platter. I cannot move, or attempt to reason, with the President, with him around."

"Probably the President may share his same philosophy."

"No, I don't think so. The Presidency is a very complicated and demanding job.

As the Head of the Nation, during the course of a day, he may get involve with fifty to one hundred issues, complaints and decisions. He makes decisions, over matters with the trust and recommendations, of his aides and advisors."

"How about our case?" She asks

"Ours is unique. He should have devoted more time to it. I personally think that he was ill advised and misled by this Mister Daggard."

"So, then you are contemplating to see him. When?"

"Yes, I will, but in a year or so, after we build the defensive measures, on the Island."

"Defenses against, whom? President? If need be, but primarily, against attacks from Daggard and his group."

"Andrius, Jason approaches him. Pardon me, Ms. Uria, Michael says that, we're approaching the island very soon. In about forty five minutes, the most."

"Thank you, Jason." He then turns to Uria.

"I must leave you, now."

"I understand, Andrius."

"Jason, we have a lot to do, before we land. Would you be able to handle the controls on the approach with Michael? If not, I'll try it myself."

"Yes, I feel all right. Nora and Dr. Alvarez did a splendid job. I guarantee that I can land this bird, without incident."

"Let's hope and pray so." Said Uria.

"Andrius, I have just heard about the Colonel. I'm so sorry." Said Jason.

"He was a good friend and we will miss him dearly."

"Even though I never got to spend a lot of time with him. In some occasions we met at Nora's cottage several times for some celebration or sort. He was some heck of a nice person and a good friend."

"He was. He was."

The two men walk off, to the front of the aircraft, after stopping and talking to some of the Orgites in the sitting area. They finally join Michael, at the controls.

While seated, Jason gives some thought to the landing approach, at the Island and turns to Andrius:

"You know something, this aircraft can't land, on that small runway. You're lucky, if you're able to land, a medium sizes cargo plane there."

"Why not?" Asks Michael

"The air strip is not long enough, Said Jason, Read your charts, Captain."

"We're crash landing on the island." Said Andrius very determined.

"Your both gone totally crazy." Said Jason

"I know, Colonel Towers was providing us with some breaking chutes, for the aircraft, but circumstances changed and it was not possible. Nevertheless, we must do, with what we have, on hand."

"Andrius, the aircraft has closed to seventy-five thousand pounds of jet fuel onboard, that must be jettison, before any attempts, to land, can be made." Said Michael.

"Right! Can you see to that?"

"I'm not too sure about the workings of one of these old jumbo jets, but I will take a look at the plans and figure them out, somehow. Colonel Towers was the right guy for this task."

"The Colonel is not here now and I elect you. This was my alternate plan, to land without fuel, by this, eliminating any chances of explosions and fires, in the event that the landing is not too successful."

"We have approximately, forty-two minutes, before landing."

"Good."

Michael starts manipulating the dials on the panel and then turns to Andrius.

"I have bad news for you, gentlemen. The fuel cannot be discharged, from the tanks."

"Why not, Michael?"

"The emergency fuel discharge system seems to be inoperative. I tried it several times it's no good. It's kaput. There's only one, out of the ten pumps, that's working."

"That's bad news." Said Jason

"That pump will take six hours to discharge the fuel. That is the best that I can do, by overriding some of the relays, from here."

"We must do better than that. Why should the pump take, so long?"

"Andrius, these jumbo jets are designed, to carry a large storage capacity of fuel, to stay aloft for longer periods, than conventional aircraft. The fuel tanks are divided into small compartments, to maintain balance in the air, while in flight."

"Can we force all the pumps, to operate at the same time?" Asks Jason

"Surely, but the main control panel and the sequential controller are five meters below us. The hatch that leads to it is locked airtight from the opposite end. This is a standard procedure for military aircraft. It's designed for safety reasons."

"That's a military ingenuity." Said Jason

"That will be risky, Andrius. If you blow out the hatch and manage to rupture any fuel lines below, we're all doomed." Said Michael

"I'll be careful." Said Andrius as he looks over the jet's blueprints, while examining how the hatch was constructed and where the locking mechanisms, are located. After a couple of seconds, he points at one area.

"We will place one ounces of C-4 explosives here, by this edge, and the rest evenly spaced over here, by the hinges. You will need to flood the top of the hatch, in order to dampen down the explosion."

"Where shall we get the water?" Asks Jason, as he approaches the men, seated by the radar console.

"That's easy, said Michael. See here, on the plans. This is a drain line from the water storage tank, which supplies, our drinking water and the water for all the laves onboard."

"Splendid! Said Andrius. There are about two thousand gallons, in that tank. It will be enough to flood the small room, below us, to about a meter deep."

"I think that should do the job." Said Michael

"Alright. Let's get to work. We have little time, left. I will go back to our storage section and get the explosives, Michael." Said Andrius

Just behind Michael's flight seat, Jason knells down and unbolts a locked cover to a manhole, which leads down to the hatch, over the pump room.

Jason then returns to the controls and presses a knob, on a side panel, which lights up, a small room, below. By the time Andrius arrives with the explosives, Michael has already begun breaking the seals off the drain valves of the water tank.

"Michael, here." Andrius said, while dropping explosives down to him.

"Very gently, please." Michael said in a very nervous voice.

"Don't be afraid. These cannot go off, unless the detonators are placed, in the charge."

"Thanks for the information, but I still don't trust explosives. They are very unstable at times. If you know, what I mean?

Andrius, back in San Augustine, I set a couple of these charges, which exploded prematurely, so be careful, they are very mean. They are nasty mean, to put it to you, bluntly."

"Catch." Andrius said again, while throwing another handful to him.

"Michael, you can only die once. It will be quick and you won't feel a thing."

"I know, I know. You don't have to remind me."

"Come on, let's get to work." Said Andrius after jumping down.

They kneel, by the hatch, and skillfully mold the explosives, around the edges and finally place an extra load on the locking mechanism.

Afterwards Michael stands up, walks to the tank and opens the valve, just as Andrius finishes placing the last detonator, on the charges. He lays the wires to the flight control deck, where Jason is sitting.

By this time, water floods the area. It covers the whole room and the level slowly rises.

The wire by this time is all stretched out. Michael while being in knee deep, frigid water quickly climbs up, with his teeth chattering.

"Andrius, do you think that is enough water?" He said while drying up himself, with a towel.

Andrius bends down, takes a look and shakes his head:

"Well, perhaps a foot or more." He gets up and joins Jason, at the controls.

"Are you feeling any weight change, up front?"

"Slightly, Andrius. The aircraft is still on auto-pilot and the onboard computers, are automatically correcting the jet's attitude, for the shifting in weight."

"What's that flashing light?" He asked.

"That's just stating that there is a malfunction, in the storage tank."

"The computer does not say who, or what is the cause."

"No, perhaps eventually in time, they will."

"That is, if there is further integration of our people into the commercial computer market and I will see to it that it will never happen." Andrius said in a stern voice.

"That wraps it up, Said Michael, everything is about ready."

"We won't be able to lock down the manhole because of the wires but brace it, somehow. We can block it up, with some of this cushioning material." Said Andrius

"Where is that from?"

"These are pieces of foam rubber pads and assorted seating materials, which were left over scraps, from the battle, in San Augustine. There were about two dozen seats destroyed, so I decided not to dump all of the debris out."

Michael takes some of the material and carefully places it in the opening, to absorb the explosion.

Andrius does a quick calculation and estimates that the explosion impact, in general will not be too severe and with the help of the water, the force will be considerably dampened.

Jason reduces the jet's air speed drastically and opens all the side vents and window shields on the aircraft, just in case Andrius' estimates are off. By this, he reasons out, that by the time the force of the explosion reaches the flight deck, it probably be dissipated enough and should not blow out the windshields of the aircraft.

Michael sits in the flight seat and straps himself in. Andrius carefully leads the wires to the radar console; he hooks it up to the detonator and finally straps himself in his seat.

"Everyone ready?" He warns.

"OK, let it go!" Michael said anticipating a worse scenario. He covers his face, as Andrius closes the contacts.

A fraction of a second later, they feel a small tremor below.

Suddenly the foam and the seating material fly upward followed, by a gush of water, which engulfs everything, in the cockpit. The aircraft sways for a few seconds then slowly stabilizes.

"Hold there, boy!" Jason yells out at the controls.

He eases up on them as the swaying ceases. Michael quickly unbuckles his seat belt, grabs a rag and wipes off the reddish brown water smears, off the windshields and the flight instrument panels. Everything in the cockpit is soaking wet and muddied. Andrius quickly goes over to the manhole and looks down.

"The lights are all out down there. Is there a flashlight, handy?"

"Over here, Andrius, by the fire extinguisher, on the wall." Jason replies.

"Thank you." Andrius goes over and climbs down the manhole to the lower compartment. Michael approaches the manhole and leans over to see, what's going on below.

"How is it, Andrius?"

"I can't tell. It is too smoky, down here. Wait a few moments until it clears up a bit."

"How about the air?"

"I don't recommend it for you, my friend. It's pretty bad." Andrius shouts up, from the lower sub deck. He finally reaches the hatch blindly and feels around it.

"Guys, the hatch is twisted out of shape and still hinged, on one side."

Andrius places the flashlight down in a puddle of water, which is draining down, through the partly opened hatch.

Once grabbing the open edge, he slowly peel off, what was left of the hinge, causing a sharp clamor and a squeaking metallic sound, as the hinge gives way and breaks off.

"What's that noise? Are you all right, down there?" Michael shouts out.

A long pause elapses. Michael becomes impatient and rushes over to Jason:

"I need a gas mask, I'm going down there. He must be in trouble."

Then a voice s heard:

"Michael, I'm OK. I just took off the hatch." Andrius finally answers.

Michael rushes back to the manhole. "Andrius, look down the hatch. Can you see anything?"

"Not a thing, but there is some kind of noise down there. It sounds like a windstorm. Michael, I'm going down, further."

"Take the flashlight."

"Sorry, but it seems to have shorted out with something in the puddle."

"I'll get you another."

"Forget it, I can manage."

Andrius lowers himself by grabbing on to a ship's ladder. Reaching further down, he notices that there's some type of diffused light below and a strong wind current blowing, throughout the pump room.

Looking down, he shines his little pocket flashlight and discovers about four feet of water and jet fuel floating, about in the room. He immediately puts out the little flashlight.

"Michael, don't attempt to put on any lights down here, or light any matches, up there. There's plenty of high volatile jet fuel, flowing all over the pump room floor."

"It's Murphy's law. If something is going to possibly go wrong, it will go wrong. The explosion must have severed, some of the fuel lines." Michael assumes.

"No, I don't think so." Andrius replies.

"It's just too much of it. I think, it must have been a mortar blast, because there's a big gaping hole, just above the fuel level and I can see blue sky, about twenty five feet away towards the stern at mid ship."

"You're right, Andrius. Jason is now registering a considerable drop, in air pressure in the cockpit."

"It's very cold down here. Don't attempt to come down."

"I can imagine. Andrius, can you see the electrical panel board?"

"Yes, it's at a distance."

"How about the sequential panel?"

"That too." It's alongside the panel."

"Can you reach them?"

"Surely, but I would have to tread through the water and fuel, to get to them. I don't know how long, I can't survive too long threading through this bone-chilling slug. Wait a minute."

Andrius slowly lowered himself very gently into the murky slimy substance and treads through it very carefully, until he finally reaches, one of the panels.

"How are you doing? Speak to me." Said Michael

"Michael, I'm already here and ready." Andrius yells out.

"Good. Andrius listen to me very closely. A wrong move could be very disastrous. So you will have to be extra careful."

"Don't worry, I will."

"On the sequential controller panel, turn off the top row of switches and the main breaker. Be super extra careful. Try not to snap them off, because they will have a tendency, to slightly ark out in their waterproofed enclosures."

"I will. I will take my good time. I know, what can happen, if I don't."

Andrius taking extreme precaution starts to gradually snap each electric breaker one by one.

Minutes pass. By this time, Michael has paced the deck, almost a hundred times. Once completing the dangerous task, Andrius calls out to Michael, again:

"Michael, the first step is completed, now I'm ready for the next one."

"Very good. Now, on that panel board there're two silver circular keys. Their handles have a nudge that is pointing up. That's their closed position."

"Yes. I see them."

"In order to turn the key knobs, they must be moved to the horizontal position towards you."

"Yes, I already moved them. They're pointing out towards me."

"Good. Now, turn the knobs clockwise to the right and press the large red button located under the raised letters that say: 'Emergency Over-Ride.' Can you see them?"

"Yes, very distinctly." He replies.

"Press them. That should override the controls and start up all the pumps."

"Hold on. Here it goes."

There's a dull flash behind the panel.

"Oh no!" Andrius cries out.

Suddenly, a rumbling noise begins throughout the pump room.

Andrius quickly pulls back from the panel, splashes across the room, scrambles up the ladder, to the small room above and up to the flight deck. He rushes to his flight seat and straps himself down securely.

"Are they pumping, or will we blow up like a sky rocket?"

"Yes. Let's wait and see, how they do." Said Jason.

Andrius sits dripping all over the console with fuel oil, all over him. Uria appears holding a couple of towels and places, all over Andrius. At one point, she hugs Andrius for a few moments.

"Thank you Uria. That felt good."

"I feared that I was going to loose you and never see you, again."

"It was closed. I thought I would blow up with the fuel down there."

"The most important thing now, is that you are safe and sound. Nothing else matters."

"Thanks." Andrius turns around and hugs her in return.

"Andrius come with me and let's get you out of the clothes, O.K. I will seal them in a plastic bag. Wow! They're smelly."

"I know, thanks."

Ten minutes pass. Jason looks at the fuel gauges and checks the fuel level. He verifies that the reserve and the wing tanks are gradually emptying out of the aircraft.

He checks his fuel reserve for the landing approach, to the Island and it's still intact.

Andrius returns to the cockpit wearing a new outfit. He goes over to the hatch and takes a last look down the manhole and discovers much to his dismay that the fuel, in the lower pump room, has not completely drained out. He stands up, throws his hands up in the air and shakes his head.

"I promised myself not to go down there anymore."

"What happen?"

"We'll have to drain off, that stuff, down there. There's still some fuel oil, thrashing about."

"Andrius, there are no drains down there." Michael confesses.

"How about a portable pump?"

"There are none available. All of the pumps are located, in the wing areas and they are not accessible. Unless you are planning to walk, on the wings to get at one."

"Not on your life time."

Andrius goes over to Jason, at the controls.

"Jason, I'm having a brainstorm. What if I were to close this manhole, would it be possible to increase the pressure in the pump room?"

"Yes, why not? But what is your angle, Andrius?"

"I think I may have a solution."

"Well, enlighten me."

"By pressurizing the room below and executing a forty-five degree angular bank, we may solve the problem. It's possible to drain off, the remaining fuel, through the hole, on the side of the aircraft."

"That's a great idea, Andrius. Let's try it." Michael asserts.

"And if this does not work, we will chance the landing, anyway."

"Guess what, gentlemen?" Jason declares.

Michael turns around. "What happened now?"

"No. Nothing happened, but looks ahead, our destination! The Island!"

"That's some beautiful sight to see. It shall be our temporary home." Andrius added.

"We should be landing, in about twenty minutes. That is, if Andrius' idea works out." Jason was pessimistic.

"I'll take bets, starting from now. What are the odds, Andrius?"

"Forget it, Michael. The odds are, in my favor."

"Well, if you win, I will lose and if you lose, I still will lose, because I will never live to collect the winnings. You're right, Andrius, forget it."

Michael goes over to the manhole and bolts it down tight. Jason manipulates the controls and pressurizes the room below. Seconds later, a warning light alarm goes on, showing low pressure, in the pump room.

Jason makes a general announcement to everyone of his intentions and pulls back on the throttle and begins banking the aircraft to one side.

"Hold on, everyone."

Michael leans by the side windshield and observes the fuel and water, spurt out and vaporize in the air stream.

He then sees an ominous object.

"Andrius, we may have a serious problem. Please come here, quick."

"What is it?"

"See those wires hanging out?"

"Yes."

"If they are live, they can possibly ignite the fuel, as it exits out."

"Let's hold our breath, just one more time and its over."

"Yes, it may be all over for everyone, here."

A minute goes by and the vapors slowly disappear as the wires slash up and down.

Andrius goes and opens the manhole and looks down through the hatch and smiles.

"It's a miracle. The fuel is all gone. Even the debris, which was scattered throughout the room."

"Good job done guys. Now let's land this baby. The aircraft will be out of fuel, in eight minutes or so." Michael announces.

"There will be enough to circle the Island, at least once." Jason adds.

"Very good. That should give me enough time, to get out of these clothes and into a fire retardant suit, just in case we have fires." Said Andrius as he turns and walks, into the troop section. "You guys are also welcome to suite up, there are four more suits back there."

Michael returns to his flight seat after putting on of the suits and gets on his radio and calls ahead to the island for landing instructions and local weather conditions.

Jason initiates the final descent and adjusts his approach attitude.

Meanwhile, back in the troop section, Dr. Alvarez stops Andrius, as he comes out, from a small dressing room.

"Mister Andrius, I must speak to you. This will only take, a few seconds of your time, son. Please hear me out."

"But Dr. Alvarez..."

"I need to speak to you. They just informed us, that you have begun the landing approach and there may be a possibility of a crash land? Am I right what I heard?"

"Yes, Doctor, but what's the urgency?"

"Andrius, for medical reasons, I would like to have Dr. Roberts stay back here, when you attempt this landing."

"You mean crash landing, Doctor."

"Oh, oh, yes, crash landing. I beg your pardon."

"Are you worried about his condition?"

"Precisely. Any harsh impact, on his head will cause internal hemorrhaging and I will not be able, to stop it, this time. He will surely die."

"I'm in full agreement, with Doctor Alvarez." Nora intrudes, in the conversation.

"Back here, we can cushion his skull, from any sudden jolt or impacts. How about it, Andrius? Can you convince him?" Nora was worried.

"I'll do my best, but you know how he is?"

"I know him, he's like a stubborn mule but someone has to care for him." Said Nora

"I can't promise anything. You both better take a seat and strap yourselves down, because we'll be landing shortly." Andrius then resumes his way to the cockpit.

Moments later, Andrius is up front, seated alongside Jason, on the controls and turns to him:

"Jason, there are a couple of people back there, who are very concerned about you and the landing."

"They are." Jason answers indifferently.

"Yes. They want you to go back and sit out the crash landing."

"Andrius let me say this. Perhaps you may or may not agree with me, but all along this whole affair, or let's call it, this escapade, I've been playing second fiddle, either to you or to Michael, my cousin, back here.

It's about time, that I contribute my services to this group. All right? I may have been hurt once before, but I feel great, now. I don't want you, or anyone else, to worry about my well being. I'm a big boy, now. Let me prove, to myself, that I'm still a man and I'm able to function, in spite of my physical handicap. OK guys?"

"Cuz Jason, I couldn't say it, any better. Those words are from a very determined individual. I salute you man for your frankness."

"Thank you, Michael." Jason replies.

"Do me a favor, Jason."

"What is it?"

"Please don't mess up. I will not forgive you, this time." Said Michael, shaking his head and making a praying gesture with his hands.

"Don't worry. You will live to get married, cousin. I will be your best man."

"I hope, I hope." Said Michael.

"Let's quit horsing around. Give me the coordinates and the altitude, every two seconds and I will land this bird, on a postage stamp."

"Jason, I think, it would be better for you, to land on the air strip, rather than on the stamp. It may be pretty messy, if you know what I mean."

"Alright. alright. I'm laughing. I get the joke, guys. Ha."

Jason picks up the hand phone and announces throughout the ship for everyone, to tighten his, or her seat belts, and to utilize the pillow for protection, against flying debris, when the jetliner lands.

Michael, now very serious, gives Jason data on the wind's direction and local weather conditions. Andrius drains off, the remaining fuel reserves.

Michael takes a last look at the radarscope and gives Jason the OK for the approach.

"You are good for the landing, cuz." Said Michael

They feel a momentary pulsation, as the jet uses up the last few gallons of jet fuel and begin its frightful, silent dead glide, towards land below.

An eerie sound begins, as the aircraft accelerates faster and faster downwards.

Michael is constantly giving Jason data on the altitude and air speed of the jet. Seconds seemed like minutes, as the jet increases its dead glide.

"Andrius, we have to jettison the jet engines. The jet is not free gliding! We're falling!"

"Tell me, what to do, Jason. I will assist."

"There, on you're left, the two black boxes. Open them and pull the lever out, as far as possible. They are pin detonators."

"Ready."

"Yes. You better get a firm hold on the controls. She will probably pull up." Said Michael

"OK."

"Now."

'Michael, assists Jason with the controls."

"Yes, I'm on it."

A flash followed by a bang on both sides of the ship occurs.

Everyone feels the concussion throughout the aircraft, as the detonators blow the holding pins on the jet engines.

They detach and slowly drift away crashing and exploding down on the sandy rocky shores. They completely disintegrate upon impact.

The mighty aircraft, once relieved of its burden of heavy engines, pulls up then levels itself.

Jason and Michael struggle to keep the nose of the aircraft low, so that it doesn't overshoot the short runway.

"Pull her down gently. Gently! Said Michael A little more, Jason."

"She's rocking and drifting too much, to the right. I'm losing her!" Jason cries out.

"Don't worry. Get that nose down! Lower those flaps! Now, pull the spoilers. Don't worry about those damn trees, Jason."

"Here we go, hold on!" Jason yells.

The mighty jet come crashing through dozen-withered trees and finally rumbles down to the runway, with a spectacular shower of sparks, from the front fuselage impacting, on the crudely built runway.

The tip of the left wing slightly touches the runway and immediately ignites on fire. Large chunks of the wing tip fall off from the intense friction, from the roadway.

The tail next impacts on the runway and it quickly collapses from the enormous pressure and friction created, by the sudden meeting of metal and concrete, at more than two hundred miles per hour.

Tremendous vibrations go out throughout the ship, again, causing all kinds of loose items and equipment stored up in storage bins, to fly about and fall, everywhere.

Some of the men fall out off their harness and slide up the aisles. Those who are seated instantly extend a helping handhold to keep them from sliding further.

Seconds seem like minutes, as the onslaught goes on.

The aircraft suddenly looses some forward advance and travels a different direction by skidding sideways after impacting some object of the runway.

A large chunk of the remaining left wing gives way and quickly disappears below the fuselage into a fire and dust storm created by the aircraft.

The aircraft looses additional momentum by making a semi circular turn and slowly comes to a rest under a cloud of debris, fire and twisted metal.

It miraculously stops short almost at the end, of the runway.

A couple of meters more; the aircraft would have fallen, into a frozen lagoon, where there would be no possible escape, for everyone.

"Jason, Michael rushes over, you did it. That's fantastic!"

"Yes. Yes, I did land it! I really did!"

"Hey, we have to get out. The aircraft is on fire!" Andrius yells aloud.

"Right. I will help the people out from the back, Andrius." Said Michael.

Jason remains motionless, for a few seconds, in his flight seat starring out the cockpit.

"Jason, are you all right?" Andrius approaches him.

"Yes. I'm a little shaken. Where's Nora? I've to get her out."

"Michael went back there for them."

"Andrius lets get out and help put the fires out. There's a lot of priceless navigational equipment in here and I hate to lose it."

"OK. Grab that fire extinguisher there and I will get the other one, in the next compartment." Said Andrius.

Andrius pushes himself out through one of the emergency doors and slides down, onto the left wing. He runs along it, to the mid-section. There, he extinguishes the smoky fire, atop of the crumpled wing section.

Jason gets down to the ground level and runs alongside of the flaming aircraft. He reaches the tail section and tries and successfully opens the rear escape door.

Nora appears.

"Honey jump." Jason catches her and embraces her. They then look up and see Uria and the others.

"OK, one at a time. You can do it."

They successfully bring everyone down safely after deploying the escape ramp.

Flames by now are engulfing almost the whole front section of the aircraft.

Ten other Orgites join Andrius, at fighting the flames around them.

Fire trucks quickly appear from the island and spray fire retardant foam all over the fuselage dowsing out most of the flames. The fire combatants standing on the wing who are fighting the fires also receive a dowsing of foam unintentionally.

An hour later after the fires are completely out, two buses followed by several vehicles arrives to the side of aircraft to provide the group with transportation, to the Island's underground installation. They bring dry clothing and winter gear to prevent exposure to the cold severe weather of the island.

As they drive off with the group, more vehicles from the underground installation arrive to the crash site, to recover the salvageable remains of the aircraft and prepare to bring them, to the installation to be used as raw materials for future projects as required.

Minutes later, at a good distance from the entrance, Andrius meets with one of the installation leaders who's a close and loyal friend. His name is Professor Jarvis, the mathematician.

Professor Jarvis is a short, chubby senior looking man, or better said, an Orgite Being who has come of age. He's a caring type person and always expressing a curious open mind, ready to hear a different point of view, even if he doesn't readily agreed with it, sometimes. He gradually became a father figure, to all the Orgites and has become a good source of inspiration, to anyone that would meets and deals with him.

"Andrius! At last, you are here. As you know, I arrived eight months ago, with a terrible fear, that you might be arrested, at any moment, by the secret police, over there. Your absence would have been a demoralizing factor here, and it would surely have worked against the success and the future, of our small community."

"Not a chance Jarvis but there were moments."

"Come here." Jarvis embraces Andrius and pats him on the back.

"It is good to see you. I rather think, Jarvis, that if you were the one, who failed to show up here, the effect would have been worse, because you portray that wholesome figure, filled with wisdom and age."

"Wisdom, yes! Age, no! My dear Andrius, I may have the physical appearance of a geriatric, but keep in mind my son that I am a wee year younger, than yours truly.

Remember, I'm number three but carrying with a little more wisdom and perfection, but with one disadvantage, I am a little older looking, but way more handsome."

"Jarvis, you're some character." They both laugh and embrace again.

"My son, we are truly glad you are here. I would be lost, without you. Honest."

"Really?"

"Yes, believe me."

"I'm kidding. Jarvis, I feel the same. By the way, I would like to present to you, some of our friends, who probably you have met in the past and who are now helping us, in our quest. They've decided to join us."

"Very well. Lead me to them, my son."

Everyone in the group, upon meeting Jarvis, gradually begins to develop a special liking for this weird looking, fast-talking, and lovable old man.

The bases' crew afterwards, removes the body of Colonel Towers and transfers it to one of the waiting buses.

Once again on their way, the buses and the vehicles drive along a small unpaved road littered by many withered trees and other variety, common to the Island, which were victims of the catastrophe that occurred in the Island, years before.

The Island ever since became desolated and inhospitable to humans, until the Orgites arrived and began cleaning and removing most of the deadly radiation debris that littered throughout the island.

Most of the deadly radioactive compositions were dumped miles out at sea and some, with lesser concentrations, were deposit to swampy regions and throughout the coastline, of the Island, as a tactical move.

The vehicles turn off the road and drive down through a long and narrow concrete ramp, which was carved into the side of the mountain that approaches a deep underground tunnel leading further down approximately thirty-five meters.

Jarvis acting as a tour guide points out, that the explosive force at the top of the complex, failed to damage little of the underground structures that surround the huge fusion research laboratory, located deep, in its center.

"Professor Jarvis, Said Nora, how are you producing the electrical power, to run this complex installation?"

"We have an auxiliary generating plant, on the other side of the Island, which utilizes natural ocean currents, to produce the required power that is needed for the moment."

"Thank you, Sir. I thought that it was being produced, by fossil fuels."

"Oh, no, my dear. That is a commodity here, which is very short handed. But we have fuel cells to sustain us, for a while, in case of an emergency. We dare not use the International Submarine Electrical Grid, for fear of alerting the authorities."

"I understand Professor, thank you, again." She answers.

"Well, thanks to Andrius, we hope to solve our electrical need requirements, very soon."

"Jarvis, I hope that you have been doing your homework, lately."

"Yes, Andrius. Those four problems, that you gave me to ponder months ago, must be better clarified. I have solutions but I also have questions of my own and theories, that will take at least a week of dialogue with you, in order to correlate them effectively."

"We have plenty of time, for that. I'm sure that you did them well." Andrius surmises.

"Yes, I did. I can't wait to show you. By the way, provisions have been made to store parts of your aircraft, in area sector 4D."

"Alright, that sounds good to me."

"You're storing the jet transport, down here?" Asked Nora

"Yes. It will be taken apart, as soon as possible and brought here, so we don't leave any traces that any aircraft ever landed on this island."

"You do intent to rebuild it again, Andrius, I guess." Nora again was curious

"No, I'm afraid not. We just don't have the fuel supply capacity for it, but we will be working on an alternate method of travel."

The vehicles come to a stop, in front of a large round entrance, in the cavern. A solid heavy looking circular metallic door, with interior hinges, slowly opens out and a mechanical ramp from within starts moving out from the interior of the chamber entrance and travels down to the floor, and stops.

The group takes a few seconds, to unload from the buses and walk up the ramp into a large entry room. Inside, they see other Orgites personnel working about and preparing for their arrival, by setting up and assigning the living quarters.

The Colonel's body is at last brought in and waits to be assign temporary quarters, like everyone else.

"This place looks like a small train terminal. Who built it, Andrius?" Asked Nora

"I believe that a good portion of it was built by American construction companies and German engineers."

"I see. For a large place like this, they keep it meticulously clean."

"Yes, it is. They have almost the same sanitary restrictions, which we have back at the Research Center, in New York." Andrius Added.

"Andrius, where did they place the Colonel's body?" Nora asked.

"It's over there, by the ramp." He shows her.

"What are the plans, for the Colonel's body?"

"Uria wants him to be buried tomorrow in the same manner by which was performed for Omar."

"I was going to recommend that, too." Nora added.

"Uria wants the services, to be done, around midday."

"Andrius, I never got to see the Colonel's body. Was it badly, disfigured?"

"No, not too much. Come here. I will show you."

They both approach a long metallic cylinder case and have one of the Orgite soldiers' open it by removing several seals around it.

Nora, instinctively, out of fear of looking at death, grabs Andrius' arm, for moral support, and looks into the metallic cylinder.

"Andrius, there's not a mark on him. My gosh, he's awfully soiled up."

"That was from the heavy smoke, of the burning vehicles, on the airfield. You see here, where his collar is torn apart on the jacket and also here. Those are probably the two fatal bullet wounds."

"Yes." She response.

"This is the area, where most of the bullets impacted. These two impacts came from the large caliber projectiles fired from the two jets."

"But where are the other penetrations, on his body? I don't see them."

"Nora, the Orgite body, alive or dead, has the capability of absorbing and healing itself from puncture or foreign bodies that invades it."

"That's phenomenal but the clothing bears witness to the impacts." She said.

"The only area, where there is little self-healing, is the central nervous system, here in the back region. Although the surface area has healed remarkably but damage internally hasn't. Humans by far, are more advanced than Orgites in that respect and to a certain extent. Your nervous system still functions after a sever life threatening injury and may heal itself with time, but we unfortunately, do not have that capability."

"I didn't know that. It must have been the field of study that the Professor knew little about."

"Yes. This is the area on his neck, where he was hit and what, unfortunately killed the Colonel."

Jason comes over and approaches them.

"Andrius, we have been assigned quarters. They are in level 'B' above the women's."

"Alright Jason thanks." He replies.

"Honey, are you all right? You look a little pale."

"I'm a little tired but come here and look at the Colonel's body."

"Yes, I did do a quick examination of the body before it was taken out of the aircraft. Its unfortunate what happened to him."

Meanwhile, as they talked, Nora takes a quick glance at the Colonel and notices a slight movement, of his hand. She turns to Andrius.

"You may not believe me but I thought, I've just seen the Colonel's hand move slightly."

"Nora, that's normal, said Jason, at times, in some situations a cadaver might turn completely around on a table, during rigor-mortis. That's due to muscle tension and internal pressures, which a body is subjected to, and where it initially expired.

So you may see slight movements, as muscles contract or relax."

"I know those things, Jason. You've forgotten that I'm also, a doctor. What I saw was something else…Oh! He did it again!" She said excitedly.

"Calm down, Nora, don't be so jumpy. You're wishing he was alive again."

"No I wasn't, Jason. You don't know me. I don't easily give into fantasies of the sort. I saw his hand move and it wasn't a twitch."

"You're freaking me out, Nora. My hairs on my back are standing up…. As I was saying…"

"Good God! She screams out. He moved his head." She rushes over to the Colonel's side and places both of her hands on his neck area.

"He's alive! Come here, he's alive! Feel for yourself. The Colonel is alive!"

Andrius and Jason rush over to Nora.

"Impossible, Said Jason, He can't be alive. Can you see that the body is constricted and well into rigor-mortis?"

"Come here and feel him. She demands. I'm not crazy, feel the pressure, here!" Jason leans down over the Colonel's body. He places his hands and squeezes both sides of the neck, to see if there are any muscle responses.

"I can't believe this, but I'm getting a reaction. It looks, like the Colonel has refused to die."

"Yes. Yes, the Colonel is alive! Thank God, for answering my prayers." Said Jenny, who suddenly appears making the sign of the cross.

"Quick, he needs stimuli, so he can be revived."

Jason stands up and waves to Dr. Alvarez to come over.

Minutes later, the Colonel's eyes slowly open and begins to inhale, only after long efforts by Jason and Dr. Alvarez. After awhile, his eyes maintain themselves open. Jason stops the infusion of the stimuli.

"Hey Colonel, welcome back, to the living." Jason said, while looking down at him.

"How do you feel my friend?" Dr. Alvarez was elated.

The Colonel raises his arm and gestures with his thumb, OK.

"You're looking great, Colonel." Nora said with tears, in her eyes.

"Can you speak?"

"The Colonel motions with his hands only and tries to force himself a bit."

"Good Colonel."

"I'm feeling a little better, now. I was semi-conscious for the past six hours. When shot, I was paralyzed instantly. My whole self went numbed and stiff. I could hardly breathe due to spasms in my throat passage. I was in and out of the state of consciousness for long periods of time."

"You'll be all right, in a couple of hours." Jason asserts.

"He's some peculiar man. How was he able to survive, from those bullet wounds?" Dr. Alvarez asked, very curiously.

"It's a miracle." Said Jason.

"Let's take him to his quarters, so he can rest." Said Nora.

"Wait a moment, please. Andrius, what exactly happened to me, out there?"

"Well, Colonel, you were manning a twin 50 caliber machine gun, at the tail section of the aircraft. You got shot by two enemy jets just before we departed from San Augustine."

"Where are we, now?" The Colonel asks, somewhat confused.

"You are at the Island. We landed, about an hour ago."

"Good to hear that. How about my men?"

"Unfortunately, we lost almost half of them, in that last battle. I'm sorry, Colonel. We will return when you get better and give all of them a proper and honorable burial."

"Thank you, Andrius."

"It was a horrific bloody scene, Colonel Towers. It was most unfortunate, that it happened." Said Dr. Alvarez.

"I expected casualties, but not this many. If I could only have been there…"

"Your men fought exemplary and they gave their lives up honorably. They preferred it this way!"

"They wished that a few of us escape and prosper, rather than trying to save all and failing, at the attempt. They literally sacrificed themselves for us." Said Doctor Alvarez.

"I must go afterwards and talk to each one of them and give them my personal thanks for their effort and support."

"In due time, Sir."

"Colonel, I owe you my personal thanks for your heroic attempt at rescuing my nurse and daughter from those evil men that forcibly took them."

"The actual merits should go to Michael and my soldiers that sacrificed their lives in this heroic attempt."

"Indeed. Those soldiers will be remembered in my prayers for the rest of my life."

"Thank you Dr. Alvarez for your kind acknowledgement."

Afterwards, the group proceeds to their assigned quarters and rest from the day's ordeal.

CHAPTER XI

Sometimes later, at McGuire Air Force Base in New Jersey, there's a knock, on Colonel Evans' door.

"Colonel Charles R. Evans?"

"Yes, can I help you?" He responds while opening the door.

"Yes, Colonel. My name is Karl Daggard; I'm a security officer for the CSA. I just flew up from Washington. I need to speak with you most urgently."

Daggard shows the Colonel his identification card. After he verifies his other credentials, Colonel Evans ushers him in and closes the door.

Another agent, who accompanied Daggard, stood outside the door and waited.

"Colonel Evans, what I'm about to talk to you, in a few seconds, is strictly confidential and top secret."

"Yes Sir, I understand."

"Military intelligence has referred this incident, to the attention of the President and he in turn, has ordered me, to get to the bottom of it."

"Mister Daggard, you have my full cooperation." The Colonel assures him

"Colonel, thirty four hours ago, one of our South Atlantic missile defense satellites, detected and recorded, a detonation of two low yields nuclear devices, off the coast of South America."

"It did, Sir?"

"Yes. It occurred Wednesday approximately at 1600 hours over the Pacific. Let me not beat around the bush, Colonel. Your recognizance aircraft bomber is missing two nuclear warheads."

"Yes, you are correct, Sir." Colonel Evans responded in a low voice.

"You should know that no military officer, has the authority, to launch or detonate any nuclear device or devices, no matter what the size, or what's situation, that may be warranting such actions, without the consent and the approval, of the President of the United States. Colonel, you know that this grounds for your immediate arrest and court-martial."

"I know, Sir." He answers quickly this time.

"Who issued you the damned authority, to launch those missiles? Tell me, now!"

"No one, Sir. It was of my own doing. I accept full responsibility for my actions, Sir."

"This had to be a joint concerted effort among all the officers in your bomber group. No one person alone is capable of launching, a nuclear device. You and your officers must have plotted this incident, to discredit the United States. Who do you really work for? Are you a supporter for the Middle Eastern movement for world domination?"

"No way, Mister Daggard. Like I said, Sir. It was all my own doing."

"You solely armed those missiles and launched them? Come on, Colonel."

"No, Sir. You know that would be impossible. I did get help, I persuaded them after personally signing an affidavit absorbing all of them from all responsibility for my decision to launch the two nuclear missiles."

"This was an insane move on your part. Do you know that this could have caused a nuclear confrontation, between the Unites States and the other super powers?"

"Yes, Sir. But no one knew that we were there."

"I know. I know. We only found out through our system of routine check and balances. We count and verify all the nukes every thirty minutes by computers and if one is missing or is misplaced; all hell breaks out, in the Pentagon and in the Defense Office Building, until there's an accounting for it. And it did. That's why I'm here."

"Sir, I'm your man. I had my men bypass all the safeties and firewalls and we got control."

"Colonel, you're under arrest, and restricted to your room. You're to be held incommunicado for six months, and be relocated to permanent incarceration at a military facility in the mid-west until we further investigate and safeguard this, from ever happening again."

"Sir, don't you wish to know why I did it?"

"I'll get to that, next. But what's more important is that this can happen again and we don't have any control, over it."

"Mister Daggard, I did it to save the lives of our American soldiers."

"Almost starting a nuclear war? That's your version of saving American lives?"

"No, Sir."

"Well Colonel, what's your reason? What lives?" He demanded.

"A U.S. Marine Troop carrier was about to be attacked, by two Migs, Sir."

"Did the Troop Carrier have its' own air cover?"

"No, Sir, they were completely alone. We were listening to their radio transmissions for a couple of hours, before we actually involved ourselves."

"Why didn't you call for help?"

"We couldn't, Sir. We were on a special reconnaissance mission, for the Pentagon."

"So you took the initiative to intercept and destroy the Migs, right?"

"Yes, Sir."

"Which marine group was that?"

"I don't know, Sir, but a closed military friend of mine, was in command of the aircraft."

"You will probably, needs his testimony to substantiate your actions, at your Court Martial hearing, if there ever is one. This incident needs to be kept classified because if this ever gets out, it will have international repercussions for a long time."

"I'm not worried Sir, Colonel Towers will come through, on my behalf."

"Did you just mention Colonel Russell Towers?" Daggard was shocked

"Yes, Sir?"

"But he is Air Force."

"Yes Sir, that's who, I helped."

"I was told that he was killed a few days ago off the coast of Trinidad, by the hurricane that devastated Panama."

"Mister Daggard, I don't quite understand."

"He's still alive and Andrius, too, I presume." He said to himself.

"Mister Daggard, you must forgive me, but I've been airborne, for the last forty hours. Can you please tell me, what's going on?"

"Colonel Tower is wanted by a special investigative committee, headed by the President. He's charged with subversion and high treason."

"The Colonel is no traitor, Sir. I've known him a longtime and I know that he doesn't share that sort of philosophy."

"Your Colonel friend is an Orgite."

"What the hell is that?"

"The Colonel is not human like you and I, but…"

"Come on. You're kidding. I've known him for years and he's a heck, of a nice guy. Sorry Mister Daggard. You're wrong. You're accusing the wrong man."

"Colonel Evans, it's a long story and by the way, this conversation is also classified. I've been after his group for months and I thought it all ended with that crash off Trinidad, but it seems that I'll be at it, again."

"Mister Daggard, I'm still totally confused, about the whole thing."

"Never mind, forget this conversation ever happened."

"Yes, Sir."

"Do you have the bomber's flight recorder?"

"Yes, Sir. I think flight operations can help you with that."

"I'm trying to find out in what direction, they might have taken."

"I could tell you, that."

"Well?"

"With the massive fuel load, that those aircraft can hold, they can be practically any place on earth, by now."

"We'll get them. I can assure you of that."

"Mister Daggard, I wish you, all the luck in the world. You'll need it."

"Colonel, as I said before. Not a word to anyone about this, or any of the other subjects, that we touched upon, over here. If you do it will influence your prison time."

"Yes Sir, you have my word."

"By the way. What was the name of the airfield that they took off from?"

"It was near a coastal city called San Augustine by the border near the country of Ecuador. It's located on the Southwest Coast of South America."

"Thank you."

Daggard rushes off, to his waiting car and immediately goes on the radiophone, with the President, after a few minutes of delay, due to more urgent Presidential matters.

"Good day Mr. President."

"Good day to you Mr. Daggered. What do you have for me today."

"Mister President, I have good and bad news for you, today."

"Well, Mister Daggard, I have a special sub-committee, waiting for me. Make it quick."

"Yes, Sir. That problem with the nuclear weapons deployed without your authority has been resolved, but another worse problem, has resurfaced."

"I hope it's not too serious. Can you speak freely?"

"Yes, Sir."

"Well, then, tell me." The President insists.

"Sir, Andrius and his group, are still alive, somewhere."

"Are you sure about that?"

"Yes, Sir, positively."

"You previously assured me, that they were all killed in that East coast hurricane."

"Yes, Sir, I did, but the Navy didn't find any traces of the second aircraft, which was supposed, to have crashed, in the same area of seas."

"But the radar confirmed a crash."

"Probably, they purposely made it look that way, Sir." He assumes

"Well, Daggard, you're back, on the case, again. I will give you, all the resources as required of the Navy to aid you, in tracking them down."

"Yes, Sir, and thank you."

"Daggard, perhaps you may be interested in this, military intelligence has just informed me, that we're missing at least one hundred and seventy-five aircraft. I don't know if this is related somehow, to Mister Andrius and his group."

"Sir, were they military?"

"Yes and some civilian ones, too."

"What type? I can't believe it."

"They range from medium sized aircraft of all types and some interceptors, including the jumbo military troop carrier, that's manned by Colonel Towers."

"I assume that they are fully armed."

"They're armed with our latest equipment, but no nukes. This is why I've placed all military bases on orange alert, here and abroad."

"But Sir. I'm at McGuire Air Force Base. With that order, I won't be able to leave the base."

"Don't worry. I'll alert General Cochrane of your whereabouts. He will send you an escort vehicle, to see you out safely, off the Base."

"Thank you, Sir. But why the strict alert?"

"I'm taking no chances, with this group. They may be crazy enough to use those aircraft and attack vital and critical areas of the United States."

"Sir, I will need a priority search and arrest or if need be kill orders from you, in order to apprehend these felons, before it's too late."

"I will confer with our overseas bases and have all of the military codes and frequencies changed, for security reasons and issue new guidelines, for all of them."

"That's great, Sir. In case they try to infiltrate our air space using our own aircraft, we will shoot them down like flies."

"Mister Daggard, I want you here, in my office, tonight."

"Yes, Sir. I'll bring a survey map, showing the possible whereabouts of the Orgites."

"Very well, don't take long."

"I won't, Sir."

CHAPTER XII

It is late November, and the greatest sea, land and air priority search ever made, has now been in progress for a month and so far, with no success.

Far away lands such as, the Northern Polar Regions and such far away places as the Himalayas, have not been overlooked, by this worldwide search. Weather and spy satellites, have also failed to detect and identify any of the suspicious renegade aircraft in question, in the skies, over the free world.

Due to the great emphasis that the United States has placed on this search, leaders of the Communist World and other world leaders also interested in this matter have joined in concert on the search, but with more of an ulterior approach.

The President and the Navy Department decide to establish an exploratory mission, by atomic submarine, in search of the Orgites, in the South Atlantic and elect Karl Daggard to head this mission. Daggard is summoned to the Oval office, to receive final briefings on the trip.

"Mister President, good afternoon."

"Come in, Karl." The President stands up and ushers him in.

"First of all, Mister President, I must congratulate you on your successful re-election. It was a true land slide, so to speak." He shakes his hand and they both sit down.

"I'm sorry, that I could not be here, for the celebration, but as you know, duty calls."

"Thank you, Daggard. I understand. Well, when are you scheduled to leave?"

"We'll be leaving from New London on Thursday, Sir."

"What region are you searching now?' He asked.

"I thought you knew, Sir."

"Yes, I have a copy of your orders, but I haven't had any time to go over them. I hope you will forgive me, Daggard. You do understand, I have a very hectic life here, I'm presently deeply engrossed with the problems of our Nations' and of the world."

"I understand, Sir. Anyway, I'll be searching two probable areas.

One is that notorious Devil's Triangle, not the one in the Caribbean area but the one in the far Pacific near Japan and the other one is, the lower South American Cape Region area."

"Looks like you have your hands full with the expedition. I wish you success in your venture."

The President then rises and walks to a wall safe and opens it. He takes out a black leather case and hands it over, to Karl Daggard.

"Tell me, Daggard. How can these people vanish into thin air like this, and leave no possible trace. It confounds me. Where do you think, they have gone to?"

"I can't imagine, Sir, but I think that our Russian friends may have them already and all these maneuvers, which they're doing in concert, is just a smoke screen, to throw us off."

"That may very well be, but I have my sources, and they say that their search is really authentic. Sources also informed me that they're also spending millions on this venture, like us."

"Oh, yes. They've been keeping close tabs, on our search and recovery ships."

"I'm afraid, if we make a sudden move and apprehend the Orgites, they'll try to intervene and attempt to rescue them, from us."

"That will be considered as an act of piracy, it's not acceptable."

"Well, most likely, we'll be in international waters and it can be expected."

"On the other hand, Mister President, we would do the same if the opportunity arises and in the process we could eliminate all traces of the intervention. If you know, what I mean, Sir."

"Daggard, I will have none of that. Those are dirty tactics that can easily involve us in a possible international conflict, with the Russians or whoever they may be."

"Sir, I'm not saying that this will happen, but if the situation warrants, we must take advantage of it. I would strongly recommend this action, for the very reason that, if the Russians or any other rogue nation manages to get their hands on the process of creating these Orgites beings, I feel sorry for the free world."

"I can't allow that to happen. I'm sorry Daggard, but no. We just have to make sure that we apprehend them before anyone does. That's why I've decided to engage you on this mission."

"Mister President, would you rather chance a small skirmish with any rogue nation now, or face millions of these Orgites later? We're no match, Sir."

"Don't worry, Professor Donnelly will provide us with sufficient numbers, to upset any gains that anyone can produce."

"Mister President, you must be kidding. I interviewed the Professor some days ago, and in my opinion, I think he is on the verge of senility. Other than him, the only one, who knows the process is Dr. Roberts and the tall one, named Andrius."

"Daggard, in that light, you must apprehend them, before any other nation does."

"At all costs, if need be, Sir?"

"We'll see. We'll take one day at a time and modify your orders accordingly as the situations warrant it, alright?"

"Thank you, Sir." Daggard answers somewhat uplifted.

"Well Mister Daggard, I'll entrust you with this mission and I expect some success. Execute the mission without complications, all right. No more embarrassments."

"Yes, Sir. I'll do my best. You can count on me."

"No Sir, you will do your utmost!" The President affirmed.

"Yes, Sir."

"Good hunting, Daggard." Said the President as he escorts him out of the door.

Once the President returns to his desk, the Secretary of State enters through a side door and sits in front of his desk.

"How did it go, Sir?"

"Just as we planned. That sea mission should entertain Mister Daggard for several months out, in the South Pacific. There he will surely not get in trouble and embarrass this administration. He'll only deal with penguins and polo bears."

"That's very funny, Sir, please stop, you're making me laugh."

"Daggard is no joke. I must do this; he has some dangerous ideas that can possibly involve us in a probable conflict with China or the Russians. This mission will keep him out of harms way and will relieve me off some of my sleepless nights."

"Good, I don't blame you, Sir"

The Island:

It's late March, and harsh Arctic winds begin to increase to cold and steady air streams, familiar to the small volcanic island, during early winter months.

It's morning and a normal workday, at the subterranean complex. Jarvis, the mathematician, has been up and working before dawn.

Andrius and other Orgites join him, at a damaged section of a particle accelerator machine that ruptured many years before and need some repair.

Andrius walks around inspecting the accelerator, as Jarvis initiates a small tour of Orgite newcomers and begins a descriptive analysis of the machine, to all who are present:

"This machine is the only one of its type and it stands alone, in the center of this deep complex, it measures approximately 250 feet in diameter, comparable to a typical particle accelerator, normally known as a cyclotron.

The Russians and the German have modified it some time ago to function slightly different from its intended use. Instead of the standard highly polished aluminum tubing, normally used as a conveying path for nuclear particles, the tube construction is now made up of a combination of glass and high density, polyvinyl material. A pipe of the same material rises from the top of the machine and terminates, high above the structure.

Attached to the circular pathways of the machine are electro magnetic rings, segmenting the surface of this translucent pipe, every three feet. Each of these rings contains massive braids of copper windings, connected to an electrical power source, suspended high above us hermetically sealed in a room.

At the upper level of the complex, is another series of electronic components, whose only function is to heat up certain elements, such as helium and die tritium to temperature levels, higher than those found, on the surface of the Sun.

In the lower section, the machine creates a very unstable future element, if when harnessed correctly; it will possess the potential, of limitless power. This element is initially created at a great energy cost and is known, in the scientific world, as super plasma.

To date, no country, in the world has been able to successfully contain this element, within a fusion reaction, no more, than a millionth, of a second. There's no containment device, yet invented, which is capable of holding the plasma, intact. Even the densest metal structure or the finest refractory that man can ever conceive is not able to sustain this potential energy source.

The required heat source to energize the process is supplied by thermal plant, located in the upper level of the plant.

The whole system is controlled and sustained at a safety level by ten giant 500-horse power pumps that circulate closed to a million tons of pure refrigerant liquid and seawater, through the inner core. It literally acts as a safeguard in preventing a melt down of the massive steel and concrete reinforced columns, which supports the complex.

In addition to this, twenty giant seawater-circulating pumps discharge the super heated spent water, into an underwater deep trench, located several miles offshore that absorbs the spent heat, that is dispersed from the thermo induction coils. The spent water mixes with an underground subzero temperature river current, which has affected the island's environmental conditions for ions."

"Interesting." Andrius is amazed, as he joins the group.

"Scientists, at the time of construction, estimated that after the spent water is discharged there would be a five to eight degree temperature rise, in the frigid seawater temperature around the island.

Records showed that most environmentalists agreed that it would be an improvement to the geological and environmental conditions, of the island. While others, on the other hand, predicted an ecological disaster, for the local marine life for years to come.

The environmental disaster never materialized, even after the plant was in operation and tests were being performed for some years."

"Professor Jarvis, where did the scientists get this abundant power to do these lavish experiments?"

"The source of the power needed came from the International Electrical Power Grid. Special permits were issued and adjustments to the power grid were modified assuring a constant supply of electrical power to all nearby countries.

As Professor Jarvis continued his lecture, a personnel elevator located, at the far level of the fusion chamber level opens. Uria appears, and joins Andrius. They both walk back to the group being lectured as Jarvis finishes his lecture at the machine.

"Good morning, Professor Jarvis."

"Good morning, Ms Uria. I trust you all had a restful night."

"Yes I did, and a well deserved one."

Jarvis turns to Andrius.

"I have that data printout that you requested yesterday, on the power demands of the accelerator and the other equipment, which you are proposing."

Jarvis hands over the papers. Andrius quickly reviews the data and returns them to him.

"Well, there you have it. What do you think Jarvis? Will it work?"

"You want my honest opinion, Andrius?"

"Well, let's have it, that's why I asked."

"You don't have the available power, for the dual operation. On paper it looks good but."

"How about the fossil fuel power plant, on the other side of the Island?"

"Perhaps, you may have some capacity there, to run all your pumps and the other systems in the complex, but I doubt that you have the combined capacity, to operate the cooling equipment and the new control devices, on the fusion machine. Anyway, that fossil fuel plant is not good for us anymore; it is running very low on fuel."

"Can you use the fuel, from all the aircraft?"

"No. That's only temporary. We need a continuous source of supply. We don't have that capability, unless we discover oil on this island and refine it for that purpose."

"Then what do I need?"

"You need a nuclear power plant, with the capacity to light up a city of about five to ten million people. We are talking GIGO watts and not mega watts."

"But how did they operate this equipment, before?"

"Equipment room records, that were found, state that the majority of the experiments on fusion were made fully with the power grid system."

"Is there such a grid in this area, this far south?"

"Yes. There's a standard domestic grid but this one is special. It's designed to carry a greater more capacity. The plans designate the location of the grid to be about a quarter of a mile offshore. To be exact, the grid is located right off the western tip of the island.

Oh, yes gentlemen, there's a power transfer station, located on the landside and there's no need for anyone to wet their feet incase we need to get access to It."

"Thank you, Jarvis. We will need the power grid for the other projects that I have scheduled for May and June."

"That much power?" Uria was concerned.

"Yes, I'll need the combined power of the fossil fuel and the grid, if the fusion generator fails to function, as planned." Said Jarvis

"We can perform some experiments, with the other smaller accelerator now, provided that all power is cut from the complex and we can utilize some power from the grid without causing any attention, to the power center located near Amazonia in Brazil."

"Think of it, Andrius if your theory works and the machine functions, as predicted; we will have all the unlimited power required to design and build the space crafts."

"I'm sure, that it will work. It has to, our future will depend on it."

Nora and Jason appear.

"Good morning everyone!" Said Nora.

"Oh, we didn't see you approach. Good morning Nora and Jason." Uria greets them.

"I'm glad that we're all together. Andrius, I have a feeling that Dr. Alvarez may be wanting to return to San Augustine, very soon." Jason declares.

"How about his daughter, Jenny?"

"Jenny is totally immersed with Michael and I doubt that she would ever want to be separated from him." Nora confesses.

"And Mrs. Mason shares the same feeling, as the Doctor, I gather?" Andrius added.

"They both are very devoted to their profession. I feel that they're being stifled out here, cut off from humanity and all its problems."

"I do realize this, Nora. I'm sorry that it turned out to be this way. I will assure you, the moment that we're able to provide them with transportation; I personally will return them to San Augustine and provide assistance to reconstruct the hospital and provide them security."

"That's very noble of you, Andrius, thank you." Nora pauses, then as if recalling something in mind.

"By the way Andrius, the other day, I saw the plans for your flying machine."

"Ah, you did. Who showed them to you?"

"Who else, Jason."

"I trust you were impressed?"

"Very much. One curious note, Andrius, I noticed that it does not have jets or rockets, as a propelling device. How does that work? Can you explain it to me in simple terms?"

"Yes, Nora. It partially works, on simple kinetic energy. This energy will propel it to velocities, beyond inconceivable speeds, similar to sailing ships of old."

"You're talking over my head again, Andrius."

"I'm sorry. The vehicle will simply fly, utilizing the natural forces that circulates throughout this Universe."

"Is this force magnetic or ionic?"

"Neither. The force is sub-atomic, in nature. It's comprised of small particles, similar to hydrogen atoms.

In layman's language, the force is called 'Solar Winds'. You may recall many years ago, when NASA landed on the moon; they brought with them experiments to test the capability of solar wind, as a propellant. They were going to develop its' use for future space travels but due to funding and lack of technology, at that time, they never took the next step to fully develop it but we eventually did. I ran with the concept and developed some theories and applications."

"Yes, I remember. While I was in England working on my Doctorate, Jason wrote to me about the research and its progress but never updated me on its final development."

"Well, at that time Professor Donnelly developed a theory how these particles may contribute to the aging process, in nature. Jason is also familiarized with the report."

"Well, yes, said Jason. Professor Donnelly theorized that if humans were to shield themselves from the constant exposure of these particles, there's a strong possibility that human life spans can be extended, perhaps, beyond a hundred years or more. People may be able to live longer than anyone can imagine."

"Is that possible, Andrius?" Nora asked.

"No, I'm afraid not, Said Jason. We experimented intensively for several years with all types of shields, some magnetic and other types that were reflective, and what not. They all were unsuccessful.

It was next to impossible to design a shield that would be impregnable enough, to resist these finite particles."

"Nora, there is presently no material on earth, that can resist this type of particle exposure. These particles traverse the earth day and night. We noticed that they're deviations of the particle, only at the core of the earth.

The deviations are not caused by the Earth's magnetic core. There is something in the core there that is causing some type of resistance to them. We suspect it has to do with mass pressure and compression." Said Jarvis.

"Andrius may have the theoretical solution." Jason added.

"Then why are we here, wasting time, hoping to fix this machine?" she asks

"My dear, this machine, if engineered correctly, will provide us with the power to transform a simple shield, into a perpetual motion engine."

"May I inquire? What is this simple shielding element that you are all talking about?"

"Nora, it is found abundantly throughout the earth and I imagine, elsewhere in the Universe." Said Jarvis.

"Nora, it is presently shielding your sensitive skin, from the destructive rays of cobalt, stored below us." Said Jason.

"I can't imagine what it can be. Water? Tell me."

"It's plain lead, Nora." Said Jason

"I thought of it, but never associated it, as being a simple element."

"But after it is refined and its' molecular structure is altered to our specifications, the new hybrid element reconfigured, will be called Plomutite." Said Jarvis

"Jarvis already calculated the level of refinement and the power needed to achieve it. We estimate it will be in the neighborhood of over four GIGO-Watts, of electrical power."

"Andrius that's enough to light up several cities like Las Vegas."

"It requires much more than that." Said Jarvis

"So, that's why, we need this machine." Said Nora

"Precisely, its potential power is limitless, if it works as we propose."

"But if other countries have tried and failed, at making these fusion machines work, how can you?" Asks Nora.

"Then she asks, why us. And we tell her that we're the best, of the best. We have triumphed over those who have failed. Did we not create the future species of mankind?" asks Jason.

"I must confess that you did and I congratulate you and Professor Donnelly for it and Andrius for refining the process." Said Nora.

"So why do you doubt us?"

"I thought you were good with biology but physics may not be your forte." Nora confesses.

"Nora, we're physicists and scientists and we deal with the unknown. Problems do come up at times and we consult and pick each other's brain till a near solution is found. We work as a team, like a well-oiled machine."

"Sorry guys, my fault. I do realize that, I apologies."

"No need to do that, we love you anyway. Getting back to the research on cold-fusion generation, the researchers approach to the problem of controlling the plasma was purely academic. They failed to apply a simple solution. We instead installed additional electro-magnetic controllers, which will simultaneously distribute and converge the plasma, at pre-determined points, along the path of the plasma.

Academia never thought about this. They only converged it at one point hoping to maintain a reaction and this was their undermining error. We in turn will do it at various points, creating a so-called simultaneous chain reaction.

This can be accomplished by rotating each of the electro magnets, counter-clockwise to each other, at various increments." Said Jarvis.

"That's right. It would be like ringing a wet cloth. You merely ring out the excited electrons by rotating each end, in an opposite direction. How clever."

"Did I not tell you, that our approach to the problem would be simple?"

"When do you think, it will be ready for testing?" Nora asks.

"We'll be through repairing this section, in a day or two, but I will have to install the additional two dozen Electro-magnets, along the pathway. I would say it might take a few weeks, the most."

"Where are you getting the material for all of this construction, Andrius?"

"We have plenty of spare parts and if we cannot find what we need, we can always make it ourselves. There are plenty of raw materials stored from the aircraft that were flown in. We have a bone yard of material to pick from and what was originally stored here."

"I would like to join the group and help, Andrius. Can I?" Asked Nora

"You can assist Uria, to set up our second project, after this is set forth."

"What other surprises, do you have up your sleeve, Professor Jarvis?" She asks.

"Another rewrite of the natural laws, my dear, it is called gravity repulsion."

"Oh! Here we go again."

"Let me explain, this one." Said Professor Jarvis.

"I'm ready."

"Andrius' vehicle will operate with two propulsion systems.

One is a linear motion solar windshield, which we already talked about, and the other, is a gravity repulsion device, installed, at the bottom section of the vehicle.

This device, will function using the laws of Physics, but in a reverse order. Let me clarify this because I'm receiving that look again.

In Physics, structures having larger masses, have the tendency, to attract smaller masses to its' center. We all know this, as Gravity or the Absolute Law of Force."

"Yes, that was Space Physics 101.1."

"O.K, All mass has a force. By suspending two circular metal shields above each other and installing on each of their surfaces, a series of insulated copper windings, in circular patterns; we can postulate that gravity can be reversed by rapidly alternating the current of each of the circular windings about a million cycles per second.

We then rotate the shields, in opposite directions, at a certain revolutions.

Pulsating magnetic lines will cause an imbalance in the atom molecule by disrupting and transposing the orbits of the proton in the nuclei and thus we change the overall structure of the atom to function negatively. The degree of disruption in the nuclei will occur as long as the frequency and pulsations are steadily maintained. We predict that a phenomenon of reverse gravity will occur and we've named it, the Negative Mass Impulse."

"So the structure having the largest mass, namely the Earth, will repel the new hybrid element, away from its center because the molecular properties of the element has changed and are no longer subjected to attraction or gravity." Said Nora.

"Precisely, you catch on quick, Nora. That is what will launch the vehicle into the outer regions of the earth's surface, or as required. By gradually decreasing the revolutions and the power to the electro windings, the vehicle will gently return to the surface of the earth."

"It will simply operate just like an elevator." She added.

"Right, and the horizontal movement of the vehicle, will be achieved by utilizing the effect of the solar winds panels, to propel it in any horizontal and vertical direction."

"Won't you have to learn how to navigate, with this new concept of space travel?"

"Eventually, but we will leave it to the global positioning satellite receiver, that Jason is installing, as primary guidance system."

"It's very fascinating; I can't wait to see it, after you build it." Nora then turns to Uria."

"I'm ready, Uria."

"Thanks."

"This way, Nora." She ushers her on.

Both women walk off and board an elevator, which takes them to the upper level of the complex. While en route, Nora turns to Uria.

"I overheard that Andrius gave orders to build defense fortifications around the Island."

"Yes he did and it was already in progress when we arrived but he later changed his mind and told me that he rather build the launch sites for the vehicles, instead. They will be our only means of escape, in the event that we are attack."

"But where can we go, if we have to leave this place?"

"I'm afraid, that I don't know. Perhaps, to some other island."

"We will constantly be on the run, for the rest of our lives. Can't you see that? Just like wanted criminals."

"Don't worry, Andrius will decide the right path to take. I place all of my trust in him."

"I trust him, too." Said Nora

"By the time the prototype is fully functional; fifty vehicles will already be built and furnished with the same components."

"Time is of essence and the probability that we will be discovered is approaching."

"I'm not worry, we're safe here."

"That's a good attitude. O.K. Nora, there are certain unknown factors, that must be dealt with, before any attempt can be made at building these marvelous flying machines."

"What are they?" Nora asked.

"One factor is the solar windshield. We will have to determine the final shape of the solar windshield, made of plomutite. Will it be circular flat, spiral or conic?

Then on the anti-gravity system, what is the immediate reaction, when one creates a negative mass element, on earth. Can it be controlled, or would it cause an unstable chain reaction, that may end up exploding, destroying everything and killing everybody, on site?"

"Yes, said Nora, there are many questions to be answered and each needs considerable time, to evaluate. Uria, the longer we stay here on this island, the greater are the odds, and that we will encounter that madman who attacked us."

"We shouldn't worry about him, now. The mental energy that you will spend worrying should be directed to more creative or positive matters. There's a lot to be accomplished in a short time and we need every single minute of it."

The elevator opens and both women disappear into a long dark corridor.

CHAPTER XIII

Weeks later, weathering a vicious storm, Andrius, Jason and Michael are on the outside fence of a structure, located about three miles from the airfield, where they landed. They park in front of the security gate, of a large concrete blockhouse, overlooking the ocean, on the northwest end of the Island.

A twenty-foot tall metal fence and barbed wire protects the blockhouse from any possible intrusion from the outside.

Approaching the security gate, there's a sign giving fair warnings in English, German and Spanish. Michael reads one of the displays:

"Keep out. High voltage." In addition, below it reads: "International Power Grid System Substation No. 258. No trespassing."

Two rugged looking heavy steel doors, fifteen feet high, prevents easy access, into the building.

After cutting through the outside fence, the men finally approach the massive doors and carefully inspect them.

"Damn it, Said Michael, the door hinges' are located, on the inside. That's bad news."

"What do you expect everything to be easy?" Said Jason.

"In my infinite wisdom, I foresaw something like this. That's why, I've brought with me, twenty pounds of plastic explosives, just for unexpected surprises."

"Will that be enough?" Asked Jason

"By looks of it, I estimate that the walls are two to three feet thick, of reinforced concrete. Those doors look no less than three inches, of solid US steel, to say the least."

"Well, Andrius, what's your assessment?"

"Michael, you are the explosive expert. I'm only here just as an observer."

"O.K. So let's get this over with. I'm wet and cold." Said Michael

"Aren't we all?" Said Jason

Michael knells down and tinkers with the detonators, for a few moments.

"Come on. Come on, Michael, Said Jason what's taking you long?"

"Wait. This is delicate work, cuz. My fuses are getting wet."

"Hey, I'm no dummy. Those fuses can be used anywhere. They're waterproof."

"I was only testing your knowledge, cuz."

"Come on, let's get on with it."

Michael places the case that he carries on the ground and opens it. Afterwards, he removes several red cards with warning labels, stating:

'High Explosives.' 'Handle and dispose of, with extreme care.'

He counts twenty separate slots. Each one contains a cylinder, with additional information written in red that said: "Eight ounces of plastic explosives. "Danger!" Please handle with care."

The men remove the explosives and spread them, on the dry concrete floor. Michael makes four groups and compresses them to various surface areas, on the steel door.

After placing the charges and the detonator devices, they quickly move away to look for cover, by shielding themselves, behind the military truck parked in front some fifty feet away."

"O.k. is everyone safely hidden?"

"We're all ready here."

Michael yells aloud "Fire in the hole!" Then triggers the switch.

Suddenly, there's a blinding flash accompanied by a loud bang.

The ground shook and the truck rises off the ground two or three inches in the air then drops abruptly.

"Wow! That's a rush."

A large section of the front wire fence flies off and falls across the side of the truck, narrowly missing the front windshield, but partially shattering the rear window.

Michael gets up gasping for air and coughing up dust. Debris and heavy dust still was falling all around.

"I can't take any more of this." He said while dusting himself, off.

"Watch out!"

The warning metal sign that was attached to the main entrance comes down and narrowly misses Michael's head.

"Thank you, guys. That would have given me a nasty cut."

"Not only that, but it would have decapitated your head." Said Andrius.

"Come on, let's see what happened." Said Jason

"Talking about heads how's your head, cuz?" Asks Michael

"Never better, with this hard hat to protect it. How's yours?"

"I still ache. Why you didn't get me one, too?"

"Blame it, on your infinite wisdom, for not bringing one with you."

"Hey, don't rub it in, cuz."

"Come on, this was the last one, in the shed. We'll probably find some inside."

They wait a while till the dust settles and approach the entrance to the blockhouse. As the dust clears, they discover that the steel gate door has not blown in, as expected, but is sufficiently damaged to allow them to pass through a small gaping hole, big enough to squeeze through in without to much difficulty.

"Michael, it looks like your ten pounds of terror, was no match for the metal door and frame. It's still standing upright and laughing at you." Said Andrius

"Gentlemen, you have to realize that this place is built like Fort Knox. Look at that steelworks, around the framing. It's massive! Probably it's designed to withstand an indirect nuclear blast."

"You may have a good point there." Said Andrius.

"The concrete gave out, long before the steel even nudged." Said Jason

"You're right, Jason." Said Andrius, while examining the structure very closely.

Once inside after breaking through the front glass doors, Andrius walks up a small ramp and locates the power electric panel and starts throwing on the light switches.

As they come on throughout the long and narrow building, they begin to see the heavy electrical and mechanical equipment, housed within.

"Look at that, Jason. Said Michael. See those gigantic transfer switches? They're isolated and hermetically sealed, within that large glass enclosure chamber. How the heck do we get in? There must be a way."

"There's no need to get to them. See here, on the right. That's the control room. The whole transfer switch operation is run from this side end, of the building." Said Andrius

"So these are, the transfer switches, I have never seen them that huge before. They must be fifteen feet high."

"Due to the extreme high voltages flowing through the feeders, the switches can only be operated, by mechanical means. They're remotely controlled and located away, from the high-tension area. The electric arc along, when switching, can probably vaporize you in an instant in there. That's why it must be isolated in its own environment."

"Wow!"

"See this glass?"

"Yeah."

"It's four inches thick. It provides isolation from the flash points of the switch."

"Thank you for the guided tour, cuz."

"Alright, let's get into the control room and see which switch will divert the flow of current, to the complex." Said Andrius

"Most likely, there has to be an open transfer switch on the floor somewhere here, which previously fed the complex. Let's look for it. We have to get in to see which one is it."

Andrius forces the door open and all three enter.

Inside, they discover another enclosed glass panel, which runs the length of the building with a narrow adjacent corridor. They walk the distance and reach the far end.

"What do you think, Andrius? Which is the right one?"

"It looks like those last two switches are open. It's a good possibility that they are the ones."

"Wait a moment, gentlemen. Said Michael, guess what, I found some power flow diagram, in this storage bin. These are probably, the flow diagrams, for all the switches."

Michael throws the roll of drawings to Jason and he immediately spreads them open on a nearby desk.

"Let's see. Said Jason, as I interpret the wiring diagram, the only means of throwing the switches, is by this generating set. We have to start it and build up the power surge and energize one switch, at a time. This is done by pressing the start button, TSB."

"TSB means throw switching bridge, said Andrius, that is the red one."

"Oh, well. Let's get on with it."

"What's your hurry, Jason? We should be very sure of what we are doing here, alright."

Michael goes over to the truck and informs Jarvis by radio, that they're ready to throw the switch.

Jason sits on the control panel and begins typing commands to the remote controller, once energized. He aligns the switches in proper sequence, before connecting them. As he does this, he turns to Andrius:

"Where's Colonel Towers? I didn't see him morning."

"He's supervising the men, at the other end of the Island. They're excavating and leveling off the area. We will soon be finish constructing the site for our launch vehicles."

"I would like to join him, after we're through, here."

"They're ready, Andrius!" Michael yells out from the truck.

"Jason, do you have power?"

"Yes, I do."

"Alright. Start the generators." Said Andrius

Jason presses the ignition buttons and it starts up. After allowing the equipment to warm up, Andrius and Jason start manipulating the relays and make the first connection, from one bridge to the main supply flow point. All watched cautiously, at the meters above, to see if there are any drastic fluctuations of current, on the bridge.

Any abnormal surge will instantly alert the power authorities that an intrusion to their system has occurred.

As the contacts mate, they only noticed slight current variations. This assures them, that the current is flowing freely to the complex's primary power panels.

The portable radio on the truck buzzes on.

"Andrius! Said Michael, Jarvis confirms the power, at the complex."

"That's it, said Andrius, now we throw the remaining two other switches and lock everything in place. We're all finished here. Thank you guys and lets get back."

"Andrius, don't forget to drop me off, at the construction site." Said Jason

"Right. Will do."

As the men exit the control room, they hear a strange creaking sound. They look ahead and see the main entrance steel doors come crashing down into the building, with a tremendous sound. The impact causes dust and debris to fly in and everywhere. The lights flicker out then come back. Andrius turns to Michael.

"See Michael, you did bring the right amount of explosives with you. You had a built-in delay reaction. That's pretty good; you have to teach me that, someday."

"You guys must be joking. I was just as surprised, as you were. That happened by pure accident. I didn't have anything to do with it."

"Come on lets go." They all leave laughing.

Late that night, as the equipment is being carefully tested at the complex, eight hundred nautical miles North of the Island, in Buenos Aires, at the Departamento de Distribucion de Energia, a technician manning the equipment, sees on one of the meters a slight fluctuation, in the power grid. Out of curiosity, one of the night superintendents, at the station, who is dozing on and off, also notices something but is not sure; he picks up the phone and places a call to another plant engineer, some fifty miles away, to verify the condition.

Unfortunately, as he establishes the contact, the fluctuation ceases and power levels go to normal. The engineer excuses the incident to equipment local sensor failure, or tiredness on his part and hangs up the phone.

Three weeks later, the construction groups, working day and night and at times, under severe conditions, are nearly finished with the launch sites.

Andrius' prototype vehicle which was hastily built, is rolled out to the site and now rests at the bottom of one of the launch silos, awaiting the installation of a final component, essential to the vehicle; the solar wind deflector discs.

The molded outer shell is in place, but the material within the shell, still waits final processing, at the complex.

Andrius is forced to schedule that week, to start-testing his improvements to the fusion machine, for reasons that he believes that the electrical grid would not be able to supply sufficient power alone, to reconfigure the molecule structure of lead into the new structure called Plomutite.

Meanwhile, Jason and Colonel Towers test the vehicles' anti-gravity system.

The new vehicle is an elongated bell like object, seventy-five feet in diameter, at the base that terminates twenty-five feet diameter at the top where the cockpit is located. The vehicle is similar in shape to NASA's old mercury capsule but way larger size and capacity.

It rests atop of a metal pedestal, at the launch pad. The outer skin material is made of heavy gage titanium. It includes three mechanical arms connected to concave discs molded to the outer curved body of the vehicle.

The discs and arms are designed to stretch out and rotate the concave discs into a position to capture the solar winds, once the vehicle reaches orbital height and speed.

The flight seats and control devices run spirally within and around the base of the vehicle and rise up to the cockpit level and terminating with three flights control seats, inside of the cockpit.

A steel monorail enables the lead pilot seated, in the center seat to move forward, into the cockpit area, giving him to view a 360-degree breathtaking unobstructed panorama while the two co-pilots remain fixed to allow free movement to the pilot.

On the exterior, just below the passenger compartment, at the base level of the vehicle, laid two circular, seventy-five feet diameter stainless steel plates, one above each other, separated by an 8-inch air space between. Each plate is reinforced with three-inch spiral ridges on the outer surface to reduce any plain distortions. They are individually driven by variable speed electric induction motors and controlled by an automatic flight modulator located in the cockpit.

Jason and Colonel Towers prepare to test the plates'anti-gravity performance.

Once ready, the immediate area is cleared off all personnel. All vital equipment is relocated, a quarter mile away and protected with fiberglass canvas covers.

All personnel are then directed to move into the Complex' control room for safety reasons.

All controls and test functions of the vehicle and results would be initiated and recorded from there.

Due to the lack of horizontal control of the unit, Andrius instructed Jason, to limit the vertical climb to just about a few feet. He feared that once it becomes airborne, the vehicle might drift away due to the variable wind gusts at the launch site. They attach a one hundred-foot 2-inch steel tether cable to the vehicle, as a precaution for safety and anchor it to a heavy concrete pylon nearby.

Jason activates the on-board fuel cell unit and connects to the base power system as back up.

The circular electro magnets surrounding both of the titanium plates become energized.

As this happens, tension between the plates releases a momentary discharge of the static energy, causing a bright flash, in all the video monitors. Jason next energizes the three circular copper windings laminated on the perimeters on both plates. They are capable of alternating the magnetic fields, up to at least a million times per second or more. Their purpose: to distort and cut, as many magnetic lines between the plates, as possible.

By this, Andrius hopes to disrupt the atomic molecular orbital make-up of the two metal plates. Once achieved, the plates will create, a negative charge within its structure and the earths' mass will repel it. It's similar to gravity but in a reverse fashion.

By gradually controlling the revolutions of the plates, Andrius believes, that the velocity of repulsion can possibly be gradually controlled, with the use of the variable speed induction motors.

Jason turns on the speed control knob. Everyone views the vehicle through closed circuit cameras, to observe a reaction if any.

At sixty revolutions per minute, they note a light bluish haze, which begins pulsating between the plates. He checks the temperature of the plates and they are normal, at twenty-two degrees ambient.

So far, they observe that no levitation of the vehicle has occurred. In Jason's eyes, Andrius' theory is now in jeopardy. The experiment continues:

"Jason, let's try one hundred and twenty revolutions, to see the effect." Said the Colonel

"Alright. Colonel, keep a sharp eye, on the radiation background and on the current that the plates are drawing, from the power cells." Said Jason

"Alright, Jason, let it go."

Jason turns the control knob higher.

"Jason, there's a marked increase, in the radiation. It has jumped from the normal background count to a whooping 165 counts, per minute."

"How about in the vehicle?"

"Negative on the vehicle. The level is normal."

"Good."

"It's now climbing to fifty percent above normal."

"That's not too drastic." Said Jason

"But, Jason, look at the screen!" said Colonel Towers

"Yes! Its spiraling outwards bluish pulsating waves."

"Perhaps if we increase more revolutions, let's see." Jason turns the knob further.

"Wow! Outside radiation is rising to nine hundred counts per minute and the plate temperature has risen to three hundred degrees and climbing."

"What's the condition inside the vehicle?"

"It's normal and 60 degrees Fahrenheit."

"Look! Pressure on the pedestals is reducing, Colonel. It's beginning to levitate. Look at all the sensors."

"Increase it, Jason just a bit more!"

At four hundred revolutions, the bluish light transforms itself, into a blinding white light, emanating away from the vehicle, in circular waves, at high at speeds.

"It looks like lightning." Jason yells out.

"Hey, I'm getting zero pressure, on the pedestal. It's rising."

"No! Can you see it? It is still on the pedestal."

"How can it be, I'm receiving, a zero readings, here?"

"Wait a second. Look at the screen. The pulsating lights stopped." Said Jason

"My instruments are showing everything is still operating and yet, I see no movement."

"I'm registering, on my instrument panel that the craft is about twenty-five feet in the air, but on that screen, it's still on the pedestal. I don't get it. Maybe the sensors have failed."

Jason takes a closer look at the screen

"Damn it! It's burnt out."

"What do you mean?" The Colonel demands,

"The photo cells on the camera have completely been burnt out. See?"

"That's why we're only seeing the ship, on the pedestal. Something burned out the camera at the moment it elevated."

"Colonel, switch on the black and white camera that is just above the launch site. At least, we will get a picture of the vehicle, from 100 meters away."

"You're right, Jason, there she is. The vehicle is in the air, but look at the ground beneath it. It's all scourged and burning. Perhaps that white light may have some kind of destructive force to it. Said Jason, We may have to check into this and report it to the Professor to evaluate."

"Ah! There goes the second camera. Another burn out occur. The light intensity is too much. I hope we can somehow reduce its destructive force." Said the Colonel

"I think it's not the light emissions, but intense micro wavelengths emissions between the rotating plates. The light source that we're seeing is just ionization of the air but what we must worry about are the waves, that elongate and disperse out." Said Jason

"Jason do you think that there may be a way to correct this?"

"Some means will have to be devised to protect ourselves from it. We may also have to inform Andrius, about this condition." Said Jason

"Andrius already knows." Said the Colonel

"Very well. Let's bring the vehicle back down and secure it, so we can install the solar panels provided, that the fusion machine proves operable and successful, tonight." Said Jason

"Alright. Bring it down very slowly. It may have drifted away from the launch pad, as we spoke." Said the Colonel

"The instruments show, that it has drifted about thirty feet to the west. I think it's still safe to bring it down, to the pad. It's wide enough."

"Very well. Here it goes." Said the Colonel

Once wrapping up the experiment, they all drive over to the vehicle and bring with them several fire extinguishers to put out the fires around the site. They finally secure the vehicle, after allowing it to cool down for an hour.

Afterwards, they return to the complex, where Andrius and Michael are prepping up, the huge fusion machine. Jason enters the sub-level, just as Michael actuates the seawater pumps.

"Congratulations cuz, on that successful tryout, of the vehicle." Said Michael

"Thank you, but the one who should receive all the honors is Andrius, for formulating the theory."

"But you must realize something. You made it work, and that's what counts."

"I'm sure of that, but…"

"Listen, Jason, Said Michael, I need your hand over here for a few moments, with this equipment."

"Alright, what seems to be the trouble?"

"Well, I'm getting a pump failure signal, from pump number three. Can you go and see what's the trouble?"

"Alright, I'll be right back. It will only take a minute."

"Thanks, Jason."

An hour later, the circulating pump is repaired and placed on-line again by midnight. The cooling equipment is started and left running overnight.

Meanwhile in Buenos Aires, at the Departamento de Distribucion de Energia, the power fluctuations, begins more dramatic fluctuations this time.

A day superintendent verifies the condition with the other distant power station and both sites upon reviewing the data cannot figure out what could be the cause. They call several scientists, at the astronomical center to see if solar flares may be affecting power transmissions. One scientist responded by saying that it may be a possibility because one flare did occur several days past and the lingering effect may be still around.

They accept the logical explanation and resume monitoring the system and their duties.

An hour later, there's a sudden power drop in the local grid, which forces the Buenos Aires central power station, to order a secondary cross feed of 15.0 GIGO-watts of power, from several auxiliary feeders and South American supply centers. All efforts to avoid power outage become fruitless.

Parts of Buenos Aires and the surrounding cities go into blackouts, as feeders from sub stations start failing throughout the country from lack of power.

Auxiliary and local emergency power equipment in hospitals and government offices, immediately are called in and activated, to provide emergency temporary power.

Radio-satellite calls for assistance are placed to power controlling centers in Spain and in Venezuela, to no avail. A last effort is made, to re-route electrical power from the North American grid but it fails due to rolling blackouts across the Northern South American Territories, that become unmanageable.

The outages begin to plague major towns and cities, throughout Argentina and the middle sectors of South America.

By mid-morning, the governments in those regions alert their National Guards and deploy them to their central cities and rural areas to maintain public safety.

They also alert the International Red Cross and request assistance and medical supplies.

Each of the affected areas begins requesting help from FEMA. FEMA in turn responds to all emergency requests and supplies all necessary medical aid and other vital power generating equipment and sends them by cargo aircraft to key critical locations in South and Central America and other critical areas as a precaution.

American agents, upon witnessing the decaying situation, send coded messages, via satellite, to Washington, the State Department and the CSA. The Secretary of State at this point does not see any serious crises that may directly affect the security of the United States and decides not to inform the President, at this time.

Power and nuclear plants on the East Coast and the Mid West are placed into alert in case the rolling power losses in the Southern Electrical grid become serious. Generating sets that were dormant for years are now being called into possible service in combating the ever-growing power losses in the International Grid.

CHAPTER XIV

It's mid-morning in Washington. The National Security Agency informs the President during breakfast of the potential disaster, which occurred overnight. The President picks up the phone and calls the Secretary of State.

"Jerry, tell me. What goes? I haven't review my security reports yet."

"Mister President, I didn't want to disturb you. I was alerted last night, of the serious situation, Sir."

"Well, you should have awakened me. How bad is this?" the President was very concerned.

"Information is coming very sketchy. They're having trouble, pinpointing the troubled power feeds, which supply Buenos Aires and parts of Northern Chile."

"I spoke to Ambassador Rodrigo, a few minutes ago. He fears that this may be possibly sabotage from some international group. Can you confirm it, Jerry?"

"Not likely, Mister President. My sources have checked into this matter already and odds are that the trouble may be accidental. It's located outside of the country. Perhaps in Europe, Sir."

"It's probably due to some burnt out subterranean feeder cable, or a malfunctioning transfer power switch somewhere between."

"It's possible, Mister President. So don't worry. They'll have it all cleared by noon."

"Keep me informed, alright. I'm very concerned over any security situation that arises in South America. It's a potential powder keg. I will make an all out response on any serious provocations on part of these insurgences. That will give me the justification to go at them with the full might of the United States and I will certainly be backed up by the free world. Jerry, get me that Intel so we can go in and eliminate this threat once and for all. I'll give a heads up to the Joint Chiefs this morning."

"Yes Sir, will do."

Meanwhile at the island, an electrical power source is switched on the panel to the accelerator.

A strange and bright purplish glow begins shining throughout the lowered laboratory of the sub-level of the complex.

Super heated plasma fed into the machine is gradually concentrated into narrow beams and flows in a circular path, waving to and fro, around the transparent encasement chamber, of the huge fusion accelerator. A low frequency hum begins and reverberates throughout the chamber making loose items to move about with no exterior visible forces acting on them.

"Goodness, Said Michael, it has taken us almost two days to produce 1800 cubic liters, of this plasma. That was some task!"

"Don't despair, Michael. Said Jason; you haven't seen anything, yet. There's more to follow. Hold on to your glasses, pens and notebooks people."

"Alright, Jason. Said Andrius. Start accelerating the plasma. Start slowly then increase gradually, when you nearly reach closed, to the speed of light. That will be in the region of 300,000 kilometers per second then begin to throttle down a bit. Don't push it."

"Alright, Andrius, but why can't we go higher?"

"I have a hunch. Researchers out in California experimented with the plasma, at levels of 1.2 of the speed of light and that was the region, where they had the fatal accidents. I don't wish to repeat, the same fatal error."

"I see why, now." Jason responded.

As the gaseous substance, in the chamber accelerates higher, the plasma becomes brighter and brighter. It exhibits an eerie reddish light with a bluish halo on the outer fringes of it.

"What's that?" Asked Michael

"That's light breaking down into some of the component parts, without the use of a prism or a spectrometer."

"Jason keep it steady. Now Michael, you see those two knobs?"

"Yes, Sir."

"Those control the electro magnet rotations. One runs clockwise and the other counter clockwise."

"I see and understand clearly."

"Now begin the rotation of the electro magnets, at one degree at a time, in opposite directions."

"Right, Andrius." Said Michael.

Andrius turns to the group of fellow scientist standing, in front of the machine.

"I will advise everyone at this time, to put on your light and heat shields, because it may become a little bright and warm in here. Please don't forget your safety gloves."

"Andrius, Said Michael, So far, twelve degrees and no reaction, yet."

"Increase it now, to two degrees, every three seconds."

"Right."

A few second lapses, when suddenly a bright flash occurs, which stays on blinding white. The assembled group, out of fear, immediately evacuates the chamber. Andrius, Michael, Jarvis and Jason remain, but shield their faces with their hands from the awesome spectacle, before them.

"Is everyone all right, here?"

"Yes, but Andrius, look at your cloths. They've been bleached white. Hey, ours too!"

"Everyone please calm down. Don't remove your gloves or your face shields. If you do you will suffer sever burns and you surely will go blind."

"This is fantastic, gentleman! We've just looked into God's eye, the source what powers the Universe." Said Jarvis

"Careful gentlemen, we have a tiger, by the tail. One wrong move and we will be instantly vaporized. Be wise and be mindful. Double check your every move." Said Andrius.

They observe that the power scales go beyond their designed limits and jam. The low harmonics end and are replaced, by a high frequency, ear-piercing sound, which becomes unbearable, together with the light and heat that's radiating, from the machine.

"Radiation levels are steadily climbing, gentlemen." Said Jarvis.

"Quickly! We can't any longer stay here. Let's all move, into the next compartment. I had our fellow scientists erected an auxiliary control panel and view screens there, in case of an emergency. We must use it now."

"Good thinking, Andrius." Said Jarvis.

"This way, please."

"Andrius, I don't wish to be the prophet of doom, but there is more than a twelve percent current reduction, throughout the complex. I don't know how long can all of the equipment holds out. It is very dangerous."

"Jarvis, we need at least, ten to fifteen more minutes. That's all."

"But Andrius, due to the low voltage, I have motors and feeders burning out throughout the complex. See the upper right sections of the monitor. Those red flashing dots are failure alarms going off in all the levels throughout the plant. They are other major breakdowns that are occurring simultaneously. I can't give you additional power."

"We must turn off the environmental control equipment. I need additional power to sustain this reaction in equilibrium."

"We can't do that, we'll all suffocate eventually but the humans will die first."

"Sorry, but I can't stop this now, Jarvis. Pull more power from the grid. It will temporarily alleviate your conditions. I need the power now and more."

"The loads on the transmission lines and feeders are now, beyond their designed limits."

"Use it, anyway! It will only be for a few more minutes. Trust me."

"Alright, Andrius. I hope we don't all go up in a gigantic flash, if the circuits cannot take the overload."

"Jarvis, I would like to give you some of the power from the fusion machines' output, but the power lines, are not capable of taking the load. I won't risk it. It will set us back months if these lines fail."

"It's all right, Andrius, I understand."

Jarvis rushes off, shaking his head and throwing his arms, in the air.

Ten minutes go by when Andrius arrives at the control point self-equilibrium on the fusion machine. He pulls back and cuts all power to it and sees that the machine sustains the chain reaction within the chamber as long as the plasma is continuously supplied at certain intervals. Andrius discovers that the machine consumes an infinitesimal quantity of the plasma in the range of less than 1 milligram per GIGO watt of sustained power.

"Congratulations again Andrius, you did it. You've successfully reached equilibrium."

"Thank you, Jarvis."

Minutes later, the power losses to the center are restored to less than five percent. Critical conditions throughout are finally alleviated. The additional power that Jarvis extracted from the power grid is felt in the main power distribution centers, in Venezuela and Spain.

Automatic power controllers, in both countries, bypass power from other sectors, to satisfy the demands. Engineers on both sides of the Atlantic, upon seeing the unusual negative surge become perplexed, over the strange situation. Particular attention is focus to the power grids supplying the Southern coast of South America.

The C.S.A. and the Europa Secret Service, take up interest, in the developing situation. One C.S.A. agent, stationed in Caracas, sends a tech message to the State Department, alerting them of the strange occurrences and the suspected area of origin.

Later that day, the Secretary of State meets again with the President.

"Hi Jerry. I hope everything has been resolved, with that problem."

"Mister President...."

"Guess what. I leave this weekend for some rest and relaxation, to the Florida White House."

"Good, Mister President. I wish you a pleasant trip."

"Jerry." Said the President

"Yes, Sir."

"You were going to tell me something. I hope I did not interrupt you."

"No, Sir. Its just, that I don't know how to start, Mister President."

"Is it about our nemesis, Mister Daggard? Is he missing?"

"No, Sir. It's much more serious than that."

"Then I think I better sit down and let's talk, alright."

"Mister President, I hope that this doesn't damper your weekend plans."

"What seems to be the problem?"

"It has to do with the electrical power problems with the power grid distribution in Europe and South America."

"Oh yes, I was thinking about that this morning. Was it resolved?"

"No Sir. It has become worst."

"What's the latest?"

"Sir, I might have that Intel that you were looking for. This might sound strange but intelligence thinks that a Middle Eastern Group and the insurgents somehow are connected with the power outages that are plaguing South America and now parts of Western Europe."

"That's very serious. Does the CSA have any evidence of this? I need that Intel."

"No Sir, no concrete proof yet."

"I should have been informed of this, much earlier."

"Mister President, we believe, that this could possible be a strategic plan by them to launch an immense economic assault, on the West."

"It's a clever move on their part. Don't you think so?"

"It is, Sir. Our best minds couldn't device such a devilish plan."

The President raises his arm, and turns around and picks up the phone.

"One moment, Jerry."

"Security, hold all calls and cancel all of my engagements for the day. Get the Vice President on line two, please and hurry." He turns to the Secretary again.

"OK Jerry, you have my full attention, now."

"As I said, Mister President, we suspect that they may be sabotaging the International Power Grid distribution from somewhere out, in the Atlantic Ocean."

The blue phone rings: "It's the Vice President, Sir." The operator announces.

"Thank you."

"Say, Hank."

"Yes, Mister President."

"Something serious has come up. Can you possibly fill in for me, for the rest of the day?"

"I have a couple of functions to attend to today; there's no problem in canceling them, Sir."

"Good."

"Mister President, are we in some state of emergency?"

"Not at present. You will be briefed on the latest situation, which is developing, as we speak. The Secretary will shortly meet with you, alright?"

"No problem, Mister President."

"Thanks."

He hangs up the phone and turns to the Secretary once more.

"Alright, Jerry. Continue. I'm sorry."

"The C.S.A. contends that it may be a small specially trained group, of approximately less than fifty men, or slightly more. Too small to be noticed and under our radar."

"Commandos?"

"Precisely. If the group was any bigger, chances are that we would have known about it earlier and taken the necessary precautions.

Small groups like this can easily slip into any country without any detection. The odds are that they are operating from a submarine, a merchant ship or hold off, in some deserted island, or even in some allied country near the power grids."

"That's a problem. Where do we begin to look and who are the nemesis that would aid them?"

"Mister President, if we're able to find their location, we can easily eliminate the threat and foil their plans. We must act very fast, Sir."

"You're talking about a world wide operation, Jerry."

"Yes Mister President, you already implemented one, in one area a months go."

"What do you mean?"

"The infamous Karl Daggard's search and destroy mission."

"Oh my God, I've completely forgotten, about him. Where is he?"

"I think he is somewhere in South Pacific, off the Coast of South America, Sir."

"We will get Mister Daggard on this mission, as soon as possible. Find out exactly, where he is and we'll issue him new orders. Coordinate this with the Joint Chiefs' and the CSA."

"Yes, Sir. Does this mean that the search for the Orgites shall be temporarily halted?"

"Yes, Jerry, just temporarily. Listen, get a complete power grid layout, from the Defense Department, showing all the undersea transmission lines, especially the ones that run from Europe and along South America's Eastern and Western coastlines."

"Yes, Sir."

"I have a feeling that the enemy might be tampering with the power grid along these areas. Also, inform Mister Daggard, that his search party will be supplemented this time, with additional air and sea support, from a small segment of the Sixth Fleet."

"Yes, Mister President."

The President picks up the phone again:

"Get me Admiral Shea, and set up an emergency meeting, with the Joint Chiefs, today."

"Mister President, how much information shall we release to the news media?"

"You tell them, that the President has alerted our Atlantic Naval forces, just as a precaution, to safeguard the security and well-being of all those countries, affected by these power black-outs. In addition, inform them, that we have FEMA and Homeland Security on board, to provide relief to those countries needing help and relief."

"Very well stated, Mister President, I will get right on it."

"Well, Jerry, after my meeting with the Chiefs, I'm finally off, to a well earned semi-work and vacation, this time. Don't forget to keep me informed. Use the blue phone, as necessary and as often."

"Rest assures, Sir. Have a nice time and enjoy your vacation."

CHAPTER XV

Later that afternoon, somewhere in the South Atlantic, on board the USS Bixby, a nuclear submarine, Daggard is awakened from his sleep, by a knock on the door.

"Sir." Said the ship's Yeoman.

"Yes, what is it?" He demands

"Sir, sorry to disturb you but I have a special communiqué here from COM-SAT for you, from Naval Communications Center in San Juan, Puerto Rico."

Daggard gets up somewhat confused, and opens the door. The Yeoman hands him over a sealed envelope.

"Thank you, you may go, now."

"Yes, Sir." The Yeoman salutes him and withdraws.

Daggard tears open the white envelope. Inside there's a blue and red sealed letter marked 'Top Secret'. He quickly returns to his bed, breaks the seal and carefully displays all the materials from inside the envelope, on his bunk bed. He reaches over to the wall and puts on a small light to help him decipher the material. Inside, there was another small envelope, containing two maps and coordinates to different points that are highlighted. He finally finds the communiqué and reads the orders, from the Secretary.

At the end of the message, he is informed that similar orders were also issued to the Commander, on board the submarine and to designated Sixth Fleet Commanders that will be involved, in the search mission. There's another knock, on the door:

"Yes, who is it?"

"Mister Daggard, this is Captain McKenna."

"Come in, Captain, I see you have also received the orders."

"Yes, Mister Daggard, it sounds very urgent."

"This is a very serious matter, I hope, we can intercept this group, before their plans are fully executed." Said Daggard

"They're giving us ninety-six hours, to find and eliminate the threat."

"Captain there isn't enough time, given the thousands of square miles that we must cover within this time limit."

"We have the additional support of sixty aircraft, to cover as much of the area as possible, but..."

"What's first on your list, Captain?"

"Mister Daggard, please join me and the exec's, in the War Room. We can talk there."

"By all means, lead the way, Captain, I haven't been in a War Room, since my early days, when I worked at the old Pentagon Building, which has subsequently been replaced by the new DOB complex."

"Oh, yes, its the first type of windowless structure, ever built. I feel well at home there, if you know what I mean."

After leaving the compartment, both men walk through the narrow submarines' passageways and enter a brightly lit circular room, near mid ship, adjacent to the cruise missile silos.

On a sidewall of the room, a viewing screen displays various sectors of the submarine and the personnel at work. Another screen displays an overhead view of the area where the submarine is navigating through. Captain McKenna pulls out a chair for Daggard and himself.

He reaches for a button located atop the desk and presses it.

A section within, slowly opens and a control panel rise from the desk and stops at arms' length. He manipulates a keyboard.

"Mister Daggard, we've programmed the sites into our computer of all the power sub stations and pin pointed the general path of the transmission lines which are routed through underwater ocean tunnels, throughout these sites. Here they are. Automatic sensors are constantly monitoring these tunnels.

As they look up at the large display screen, Daggard picks up a laser-pointing pen.

"Which are these ones, Captain?" He asks.

"The red flashing points represent the power transfer sub-stations and the green lines as you see, are the deep sea, transmission lines."

"I see, Captain." He responds.

"Now, these white triangulations are the sectors and transfer stations that have been selected for our group to land and investigate for any subversive activity."

"Which ones are assigned to us?"

"These. The lower four sites, on the corner. They are a group of small islands, which belong to the various nations, in the region. The majority of them, are uninhabited, but would be enticing targets, for a subversive group, to set up operations, there."

"Do we have clearances from the local governments, to land on these properties?"

"The Defense Department is handling that phase of the project. We should be getting the green light, by the earliest midnight tonight, or morning."

"Which is our first target?"

"You see this small one here?"

"Yes Captain."

"That is the island of Marina. We will be reaching it by two or three o'clock in the morning, so you better get some sleep. I believe it belongs to Brazil. It was previously used as a coaling station, but with the advent of nuclear fuel, it was abandoned about ten years ago."

"It looks very suspicious."

"They all do, Mister Daggard. The last island, on our list is this little ugly one. It's just a few hundred miles south, from an island chain called 'Isla Del Fuego'. They are named, in that fashion, due to the island's severe conditions. The only search group, who's equipped to land on it safely, will be our team."

"What do you mean, Captain?"

"The Island is off limits. It is deadly poisonous there and extremely contaminated, with radioactivity. It was previously contaminated by a freak industrial accident, by research groups there, some years ago."

"I see."

"It's so toxic that anyone without sufficient protection, would probably last a few hours out there. There's no cause to be alarmed, Mister Daggard. We have specially designed suits, which will withstand these types of severe conditions."

"Captain, I'd rather not commit a large landing force, on that Island. You can never tell, what can happen to a person, if one of the suits proves to be defective. Damn it! I don't trust them."

"I would agree with you. There's a limit to the type of radiation, which they can resist. Most likely, some radioactivity is bound to infiltrate. Anyway, the suites have been certified two weeks ago by the AEC Safety Division."

"Captain, believe me, I know of some cases." Said Daggard

"Alright, we will limit the investigation, to less than a dozen men."

"Thank you. I don't see the case for any more, but if I need more, then I will call you, alright?"

"That will be fine with me, Mister Daggard."

"Are we all through here?" He asks.

"Yes Sir."

"I'll be in my quarters. Please wake me, when we reach near the Island."

"Yes Sir." Said the Captain

Daggard gets up and the Yeoman approaches and escorts him, to his cabin.

A good distance away from the mainland, of one of Florida Keys, a navy helicopter lands on a public baseball field owned by the town. As the President exits his aircraft, he greets the locals and apologizes for temporary halting a game between two of the area schools.

Afterwards he's escorted to his waiting limousine and is driven off.

Three Secret Service vehicles led by four state police officers on motorcycles and a police helicopter follow the entourage.

Minutes later, half a mile away, they stop in front of a white, Southern style house, situated on a ten-acre plot owned by the President.

As he arrives, other Secret Service personnel emerge from the house and greet him.

They all shake hands and the entourage disappear into the house.

The police and the local security linger about for a while then depart, after a signal from the Secret Service, is given.

It's mid afternoon; the President is in the garden having lunch with Florida's Governor Friendly, and two other political aids. The men are deep in conversations over the latest world and national economic affairs.

"Mister President, if you sign the bill for raising the tariff on these commodities, I'm afraid, that it will cause an additional jolt, in home market prices of these products, here."

"Not quite, Governor. I'm attempting to reduce foreign competition to a certain degree and we must do it. It is the survival of our small home markets, what's at stake."

"No, I don't think so, Mister President. In my opinion, you would be creating a monopoly situation. You and I surely know, that some of our major state side corporations, are talking mergers, in a year or so, and all of the competitive prices, will shortly disappear."

"That's just here say, Governor. I don't believe that these two commodity giants can ever merge but become a joint venture experiment. There will be too much fear across the board. Who will have the controlling factor? Will it be Pacific Nationals or America Mercantile? They're both too big, to relinquish power, to the other. It's just impossible. Trust me."

"Mister President, right now they are each worth in the range of about $800 billion.

I have a feeling, that they are exerting, a lot of lobby influence. They may be somewhat, influencing some people's point of view. Don't you think so?"

"I would like to answer that, with a question of my own, Governor."

"Sir?"

"What would you rather have…?" An aid appears and interrupts the President.

"Pardon me, gentlemen. Mister President?"

"Yes?"

"There's an urgent call for you, from the Secretary."

The President quickly rises from his chair and wipes his lips.

"Excuse me gentlemen, Governor, can we continue this very interesting conversation at some other time? I love to sit and chat with you all, again."

"By all means, Sir. We will look forward and plan having another talk with you."

"Good. Gentlemen, thank you all for coming. You must forgive me, but I have the Secretary locking horns with a hot task and needs my immediate attention."

"Mister President, by all means. We will make arrangements to meet later with you, again."

"That will be fine, guys" He responds

"Good day, Mister President."

The President quickly moves inside, closes the door behind him, walks over and picks up the blue phone by his study.

"Jerry, are you there?"

"Yes, Mister President."

"What's the latest? Any contact yet?" He queried extremely interested.

"Mister President, I've just received a COM-SAT message from operations."

"And?"

"So far, after boarding several ships in the area, and landing on six sub-stations, there's no contact, yet."

"How about Daggard? How's he doing?"

"He's just arrived from the Island of Marina and also reports no contact or evidence of sabotage with those transfers' stations, or any indication, of subversive activity on the Island."

"How many additional sites is he scheduled for?"

"Five more, Sir."

"And the power problems, in that area? How are they doing?"

"Sir, so far, the sever fluctuations have subsided but there's still a sizable reduction in the whole southern hemispheric region."

"Damn it. Why can't we pin-point, where the power drop is originating?"

"Mister President, it can be done, if only one or several power grids existed, between two points but there are multiple grids, cries crossing each other. Then there are the transfer power stations, which periodically, alter the path, to different distribution centers. One must physically inspect each station and the individual position, of the switches."

"That sounds complicated, ah."

"Yes, Sir. It's pure detective work."

"Alright, Jerry. Call me the moment you make contact or find anything. I need the Intel."

"Yes, Sir."

"By the way Jerry, tonight I'll be with the First Lady, at the annual Maritime Banquet in Miami. Use the I.S.C. Communications System, for a faster connection."

"Yes, Mister President, and thank you, Sir."

"Jerry, we all must keep a good public image. I'm afraid that, if the media suspects, that a special operation is taking place out there, without their knowledge, there maybe legal ramifications. They may accuse me of launching, a major offensive against the Insurgents in South America, without the blessings of Congress."

"I'll do my best, Sir and keep a poker face and deny everything when asked."

"Good day, Jerry. Call me, in the morning."

"Yes, Sir."

The President hangs up and goes to an aid in the next room.

"Please get me Mister Rodrigo, the Argentinean Ambassador on the phone."

"Yes, Sir. He will be right with you."

Meanwhile back in the South Atlantic, it's mid-day, at the complex. Andrius is almost finishing inspecting the last ten launch vehicles, with Colonel Towers.

"Andrius, we may have to construct the fire walls between the ships, to prevent them, from incinerating each other, as they are launched."

"Good thinking, Colonel, I hope we don't ever have to launch them in haste."

"Andrius, I have to speak to you, about Dr. Alvarez."

"Colonel, is there a problem?"

"When are we returning the doctor and the nurse back to San Augustine?"

"That will depend on you. How much more time do you need to finish here?"

"All of the vehicles will be ready for operation, in two or three days, the most."

"That sounds good. How about the prototype?"

"It's nearly ready, I would say, late this afternoon."

"Good. Tell Dr. Alvarez to get ready. Tonight he shall be in San Augustine."

"Andrius, I would like to go along, on that initial trip."

"Yes, why not, I'm also inviting, Jason and Michael."

"That sounds great. Our team is back in action."

"By this, we shall all learn first hand, how to maneuver the craft, without the use, of the on-board navigation system." Said Andrius

"That's perfect, now I will get to learn space navigation."

"After we leave the Doctor in San Augustine, I will like to pay the President of the United States a personal visit to parley our situation and also convince him to allow us time on the island, until our crafts are finished."

"And if he refuses?'

"Then we'll barter with him using some of our new toys as a bargaining tool."

"Do you know where he is?"

"No but you do."

"Yes, the President is not in Washington."

"I know."

"This morning, the BBC, said that he's meeting with a couple of European Chiefs of State, at his summer home."

"Do you know exactly where that is, Colonel?"

"Surely, I flew over that area many a times on maneuvers, when I was stationed a couple of miles north at Homestead Air Force Base."

"Give Jarvis the coordinates, so he can program the on-board computer on the spacecraft, to take us there. I don't wish to fly there manually and destroy the element of surprise, by getting lost out there, in the heavens over the Florida Keys."

"Andrius, it's customary to initially christen all aircraft, on their maiden voyage. What shall we name your prototype?"

"Colonel, let me see. Let's call it, The Titan. I'm naming it, after that mysterious earth like planet, which orbits Saturn."

"Yes, of course. Said Colonel Towers. It has the promise of life for future travelers."

"I would like to go and explore it, some day, if we are eventually forced to leave the Island."

"I believe that NASA landed a space probe there over a decade ago."

"Yes, but it failed to send back data. The United States had to scrap the project, because the government thought that it wasn't feasible, due to the enormous distances and the time required to reach it."

"I will bet, that if the solar wind panels prove to be successful, out there in space, we could attempt, such a distance."

"I have Jarvis working on the problem."

"Probably, we will have to travel through space, for years."

"No, I don't think so. Perhaps fourteen to eighteen months, the most."

"I would think that the force of acceleration will definitely affect the human body as a whole and may affect the normal workings of human organs."

"I don't think so. Jarvis is calculating the maximum rate of acceleration and the deceleration that will produce artificial gravity, within the craft and would assure the safest and uttermost conditions, for everyone on board."

"How can you create gravity in a craft, while still on flight? I would think it would be impossible."

"Colonel, we will do it, by accelerating from earth's gravity, at an increasing rate of thirty-two feet per second, per second. By using this rate of increase, we will imitate the earth's gravitational pull once we are out in space. At maximum speed, we will be traveling close or a little more than a million miles per hour. When we reach the halfway point of our destination, the ship will then swing around in space. At this time, the vehicle will decelerate, at the same rate of thirty two feet per second, per second."

"It sounds logical, but can it work?"

"Let's hope so. And if it does not, we'll crash into the planet, at almost the speed of light."

"Such speeds are incomprehensive."

"Well, the hydrogen particles travel over a million miles per hour. We will probably can go the same rate and greater with some our improvements to the shield."

"Incredible! We just disproved and surpassed Einstein's theory."

"Colonel, let's not get beyond ourselves, anyway, has the construction crew installed the liquid oxygen tanks and the compressors on the Titan?"

"I believe that they're just finishing up with the compressors and the food storage units."

"Alright. Let's return to the complex and see the Doctor. Perhaps he may have changed his mind, about wanting to return, to San Augustine."

Meanwhile, three hundred miles north of the Island, at evening time, Daggard is seating having dinner, before his final landfall expedition, to the contaminated island.

"Mister Daggard, I hope that this will not be your last meal with us, said the Captain, I've truly enjoyed your stay here."

"Captain, you must be optimistic. I'm very sure, that this island is the last place on earth, where a bunch of subversives, would ever want to be. I rather bypass, this infernal volcanic rock and look elsewhere but I have my orders."

Captain McKenna nods his head in agreement and looks at his wristwatch.

"We shall be reaching the eastern coast, at about twenty-one hundred hours. That will be, in about three hours or so."

"That gives us enough time, to prepare and inspect my gear."

"Mister Daggard, at eighteen hundred hours, I would like you to put on the radiation suits, just as a pre-caution."

"Why, Captain?"

"Our long range Geiger counters, are registering up to a thousand roentgens, at almost a hundred miles out, from the Island. It's drastically high, compared to the normal background count, of one hundred and twenty-five counts per minute. Everyone on board will also, put on their radiation suits."

"Very well, Captain. Said Karl Daggard. I will see you soon." He gets up and walks away.

While back at the launch site, Andrius assists Dr. Alvarez and Mrs. Mason, up a metal ramp that leads into the Titan spacecraft.

"It's a challenge in getting into the spacecraft. Please be careful folks."

"Thank you, Mister Andrius. My aging bones and joints need a bit of lubrication."

"This way please." Said Michael, as he directs them, towards the central seating area, of the spacecraft.

"What a strange looking jet plane." Mrs. Mason remarks.

"It's not quite a jet plane, Mrs. Mason. This aircraft is more, like a sailing ship. The type that runs with the natural currents, which Mother Nature provides us with."

"Please be seated and place your safety belts on. We should be embarking shortly, after all the supplies and survival gear are loaded."

A mile and a half above the launch site, on shore, four rubber boats make landfall on the rocky beach.

Daggard and twelve Navy men, dressed up in the special radiation suits disembark. They slowly make their way, through the semi-frozen swamp areas and the unfriendly rocky terrain before them. An hour later, the detachment finally reaches the outpost transfer station and regretfully discover that it has been forcibly broken into.

Daggard quickly radios the submarine and reports the possible contact with the enemy and informs the Captain, that he will further explore the northern side of the Island for any signs of the subversives. They decide to meet with another recovery team from the submarine on the other side of the island, in two hours.

The submarine then submerges and begins its' slow trek through many subterranean obstructions that lay along its path to reach to the other side of the island.

Daggard and the men enter the transfer station together with technicians who come along to reposition the switches, assisted by the power grid engineers of Argentina, which are contacted by radiophone.

By now, all is ready, at the spacecraft site. Andrius and the Colonel go through a pre-lunge safety list then activate switches and energize the ship's anti-gravity system.

At that instant, a guard who is posted outside of the transfer station observes a strange pulsating light reflection, in the skies. He quickly rushes into the station and alerts Daggard, of his strange sighting.

After Daggard confirms the sighting, he picks up the radiophone and tries to contact the submarine, but there's no response.

There is some strange static, in the radio, which blocks his reception as well as the radio transmissions. He orders some of the technicians to stay and fix the switches.

Unable to call for additional help, he decides to break up his group into two search parties. He sends four men and some of the power technicians out to the North Coast, along the shoreline and the rest of his men to go with him to investigate the site of the strange lights in the skies.

At this time, Andrius is just about to increase the revolution on the controller, when he receives a call from the complex.

"Andrius, this is Jarvis. We've just suffered a major power failure, out here."

"What's the trouble?"

"There's no power coming in, from the transfer station."

"That's very strange." Andrius responds.

"I'm afraid, that you will have to wait a couple of minutes, until I by-pass some additional power needed, from the fusion machine without over loading the lines."

"Jarvis, I can easily use the on board fuel cells, in the space craft."

"No, you need the power, for your return trip."

"How much longer, do we have to wait?"

"Just a couple of more minutes my son until I make the final adjustments."

"Alright. We'll seat tight here meanwhile and acquaint ourselves with the controls."

"Andrius, please maintain the plates rotating. If they cool down, it may take longer, to start the reaction, again."

"Will do." He answers.

Daggard and his men by now reach the top of a low ridge and discover a strange ground depression stretching outward from a side of a hill. Still being somewhat perplexed about the strange light flashing in the foreground, he decides to investigate the site first. He pulls out a flare gun and launches a flare, high across the hillside.

As it lights up the sky, the view of the launch sites are exposed. One Navy man comments:

"Mister Daggard, those things out there, looks like ICBM missile silos, but they are much wider. They are neither our type nor the Russians'. Can they be Chinese?"

"I have no idea."

Another Navy man along side of him turns to him:

"Look at that strange metallic object, standing in the center, of one of them."

As the flare burns out and slowly falls to Earth, Daggard manages to count at least thirty silos with these objects. He turns to the Lieutenant Commander beside him.

"You did see them, too?"

"Yes, Sir. I estimate they're about sixty to eighty feet diameter silos and the site is approximately fifty acres. It's immense. I've never seen anything like this before."

"What are they, Sir?" The Second Lieutenant queried.

"It beats me. Perhaps it's some type of new missile. A saucer shape secret weapon, which the enemy is planning to use as a threat against the free world."

"Sir, we better get out of here." Said the Lieutenant, with a concerned voice.

"Wait. I want to know about those objects, out there. Have your man, go over the ridge and photograph the silos and whatever is creating the bright flashes, in the skies. I need proof."

"Sir, we are not equipped to engage with the enemy, at this time. In addition, your flare probably has alerted them by now. We should leave this place now, before it is too late."

"Lieutenant, are you disobeying my orders?"

"Sir, I must decline to do so. I wish to repeat myself. My men are not soldiers. We are only a recon unit. We don't engage in combat, Sir. I'm sorry, but I cannot order them."

"Lieutenant, please come here a second. I would like you to look at something."

"Yes, Mister Daggard."

As the Lieutenant nears him, Daggard pulls out his weapon and puts a full clip of bullets into the gun's chamber. He suddenly turns around and grabs the Lieutenant by his radiation suit and aims his weapon, at his head.

"Listen to me very carefully. If I squeeze this trigger, your brains and this helmet will be splattered, all over this hillside.

Lieutenant, you do not know me and what I'm capable of doing. I'm not leaving this place, without the information, which I came here for. I don't care if you previously were doing kitchen detail. You're all now combat soldiers."

"Yes, Sir." The Lieutenant reluctantly answers.

"Order your men up the ridge now, and move it!"

Shortly afterward, the men begin to climb up and slowly approach the ridge where the foreboding light flashes, are emanating, in the skies. There's an eerie feeling felt by all.

Daggard, somewhat fearful himself, decides to slow up a bit. Four of the men reach the top and walk along the rim to get a better view, of the partly concealed object with the pulsating lights, in the mist. Two more of the men reach the top.

One of the men calls down to the Lieutenant:

"Sir, we're looking directly, at the light source."

"Can you see, any shape to it?"

"Heck no, it's eerie and too foggy down there, I guess the object is sitting about thirty meters below the ridge, Sir. It's metallic and shinny. I can't figure out the shape."

"Lieutenant, tell your man, to go down and get a better view. Tell them to photograph it, whatever it is."

"Yes, Sir."

Meanwhile, as the soldiers on the ridge slowly descend into the far side, Jarvis who is at the research lab calls again.

"Sorry, Andrius, for taking too long, but one of the switches jammed. We had to use a small jack, to unbuckle it. I'll have you on your way, in no time, now. Hold tight a few seconds."

"Jarvis, how much more time, now?" Andrius becomes impatient.

"Thirty seconds, to be exact."

"Good!" Andrius and everyone onboard are now contented.

"Andrius, you may pressurize the ship, now. You have power. I'm initiating it. Yes! You now have full power. Have a nice trip. Don't forget to come back to us, again."

"You bet. So long and thanks, Jarvis."

Andrius gradually increases the revolutions on the plates and the spacecraft starts producing a winding sound.

"Mister Andrius, I'm beginning to feel pins and needles, throughout my body." Dr. Alvarez remarks.

"I'm also feeling it, Doctor." Said Mrs. Mason

"Oh, so it's not only me." Said Dr. Alvarez.

"Doctor, Said Andrius. Don't be afraid; it's only temporary. The tingling, in your body is coming from the enormous electro-magnetic fields, that are being generated, below us. It will stop shortly."

Meanwhile as the revolutions reach their peak levels, the soldiers, at that very moment, reach a quarter of the way down, the side of the hill.

The spacecraft suddenly looses gravity, breaks from its' power connections and elevates. Waves of destructive light emit all around at lightning speed, as it slowly rises above the silo. Above ground the waves expand and radiate everywhere in site.

Suddenly, screams are heard from the soldiers, as their radiation suit burst into flames. The fires instantly engulf all of them without any warning.

One-soldier panics, trips and falls down the side of the hill towards the ascending vehicle. His body receives the maximum exposure of deadly waves and instantly dies in a ball of fire.

The lieutenant, upon witnessing this, quickly leaps backwards, off the side of the ridge and heads for cover, as the deadly waves, impact the top of the ridge, causing everything on site to burst into flames.

He hears the mournful cry of his other men, as the spacecraft, rapidly elevates high above and disappears, in the heavens. He quickly heads for cover as the deadly waves passes by.

With some of his men dead and critically injured, he could only think of one person to blame for this, and that person is Daggard.

He climbs down the ridge and finds Daggard on the ground partly smoldering, in smoke and flames. He quickly stamps out the flames by using the wet dead vegetation and swamp material on the ground by his side. He then pulls off Daggard's helmet.

"You bastard! You better not die on me, now." He screams at him.

He takes off his helmet and administers mouth-to-mouth resuscitation, for a long time, until he slowly brings Daggard back to life again.

A few minutes pass by and he finally comes to.

Out of rage, the Lieutenant grabs him by the metal collar of his suit.

"All of my men are dead up there, on the ridge and it's all my entire fault.

I feel bad and disgusted because I had to listen to and your rhetoric. Damn it! I have a good mind to leave you here, to burn in hell, but I don't also want your blood, on my hands."

The Lieutenant turns around and throws up, on the side the hill.

Daggard suddenly realizes that the Lieutenant removed his helmet and cries out.

"We'll all die soon, anyway. You've broken the air seal, on the suites. We're all exposed, to the deadly radiation."

"Good, we both deserve it."

"We're going to die all alone on this cold and muddy hill."

"No, you won't but I wish you would. There's no radiation, here. It's somehow free of it. See?" The Lieutenant shows him, his wrist's Geiger counter then pulls Daggard up on his feet. "Come on let's go."

They both begin climbing slowly down the hill.

After reaching level ground, the lieutenant not trusting Daggard, makes him walk in front of him.

"You will have to answer to someone about what you did here."

"Do I have a choice?" Daggard replies.

"I don't think so."

"I was just doing my job. I follow orders just like you do."

"You couldn't wait until we got more help, right?"

"There wasn't any time."

"How about now?"

"I guess you are in charge of that."

Daggard, meanwhile as he walks in front of the Lieutenant, he slowly pulls out a pistol, in front of him and cocks it.

"Lieutenant, Daggard speaks to him in a conniving manner. Let's be sensible about this. It will be my word against yours. Let's forget all about what happened out here, tonight. I will definitely put in a good word, for you. They will make you a full Captain, alright."

"For doing what?"

"For outstanding actions beyond the call of duty."

"How about my dead comrades? What will they receive out of this?"

"I'm sure, that we can work something out for them and their families. Perhaps meritorious medals, for valor given, to their survivors."

"I realize that they will have a rough time convicting you, let me think about it."

"Think of it. A Captain in the Submarine Service and in charge of your own Atomic sub."

"Alright Daggard, that's enough, I'm not interested, but keep your promise to my men."

"Good. Let's shake on it."

"Forget it. Keep on walking."

The Lieutenant lowers his guard for a moment; Daggard swings around without warning and fires two shots directly into the Lieutenant's chest. As he falls to the ground, Daggard quickly rushes over, kicks the weapon off his side, and takes possession of it.

"I knew I couldn't trust you. You bastard." The Lieutenant slowly closes his eyes and dies.

As Daggard picks up the portable radio and straps it on, he mutters.

"I told you so. I'll do whatever it takes, to get my way. Sorry, you loose."

He drags the Lieutenants' body down into the swamp and slowly sinks it. After he watches it disappear from view, he gets up and marches off to his rendezvous with the submarine and the other recovery team.

After a couple of minutes into the flight, high above the Earth's surface, the spacecraft initiates a slight curve toward the horizon. Automatic controls, guided by the global positioning satellite, gradually reduces power to the rotating plates and slowly extend outward the mechanical arms, of the solar wind panels, into position. As this happens, the vehicle then gradually picks up momentum and approaching near orbital speed.

"Look at that how the solar winds ionizes the panels with brilliant arrays of colors."

"Its actually the sub atomic particle impacting the almost impenetrable electron shield is what causing the colorful light show."

"Wow! Its like the aurora-borealis in miniature form." Said Michael

Michael then calls out to Andrius, who is perched high up front in the pilots' seat of the vehicle, manning the controls:

"Andrius, where are we now?"

"We're approximately, one hundred and twenty five miles above the earth's surface and traveling at over ten thousand miles, per hour. The vehicle will level off automatically, at eighteen thousand."

"Would we overshoot San Augustine?"

"No. The spacecraft is programmed to do one complete orbit, around the earth, before we land again."

"Then we should all sit back and enjoy the flight."

Ninety minutes later, after executing a 180-degree spacecraft swing around, the control system energizes and increases the revolutions on the rotating plates, as it starts a controlled free-fall to earth by throttling the gravity controls from time to time.

The outer shell temperature of the spacecraft rises over twelve hundred degrees, as it penetrates the upper air layers of the earth's surface. Michael looks out through a small porthole:

"From up here, you can't determine, which way is up or down. There's the beginnings of blue skies below and above, at the same time."

"Michael, you must have experienced this strange phenomenon, when you fly your jet higher than sixty thousand feet altitude."

"I wish. Commercial aircraft are not equipped for such altitudes. You need lots of fuel.

At lower altitudes, I did witness the phenomenon. It was almost as brilliant as this.

Hey, I'm beginning to see the West Coast of Africa. Looks a pale brown dark green color. Wow! What details? Andrius, we're flying backwards. When did that happen?"

"Just as we started descending, the aircraft did an automatic mid course maneuver. It automatically rotated in space to make the initial re-entry."

"Wow! I can see clearer now."

"You can probably see more details in daylight." Said Andrius

"Mister Andrius, I'm feeling that funny sensation, again." Said Mrs. Mason

"Yes. We're landing, soon. The vehicle will not land exactly at San Augustine, but a mile or two, from The Villa Rosa. We will leave you outside of the town, by a dried riverbank. It is only a short walk from there."

"Oh, excellent, Mister Andrius, I'm very familiar with the area." Said Dr. Alvarez

"I've also traveled through that region, plenty of times. I believe that the insurgents never went near that area, because of its proximity to Chile." Added Mrs. Mason

"Doctor, once we leave you there, please move away from the spacecraft, as far as possible. The engine emits a deadly heat wave that may cause burns on your skin, if you are too close." Said Andrius

"I understand, Mister Andrius. We will take proper precautions."

The spacecraft streaks across the Southern skies looking more like a meteor than a spacecraft. It gradually reduces its speed and makes an uneventful landing.

Surprisingly, the area was rain soaked due to a sudden heavy downpour, which occurred minutes before their arrival. Once on the ground, no fires in the immediate area are seen due to the wet vegetation and muddy ground.

Andrius and Michael exit the aircraft and help the couple off.

"Thank you Doctor Alvarez, we will visit you soon, after we iron out, some of our transportation problems. Our technical people will be arriving later on today or tomorrow with equipment and service personnel to assist you to put your house and clinic in order."

"That's great and generous of you Mister Andrius. Thank you."

"Dr. Alvarez, it is a pleasure to have met you and I thank you for your hospitality in assisting and treating Dr. Roberts during his time of need."

"You're welcome, Sir and I thank you also for rescuing my daughter and my nurse."

"You're also welcome and so long for now."

"Alright, Mister Andrius. Good bye and we'll look forward to seeing you soon."

Dr. Alvarez helps bring down Mrs. Mason's handbag off the aircraft and immediately after, they both hurry off the site to avoid being exposed to the vehicle destructive wave emissions.

Shortly after, Michael and Andrius inspect the vehicle and wait a while longer to make sure that the couple safely reaches their destination and climb into the spacecraft.

Minutes later the spacecraft takes off this time, using its own power and disappears from view, in the night sky.

At the island, Daggard by this time reaches the other side of the island and joins the other Navy men, as radio contact is reestablished, with the submarine.

Minutes later, once on board, Daggard describes to the Captain and the ship's officers, the ill-fate of the men and their harrowing experience, facing death, by the hands of an unseen enemy, who viciously attacked them, using some type of lethal weapons that instantly incinerated everyone in site.

He displayed his burnt radiation suit, bearing witness to the ordeal, which he miraculously survived. He promises them that their untimely death, will not be in vain and those who are responsible, will be brought to justice and punished, for this malicious unprovoked attack.

Afterwards, Daggard goes into sickbay, for medical treatment, for the burns on his shoulders and arms that he received from his attackers.

A few hours' later, he meets privately with the Captain after arranging a special memorial for the men that perished on the Island.

"Captain, we must now speak in private. I have some vital information to talk to you about. Its about classified military intelligence that was discovered by your navy people, on the island."

"Please step in here, Sir."

"Thank you."

The Captain closes the door behind him and both men sit down on a small table.

"Captain, the Chinese Reds or whoever is out there have erected a vast missile launch complex and a control center, at the other end of the Island. We must alert the President and our military of the serious situation, so he can give me the authority to launch a major offensive against the Island."

"Are you sure?"

"Yes. If this doesn't give me the opportunity to become Presidency, nothing will."

"Mister Daggard, put your future presidential plans on temporary hold because I'm afraid, that you will not be able to speak to the President, for some time. Not today, nor tomorrow."

"What do you mean?" He focuses his eyes on the Captain.

"Right after your last radio message with us, early this evening, we've suffered a complete lost of all communications and radar. Your hand radio was the only communications device that was able to get through to us because it was site on line transmission."

"How is that possible?"

"Our equipment just became inoperative. All the communication equipment has been checked and double-checked. Theoretically, it should function, but it just simply, doesn't. Some exterior electro magnetic force has neutralized our radar signals and has fried some of our electronics circuits. We're working around the clock repairing and restoring the burnt out units. For others there are no replacements. This may be just a phenomenon, which only occurs in the Southern Hemisphere. I'm assuming another worse possibility, that nuclear weapons have been detonated somewhere in this area or elsewhere and we are possibly, at a state of war at this moment perhaps with the Russians or China."

"I can't believe this. Is there any other method available, to make contact with Washington?"

"Not by military radio or our special submarine link system. They are all out of commission. We're sitting blind and cut off from the rest of the world, if there's still one."

"There has to be some other means that we can link up with Washington."

"We can possibly splice into one of those defunct deep sea telephone cable now being used by the motion picture industry. It will take at least six to eight hours, to get to it."

"No. No. That won't work." Said Daggard

The Captain opens up a chart and looks up at Daggard.

"How about the Sixth Fleet? Supposedly, it should be about six hours southeast of here, if not ordered elsewhere and if we travel at high speed on the surface, we can intercept them."

"That's better."

"But there's a problem. Our ID code transmitter is inoperative. They may detect and confuse us as an unfriendly and fire an anti-sub missile against us before we are able to communicate with them. Remember, we only have line of site communications."

"Not a good idea. It will be suicide to attempt to reach them like that."

"We can sail parallel with the fleet and launch distress flares at random and force them to investigate."

"That's better, Captain. That's one option. You do know that I have the authority, to launch a conventional limited offensive weapons, against the Island."

"Yes, Mister Daggard. I know that."

"A small assault of the Island will be sufficient, for the present time, but I want, on a moments notice, the flexibility to clear out, all of the assault forces, off the island."

"Mister Daggard, what do you have in mind?"

"The use of nuclear weapons, if need be. The enemy may be able to repel our first assault. We can't take any chances. If they launch those missiles, the whole world is doomed."

"You'll need the President's authority for that."

"Captain, let's get on the way. By standing here talking, we're not accomplishing anything. The President may be anxiously waiting, for my call."

"You're right, Sir." Both men exit the small room and walk off, to carry on with the mission.

CHAPTER XVI

The Titan spacecraft streaks down across the night sky and finally land on a tennis field beside a swimming pool in Key Largo, which are private properties owned by the President.

Besides creating numerous small brush fires for a radius of a half-mile throughout the area, the spacecraft, also causes power blackouts and local breakdown of all radio and telephone communication transmissions.

Due to the size of the small community, local volunteer fire stations are the only means to fight fires. The South Miami Fire Department responds only to mayor calls for help, when made, to the mainland. Helicopters ready equipped with the latest fire fighting equipment are placed on alert, when the President is in Key Largo.

The commotion that night, outside and around the Florida White House, awakens the President. He gets up, looks out the window and sees a strange glow, in the sky.

Somewhat curious, he quietly leaves the bedroom and meets outside, with the Secret Service people. They try to explain the situation, but cannot come up with a logical reason for the strange fires, which suddenly lit up, around the compound.

Confused by the situation, the President recommends that the remaining agents that are stationed around the house should join the other security and neighbors, in putting out the fires and further ads:

"Mister West, don't worry about the first Lady and I. We will keep our doors locked. Please join the others. They need your help.

If possible get in contact with the neighboring volunteer fire fighting stations, if you need additional help in fighting these small brush fires."

"Alright, Mister President, if you say so. Please go inside now, before we leave. Thanks."

The six agents then quickly hurry off and join the rest of the local fire brigade.

At this time, Colonel Towers and the others luckily find a path, through the smoke cluttered gardens and unknowingly, walked right by the Secret Service, who is busy fighting the multiple fires, around the grounds. Any attempts by the Secret Service, to call for additional help to the mainland, either by radio, or by telephone, proved to be fruitless.

Once the party reaches the house, they separated into two small groups and enter the house through the garden and the servant's quarters. Wearing night vision equipment they simultaneously converge in the bedroom. The sudden invasion startles the President and his wife who were conversing about the strange occurrences outside in bed.

The First Lady gives a short scream, thinking that the group are subversives and are there to kill them. She quickly moves to the President's side out of fear for safety.

"No! Said Andrius, he raises his hand. Do not be afraid, Mister President. We are not here to hurt you, nor your family."

"What is the meaning of this?" The President demands.

"Please lower your voice." Said Michael, while displaying his automatic weapon."

"Who are you and what do you want with us?" The President asked while holding his wife in his arms.

"We only wish to speak to you, Mister President." Said Andrius

"Armed with guns and automatic weapons, and you wish only, to speak to me?"

"No. This is just for our protection. We have no choice."

"You look familiar. Do I know you?"

"No, I'm afraid not. We haven't met before, but you know of me."

"Of you? He questioned. From where?" He queried.

"I am Andrius." He said in a low voice.

"Andrius? Andrius? I don't quite recall that name. Oh, yes, I remember, now. You are Andrius, the researcher and the leader of that group called 'Orgites', right? He pauses and thinks for a few seconds.

Why are you here? I thought you and your friends were all dead. Reports said that you all perished in an airline crash off the coast of South America."

"Apparently, we did not."

"I'm now curious. Why are you here?"

"As I said before, I wish to speak to you, Mister President."

"I can't imagine, why. Tell me, how did you get through our security bearing with all those weapons?"

"Security? We didn't see any, Sir."

The First Lady interrupts the conversation.

"Honey, who are the Orgites? Are they some political anti-social group?"

"It's a long story, honey. They're a new species, of humans."

"I don't understand, you are saying, a new species of humans? Is that possible?"

"Janet, they are a secret race that was created, through scientific research."

"By who?"

"By our Government."

"For what purpose?"

"Our government was interested, in their potential and their far superior abilities."

"My lord. Since when do you know of this awful thing?"

"I've known about this for quite some time, dear. Some of our people that work in the Intelligence sector of the government decided to keep their existence a secret, until we can find some method of introducing them, to the world."

"How as equals or as slaves. I believe I heard two or three years ago, a public announcement was made, but people refused to believe, which caused some confusion and strive to many. Days later, the disclosure was retracted and people quickly forgot, about the whole incident."

"You do remember dear."

"Yes, I do remember it very clearly. It happened in New York City and it was disturbing."

"A lot has happened, ever since. Our country is presently being threatened from abroad and some in the Government found a potential military use, for this new species."

"I assume that the United States wanted to use them in some way, or another."

"Yes, we wanted them to help us militarily, but their leaders refused and have caused sedition and crimes, against the United States."

"Mister President, may I intervene in your conversation because we need to clarify your statement."

"And what is that, Mister Andrius or whatever your name is."

"Sir to clarify the situation, we have been unjustly accused." Said Andrius

"I understand now what's going on. You do know that there are Federal warrants out, for your arrest and your other friends, here."

"Yes, I know, Sir. I wish you would retract those orders."

"That's why you're here and why should I do such a thing? Do you have plans to hold us hostage?"

"No Sir."

"You've broken our laws and now it's up to the Justice Department, to determine your guilt, or innocence."

"What exactly are the charges that I'm accused of, Sir?"

"I believe, various counts of murder, insurrection, and high-jacking. Is that not enough?"

"Oh my dear they're harden criminals." Janet, the Presidents' wife exclaims,

"Sir, I haven't murder anyone." Andrius affirms.

"You murdered a federal agent, in New York City and two others, in New York State."

"I regretfully did terminate the life of a person, but strictly in self defense. The others were accidental.

I leaped from an aircraft and fell upon a person who died as a result. That occurred in Upstate New York. My race doesn't kill in cold blood. I will prove my innocence."

"So, you do not deny those killings?"

"No, Sir. These individuals were trying to kill members, of my family and succeeded killing a colleague of mine who was not able to defend himself. It was a cold-blooded murder without mercy. Like I explained, I acted in self defense, when our lives were being unjustly threatened to a point of death."

"I believe that this gentleman is really telling the truth. I believe him."

"Dear, let me handle this. I will get to the truth somehow."

"Alright, go on."

"Then who killed the police officer? Perhaps your comrades, over there?"

"No, Sir. I'm afraid not."

"Well, then, who?" The President demands an answer.

"I believe it was an evil and sadistic individual, answering to the name, of Karl Daggard."

"Oh no, not him." The President's wife cries out.

"Are you leveling with me, Mister Andrius?"

"Would I deny it if I were the one? I have nothing to hide, Mister President."

"No, I'm afraid not."

"The policeman would testify in my behalf, if he were alive, today. Daggard shot him in the back. If you test his weapon, you will find that he killed the policeman, in cold blood."

The President thinks about what Andrius said.

"My God! I cannot believe that my step brother is capable of murder." Janet confesses

"I'm afraid it is true, Janet. I also had that awful gut feeling about him.

It was Daggard all the time, after all. He was responsible, for all of these senseless killings. At first, when I heard of all the incidents and his phony excuses, I refused to believe that he was capable, of committing these horrible things. I know now."

"I'm positively certain too, without a doubt Sir." Andrius added.

"Mister Andrius, my brother was adopted, at a very late age of fourteen years old. He came from a broken family and was troubled, all his life.

My parents made sure that he received a good education, because we were well off and my father had a special liking to him. Karl was the only male, among six female siblings, in the family. He was spoiled and he took advantage of it and my parents, in many ways.

In a way, I feel sorry for him, because he never overcame his demons. He suffered from an inferiority complex and became very ambitious and heartless. My parents were always covering up his faults and bad deeds. He had a dark side to him that was hard to unravel by many of the doctors that were consulted."

"I must deal with him, on my own terms." The President walks over to the window and looks at the people, fighting the brush fires, in the far distance.

"Daggard must be brought to justice and he must answer for his crimes."

The President turns to Janet his wife again:

"Sweetheart, he's not in his right mind. We must commit him before he does more damage to us and to everyone around."

"I'm so sorry for my brother, dear. I've should have told you years ago. I feel it's my fault."

"Mister Andrius, how about your refusal, to join our cause?"

"Sir, I never had the chance to rightfully refused nor I was ever consulted."

"But you ran off, before anyone, could speak to you."

"Sir, I panicked by the manner your security people tried to approach me. It was scary.

I was simply trying to let everyone know that I would not commit my people, to a cause, that would perpetuate our involvement, in all future military conflicts, throughout this world. That is all, Sir."

"You mean that the Government wanted to use your people for warfare." Janet asks.

"Unfortunately, this was their plan."

"That's unheard of. How could they force a new race of people, which are not even citizens, to fight and defend our country? It makes no sense."

"Janet, the American people are tired of sending their son's and daughters out to fight foreign wars, or any kind of war. Too much blood has been spilled and more possibly, in the future. The Orgites was the solution to this monumental problem of National Defense. I realize now that it was morally wrong to do this."

"This proposal dwarfs my brother's evil deeds by light years. You, I mean, this Government was planning to subjugate these benign people, to fight all our foreign wars?"

"That was the idea, at the time but I was thoroughly against it at first, until the situation in South America worsen. I also panicked, too. I became blind with fear and uncertainty."

"Do you know that this is morally wrong and it can cause you to loose your re-election and the downfall of the Party, if it's ever made public? You would be impeached."

"Yes, I'm well aware of that, sweetheart I've now decided to do the correct thing."

"Good."

"So then, in what other means can you help our country with, Mister Andrius?"

"Sir, I simply don't know. Perhaps a new weapon or something worthwhile."

"Perhaps something like the diversion, which you caused, to get to see me?"

"Sir, that was no diversion, it's simply an electro-magnetic force that's generated from our spacecraft's propulsion system."

"Electro magnetic? Never heard of such a thing. I hope this is not the so-called reverse engineering that some are claiming, that's secretly being extracted from the extra terrestrials. I doubt it, if they actually exists."

"No Sir, my people invented it. It's actually an inductive flux that's used for navigating in space. The force is so great, that it literally incinerates everything, on sight. We're presently working at reducing its' destructive effects."

"Mister Andrius, can you give the United States this new type of propulsion system?"

"Mister President, that's why I've come here; I wish to negotiate with you. I will give you this new technology and other inventions, which will revolutionize all energy and weapon systems here in America. I will ease all of your transportation problems, on this planet."

"I'm glad that you decided to see me first, before any other country, Mister Andrius."

"Mister President, I love the American people and the way of life in our country and I will never trade it for any place else."

"Well said, young man. You are an honest man."

"Thank you. Well, you hold all the cards now, Mister President."

"Can I ask you, where are you and your people hiding?"

"Sir we are not hiding from anyone but for our security sake, I cannot answer that, Mister President, but I will give you my word and I will surrender personally to you and turn over all our research materials in return, if we can reach a mutual understanding."

The President turns away from the window, goes to his study and sits down.

"You are willing to do all of that?"

"Yes, Sir."

"I've the orders here incriminating each and every one of you, of high crimes and treason. They're waiting, my signature. If convicted of all these crimes, all of you will serve many years in jail and most likely you will never see light of freedom, in your lifetimes."

Andrius takes a deep swallow realizing that his sentence would commit him to an eternity in jail because he was created possibly to be immortal.

"Yes Sir. If this will free my people, I'm willing to face all the consequences."

"Andrius, to prove my sincerity, I will forgo these orders. Even if we do not reach an accord, I believe you're innocent of all these charges. I personally don't agree with your weapons offer that you're willing to give to the United States. Nevertheless, OK, I would accept your new energy force, but nay on the weapons O.K. Lets keep that offer between us.

Remember one thing is that power corrupts even those with the very best of intentions. Can we agree to this?"

"Mister President, I must apologize, I underestimated you. I thought you would embrace the idea, of having the advantage, over all your adversaries, with such a weapon system."

"No. I deplore it."

"Mister President, I have to confess that American Presidents are born to lead this country. They are specifically chosen by God as special leaders of America."

At that moment, the telephone rings, causing Andrius to jump.

"Please do not answer that, Mister President." Said Andrius

"Trust me, Mister Andrius, I must. It's a national security phone. We may be in the state of war."

"Alright, Mister President."

The President quickly goes over to the phone, presses a five-digit combination and disengages the phone from its' locked brace.

"This is the President."

"Mister President, this is Daggard. I'm on board the Naval Destroyer, The McCormick."

"Yes, I know. What is the urgency for this call?"

"We've made contact with the enemy, tonight. They're preparing to launch a massive missile attack against the United States and the free world at any moments time."

"How? With nuclear weapons?"

"No Sir. They are using some strange looking type of aircraft. I've never seen anything like that ever in my life. The aircraft looks more powerful, than anything we have."

"How many of these aircraft did you see?"

"Mister President, literally hundreds, as far as the eye, can see. We must destroy them. Sir, I'm requesting permission to launch nukes against the Eastern coast of this Island. We must launch them as soon as possible. Time is of essence."

"Which island is it?"

"I believe it is called The Isle of Corazon, Sir. It was formerly a research outpost now abandoned."

"You presently have limited authority to confront them once you confirmed that there's a hostile intent to attack the United States. For now you use conventional weapons, Mister Daggard, but I will make the final decision, on the use of nuclear weapons."

"Sir, I will commence with an amphibious assault group, on the northwest coast.

Intel has discovered, a subterranean command center, in the island.

They estimate that there are about two to three thousand men there. If I can take out the command center, we could avoid the use of the nukes, Sir."

"Do they have any coastal defenses?"

"Not that I can see, Sir. I would say, no at this time but there may be."

"Very good. You have the authorization to proceed with your plan. As I speak, I'm patching you up to the Joint Chiefs, to work out your plans and execution."

"Thank you, Sir."

Minutes later, after working out the military tactics with the Defense Office, the President hangs up the phone and sits quietly while meditating on the situation. He then gets up and turns to Andrius.

"Mister Andrius, I hope you forgive me. For the past forty-eight hours, we've been going through hell here."

"Sir, I don't understand." Andrius was somewhat alarmed.

"Not because of your group, but of a sizable insurgent movement coupled with a Middle Eastern group who have been systematically sabotaging the Southern International Power Grid System, in the South Atlantic and now Europe.

Their aim is the economic destruction of the West by any means put forward. One is by political over throw of Democratic Governments in South America and the other is the sabotaging of the world economic support systems."

"Oh, how strange." Andrius was now very concerned. He quickly thought that he might help the President with this situation.

"Luckily, Mister Daggard has located them and will soon stop their offensive.

I believe, he said, that they are located on a volcanic island, a couple hundred miles south of the Island of Marina and Tierra del Fuego, in the South Atlantic, an Island called Corazon."

As the President further explains the scenario, Andrius realizes the troubling dilemma.

"This may come as a big surprise to you, Sir. My people unfortunately are on that Island.

I'm afraid, that we are the ones responsible, for the power losses. Not that we caused them intentionally. I needed the electrical power, to construct my spacecraft and to repair an abandoned fusion cyclotron, in a lab, which was previously used for a research program. This is part of the partial list of equipment and other new technologies that I plan on to give to the United States of America."

"Mister Andrius, this puts a different light, on the whole mystery. So, actually, the Insurgents and the Middle Eastern group are not on that island but Mister Daggard, believes otherwise."

"Mister President, my people will be in great danger, once Mister Daggard discovers who they are."

"I do agree with you. Mister Daggard is a megalomaniac and a psychopath. Your people will not stand a chance."

"I have to go back and stop him somehow."

"You must. He will confiscate all the spacecraft and the fusion generators, as spoils of war and probably claim it for himself. I'm afraid that he will use it as a political stepping-stone for fame and power. I cannot let that happen. He's too ambitious and dangerous."

"What do you propose, Sir?"

"Mister Andrius, you better leave for your island, as soon as possible. Remove all your people, at once.

I'll make sure, that Mister Daggard never gets his hands, on these items. I have a plan of my own, to deal with him and eliminate any threats to your people."

"Thank you, Sir. How about your Secret Service? They're out there, all around."

"Don't worry about them. I will order them to come in to prepare for my immediate departure. I've decided to make a special trip but I must first return to Washington."

Suddenly, the lights go on, throughout the house.

"Ah. That's better. Oh, Mister Andrius, I see you much better, now. You're somewhat a little different, from what I pictured you, before."

"Yes, Sir. A great many people have the same opinion."

"I now see your other comrades. I believe you must be, Colonel Towers."

"Yes, Sir."

"You've some fantastic military record, son. I wish you would reconsider staying with us."

"Sir, I would like to, but not under these circumstances. Perhaps later."

"Yes. Yes, perhaps later, I invite all of you, to be my guests in Washington. I know that we can work out some accord to have your people return to the United States, with all rights as citizens fully guaranteed and protected."

"Mister President, thank you. That's a very kind gesture, on your part. I hope, to see you in the near future, so that we can discuss this, again."

"Good. At least, that will be a start. Well Mister Andrius, the First Lady and I will not hold you any longer. You have important things to do, now."

"I wish to thank you both again for your understanding and hospitality."

"O.K lets get this show on the go. Please gentlemen, move to the back porch and wait there, a few minutes, after I call in the Secret Service. All right?"

"Yes, Sir. Once again, it's a great honor to have met you, Mister President."

"The same here, Mister Andrius. This way, please." The President ushers the group, to the rear of the house.

Minutes later, Andrius and the others, find their way back to the spacecraft without ever crossing paths with the security people fighting the brush fires and take off to an encounter with Daggard back at the Island.

When the lights, again go out in the house, the President speaks out to everyone:

"Don't be alarmed, gentlemen. It's only a temporary condition. A call has been placed to the Coast Guard fireboats. They should be arriving shortly and they will put out all the fires that have started up, again. So lets relax and savor the moment."

"Sir, has this happened before?"

"It's a normal condition out here on the Islands. You have to learn to bear with it."

A confused group leader looks at the President and wonders why is he so confidant, that what is happening, is only temporary? Frustrated, the agent walks out of the house and looks, at all the brush fires, in the distance. He shakes his head in dismay and looks up, and sees a bright glowing object, streaking across the heavens and wonders.

"Ah that must be the International Space Station." He grunts out a few other words to himself and walks into the house.

CHAPTER XVII

Twilight, in the Southern Hemisphere, brings six destroyers, two heavy cruisers, a missile launcher and two aircraft carriers, twelve miles off the coast, of the small volcanic island.

At least three-fourths of the population of the complex has already boarded the spacecraft and await Andrius' arrival.

Jarvis, at this time, anticipating an amphibious invasion, deploys five hundred and fifty fellows Orgites, as a first line of defense, of the Island. He has them install high density directional loud speakers, on the beachfronts, as a last attempt to convince the landing forces, that needless blood and loss of lives, on both sides, can be avoided, if they refrain themselves, from invading the Island.

One hundred amphibious sea-craft, loaded with marines spearheaded, by a special detachment of C.S.A. agents, flown, in earlier that day, begin their slow trek, across the frigid choppy seas.

Men wearing special weatherproof gear and weapons specially designed to weather the treacherous conditions, which they are about to embark.

Jarvis makes a calculated guess that this was the only approach, that the military would use, because three fourths of the coastline is physically impassable due to ocean currents, many submarine rocks and coral structures, that litters the ocean floor and shore.

The ocean temperatures due to the high salt concentration, tethers at twelve degrees Fahrenheit, guarantying a quick death, to anyone who falls in and is exposed to the waters, for more than a minute.

An aerial approach was seriously considered but due to a steady strong 60-mile per hour turbulent wind currents would pose a greater danger for the paratroopers than an actual combat scenarios.

Aerial support was also ruled out due to strong electro-magnetic disturbance, in the area would cause aircraft to malfunction while in flight. The decision was to use the combat soldier as the best approach for this interdiction. The only problem before them would be the harsh and hellish environmental conditions of the island.

The fully covered and internally heated assault boats, slowly coasted on the seas for an hour, toward the island, meanwhile receiving individual group instructions via video monitors, from their commanders.

Once they reach a rendezvous point of four miles out, all the sea-crafts begin circular patterns, awaiting the final orders, to start the insertion.

Jarvis using a radiophone and high intensity directional loud speakers pleads, with the invading forces, but all attempts prove fruitless.

At a pre-planned designated time, cruisers out at sea, begin firing hundreds of non-guided rockets, along the coastline of the island, saturating the beachfront and all the inland areas.

Strong concussion, from exploding shells, is felt throughout the Center, as naval guns aim, at strategic targets and suspicious enemy concentrations. Due to their deep location within the mountain, no damage is made or reported. The aerial attacks goes on for two hours with no end in sight.

Crude oil, mixed with a combination of jet fuel and industrial alcohol, are piped in from area storage tanks. They are set ablaze, by the fellow Orgites, as a contra measure to disguise key landmarks and roads, which will be used, as an escape route, if other counter measures fail to dampen the invasion.

In addition, Jarvis has hundreds of used jet fuel oil tanks and oil storage drums, linked up by heavy chains, are floated out three miles off shore, and sit waiting for the right moment, to be set on fire, as a final deterrent, against the invasion. The tank contains a special mixture of highly volatile substance of solid and liquid fuels designed to burn brighter and longer than the standard fuel.

At this time, Daggard boards one of the landing craft, and heads forward to spearhead his invasion group.

After the aerial and rocket onslaught is completed, smaller cruisers ahead of the assault craft, begin laying thick heavy smoke, to camouflage their planned beachhead.

Some of the smoke laying sea craft accidentally collide with submerged submarine boulders and explode into flames becoming the first casualties of the invasion.

Rescue boats immediately are launched from various ships and rescue the survivors giving the men in the assault boats an omen of worse scenarios to follow. The moral amongst the men is pretty shaken but not fully destroyed.

Daggard, somewhat alarmed by the untimely occurrence arrives to the assault boat well resigned and takes his position of Commander.

He gives the word and the first step to the invasion commences.

As the crafts reach three miles off shore, Jarvis launches several small aerial rockets across the waters and successfully ignites numerous floating fuel oil drums and the aircraft fuel oil tanks, fed by additional oil tanks, located below the surface supplied by fire hoses from shore supply tanks.

The exploding fuel forms a spectacular 100 feet solid firewall and black smoke, which immediately stops the sea-crafts, from advancing further.

The crafts immediately veer off and retreat, to safer locations, to await new orders.

Daggard, upon seeing this, quickly give out orders to the captains to crash the wall of flames. The assault-craft group leaders hesitate and call the Fleet Captains for assistance.

The Marine Commander, upon seeing the sudden turn of events and the momentary confusion among the marines, calls Daggard, on the radio for consultation.

"Mister Daggard, we must talk strategy, here and now. This is not good."

"Commander, you should order your men to crash the fire-wall, it's only a ploy to slow us down. The assault crafts can easily navigate through the thin layer of flames and will not, suffer any serious damages. I've seen this ploy before in the Middle East. We cannot allow them to sway us by a little fire. Where is your sense of adventure and military pride?"

"Sir, with due respect, we should wait for the fires to die down, before we commit the men. The Seals were not given enough time to go out and neutralize those floating fuel oil tanks. There may be mines, underwater traps, and all kinds of obstacles, which will cause the needless loss of lives of the men. We must reconfigure a safer approach."

"I can't wait; this has to be done, now. Time is critical, Commander."

"I understand the gravity of the situation, but at this moment and time, I must stand down, Sir."

"Commander, if you have no stomach for it, you should relinquish your command position and surrender it, to a real commander that's able."

"Thank you; I will do that if you wish me to, Sir."

"You'll be Court Marshaled, for not following a direct order from the President of the United States and cowardliness, in the face of battle."

"Sir, you are a civilian and you have no authority to question or direct any of my military decisions, whatsoever, unless, such orders originate directly, from a Senior Commander or from the President of the United States himself."

Daggard infuriated by the Commanders response throws the radiophone on the deck and curses at him.

"You son of a bitch!"

He picks up another communications phone and orders the helm man to move on.

The crafts, which the marines began a circular pattern, maintain their pattern and await further orders from their commanders.

Meanwhile, Daggard reaches up to the head of his CSA forces and orders to his group, to form a separate attack formation.

"Men, follow me." He yells into the radiophone. He heads a spearhead, with twenty assault crafts and begins the assault.

All the sea-crafts' engines roar to high gear and anticipation. The men zipper up the special combat suits and secures their headgear and weapons.

Air horns from each of the crafts sounds out, as a means to cause confusion, to the enemy on shore.

The Marines, eager to join the invasion, upon hearing the attack horns, are unable to join the assault group; instead they also sound their horns as a show of support for the invading group.

The attack formation, charges forward at full speed.

The spearhead approaches the fire-line and all the assault-craft disappear as they crash through the wall of flames, smoke and black muck, while throwing caution, to the wind. Chaos immediately ensues as this happens.

Many of the sea craft crash into submerged obstacles. Others become entangled on the heavy chains, which are fastened together to the fuel oil drums, as a deterrent.

The large assault boats crash into submarine boulders. Some explode upon impact. The heavy smoke causes terror and disorientation amongst them. The heavy smoke causes poor visibility and some of the crafts crash into each other. Many of the boats sink with all hands on board.

From the ships they observe men jumping off their fiery crafts and succumbing, to the burning fuel.

Many die, in the frigid waters attesting to Daggard's fruitless attempt and disregard.

Eight sea crafts, manage to survive the ordeal and land on shore, under a hale of fire, from automatic coastal defense guns, installed by Jarvis and the fellow Orgites from atop of a hill that overlooks the shoreline.

Once on land, the amphibious crafts move inland through the swamps and desolated woodlands, stopping occasionally, to reconnoiter and eliminate small pockets of resistance from Orgites, who decide to remain, as sacrificial victims as a slow down tactic, in order to allow the others to survive and reach safely to the launch sites.

As additional forces make landfall and reconnoiter their position, they receive equipment to aid them, in combating the enemy forces, on the island.

The equipment is delivered by unmanned sea craft and other special tools delivered by high altitude aircraft using parachutes guided by remote control, from the fleet assembled, twelve miles off shore. Unfortunately the remote control equipment misses their target due to the electrical impulses that affect all electronics and land miles away from the intended place.

An hour before sunset, Daggard rides, in a land rover vehicle, with the rest of his expeditionary force and reaches the heavily protected outskirts of the complex.

With the aid of global positioning satellites, missiles are launch against all the automatic gun positions, installed on the mountains, overlooking the invasion site and the complex. They eliminate many of the sites except those, which are in inaccessible places and many of the aerial weapons go astray due to disruptions of their guided systems.

The remaining Orgites flee in various directions and create separate guerrilla fighting groups, causing additional problems, for the military to target.

With the elimination of most of the resistance, Daggard finally reaches the research center and concentrates all his efforts, in penetrating the heavy metallic entrance doors, with high explosives and special laser equipment flown in, by marine copters.

The main marine forces finally arrive and take over, key positions along the landing zones and approaches to the center complex. They receive a welcome relieve from the exhausted and battle ridden CSA agents.

After two hours, the CSA agents finally break through the heavy fortified entrance and the troops quickly take charge of the vacated upper levels of the complex, which are without electrical power, at this time thanks to the technicians' efforts at the power transfer station.

They bring with them, electric winches and portable lights to aid them in searching through the abandon labs for any remnants of the enemy.

As they carefully move about, one of the marines Sergeants senses some type of vibration on one of the steel column supports. This was very odd and he reports the strange occurrence, to Daggard.

After confirming it with the soldier, Daggard takes six of his armed CSA men and locate a shaft near the column and sets up a winch assembly to go down and investigate.

Several of them loaded with lighting equipment ride down on the steel winch cables to one of the lower levels of the complex. They carefully investigate the level and realize that the vibrations are coming from an even lower level, of the complex. They set up another winch and decide to go down.

At the lower level, the shaft becomes narrower and Daggard decides to go down by himself with another agent, to investigate the paradox.

The agent sets up another portable electric winch, which is lowered from the surface. He and another agent begin to go down the narrow shaft.

"Hey are you all right?"

"Yes Sir. This shaft is deep. I can't see bottom yet."

"Just be careful. Tell me the moment you see anything, all right?"

"Yes Sir."

Daggard had no clue, that he was being lowered, to a room adjacent to the main corridor, that leads to the Fusion Generator machine.

Once touching down on the floor of the lab, they put on their flashlight headgear and slowly walk towards the source, of the strange vibrations and sound.

Taking some precaution, he swings his weapon around and lights up a laser pointer, to the muzzle of his weapon. They then carefully push themselves through a heavy steel door into the main corridor.

As he does, a bright light, like the size of a silver dollar, at a distance beyond, temporary blinds both men. Fearing that they will shortly confront the enemy, Daggard cocks his weapon, to catch them by surprise. He reaches into his backpack and pulls out light gargles and puts them on to protect his eyes from gun flashes.

They both rush into the outer chamber, of the lab and suddenly confront Jarvis, who is busy working and is equally surprised, to see them.

"Please, please, Sir." Jarvis waves up his hands. "Don't shoot. Please don't shoot me. I'm unarmed, Mister Daggard."

Daggard was also equally surprised that this strange little man knew his name.

"Come here very slowly, old man." Daggard said in a low voice, while looking all around him, for any other person, in the chamber.

"Don't worry, I am all alone."

"I said come here, old man."

"Yes Sir, as you say." Jarvis slowly inches tiptoes towards him.

"How do you know my name? Daggard looks at him, intensely. I don't know you."

"Only by reputation, Sir. I knew you were coming for quite some time."

"Wait a minute. Who are you? You don't look Asian or Middle Eastern. Are you being held down here, as a prisoner by them?"

"No, Sir. Not in the least bit."

"Well, who the hell, are you?" He demands.

"My name is Jarvis and I work here."

"You work here, all by yourself?"

"Not entirely. I work down here by myself and the others work, at the upper levels."

"There's no one up there."

"Oh, they are all gone, already? I have been so busy, that I forgot to join them."

"Join who?"

"Them." He points up with a strange look in his eyes.

"You sound crazy."

"Not a bit."

"You are crazy."

At that moment, a portable radio sounds out:

"Jarvis, this is Andrius. Everyone is almost board. What's taking you so long, old man?"

Jarvis makes a move to answer, but is pushed off, by Daggard.

"Please do not hurt me, Mister Daggard."

"Don't you move a muscle, old man, or I'll surely blow you to kingdom come?"

After a few seconds, Daggard suddenly realizes that the voice on the radio is his old nemesis, Andrius, the leader of the Orgites.

Meanwhile, other agents arrive at the scene. Daggard calls over one of the agents and whispers an order to him then approaches Jarvis.

"Listen, old man, tells Andrius, your leader, that there's someone here, who wishes to meet with him."

"Yes, Sir." Jarvis quickly picks up the phone.

"Andrius, are you still there?"

"Yes. What is the trouble? Don't tell me." Andrius suddenly realized, what was happening.

"Your friend, Daggard, is here, but he…." Suddenly, Daggard's men rush over and hit Jarvis across the head, with a rifle butt. He falls unconscious to the floor. Then Daggard walks over and picks up the phone:

"Hello Andrius, are you there?"

"Daggard, what happened, to the old man?"

"He's standing right here, next to me."

Andrius perceives that he wasn't. He then responds.

"What do you want? You better not hurt him."

"Listen. The next sound you hear will be the old man's head, bursting into bits."

"You'd better not, Daggard. I will get you. I swear." Daggard sets his rifle on automatic and fires several rounds.

"I'll do the same to you, when I see you. Do you hear me? Come and pick up the pieces."

Not caring to wait for the response, Daggard shoots out the radio.

Andrius, after hearing the gun discharge, tries to sense any telepathy from Jarvis, but is unable. Andrius puts his hands to his face in anguish after realizing that Jarvis has been murdered, he then decides once for all, to go to the complex and avenge Jarvis' death and the deaths of all of his fallen comrades.

"He was like a father to me and this hideous monster of a man had to kill him in cold blood.

There's no forgiving him. Daggard will pay dearly for this with his life."

Andrius gives out the orders to begin launching the spacecraft and informs everyone that he would join them later, in orbit, around the earth when he returns from the Complex.

After receiving word, that the complex is secured, Daggard drags the unconscious Jarvis into a room, adjacent to the control room. Still curious about the low hum noise down the corridor, he ventures forward to investigate.

As he opens another heavy steel door, he discovers the strange alluring light being emitted from the cracks along the edges of the doors in the adjacent room. He finds a face and an eye shield and places it on. As he approaches the door he reads on the door CYCLOTRON ROOM/FUSION GENERATOR. He opens the door and walks into the sunburst before him.

"My God!" Daggard is held captive for several seconds.

Somewhat familiar with the Russian Tokomak machines, he is in awe and in disbelief, at witnessing the awesome power, being created, in front of him.

After a few minutes he realizes its' world wide potential. "This is all mine." He then exits the room and discovers that his military outfit is completely bleached white. He then walks out to the other lab and approaches the other agent.

"What happened to your fatigues, Sir?"

"I'm lucky, that I decided not to shoot the old man. He's just become a highly valuable commodity for me. I can use his genius, to my advantage."

"What's that awful light, Mister Daggard?" The agent asked.

"Don't get closed to it. It's awesome power, unlimited power beyond anyone's concept. That's the fuel, which powers the stars, in our Universe and I have it in the palms of my hand. It will be all mine.

The old man has fortunately unlocked its' secret. The genie is finally out of the bottle."

"It must be some kind, of atomic power." The agent comment.

"It is far better. Whoever owns such a power, will rule the world."

"But Mister Daggard, how about the Orgite, Andrius?"

"He's coming here, just as I planned. Listen, bind the old man's arms and legs and take him to the beach. Wait for me there. You are not to say a word to anyone of what you just seen, O.K? This is a military TOP SECRET."

"Yes, Sir."

"Make sure, that he speaks to no one and make sure, that nothing happens to him, alright? You will answer to me, personally, if anything happens to him. Have the medic, look him over, for any damages and treat his head wound, alright."

"Yes. Right away, Sir."

Another soldier comes rushing to Daggard.

"Sir. Sir, we just received word. We have to evacuate the Island fast. We tried to call you on the radio, but couldn't get through."

"What do you mean?" Daggard demands.

"The President has ordered everyone to evacuate. He has decided to destroy the island, with a nuke."

"Give me your radio. Damn it! I gave the President explicit instructions, to drop the missiles, at the other end but not here. They will destroy my machine; he can't do that! Daggard clenches his fist in defiance.

"Damn it! He's carrying out my original wishes. I just did another fatal mistake. I have to stop him at all cause."

"Sir, the radio is not working down here but the other one that you shot did."

"Go ahead and send a message, to hold the launching, until I speak to him. Hurry go!"

"Yes, Sir."

Minutes later, the soldier comes rushing back again, to Daggard.

"Sir, we tried to get back to the ship, but none of the portable radios are working again and the strange missile weapons, are starting to take off on the other side, of the island."

"This is not my day. I must first kill Andrius and afterwards stop the President, from doing this stupid thing. It's not his fault but mine. I asked him to do it. Damn it!"

Daggard reloads his weapon and hurries off, to rendezvous with Andrius.

Once outside the complex, he boards an amphibious craft and makes his way through the semi-frozen swamps, towards the spacecraft launch area.

A few miles down, as Daggard clears a small mound, Andrius suddenly appears and leaps across into his vehicle, knocking Daggard, completely off. The amphibious craft goes astray and crashes into a small withered tree and comes to a stop.

Both men engage, rolls down a small slope over each other and violently struggle with each other in the midst of swampy ground. Daggard quickly gets up and kicks Andrius, in the face and races back to the craft, to retrieve his weapon.

Andrius recovers; he chases after him and grabs Daggard just as he reaches the craft. With the weapon in hand, Daggard quickly cocks it, swings around, gets off two shots and misses. He slips and falls backwards, on the wet ice.

Andrius leaps after him and both men roll into the mud again. Daggard kicks Andrius and flees off again but as he does, he pulls out his side arm from his belt.

Andrius recovers once again from the kick in the face and rushes towards him. Daggard suddenly stops, turns around with the gun in his hand. He takes dead aim at Andrius, pulls the trigger but the weapon jams. He quickly swings and hits Andrius again, across the side of his head, with the butt of the gun. Andrius falls backwards and hits the ground hard. He's now dazed and disorientated.

Daggard runs off and disappears as Andrius slowly gets his wits back and begins to follows Daggard's foot trails, in the snowy swamp.

Minutes later, Daggard reaches the beach and runs along the edge looking for his other agents for support but they are nowhere, to be found.

Upon failing at this, he makes a wide circle and climbs up a small hill to avoid Andrius, who is now bleeding profusely, from his face and determined to get him, at all cost.

Daggard reaches the top of the hill completely exhausted. He unjambs his weapon, when Andrius suddenly appears and knocks the gun out of his hands, as it fires and grazes him.

As the two men struggle, atop the hill, without warning, one of the spacecraft, rising from the silos, drifts across over the edge of the launch site and incinerates the hillside, together with the two combatants, just below the crest of the hill.

Both burst into flames and roll down, the side of the hill, while still fighting each other.

At the bottom, they break through the icy covered swamp and disappear.

The swamp luckily saves their lives, by snuffing out the flames. A minute goes by and there is no movement in the swamp. Both men remain submerged.

Andrius finally knocked out Daggard unconscious below the surface of the swamp and climbs out alone.

Once on the ground, after a short spell, he turns, kneels down and extends his arm down into the depths of the swamp and feels for Daggard's body. He finally locates him and pulls him out by the collar of his flak jacket and drags him, to a small clearing, in the marsh.

Both men are badly singed black and muddied all over.

Daggard lays unconscious on the semi frozen murky ground. His clothing still smothering from the exposures to the deadly wave emissions, even after being submerged in the mock.

Andrius looks up in the sky, and he sees a long outstretched column of his spacecraft streaking across the skies and he falls back on the ground, after loosing his balance.

Completely exhausted he rests for a few moments. He then gets up and in an oblivious state of mind; picks up a large bolder, weighing many times his weight and brings it over to drop it on Daggard body, as a repayment for what he did to him and Jarvis.

He suspends it with his arms outstretched and looks down on him and lingers and waits until Daggard comes to and finally sees him.

As he does, Daggard stares at Andrius unable to do anything but just stares aimlessly.

"Daggard, this is for the suffering that you have inflicted, on my people and for killing of my adopted father." Andrius displays emotions and feelings that were never expressed before in his life.

As he motions to drop the bolder when suddenly he hears a woman's voice:

"Andrius, no! Please, do not kill him." It is Uria who yells out, at top of her lungs.

"He must die. He killed Jarvis."

"No, no Andrius, there has been enough deaths, today. Jarvis is alive. Look here, he lives."

Jarvis, Michael and the Colonel immediately appear and join Uria.

"Please, Andrius, he's not worth it. Allow the authorities, to punish him, for his transgressions. If you love me, please don't do it."

Andrius takes a deep breath and upon seeing his family and friends, falls backwards completely exhausted with the large boulder, to the ground.

Everyone rushes to his side. Andrius face was all blackened and his clothing torn to shreds and still smoldering.

"My love, you've been hurt bad." Uria cradles him against her bosoms and embraces him.

"I'm very tired of fighting and running. No more."

Uria allows Andrius to lie on the ground, with his head on her lap, for a long while.

"I'm dying." Andrius closes his eyes for a short spell. Uria pulls his head closer to her.

"No Andrius, you must live for me. My love, you will rest and get well, again."

A few minutes later, Andrius opens his eyes, reaches out, and touches Jarvis' hand.

"My son, see I am alive and well."

"But I thought he killed you."

"Your nemesis had me plunked on the head, by his comrade. That's how, they persuaded you, to come to him. It's an old trick to lure you to him, so he could kill you himself."

"But how did you all get here?"

"We took the half-track and drove across the swamps. By the time we arrived, at the complex, all of the troops were gone, except for Jarvis and two soldiers, who were holding him, at the shoreline." Said Michael

"We have them all tied up, at the beach." Said Jason and Michael joining them.

"Gentlemen, we must evacuate the island. There is about a two hour window left, before the Island is destroyed." Said Colonel Towers as he helps Andrius up, on his feet.

"There you are. Can you walk?"

"Yes, I think so. My legs feel, a little wobbly."

"Our friend there is worst off. Said Jason, he will require mayor medical help. I doubt that he will ever survive this."

"How serious is he, Jason?" Asked Jarvis

"The poor devil has burns, over seventy-five percent of his body. We cannot take him with us, guys. I don't have the medical equipment, or the supplies, to treat his burns." Said Jason

"Let's send him back to his ship, with the other two soldiers." Said Andrius

"That's a good idea. You go ahead Jason with the Colonel and Uria, to the spacecraft, while Michael and I, deliver Mister Daggard, to the two soldiers, on the beach. Nora will wait for us, at the spacecraft, as long as possible, even till the very last second."

"How are you feeling, Andrius?" Michael asks

"Much better, now. Thanks."

"Its incredible how the Orgite body replenishes itself after severs exposures to fire and injuries." Said Jason.

"That's fifty thousand years of evolution, before your eyes." Said Jarvis.

"Amazing." Said Nora.

"Please don't take any more chances, Andrius." Uria pleads.

"We'll be back shortly, I promise you."

Minutes later, Daggard, semi-conscious, is brought to the beach. The two soldiers are set free to join him at the sea craft and are set off on their way back to the naval ship stationed off shore.

Meanwhile, the President of the United States arrives, to the naval flagship, after all the combatants return to their ships. The President stands with Admiral Clark on the bridge, observing numerous strange fiery objects ascending, from the Island and disappearing, in the skies.

"Mister President isn't it obvious, that you and I can readily see these luminous objects flying off and yet the darn things don't register, on radar. We cannot even aim our missiles, at them."

"That's strange to say the least."

"Can they be ghostly light apparitions or some type of laser projections designed to distract us, some way?"

"I know about this, Admiral. This phenomenon has happened, once before."

"I've counted about twenty so far, and more are still ascending. What can they be?

We've sent reconnaissance aircraft to investigate but midway to the site, they suddenly developed mechanical problems and had to abort the missions.

What's going on? Are these things extraterrestrial? Are we witnessing the first contact, with an alien race? You must know, Sir."

"They're not aliens; I can assure you of that. Trust me, Admiral."

"That's a relief, Sir. It's probably one of those new secret weapons, that only the top government officials, know about."

The President looks at the Admiral and smiles.

"Admiral, has Mister Daggard arrived, yet?"

"Yes, Sir. They took him to one of the helicopter ships; there he receiving first aid. Once he's stabilized, he'll be brought here for further medical treatment.

The commander of the vessel reports that he's critically burned and they fear, that he may not survive, Mister President."

"Sorry to hear that, Admiral. I believe that he sustained those injuries, when he and his men crashed through the fire-wall, at the beachhead."

"Most probably, Sir."

A Naval helicopter appears an hour later and lands on the stern section of the ship. Navy corps carried Daggard on a stretcher and bring him sickbay.

A few minutes later, the President and the Admiral decide to make their way to sickbay.

At a good distance from the room, the President hears Daggard's chilling sounds of agony from his excruciating pain, from the burns, throughout his body.

The ship's head doctor approaches the President and prevents them from getting closer:

"Mister President, I have given him all the pain killers that his body can possibly tolerate. It is a miracle, that he is still alive."

"Thank you doctor for your effort."

"Sir, off the record, this man is expressing some type of hate or extreme anger. You can see it, in his eyes. His body is very tensed and constricted. I've never seen this, before. He's constantly mumbling some words. One name for sure, I heard he said was some one named 'Andrius'. He grinds his teeth, after pronouncing that name. He's very delirious. We had to install suppressers in his mouth, to prevent further damage to his teeth and tongue. He also has some damage to his lower jaw. It could have been from some impact, or it was self-inflicted.

Mister President, does the name Andrius have any significance to you, Sir?"

"Perhaps Doctor, It's just the name of an important person, who he tried to surpass, but never quite, succeeded at it."

"Oh yes, some great leader or a true military hero, ah?"

"Yes, doctor, a true damn hero and a great man, to say the least."

The President turns and walks out of the entrance to sickbay and returns to the bridge.

"Mister President, Said the Admiral, thirty objects, so far, Sir. They keep coming."

"Say Admiral Clark, how long would it take you, to pipe me up to the P.A. systems, on all the ships, out here?"

"Mister President, right away, Sir. In about two minutes."

"Good. Do it. After you hook me up, please start the final count down. I want everything above and below that island destroyed. There are things there, that may be detrimental to these times and in the wrong hands, they may usher worldwide tyrannies by those, who may possess these objects. I rather not have them at all, at this time and place."

"Yes, Mister President."

"I wish I were going with them." The President muttered

"Excuse me, Sir, did you say something?"

"No, no. He smiles again at him. I was just talking to myself, Admiral. It's been a long day."

"Mister President, you have center stage. I will be honored to announce you, Sir."

"Thank you, Admiral."

"Men, this is Admiral Clark speaking to you from the flag ship. I must congratulate all of you for the splendid well executed job that each of you performed today. I'm especially proud of our marines and their ease, in securing the island, without too many casualties.

Good job, men. I present to you the President of the United States."

"Thank you, Admiral Clark. I like to thank the men, and women amongst us who have witnessed and have been part of this mission in protecting America.

Today, that makes me proud to be an American.

I salute each one of you for a job well done. You all should be proud today.

Gentlemen, we are all witnessing in our culture at home and out here today the mindless persecution of a new race of people, in a free democracy.

These objects that you see in the skies are people fleeing not from justice, but from our own misguided attitudes. We have unjustly enslaved, persecuted and selfishly tried to stifle and suppress a new race born to us freely, and have also tried to manipulate them for our own selfish gains.

Unbelievably, we did this also, to one innocent individual two thousand years ago and we all know who that is.

Let's all hope, that our democratic way of life doesn't ever erode to low ebb, and dangerous levels, that our very own fundamental principles of our country, which include our Constitution and basic human rights can possibly be diluted and perverted, by those who care not.

I warn you to be always, on your guard against any kind of erosion of human dignity, because tyranny will surely follow in its quake as day follows night.

Freedom is not a gift bestowed on us by governments but it is a natural right or better said it is a universal right to be shared by all mankind whether you are human or this new human species called Orgites.

Preserve and cherish your freedom; defend it against all forms of tyranny at home and from abroad. The future of all our species and all others will depend on it.

Lastly, remember when any race thinks of itself as superior to another and begins to restrict the civil rights and freedoms of that other, such actions or attitudes will revert eventually and affect you, personally. You will have the establishment of anarchy and a Totalitarian Society.

Wherever this wonderful and unique new race of mankind decides to travel to live in this universe, let us hope and pray, that freedom, justice and their pursue of happiness will always prevail with them. I have also given them an open invitation to live here on Earth and join us to create a new earth, free of hunger, deceases and provide decent living conditions for all the peoples of Earth.

Thank you, for allowing me to share some words with you today."

"Thank you, Mister President for those words on encouragement.

Gentlemen in a few moments a small portion of the Island will be destroyed by a 150 Kiloton nuke. Please be advised that special eye protection gear is required if you wish to witness the blast. Thank you."

As the last luminous object disappears in the heavens, the President turns to the Admiral.

"What adventures await them? I wish I were also going with them."

"I too, Mr. President. Will we ever hear from them again, Sir?"

"I will be surprised, if we never do. We need them, just as well as they need us in many ways."

"Thank you, Mister President."

A New Beginning